DAVID CLEMENT-DAVIES

AMULET BOOKS

NEW YORK AND LONDON

A catalogue record for this book is available
from the British Library.
ISBN-13: 978-0-8109-9470-6
ISBN-10: 0-8109-9470-4

Text copyright © 2007 David Clement-Davies

Book design by Chad W. Beckerman

Printed and bound in U.S.A.
10 9 8 7 6 5 4 3 2 1

HNA
harry n. abrams, inc.
a subsidiary of La Martinière Groupe

The Market Building
72-82 Rosebery Avenue
London, U.K. EC1R 4RW
www.hnabooks.com

For Hen, Patrick, and Honor—at last

... BURN, BURN, BURN,

LIKE FABULOUS YELLOW

ROMAN CANDLES ...

—JACK KEROUAC

CONTENTS

PART TWO
The Past

ACKNOWLEDGEMENTS

I WOULD LIKE TO THANK EVERYONE AT
ABRAMS; CHAD W. BECKERMAN FOR
HIS THOROUGHLY GROOVY DESIGNS;
SCOTT AUERBACH FOR HIS KEEN EYE
AND HARD WORK; BUT ABOVE ALL MY
EDITOR, SUSAN VAN METRE, FOR HER
SKILL, SUGGESTIONS, ENTHUSIASM, AND
CONSTANT SUPPORT.

PART ONE
THE FUTURE

ONE

GHOSTS

In the shadows of a looming mountain, deep within the mysterious land beyond the forest, a small grey wolf pack came weaving invisibly through the red gold trees and soaring pines. For a month the wolves had been fleeing for their lives, but their growing fear now was for their new surroundings, for they were passing through one of the most haunted regions in all of Transylvania, or so it was said.

They came as silently as ghosts themselves, swept along like leaves being scattered about them in the scurrying east wind. Yet their running forms seemed carved out by the wild landscape, in the natural facts of evolution, so they were almost perfectly camouflaged, shielded by the deepening colours of autumn change.

As they broke from the trees a Dragga and a Drappa appeared— the wolves' own words for an Alpha male and female—running side by side, their fine heads up, their ears cocked forwards for any sounds of danger. They were followed into the open by four other healthy grey wolves, including a Beta male, two large cubs, and the smallest and weakest of the group, the Sikla, or Omega, wolf.

The Sikla had been trailing all day, and suddenly caught his front leg on a branch and went tumbling painfully forwards. His startled yelping was snatched away by the howling wind as he disappeared in a cloud of leaves and twigs, and the rest of the wolf pack turned and raced back towards him.

Wild wolves are group animals, fierce in their competitions and rivalries, but also deeply social creatures, pack beings who, when not battling for dominance, will work for the good of the whole. If one falters, or is injured, in the wild, they will do all they can to aid him, and then work to restore the balance of the group. Only when nature itself becomes the enemy of all might they abandon an injured pack member to his fate.

As the grey wolves surrounded the Sikla, the Dragga saw quickly that he was not injured after all, as he picked himself up and shook out his coat, and the Dragga's look changed from concern to anger that this clumsiness had slowed their pace.

"Forgive me," whispered the Sikla, "but I had a feeling that distracted me."

"Feeling?" growled the Drappa, stepping up beside her mate. "What feeling?"

Wolves command the kingdom of the senses, and females especially trust their instincts completely. This Drappa had felt something too. Danger.

"I don't really know," answered the Sikla softly, but thinking nervously of ghosts. "I felt as if we're being watched."

"And I," growled the Drappa, looking around gravely and scenting the air. "I've felt it for a while now. Could it still be the Vengerid?"

The cubs, a male and female as large as Alsatian dogs, but

far more sinewy and vigorous than dogs, suddenly looked terrified.

"Hush," snapped the Dragga. "Jalgan's curs are long gone by now. I've led you all to safety."

The Drappa growled, and the female cub wondered if her parents would argue again. With all the trials of the last few months, the adults had fought terribly on many occasions— loud, angry growls in the night—and the young cub hated it. It had made her so miserable, in fact, she had even thought of running away.

"Perhaps it's man," said the Beta wolf, scratching at the ground with his right paw and scenting too.

"No," said the Dragga, "I always know when they're about."

The Sikla's eyes narrowed.

"Another Varg then?" he suggested, using the wolf's name for their own kind.

"I saw something," ventured the female cub, "just after we crossed the stream back there, high up on the mountaintop. I think it's a Kerl, Father."

The powerful Dragga dropped his forehead in the gathering twilight and gave a low snarl, which made the Sikla back away. Apart from predators and common accidents, few things are more threatening to a wild wolf pack than a Kerl—a lone wolf. To highly sociable beings like grey wolves, a Kerl is surrounded with sadness and thoughts of bitter failure, but its presence also represents the mystery and threat of the dangerous world.

"No ghost then," said the Sikla, trying to be reassuring.

THE FUTURE

"There's something else though, Father," said the she-cub nervously, "the shape I saw. Just for a moment, I thought it was pure black."

The pack, who so often avoided direct eye contact for fear of arousing one another's anger, were searching back and forth in the sudden silence, for the wind had dropped.

"You're sure of this, child?" growled the Dragga.

A lone buzzard cried on the air and the she-cub shivered a little, but wagged her tail and nodded. "Yes, Father."

"Oh, stop showing off," said her brother suddenly. "You're just telling stories of black wolves to get attention."

"I'm not telling stories," his sister snapped indignantly. "I did see it."

They had been quarrelling all day too, and the young she-wolf glared at her sibling.

"Do you think it could be *him*, Father?" she said. "Fell. They say he haunts these parts."

The Sikla whimpered at the name. These wolves were not of the region, for they were fleeing the Vengerid, a band of renegade wolves lead by the murderous Jalgan. But if Jalgan was to be feared, the name of Fell was like a curse to all the Varg of Transylvania.

Some said the lone black wolf was a ghost himself, whose spirit had returned from the Balkar Wars of more than five years before, to haunt the mountains and bring fear and hatred to the Free Wolves of Transylvania. To impressionable young cubs like these, although growing fast and less gullible by the day, Fell was associated with extraordinary powers too: from the ability to make himself invisible, and to send bolts of pain through his victims and

4

blind them, to the power to fly and swoop through the night like a horrible winged grasht—a vampire.

When Varg cubs misbehaved, Fell was often invoked to discipline them. "Stop biting your sister, Child, or Fell will strike," the adults might whisper ominously, or "Eat up your rabbit, or Fell will eat it for you. Then snap you up into the bargain." His name was almost as fearful as the name of Wolfbane himself, the Evil One.

Of all the terrible tales told of the black loner though, living on his own high in the wild mountains, the one that troubled the grey wolves most was that Fell was said to possess the dark powers of the Sight.

The Sight was the ancient gift that the Putnar, the predators of the land and forests, had believed in since the dawn of time. A gift which only a rare few were born with. It was the power that comes through the forehead to talk to some of the animals, and to look into water—a river, or pool, or mountain stream—and see visions there of past, present, and future. The power to glimpse the thoughts of others too, and control wills and actions, and even to look into the very mind of man—a world as closed to the rest of the Lera as an island in a stormy sea.

"Mother," said the she-cub suddenly, "is it true what they say of the Sight? That those who possess it can feel the pain of their own prey, even as they strike?"

The Drappa couldn't answer her daughter, but she shivered and the she-cub wondered if a shape would suddenly swoop down on great black wings and drink her blood.

"And if it's true Fell's around here, Father," whispered her brother, gulping now and wondering if the wild expanses around them were really haunted, "was such an evil wolf truly Larka's brother?"

As he said it, a howl came to the pack's ears that froze them in their paw marks. Wolves have many different calls in their journeys; howls of loneliness and of anger, howls of warning and of friendship. But this powerful cry, high up on the cliff above them, was so deep and filled with intelligence and longing, with pain and searching, that the very air seemed to grow chill, and the trees to drop their autumn leaves in sadness.

"Look, Father!" cried the male cub in terror. "Up there."

The worried little family had seen it now, a dark speck on the jagged cliff edge, high above them. A single black wolf was standing on a beetling precipice, and looking down.

Up there it was as if the wolf had heard the family's words and, in the naming of Larka, had been unable to keep silent. His strong black mouth opened even wider as he howled—a muzzle that had once carried terrible lies and anger within it—and his sharp fangs glittered savagely.

"It's a Kerl, all right, and as black as night," growled the Dragga far below. "Perhaps it really is Fell."

It was hard to impress a brave Dragga like this one, but he had fear in his eyes, until the Sikla spoke.

"Perhaps we should never have left." He trembled furiously. "Perhaps you should have taken Jalgan's challenge."

The Dragga glared at the Sikla, but his Drappa spoke again.

"He looks so strong," she whispered as she peered up at the black wolf on the cliff's edge. "Yet they say it all happened before I was even born. Fell should be old and grey by now, or even dead."

"Then perhaps he really is a ghost," growled her mate.

"Hush now. There's no such thing. Not even in these parts."

It wasn't quite true what the Drappa said about Fell, even though she was talking of one of her own. If they survive infancy, wolves commonly live to about seven or eight, but they can last for twice as long in captivity. In nature it is not so much old age that takes them, but their failing strength in their struggles in the wild.

Yet there was something strangely youthful in the seven-year-old up there on the mountaintop, who turned suddenly and was gone. Fell began to climb, the hardened pads on his paws clawing vigorously on the leafy ground, lifting him higher and higher into the great Carpathian Mountains.

His yellow gold eyes, flecked with a sliver of pure green below the right iris, searched the distances ahead of him again, taking him away from the little wolf pack, and out once more into the lonely world.

The black wolf had made an easy kill that afternoon, a weak roebuck, and he could still taste meat and musk on his tongue. His belly was full, and he knew where he would rest for the night, in a low cave out of the fury of the east wind, bringing its scent of winter snows to Transylvania, carried from the great Russian Steppes and the freezing expanses of Siberia.

There the lone black wolf would sleep safe and warm, with no threat of other Putnar—other predators—to trouble his dreams. Dreams that were troubled enough already. Predators were plentiful in Transylvania, but apart from man and nature, only Putnar like the mountain bears posed any real threat to an Alpha wolf like Fell. He had scouted the cave the day before, marking it with his scent and eating a meal there, and had seen no sign of bear tracks at all.

With his recent kill, and this guarantee of a safe resting place for the night, the black wolf should have been in his element, even though Fell had also heard rumours of the ghosts in these parts. Yet the Kerl felt a pang in his heart, which made him whimper softly as he bounded upwards.

It was not the thought of ghosts, but the sight of the little wolf pack that had troubled Fell so deeply, for all morning he had been thinking of his own family, and just for a moment when he had first spied them, had wondered if it might be them; his parents Huttser and Palla, or his adopted brother Kar. Their fine new cubs too, his younger brothers and sisters. They should be five years old by now, and fully grown, and Fell wondered if they had cubs of their own.

His keen eyes darkened, and he asked himself where, in the great expanses of the land beyond the forest, they might be, or if his parents were even still alive. Huttser and Palla would be almost fourteen by now, if they had survived so long. It might be good to see them again, if only for a moment—a distant glimpse of the happy life of a wolf pack.

It had been Fell's own choice to leave them, one sun long ago, and become a Kerl. After what had happened to him—how he had felt he had betrayed them—Fell had needed to hunt down the truth of life for himself. But it was all that Fell had seen and suffered, and all that he had learnt of wolf and man too in his dark journey, that had really driven him away.

The story had all begun more than seven years before, with the birth of two wolf cubs, Larka and Fell—one white and one black—in a cave below a great stone castle. Wolf cubs with an unusual gift that had attracted the attention of their wicked aunt Morgra. Their brave little family had protected them, defeated a curse, and wrestled with a legend, even at the cost of their own lives.

The white she-wolf Larka, Fell's sister, had journeyed up to a mountain citadel called Harja, to confront Morgra and free a human child, snatched from a village below the castle. There, Larka had used the Sight to touch the child's mind, bringing a vision of man and nature that had opened the minds of all animals, the Lera, to the Great Secret: that man is an animal too. She herself had fulfilled a legend that had promised to bring forth the greatest Putnar the world had ever seen.

For ordinary Varg the stories of it were now largely myths shared in the pack dens, or during a hunt to lighten a weary day. But they persisted, for the defeat of Morgra and her pack of male killers—the Balkar—and the return of the stolen human child to its own, allowed the grey wolves of Transylvania to roam at will again; in freedom and peace through these beautiful lands, hunting and living as they wished.

These days whenever wolf packs crossed one another's boundaries, they made sure to give a traditional greeting, which they called Larka's Blessing, in honour of the white she-wolf who had saved them all. But while Larka's name had become a word for peace in the land beyond the forest, Fell's was associated with fear, uncertainty, and even evil.

Fell looked up the slope. On the rise of the bank above him he saw the mouth of the cave, a small, dark scar in the mountainside, and quickened his pace. For tonight at least the lone black wolf was safe.

But as he approached, Fell heard a kind of restless chattering and spotted a squirrel and its mate in the coming moonlight, perched on the branch of a tree high above. Their bushy red tails were raised amongst the snowy leaves, and the male was clutching a large acorn in its nervous paws, as a kind of clicking came from its chubby little mouth. As Fell listened, his eyes opened wider, for the sound suddenly changed into a voice.

"Can't you feel it?" said the male squirrel loudly. "Something strange is happening. Something in nature."

Fell blinked in astonishment. The Sight bestowed on the wolf the gift to talk to some animals—birds—but only Larka had ever reached all the Lera, with her mind and her understanding. Fell had never understood animals such as these before. Was he haunted?

"What is happening, Cosmo?" whispered the second squirrel.

"I don't know," answered her mate, "but I feel it everywhere. On the air and in the undergrowth. I feel it in the very elements themselves. Some great change comes."

Fell stirred at the strange words and noticed storm clouds massing in the skies, and he gave a low growl. As soon as the wary squirrels heard the wolf, Cosmo and his mate vanished higher up their tree, and Fell shook his head, telling himself that he must be imagining it.

He padded into the cave and stopped in front of a little pile of gnawed rabbit bones, his huge pink tongue lolling from his mouth. Inside he heard the whispering plash of water and a voice in his head saying: "Fear it, wolf. Fear death by water." It made him brace instinctively for wolves fear nothing so much as a watery death, a death Fell had once faced himself. But this pool, fed by a spring guttering from the belly of the mountain, was only a small one. It was the Sight which frightened Fell now, and its second power to bring on sudden visions in water.

He walked forwards hesitantly, then dropped his muzzle to drink. The water tasted so good, clean and delicious, as Fell stilled his thirst. He caught his own reflection and his face surprised him. Fell had often asked himself if it was the power of the Sight that kept him in his prime, and thoughts of the Sight brought back thoughts of the past.

Try as he might to push it away, the past was hunting Fell today, and he growled again. The black wolf had been fooled so perfectly by his aunt Morgra, who had known all along that it wasn't only Larka who possessed the Sight. The powers still burned inside the black wolf, and set him apart from the Varg. How could a creature such as Fell, touched by powers beyond his control, and which sometimes filled him with fear, live amongst others as a normal wolf? A creature who had known such hate and fury, and learnt to kill with such passion, whenever the bloodlust gripped him, as it does all wolves at times. He shuddered as he remembered how his powers had allowed him to blind Morgra's fighters, the Balkar, the Night Hunters as they were also called.

He hardly knew himself how Morgra had got to him, but using her own power, she had touched Fell's mind and taught him terrible things. She had filled his heart with darkness, telling him that like her he was evil. Fell had believed it too, until Larka had come.

Yet that was all long ago, and dear Larka was dead. She had gone beyond even the Red Meadow, where wolves first go when they die and become shadow memories of what has been. Morgra and her Balkar were defeated now, and the wolves were free again. The human child, through whom Morgra had hoped to control all mankind, had been returned to its own village by Fell himself.

As the wolf stood there looking down, a gust of wind came breathing through the cave mouth, and for a moment Fell thought he heard a ghostly sigh. He dismissed it, but the wintry wind rose and suddenly Fell heard a voice.

"Help the child," it seemed to say.

Fell swung his head, but there was no one there, not even the squirrels, and the wolf told himself he must be imagining things. He looked back into the pool, and his huge eyes seemed drawn deeper into the water. Suddenly Fell snarled. There was a human. The Sight had come on him again, more clearly than it had in ages, and Fell saw a boy in the pool, with a handsome face, cropped red hair, and sparkling hazel eyes. He was sitting on a rock, and in the snowy background, three black-and-white birds hopped about. Fell was mesmerised, and he knew that what he was seeing lay somewhere in the future. The Sight was giving him a vision of what was to come.

The boy in the water pushed up his right shirtsleeve. On his thin forearm was a strange mark. It seemed etched in blood, but Fell could not make out the shape, except that it reminded him somehow of a bird.

Humans, thought Fell gravely. After the animals had learned the Great Secret, that humans were animals too, it was man whom Fell had watched for five long years, disobeying the oldest Varg law— to have nothing to do with their kind—and using the power of the Sight to look into their minds, and trying to read their thoughts.

It would come on him quite suddenly, when he was near their tents, or when he stumbled on a human trap in the forest, and when he watched the Tsingani, the gypsies of the forests, and their hidden campfires from the trees. A flash of vision, showing him pictures of their lives. The third power of the Sight.

On many occasions this closeness to the humans had nearly cost Fell his life, for with their beliefs in their gods and demons, with their ignorance and fear of nature, they hated wolves as no other animal in the wild.

With flaming tapers and shouts of fear and hate, they had tried to drive the black wolf out, and so in their angry minds, Fell had seen little but life's ruthless struggle for survival. Yet the wolf had kept returning to them, driven by a power that he knew was greater than himself, and by a longing to understand them and the Sight that tormented his dreams.

Fell tried to shrug off the image of the boy, but although the picture seemed to sink deeper into the water, it did not vanish. Now it appeared as if a dusting of snow was falling on its surface. Fell blinked in utter astonishment. Another face was forming: not a human's this time, but a beautiful white muzzle and yellow gold eyes. Above the image of the boy, a she-wolf was staring back at Fell, and not just any wolf.

"Larka," he gasped.

Fell had not seen Larka in over five years. After Morgra had seized his mind, it was his sister who had shown Fell the truth again, and made him remember who he really was. Dear Larka had convinced Fell that Morgra's was the real darkness, and reminded him that as much as life can be filled with anger and struggle—the feelings he had always wrestled with as a growing Varg—it is also filled with love and courage and sacrifice. Her own.

The beautiful she-wolf said nothing in the water. Her eyes smiled back gently, and Fell lifted a paw and whined softly, stroking tenderly at the water, frightened to break the delicate image of his sister.

"Larka. How I miss you, sister."

Still the white wolf looked back, unspeaking, and Fell shook his muzzle, feeling lonelier than ever, but dismissing stories of ghosts in these parts.

"It's just the past, Larka," he murmured. "Always the past. You're dead and gone. We lose everything in the end."

As Fell said it, the wind came licking furiously into the cave, and on its back Fell heard that voice a second time. Distinctly.

"Help the changeling, Fell. The child is close."

Fell started violently, almost convinced he was being haunted now.

"Larka?"

"You must help the human, Fell."

The wind rose, and Fell could not tell if it was the breeze speaking, or his sister in the water. He wondered. He had often sensed that Larka had gone beyond the Red Meadow, where the dead first gather, to a place from where none returned. How could this be?

"Destiny," the voice seemed to whisper. "The child has a great destiny, Fell. It is marked."

Fell's tail lifted. The boy he could still see faintly below Larka's face had a mark on his arm. He remembered too the words of a blind old fortune-teller called Tsinga he had met long ago. She had spoken of Fell's destiny—*"Perhaps as important as any. Everything has a destiny."*

"Aid it, Fell, to fulfil its destiny. For all of us. For nature itself."

"Nature itself?" whispered the black wolf in astonishment.

As he spoke, Larka's face seemed to grow fainter in the pool again, fractured by the breeze stirring the water's surface.

"Great confusion, brother. Great evil. Hurry."

Fell whined. Larka was beginning to disappear altogether.

"Stay, Larka," he cried. "Tell me more of this. Where is this child?"

"Gone," the wind answered hauntingly. "Can no longer see, Fell. So faint now. All my strength to speak. Seek out friends, dear Fell. The Helpers. Find the Guardian."

"Please, Larka," growled Fell, wondering who this Guardian was, and if this voice was really in his own mind. "Don't go."

"Nature and the child's survival are one. Hurry."

Larka vanished and Fell stood there shuddering, as a breath of ice came on the autumn breeze, and outside great smudges of white began to float down from the heavens. It had started to snow.

The wolf was amazed and terrified, and wondered if he were dreaming. What could it mean, and had it really been Larka's ghost talking to him? What of these strange words of a Guardian and the Helpers?

Fell thought of Skart, the wise steppe eagle who had aided Larka in her own journey. Skart had been one of the Helpers, the birds of the air, through whose eyes those with the Sight could travel out of their bodies and see the whole world from the skies. The first power of the Sight. He shivered unhappily at the thought. The black wolf had seen far too much of the world already and wanted nothing to do with this strange injunction.

He could see the boy still, though, and the image in the water grew closer again, although it changed now into a different picture of the future. Or was it the future? For now it felt like the present. As Fell looked at the boy, he had the most extraordinary thought. Could it be the same baby he had returned to the human village, five years before? Fell didn't know that this boy was much older than the child would be, for he had no real knowledge of a human's life span, compared to a Varg's.

He looked down into the pool, and as the snowfall grew heavier, felt as if he were looking through a doorway into another world entirely. The boy's eyes were closed this time, and the sweating passion of a dream gripped his young face. A human.

TWO

THE CHANGELING STORYTELLER

Wake up quickly, Alin, Uncle's coming," said a nervous little voice in the human den. The dreamer heard it faintly, and hazel eyes opened suddenly and looked up anxiously at the little girl. It was the same boyish face that Fell had just spied in the cave pool, with the powers of the Sight, and in the left pupil was a fleck of green, like his own.

"You're just having another bad dream," whispered the little girl, with a kindly smile. Her name was Mia.

The dreamer smiled back at Mia. The dream had been full of noisy shouts and arguing adult voices, and thank heavens it was over now.

Mia was clothed simply, in a plain little peasant dress, as she looked down at the strange mark on her friend's arm. The faint symbol etched there was of a bird of prey, an eagle with opening wings, and Mia had often wondered what it meant, and if the goblins had really made it. After what Mia had discovered today, she was keener than ever to know what it really was.

Alina stirred on the bench and got up, as Mia grinned and held up a pair of rusting sheep sheers.

"Shall I cut your hair again?" she asked her friend softly.

The dreamer shook her head sleepily, although she knew she

would have to cut her hair soon, for it was starting to grow out again. With her cropped red hair and rough shepherd's clothes, the older girl might have been a boy of twelve or thirteen, for everything about Alina Sculcuvant, or Alin as Mia had just called her, was designed to conceal the strange secret that she was really a girl.

In this household Alina was treated as toughly as any boy though, and made to work twice as hard. With all the chores she had to do about the place, she rarely got enough rest, but if the old shepherd Malduk ever caught her napping like this, poor Alina knew there'd be the devil to pay. She was nervous too, because that same morning she had had one of her strange feelings, which she believed always meant something special was about to happen.

The pretence surrounding Alina Sculcuvant had begun seven years before, when Mia's uncle Malduk had found her up there in the snows, unconscious, and had taken her to see the old woman on the mountain. The strange girl had received a blow to her head and been desperately bewildered and confused, hardly able to speak, except to mutter her name and a plaintive apology. But the witch had placed her spindly fingers on a glass sphere and gasped at what she had seen there.

"A changeling," she'd hissed, "she's a changeling child."

The witch had turned to old Malduk then and clutched his hands fearfully.

"She may have been born a human, Malduk, and stolen long ago, or she may be one of their own. But you must conceal her, man, lest the goblins and fairies come to snatch her back again. Hide the child."

The old witch had spoken to Alina too, and persuaded her that she had come by magic out of the winter wilds into the world of men, perhaps found first by the Tsingani in the forest and then discarded, or perhaps escaping from the fairies. She had clasped little Alina's hands too and told her that she must accept her new life with gratitude and humility, and never look back at her origins, lest she bring down a terrible curse on them all. At eight, poor little Alina had succumbed easily enough, just as she had accepted Malduk's orders that she must cut her hair and dress as a boy.

That whole first year, in the shepherd's home, twelve long months, Alina had not been able to speak a word to anyone, and instead had looked out on the life with fixed and frightened eyes. Since then she had grown into a life filled with strange dreams.

Mia put down the shears, and now she looked at Alina excitedly. She had just had a thought.

"What is it, Mia?"

"Alina, will you tell me another story?"

"A story?"

Mia nodded enthusiastically.

Alina was well known around the village of Moldov for her fabulous stories—tales of fairies and sprites and witches, of lost children, or of the creatures she saw in nature—and she had often used them to stop the other boys teasing and bullying her.

"Yes, Alina. Like that story you made up of those children and the pebbles in the forest, and their horrid stepmother," said Mia eagerly. "Or that tale of wild animals that can talk. That was so wonderful. It made me feel so much better, Alina, and so much braver somehow."

Alina smiled warmly at her little friend. Many of the village children, when they weren't feeling jealous, marvelled at how easily the boy Alin could spin a yarn, and some said it was a fairy gift. The children had even given the strange boy a name—Sculcuvant. It literally meant "word" and a "sheep's skein," or something like Alin WovenWord, or when they were trying to be cruel, Alin SkeinTale.

There was a heavy cough in the yard outside, and Alina saw old Malduk through the cottage window, approaching the hovel. She quickly covered the mark on her arm with her sleeve and straightened her thin woollen coat.

"Later, Mia."

The old shepherd pushed open the door and stepped inside the humble dwelling. Malduk had a hard and deeply lined face, and he was carrying a little slingshot in his right hand, which he often used to throw stones at the sheep. He snapped it on the air and cursed loudly, and Alina saw from his coat that it was snowing heavily outside. As the slingshot gave a sharp "crack," Mia clenched her right hand into a small fist, her eyes flickering warily between her uncle and an old wooden chest in the middle of the smoky room. Malduk and her aunt Ranna had repeatedly warned the children never to go near it.

"What are you staring at?" grunted the shepherd, as he saw the children standing there.

"Nothing, Uncle," answered Mia quickly.

"Then fetch me a bowl of hot broth. I'm famished, and freezing too."

"Yes, Uncle," said the little girl immediately, darting towards the stove and kitchen area at the side of the room. As she went, Mia glanced back nervously at the chest, and slipped something into her pocket, something she had meant to show Alina before being distracted with thoughts of stories. A little metal key.

"And you," Malduk snapped at Alina, "don't just stand about like a dolt. Help me pull off my boots, girl."

The shepherd slammed the door shut, crossed the room, and sat down on the chest, near a huge pile of old sheepskins, rubbing his back painfully and putting a booted foot up on a milking stool. The boot was made of rough deerskin, tied in the manner of local shepherds, with bindings of cured wool. Alina took her dagger from her belt, a simple thing with a handle made of antler horn, and placed it on the chest, lest it get in the way, then knelt down meekly to undo Malduk's boot. The shepherd watched her coldly.

Ranna's right, he thought as he sat there, *the girl's certainly growing up fast. She's almost as big as me now.* At fifteen Alina Sculcuvant had suddenly shot up, and she was unusually tall for her age. As he watched her, Malduk thought of the son he had always longed for, a son he had never been able to have with his wife, Ranna.

At least they could make Alin do a man's work in the open, he told himself, which Malduk's advancing years, and a back strained badly in a fall, were making harder for him by the day. Without the gossipy backbiting from the rival shepherds, either, that would certainly have ensued if they'd sent a girl out into the fields. Malduk consoled himself too that a son would probably never have been so pliant as she. Alina had always been easy enough to bully and control, and with the little food they allowed her, and the constant hard work they had for years set her on their farm, she was like clay in their hands.

Apart from the witch's injunction that Alina should hide herself from the fairies and goblins of the forest, Malduk and Ranna had told the little girl that it was best to conceal herself like this because, in the wars that gripped Transylvania, and the frequent raids by the Turks, girls were highly prized and often carried away like cattle.

For Alina, her strange concealment called to a darkness she felt deep within. With time she had begun to question the changeling story, yet for years her sleep had been filled with those strange dreams. Of a great fairy-tale palace high in the clouds, and mysterious elven folk, who carried antlers in their hands like swords. Of being held safe for a time in a pair of strong, loving arms, and a grand household where she heard the sound of a haunting fairy lullaby in the night. Sleep pictures too of a woman with curling black hair and a man with red hair like her own, who she thought and hoped might have been her real parents. Not goblins at all, but people.

They made her happy sometimes, until a dream came that frightened Alina Sculcuvant horribly. It was of a creature with great, slavering fangs, flying at her from the shadows to drink her blood. That was the dream that made Alina turn away from the past, whatever it was.

Little Mia, who had come to the household only two years

before—after her own parents' deaths from a sudden fever that had swept the region—often wondered about Alina and the story of fairies. To Mia, Alina certainly had the air of a changeling, with her skill with animals, her love of the wild, and her thoughtful, piercing eyes. With the power to know things too before they happened. It was never anything dramatic. A dream of rain the next day perhaps, or of a sudden meeting, but it added to the air of mystery surrounding the older girl. A mystery that her aunt and uncle had ordered Mia to keep secret too, with threats of a beating.

Mia admired Alina deeply, and she was sad that her aunt and uncle treated the older girl so cruelly. Sad too that the village children and the shepherds never stopped picking on Alin when they were out at work in the fields. They also muttered of changeling origins but, not knowing what the witch had said of hiding a girl from the fairies, had no reason to believe Alin wasn't a boy.

The villagers still mistrusted him deeply though, not only as a changeling, but for the Saxon blood they saw in his red hair. They were Vlaks, deeply clannish and naturally frightened of strangers in their tiny town, clustered around a little stream and surrounded by great forests and soaring mountains, shielding them from the outside world.

"Be careful there, damn it," growled Malduk, as Alina's efforts to remove his second boot twisted a painful blister on his foot.

"I'm sorry, Malduk . . ."

"So you should be," snapped the old man. "I wonder sometimes why we ever took in a stupid, good-for-nothing girl. The other shepherds are always complaining about you, daydreaming, inventing lying stories, or talking of better things."

It was a complaint Alina had often heard over the years, but with the bitter cold snap, Malduk seemed especially irritable today. Alina dropped her gaze, telling herself, as she always did, that she ought to be grateful to the shepherd and his hard, old wife.

The girl could remember so little of her true origins, and where she had really come from. Of what the mysterious eagle on her arm was, or where she had been going in the snows. She did have sudden flashbacks though, and over these last few years had tried to piece together a fractured story of who she might really be.

She often told herself that she wasn't a fairy child at all, but that she had been snatched as a baby from a human home by goblins. That home she peopled with those half-seen figures of her dreams. The man with red hair, who she felt a great tenderness towards, although he seemed distant and aloof too. The dark-haired woman Alina made her human mother, because she felt so powerfully drawn to her. Yet in the ensuing dreams the woman was always harsh and cold with her, and would give her orders and treat her just as cruelly as Malduk and Ranna. And the red-haired man and the black-haired woman had often argued bitterly.

At last Alina Sculcuvant had decided that if she had been taken by fairies, or even gypsies, as a little girl, then she must have been some kind of servant in her past too, for she half remembered a bare room where she had slept, and other working people around her, who would scold her for her laziness. Perhaps that was better than being a true fairy, Alina sometimes tried to console herself by thinking.

There was something else in poor Alina's heart though—a feeling that she had done something terribly wrong. Alina didn't know where this dreadful guilt came from, but it always made her sorrowful and timid, and it grew far worse when she dreamt one dream in particular.

She was standing in a kind of hall, with a little wooden cot swaying beside her, and behind her that dark-haired woman was shouting angrily, and a face would come to her of a smiling baby boy in the cradle, looking up and gurgling happily at her. She felt it was her brother, and felt love for the child too, but then that shadow and those teeth would suddenly appear—the vampire—and the child would vanish. Alina would wake from this ghastly nightmare, trying to hold onto the image of the baby's face, sweating and feeling like a traitor, or a murderer. Alina was certain then that she had done something terribly wrong, and thus that she was really in exile.

"Pull harder there, girl."

She yanked at the second boot, and nearly fell backwards as it came off too. Malduk sighed contentedly and even smiled at Alina, as he stretched and wiggled his feet in his filthy woollen stockings.

"There now, that's better. Where's that damned food, Mia?"

Mia came back into the middle of the room and placed a bowl of steaming broth carefully on a low three-legged table next to her uncle. As the old shepherd sat up and leaned forwards, Mia almost gasped. She was looking at the wooden chest, and could see the corner of a parchment peeping from the lid. She hadn't put it back properly.

Malduk and Alina might have noticed it too, if the door hadn't opened again and, from the growing blizzard outside, an old woman bustled noisily into the shepherd's hovel.

"Wife," grunted Malduk, "Mia has had to warm my soup, and she's hardly old enough."

Ranna's head was heavily shawled, and she was carrying a bundle of firewood in her spindly arms.

"Which will teach the child the meaning of hard work," snapped Ranna irritably. "I've had to carry this on my back half a mile or more, husband, and in a snowstorm too. Stop your griping."

The old shepherd fell silent before his angry wife. Ranna was far more capable of carrying wood than he, and in truth he was frightened of her.

"And what's the changeling doing standing there idly?" said Ranna, moving over to the simple kitchen area, where she dropped the wood on the floor. "Shouldn't she be out in the barn by now?"

"Yes, Ranna. I'll send Alin out soon enough," answered Malduk. "You know they saw wolves last week, close to the village."

Ranna swung her head. "And they'll be down hunting soon," she said.

"Indeed, wife. That black loner has been seen in the forests again."

Alina Sculcuvant looked up immediately. There was a new dream that came to her in the night, and it had been growing stronger and stronger in the past few months. The dream of a lone, black wolf.

"But with these raiders from the East," said Ranna, "we've worse things to worry us now than wolves."

Turks from the Ottoman lands had been raiding again, plundering homesteads and setting fire to the wooden churches that dotted the countryside. They had grown bolder and bolder after their great victory over the Christian stronghold of Byzantium in the East, twenty-five years before.

Mia was listening nervously, but Ranna's words about Turks made Alina stand a little straighter.

"The shepherds say we've nothing to fear from raiders, Ranna," she ventured, hoping to reassure the old couple, "and that the King will drive them off. The King, or the Order of the Griffin."

Mia's ears perked up. She had heard rumours of the secret Orders in the lands beyond the forest, like the Order of the Dragon and the Order of the Griffin, many tales good and even more bad, and she wanted to hear more.

"And Lord Vladeran's strength and cunning protect all the lands down to the great river too," Alina finished. "That soldier said so."

Ranna swung round, a murderous look in the old woman's eyes. "What soldier?" she snapped.

"I was talking to him at market. One of Lord Vladeran's men."

Ranna was always furious at Alina for speaking out of turn, but the mention of a soldier and Lord Vladeran, whose palace lay far to the Northwest, had an especially strange effect on the adults.

The couple cast each other a secretive glance, and Malduk put a hand on the chest he was sitting on, almost protectively. Little Mia shivered as he nearly touched the parchment poking from the lid.

"Do adults need the words of a servant to reassure us?" snapped Ranna scornfully. "Mind your tongue, changeling."

"I was only trying to . . ."

"Ranna's right," growled Malduk, standing up. "Now go to the barn, and get some rest, and I'll wake you well before sunup. You'll have a long day tomorrow, with this weather worsening and wolves to watch for."

Alina shrugged, but she turned to leave.

"Wait, girl," said Ranna suddenly.

The old woman bustled over to the stove and poured some hot water into a wooden bowl, then pulled a pouch of herbs down from a cupboard, which she opened and stirred carefully into the bowl. She added a thin drizzle of broth, then turned and held it up to Alina with sparking eyes.

"Take that to warm you," she said in a softer voice, but with a sly, menacing smile. "Your favourite brew, my dear. To protect you from *them*."

Alina stared at the broth. The old witch on the mountain had first given it to her, as a charm to help protect her from discovery by the fairy people of the forest. She was none too fond of the strange herbal concoction and its sharp, acrid taste, although Alina did admit that it made her feel stronger for a while, probably because she was given so little to eat. It always made her sleep deeply too. The girl hesitated.

"Do as you're told, Alin," ordered Malduk. His face softened a little. "You know it's for your own good. Like a magic cloak."

Alina felt Malduk and Ranna's eyes watching her closely, until she had drunk the whole draft. She put down the bowl again to wipe her mouth, but it slipped from the edge of the table and clattered to the floor.

"Stupid girl," snapped the old woman.

"I'm sorry, Ranna, I . . ."

"Give me that," said Ranna irritably, looking at a handkerchief poking from Alina's pocket. Alina pulled it out and Ranna snatched it away from her, bending down to wipe the floor.

"Let me, Ranna," said Alina.

"Oh, get to bed with you."

Alina hovered there still.

"What's wrong with you now, changeling?" said Ranna, standing straight again.

"Please, Ranna. May I have some food, first?"

Ranna frowned, but went over to a cupboard and pulled out some stale bread. Alina looked imploringly at Malduk's delicious bowl of mutton soup, but Ranna just broke the bread in half and handed a piece to her with a grunt. Without another word the young woman turned and disappeared through the cottage door into the falling snow.

"And Mia," said Ranna, turning to her little niece, "put your coat on and fetch me that axe at the back. And some kindling too, from the edge of the forest. We'll stoke the fire. It's freezing in here."

Outside the snow was falling thickly, and Alina pulled her tunic tightly about her. She realised she had left her dagger on the chest inside but decided to get it in the morning, then ran towards the little barn beyond the yard, where she slept alone each night. The wooden doors were banging on their creaking hinges. There was a break in the cloud above and Alina looked up sadly at the moon. Often in the darkness she would spy shapes in its shining surface and wonder what it really was. It had almost seemed a friend to her, and whenever Alina was troubled by confusion or doubt, by fear and sadness, she would look up and hold onto it like a truth, while the moon would often seem to look down kindly too and whisper— *"Hold on, Alina. Keep on trying."*

Mia emerged from the house, and Alina smiled at her friend across the yard, then sighed and pulled the barn door fast behind her. The door blocked out most of the wind, although it still whistled mournfully through the rickety slats.

Alina shivered and felt a familiar loneliness and resentment deep in her heart. It wasn't only that Malduk and Ranna were so terribly hard on her. She had been with them for six or seven long years— she hardly remembered now—and had come to know most of the villagers and shepherds who cultivated these hills. Yet Alina was still treated as an outsider.

The other boys thought "Alin's" ways strange, for he had a much softer, finer quality than they, and his piercing eyes frightened them, while they often teased him for his red hair. The rumours about goblin origins were bad enough, but Alin was often daydreaming too and asking about the world beyond the village, which they all resented. Alina's only real friend was Mia, but although Alina was desperately fond of the child, little Mia was only nine, so how could she really share the feelings and hopes that were coursing through a growing girl's blood?

Alina cast her huge, clever eyes cheerlessly around the scrubby barn. It was so familiar to her now, this gloomy place, that she could see her way around it in the dark, yet a barn had never felt like a real home.

She thought a little jealously of the blazing stove that the couple would soon be warming themselves by that night, and wondered if the hopeless feeling in her stomach would ever leave her. Alina longed to have proper friends, to talk and dream with other girls her own age, yet her endless chores and thoughts of her origins kept her apart. Perhaps she really was a changeling, and not meant to be amongst humans at all.

Then what of this human life? It was all right, tending sheep, better than much of the hard work about the farm, and Alina had grown very close to Malduk's two sheepdogs, Teela and Elak. Just as she loved the animals she saw running free in the forests and the mountains. The lessons that she had been learning from Malduk and the others about shepherding had strengthened her natural instincts as a tomboy too. Yet she felt that there must be more to life than dreaming alone on a mountainside and watching sheep, especially for a fairy child.

Alina thought suddenly of King Stefan Cel Mare, of Lord Vladeran, and of the famous Order of the Griffin. She loved to hear tales of the secret Orders, but even more of the King, who in her mind was a strong and protective presence, almost the father figure she lacked. She often pictured him on a fine horse, wielding a sword to defend justice and the right. She often wondered too what it would be like to ride into battle serving a proud monarch, or one of the King's brave liege lords in the lands beyond the forest, like Lord Vladeran.

Alina sighed, walked over to the pile of dank straw at the back of the barn, and lay down cheerlessly in the growing darkness, drawing a thin, dirty blanket over her shivering body. On the floor beside her was more of the muslin cloth that she used to bind her upper body under her shirt, to help conceal the fact of her sex from the outside world. It made her almost ashamed to be a girl, let alone the child of goblins.

She was very cold, but the herb drink was working warmth through her veins, and bringing that familiar headiness that made her eyelids feel like leaden weights. Alina gave a loud yawn, wondering if the mixture really protected her from the spirits of the forest, and lay back, trying to keep her hazel eyes open. She was wondering fearfully what sleep would show her this time, or if the goblins would come in the night and tell her the truth of her changeling past.

THREE

THE PARCHMENT

I n the hovel old Ranna was glaring angrily at her husband, and the light from the kitchen fire sent sinister red shadows dancing about the walls. They were both standing by the kitchen now and whispering darkly together, as Alina lay in the barn and tried to sleep.

"You heard what she said," hissed Ranna. "She was talking to one of Vladeran's soldiers. There've been several around of late. If the girl remembers anything, we'll—"

"Of course she won't remember," snapped Malduk. "Do we have to go through this again, woman? What about the potion?"

Ranna cast a nervous look at the locked chest, which Malduk had sat on earlier, and on which now sat Alina's knife.

"Perhaps you're right," she muttered. "And I've always told them you'll beat them both, if they go near the chest."

Ranna seemed a little reassured, but then her cruel eyes darkened again.

"But what if someone recognises her, husband? One of his soldiers."

"Why do you think we make her cut her hair and dress as a boy?" answered Malduk. "Besides, you see how she's really changed. Nothing like she was."

"It's the change in her I'm worried about, fool," grumbled Ranna.

"We can't keep her nature a secret much longer. She's growing up so fast. Others are married far earlier than a girl like her, and there are already rumours about it in the village. I've heard some of the women muttering, busybodies that they are, and now Lord Vladeran's men are nosing about. What about Mia? She's always chattering."

"How could I foresee that your sister and her husband would drop down dead," growled Malduk accusingly, "and we'd have to take her in."

"It's going wrong," said Ranna fearfully. "I always warned you it would come to no good. After you found her."

"Oh, stop your whining, Ranna. And what about all the work she does? She's a help to us, ain't she?" Malduk said. "Humble Vlak shepherds with a servant, and a Saxon servant too," he added proudly. "That's rich. How the others marvelled at us when I found her. Or him. A Saxon waif, eternally in the debt of good old Malduk and his dear, kind wife, Ranna."

Malduk chuckled and rubbed his hands, thinking of something else too.

"Bogdan's as jealous of us as ever," he said with satisfaction. "Always calling Alin a warlock, and saying he'll bring the devil down on us. It's only because he wants a servant himself."

"Bogdan," snorted Ranna. "I saw him just now, lurking about near the end of the farm again."

Malduk scowled. They both hated Bogdan, because he had a claim on part of their land, while he and Malduk were always arguing furiously about rumours that Malduk had eyes for his wife.

"I'll fix him one day," said Malduk angrily.

But Ranna was thinking of Alina again. "More than just any Saxon though," she said sourly, "if that parchment in the chest means what I think it means. How could you take such a risk with the likes of them?"

Malduk's dark eyes flickered. The suspicion of who the girl really was had begun to haunt Malduk's mind. It was hinted at in the parchment he had found on the soldier seven years before, when he had stumbled on Alina in the snow. He had sometimes hoped that he might use it one day to make himself and Ranna a real fortune, yet with that greedy hope had come a terrible fear of the man who had written it, and memories of something the parchment had said. He could never let it be discovered who she really was, or their part in her survival.

Suddenly there was a hiss from Ranna. She was staring in horror at the wooden chest. She hadn't noticed it before, but now she could see the parchment poking from the lid.

"Look, Malduk. The letter."

"What the devil?" cried her husband, and the old shepherd began fumbling in his jerkin. "The key, Ranna. It's gone."

Ranna hurried into the kitchen and started looking frantically amongst the bowls where she had found the herbs. At last she pulled out another key, exactly like the one Mia had in her pocket, although covered in dust, and handed it to her husband. Malduk put Alina's knife on the milking stool, thrust the key into the lock, turned it, and threw back the lid. He snatched up the parchment from a pile of threadbare linen.

It was the letter, along with a bag of gold, he had discovered on the sodiers dead body, lying next to his dead horse, with Alina nearby unconscious. The letter Mia had seen that very morning, when she had found the key on the ground outside the hovel and opened the chest in secret.

After Malduk had first found Alina, and her shock had begun to wear off, she had sometimes asked the couple what was inside the chest, but she had long since lost interest, and so the old couple had almost forgotten to worry about it. But for a girl of Mia's age, it had held irresistible secrets.

"Someone's opened it and looked, all right," growled Malduk, glaring at the paper. It was covered in writing and at the top was a red crest, finely drawn, showing an eagle with open wings just like the mark on Alina's arm. It had already convinced little Mia that the parchment was something terribly important. Mia couldn't read, of course, but she had recognised the mark immediately.

"Alina must have stolen your key and looked inside," said Ranna.

"And she acted very odd when I came in. Perhaps she meant to return the key later."

"Wicked sprite. Do you think she could read it?"

The shepherd wondered to himself.

"Perhaps. A girl like her may have learned Latin letters with the monks."

"Then she knows," hissed Ranna, looking truly terrified now.

"Maybe she didn't understand what it really means," said Malduk doubtfully, "or realise that it speaks of her."

"And maybe she did. It may not name her, but she'd recognise the crest. Maybe that's why she was talking to Vladeran's men."

The old couple stood there in the flickering shadows, and both were shaking terribly with the revelation.

"What are you thinking, wife?" said Malduk, after a while. He knew his wife was much brighter than he.

"I'm thinking how vulnerable the girl is," answered Ranna. "She's often alone with the sheep on the mountain, ain't she, and with wolves prowling and the snow coming thicker and thicker, who knows what might befall a helpless shepherd boy out there? They'll only say the fairies took Alin back again."

Ranna's eyes twinkled, but something confused came into Malduk's face. He had saved Alina from the snows once, and somewhere he even felt a fondness for the girl because of it, and he still feared to have the sin of blood on his hands, and his conscience too, feeble as it was.

Ranna suddenly saw Alina's antler-handled dagger lying on the milking stool and snatched it up, as her head swung towards the door.

"What are you going to do, wife?" whispered Malduk.

Ranna looked back coldly at her husband, and her eyes glittered viciously.

"Do, man? Do what you should have done seven long years back," Ranna answered murderously. "Kill the changeling, of course. Or even better, turn the whole village to the job of murdering Alin Sculcuvant for us."

. . .

Alina Sculcuvant's sleepy eyes were growing heavy in the freezing barn, blurred by the witch's brew. She felt as if she were floating, and fairy arms were carrying her away into the forest. The herb potion, which she had just told herself was really honeydew, was hanging heavy in her blood, and her thoughts were already beginning to roam towards dreams.

"Roma," she whispered suddenly, rolling the word around her tongue, as if she was eating something tasty. Alina had been thinking of that woman of her dreams, with curling black hair, and the night before in the barn a name had come to her in her sleep. "Roma" was another word for Tsingani, the gypsies in the lands beyond the forest, and it seemed somehow fitting for a goblin or fairy mother. But Alina sighed. Roma wasn't right, and the memories just wouldn't come.

A note came on the wind though that filled the snowy air. It was the song that often came down from the mountains, with the darkness of the Transylvanian night, the call of the wild wolf.

Alina shivered, yet she felt her heart stir excitedly. So many times, as she laboured chopping wood, or sat with her crook in the fields watching over the bleating sheep, Alina had dreamt of climbing into the soaring mountains and hunting alone and free in the great valleys, or swimming in fresh rivers and bathing her face in new-fallen snow.

Dreamt of going out, alone and unchallenged by the shepherds and their stupid, fighting children, or the stern rules of the murderous old couple, to whom Alina believed she owed her life. Unburdened of her own dark dreams. She often wondered if it was her mysterious changeling origins that made her think so much of going into the wild, like a real goblin, and she loved listening to wolf song.

Alina yawned, as her huge hazel eyes closed, and immediately she was out there, running in her bare feet over grass and rock and stone. She felt like a wild animal herself, hunted by something she could neither see nor understand, and suddenly before her was the face she had seen more and more in her sleep. Not the face that came to drink a child's blood—the vampire—but another face entirely. Its great yellow gold eyes looked back at her, with anger and hunger at first, but then softening to a strange, barely fathomable question. Eyes set above a row of sharp and shining teeth, in a muzzle of pure black.

As she stared at the black wolf in her dream, Alina heard a sharp creaking from across the barn and opened her eyes again to the real world.

"Who's there?" she whispered, sitting up, and thinking nervously of the feeling she had had that morning. Over the years Alina had grown especially used to reacting quickly to sudden noises as she guarded the sheep on the mountain, and her eyes strained to see through the darkness.

Suddenly a shape was rushing at Alina across the barn, but her beating heart calmed as soon as she saw what it was. Malduk's black-and-white collie Elak came bounding towards her, and jumped up, covering Alina's face in warm, wet licks. It made her feel wide awake again, and sent the girl into peels of delighted laughter.

"Elak, stop it now," she giggled, pushing him down fondly.

"Shouldn't you be in the meadow with Teela? Why did you sneak away, boy?"

The sheepdog whined softly and lay down beside her, his huge black eyes looking up guiltily and his tail wagging. He was often sneaking off to be with Alina. How different Elak was to the savage creature she had just seen in her dream, and how glad Alina was of it.

"You mustn't run off like that, boy. Malduk will punish you, and me too," whispered Alina tenderly. "But it's so good to see you."

The girl smiled and stroked the collie's furry head. He felt so warm and soft, and she suddenly realised how desperately fond she was of Elak, and his sister, Teela.

"Dear Elak, you're my friend, at least," said Alina. "Animals don't mind if I'm a changeling or not, do they? Not like the stupid villagers."

Alina lay there stroking her friend, and she smiled to herself at her own foolishness.

"You don't understand me, do you, Elak?" she whispered. "Oh, I know you and Teela answer the whistles Malduk taught me, but it's not as if animals are like people, is it, really thinking and feeling, I mean?"

Alina sighed, wishing that people were as nice as animals, and Elak gave a whimper, but of course he said nothing. If little Mia had been there, she might have argued. She had said something to the older girl only two days before that Alina remembered now. "Not just anyone can reach animals like you, Alina, and not even the fairies know their hearts as well. Father always said animals sense what's inside a person. That's why they trust you."

But Alina thought of a day in the little wooden church in Moldov, when the priest had talked so scornfully about animals. "The holy Church teaches that God made man above all the animals," he had sermonised loudly, "and we must trust in His power." The priest was a cruel man, very unkind to the dogs in the village, and Alina suddenly wondered if animals could really think like people, and if they could what it was they thought about.

"What do sheep dream about, Elak?" she asked the dog suddenly, but he just whimpered again and licked her hand.

"Nothing but grass, I bet, Elak, or warm milk and a hole in a fence?"

Alina yawned and so did the collie.

"It's such a silly life, Elak, a sheep's. Munching on grass and drifting about in a flock, just to be shorn for your wool, or slaughtered at the Christ Mass. What's the point of it, and why do they group together so stupidly like that?"

Elak lay there dumbly, and Alina ruffled the fur on his head with a grin, then answered her own question. "Perhaps they feel safer in the fold, dear Elak. Like most things do."

The conversation had been rather one-sided, and Alina began to feel dizzy again. She lay back once more, but found herself still awake, staring mournfully at the slats in the old wooden ceiling, letting in the bitter weather, and the little flakes of snow that fluttered down, but vanished before they even reached her.

Alina was beginning to doze again when the hackles rose on

Elak's back. There was another noise, outside this time, and the dog started to growl furiously at the barn door.

"What is it, boy?"

The door opened and closed again noiselessly, and there in the darkness Alina Sculcuvant saw the glint of an axe blade. Elak sprang up with a snarl, but Alina caught hold of the dog as she realised who was standing there.

"No, Elak, don't, it's only Mia."

Across the barn the little girl put the axe down carefully against the door and walked towards her friend. She was carrying a heavy sheepskin coat under her right arm and a cloth bundle in her left. The thick woollen coat was an old one that Malduk used to wear up in the mountains with the sheep, and was almost bigger than Mia was.

"For you, Alina," said Mia, as she reached her bed. "You'll need it on a bitter night like this."

She held it out proudly to Alina, as Elak lay down again and put his head on his paws. Mia looked a little nervously at the large collie, for his sister Teela had snapped at her the week before. Elak was wagging his tail though, for he knew he was amongst friends.

"Thank you, Mia," said Alina gratefully, "but what if your uncle finds out that you've . . ."

Mia could still hear the old couple's arguing voices in her head, which had begun to rise as she had left the house and Ranna and Malduk had started to discuss Alina's fate. She hated arguments so much, and the little girl felt sick, wondering fearfully if they had discovered what she had done that morning.

"Uncle won't notice, Alina," she answered. "I hid it at the back of the house the other day."

42

Mia grinned as Alina wrapped the coat warmly about her. But her eyes darkened as she thought of what she had discovered in the chest. The little girl had realised it was a letter of some sort, and even at nine, Mia doubted that fairies and goblins wrote letters. Mia was desperately guilty, and almost frightened to speak of it.

"That mark on your arm, Alina," she said, "are you sure you can't remember what . . ."

"No, Mia. I've told you before. Please don't ask again."

Mia was going to say something about her discovery, when the barn door creaked loudly, and they both swung their heads. But the door just rattled on its own in the wind, then fell silent again.

"Nothing." Alina sighed, looking at the bundle in Mia's hands. "What's that, Mia?"

Mia held up the parcel and unwrapped it carefully. Inside was some freshly baked bread, two large pieces of cheese, and a whole onion.

"Mia!"

"Don't worry, Alina. I've been saving it up from my own meals."

Alina took it gratefully, but she wasn't hungry anymore; she was far too sleepy now. Instead she placed it carefully by her pillow, like some wonderful treasure.

"You'd better get back," she whispered, with a heavy yawn. "They'll be wondering."

"No," said Mia, sitting down beside Alina, "they've gone off somewhere."

Alina looked back at Mia in surprise.

"Gone off? Where?"

"Don't know." Mia shrugged. "Maybe to buy some more tsuika. I saw them going down the track together."

Alina wondered where they could be going at night, but almost wished that she had some fiery tsuika to drink herself—the local plum brandy that in winter was the surest way to warm the belly and fire the heart. The surest way to make your head ache too.

"I'll sleep here too tonight, if you like," whispered Mia. "It'll be warmer, and perhaps we can try to share our dreams."

It was a game Mia loved playing, getting Alina to close her eyes next to her, and seeing if they might have the same dream as they slept, because above all Mia wanted to dream of fairy kingdoms. Alina Sculcuvant, on the other hand, wanted to wake up to another world entirely.

"No, Mia," she said. "It will only make them cross when they get back. You'd better not."

Mia looked sadly at her friend.

"I don't understand why they're so hard on you," she whispered glumly.

Alina had often asked herself the same question, and she had come to believe that it must be because they feared her link to the goblins, especially old Ranna. Alina was already old enough to know that nothing produces unkindness and cruelty so much as fear.

"It's all right," said the older girl, "at least a changeling has a roof over her head, thanks to them. Far warmer than many, and food and water too. We must all count our blessings. That's what Ivan always says."

Mia grinned at the thought old Ivan, a good friend to "Alin" over the years, and his only champion amongst the shepherds, probably because he so loved listening to Alin's stories. Ivan had been there in the village last month, when Alin made up that wonderful tale of a girl, cruelly treated by her two elder sisters and made to work her fingers to the bone. Until she had found a fine silken dress in a hazel thicket, left by the fairies, and been seen by the handsome son of the village elder at festival, who had searched for her and taken her away to a better life. The boys had laughed at Alin cruelly for telling such a stupid, girly story, but wise old Ivan never laughed at Alin.

Alina's remark about a changeling might have made Mia think of the mysterious parchment, but she was feeling very sorry for her friend, and instead she had another thought entirely.

"Well, if you really are a changeling, Alina," she whispered, with a grin, "a goblin child, I mean, then perhaps you should teach my aunt and uncle a lesson."

Alina looked up in surprise.

"A lesson? What on earth do you mean, Mia?"

"Oh, nothing too bad, Alina. But couldn't you use your powers to stop them? Cast a spell or something. To make them kinder."

Alina sat staring back at Mia, little knowing how badly she needed such a power that terrible night. If the sense of things that sometimes really did happen was a power, it was a very faint one. And though Alina had no idea where all the stories she wove came from, she didn't see it as magic as some of the other children did.

Yet when she had been sad or hurt or frightened, she had often had the same thought herself. She would tell herself then that she was the daughter of a goblin queen, born in the heart of a magic flower, and suckled on honeydew, and could punish any who wished her harm, at will. That she could make their noses grow longer or their hair turn blue, that she could stop their voices with a wave of her hand, or make weeds sprout from their ears.

Yet Alina was fifteen now, and with time she had realised that she could do none of these things. She still asked herself whether that meant that she was no changeling, or simply that there was no magic in the world at all. In truth, at times she didn't want there to be any magic, because the one thing that Alina Sculcuvant wanted above all others, and with all the strength of her passionate heart, was to be a normal girl.

"No, Mia. I couldn't do any such thing," she whispered gloomily. "Besides, do other children fare any better than me?"

The two children wondered at that strange thought. They had no idea how children beyond the village lived their lives.

"But they never stop scolding you," said Mia indignantly, with all the deep sense of injustice of the young. "Even when I do something wrong, they punish you for it. It's just not fair, Alina. It's wrong. My parents would never . . . "

Mia's little blue eyes were suddenly wet with tears, and Alina sat up and hugged the little girl, feeling bitterly resentful that children should so be in the power of adults.

"We've each other, Mia," she whispered kindly. "Always remember that. And I'm fine. Really. Don't you trouble yourself about a changeling. I'm no more important than anyone else."

Mia sniffed and wiped her eyes.

"You are. And at least you get to learn some wonderful things as a boy," she said encouragingly, as Alina lay back again, and Mia reached down gingerly to touch Elak's nose. "Things that ordinary girls never usually do."

That was true enough. Malduk had taught "Alin" to count sheep on the mountains and read the seasons, to slaughter a lamb for festival and make Teela and Elak herd the dumb sheep about the valleys. To Mia these things made Alina seem as special as any goblin maiden, or the hireling of a fairy king. But although Alina always told herself that she should be grateful for it, with such useful knowledge came Malduk's constant criticisms and threats, which only added to the deep sadness in poor Alina's heart.

"Though who would really want to be a boy?" added Mia hotly. "They're always arguing, or fighting and bullying each other."

Alina smiled again. As she had sat by their fires listening to the shepherds, and deepening her voice to convince them she was a boy, she had often seen how tough they were on one another, and how hard a man's life could be.

"Yes, Mia. They are."

"I think you're special, Alina," said Mia, "and sometimes I don't understand why you don't . . ."

Mia paused helplessly, and Elak whined.

"What, Mia?"

"Oh, I don't know," answered the kindly little child. "What can girls do in the world anyway?"

Alina looked up and the barn door rattled again.

"You know, Mia," she whispered ruefully, "I've sometimes thought of running away. Of going back into the mountains and the forests and finding out who I really am."

47

Alina's hazel eyes suddenly glittered.

"Of finding the goblins and the fairies and asking them if they stole me from a human home, long ago. Or, if I'm really one of them, why they abandoned me in the snow. Of seeking out Baba Yaga."

Mia's face was suddenly filled with fear. There was no figure more terrifying to the little girl than Baba Yaga. Tales of her came like bad weather from the Eastern lands, a hag who lived in a wooden house, supported on chickens claws, that walked around the forest on its own. A witch who flew through the night, in a huge stone mortar, using the pestle as her rudder and sweeping away any trace of her passing with a broom of silver birch as she spread her evil. But now there was an even greater fear than the one of Baba Yaga in the little girl's heart.

"And leaving me here all alone?" Mia gulped, on the edge of tears again. "Shouldn't you keep hiding from the fairies, Alina?"

Alina looked back at Mia and shook her head with a smile.

"I'm tired of hiding all the time, Mia. But don't you worry. I'll never leave you alone, I promise. I've a debt to your uncle and aunt too. They saved my life."

"Only to make you their servant and scold you."

The older girl winced inwardly. Alina Sculcuvant felt—no, she knew—that she was better than a servant, whether she was human or changeling, and this life of work and care seemed wrong. Yet her dim recollections of the past had made her feel that perhaps she had always been a servant. She patted Elak again and wanted to cry.

"Does a changeling deserve any more?" she said gloomily. "But you'd better get back now, Mia."

Reluctantly little Mia got to her feet.

"All right then, Alina. Good night."

Mia crossed the barn with a heavy heart and picked up the axe propped against the door.

"And Mia," called Alina softly after her. "Thank you again."

"That's all right, dear Alina. Sleep safe."

Mia was about to slip away, when she suddenly stopped and slapped her hand to her forehead.

"Silly Mia," she cried. "I'm so forgetful."

"What is it?" sighed Alina, feeling really sleepy now.

"I forgot to tell you again what I discovered this morning."

Alina lay there listening, wondering where Malduk and Ranna could have gone.

"What, Mia?" she asked with another yawn.

The little girl frowned nervously.

"You must promise not to tell Uncle, Alina, or he'll punish me."

"Me, more like. I promise, though."

The little girl reached into her pocket and pulled out the key.

"I found it this morning, and opened the old chest. They went to market early and I waited until I was alone," said Mia, and in the darkness Alina couldn't see her blushes. "There was a paper inside it, Alina. I tried to tell you before. Something to do with you."

Elak's ears had come forwards, as he sensed the sudden tension in the air, and Alina Sculcuvant was fully awake again. She sat up sharply.

"With me?"

"Yes, Alina. I'm sure of it. There was a picture at the top, just like that mark on your arm, and lots of words, I think. Could you read them?"

Alina was having exactly the same thought that Mia had had that morning, that goblins don't write letters, and she got to her feet.

"Can you show me?" she said gravely, trying to throw off the effect of the potion. "Now, Mia?"

Mia's little face showed her fear.

"But Alina, Malduk and Ranna—"

"If they've gone down to Moldov, there'll still be time," whispered Alina, rubbing her eyes. "We can look again, then return it before they get back."

Mia was shaking, but she nodded slowly.

"All right then."

"Elak, stay there, boy," said Alina, as she walked unsteadily towards Mia. "And be as silent as the grave."

With that Alina and little Mia slipped through the barn door, leaving the axe behind. Outside, the yard was eerily empty and the snow was getting thicker, heaping around the stone well and laying its heavy, silent carpet over the shepherd's thatched house and the cluttered yard around it. There seemed to be no one about, and no noise from the hovel. The adults had gone all right.

Alina had her thoughts on the chest in the house, but Mia was still a child and delighted by the magic of snowfall, feeling her footfall light and springy on the strange new ground, almost giggling as the snowflakes melted on her cheeks and nose. In that muffling fall they could hardly have made a sound if they'd wanted to, creeping like thieves through the night towards the house. But the children suddenly stopped dead.

"Hush," hissed Alina, swinging round fearfully. "What's that?"

Mia's face screwed up like a walnut, and as they strained to listen in the darkness, the little girl suddenly caught a sound on the snowy air, like a distant drumming.

"Horses," gasped Alina.

They were both looking towards the path that ran along the side of Malduk's farm, and through the break in a wooden palisade that had been built a hundred years before, in one of the wars that had lit the region in fire and blood. It protected the track for nearly a quarter of a mile, running straight past Malduk's homestead down to the village of Moldov, but nowadays it was particularly useful when the shepherds were droving sheep to market, as it prevented the animals from slipping away down the bank, to a little stream that meandered along its far side.

The girls could both hear the sound of horses clearly now from the hard track. Riders were coming towards them in the snowy night.

"Perhaps it's Turks," whispered Mia, gulping and clutching Alina's arm.

"Don't be frightened, Mia. I'm here."

Alina was terrified. She had never fought anyone before, let alone a Muselman soldier, and the girl had no idea how she might confront something so terrible as a heathen and defend the little girl. She reached for her knife, but realised again that she'd left it in the house. The children's pounding hearts calmed a little though as they saw who came riding into the yard. They were two soldiers from the lands beyond the forest, one of whom Alina had seen before at market. He was one of Lord Vladeran's men, though not the one she had spoken with. He had a deep scar on his right cheek.

"You there," cried the other soldier, reining in his sweating animal. "I was on the hill and saw Turks riding east."

"Only three," said the scarred soldier at his side, "but they'll be others all right. The heathen never travel so far alone."

"Hurry, children," said the first soldier, "tell the household, then get the adults to raise Moldov. They must light the beacon fires."

Mia was shaking, yet she had never heard anything so exciting in all her life.

"Can we trust you, children?" asked the soldier who had just spoken.

"Yes, sir," answered Alina, deepening her voice and stepping forwards.

"Good lad. Then we've nothing to fear at all, with a David in our midst, ready to slay a hundred Goliaths. Or an Achil."

"Achil," said Mia nervously.

"Achilles, child," said the soldier with a smile, glad to take a rest from his gallop. "Your brother may look like a girl, but he's clearly bold. Don't you know the story? They tried to hide Achilles away dressed as a girl, but when they suspected him, and offered him many gifts, it was a sword he went for straight."

Alina suddenly felt her cheeks grow hot, but pride grew in her too, and Mia felt a little jealous. But the soldier with the scar was suddenly looking at Alina strangely.

"I want to be a soldier," said Alina boldly.

"Be content to be messengers first," said the first soldier, "for a warrior's is a hard, lonely way, full of death and sorrow. A boy couldn't know that yet."

Alina looked down. She thought sadly that a girl couldn't know it either, but that any life would be less lonely than hers. The soldier with the scar was speaking now.

"You sound like a priest, man," he said angrily, "giving advice and talking of Achil. You'll not waste any more of my time. I've helped by riding with you this far, but now I must get back to my own men and warn them. Besides, I have more important affairs."

"Then I'll ride to the troop of King Stefan's men camped beyond," said the first soldier, and he turned back to Alina and Mia. "Hurry, children."

They nodded as the men turned their horses and galloped away, although the soldier with the scar cast another enquiring look back at Alina.

"What do we do now?" whispered Mia. "Shall I run to Moldov to find them?"

Alina felt a dreadful sadness in her gut. Her natural instinct was to help, but she wished suddenly that it was her own parents that she had been asked to aid, whoever they were, and now she desperately wanted to know what was in the chest.

"No, Mia. First I'll get my knife from the house, then we'll go together. After we've looked."

Alina led Mia quickly up the steps and opened the door. There was no one inside either, and the room felt warm as they hurried towards the chest. Mia gave Alina the key, and she was trembling as she opened it, and took out the large paper, curled at the edges. At the top she could already see the shape of that eagle, etched in blood red, with opening wings. Exactly the same as the mark on her arm.

"Those other things on it," whispered Mia, at her side. "They're words, aren't they, Alina? I know they are. It was silly of me to try to read them, but I'm not wicked, I promise. You'll tell them, won't you, if they find out?"

Alina held the parchment with a sense of dread, and seeing the mark closer up made her shiver again. But not as hard as when she looked at the fine lettering written in pigment across the parchment and suddenly realised that she could decipher it. She began to mouth the words silently. It was extraordinary enough for a girl to be able to read, but how she could do so, Alina Sculcuvant had no idea at all. Perhaps it was a fairy spell.

"You can read it," whispered Mia wonderingly. "What does it say?"

"It says . . . 'To his lieutenant, from the hand of Lord Vladeran, written this day of our Lord and Holy Saviour 1479.'"

"Lord Vladeran," gasped Mia.

"Hush now, Mia. 'May this be a proof of the pact between us, and his orders regarding the disposal of a child. A traitor.'"

Its meaning came slowly, and Alina looked up. "Child?" she wondered out loud.

"What can it mean?" asked Mia.

"I don't know yet. It's about some child. But why does it say, 'disposal'?"

"Read on, Alina."

The girl continued, haltingly.

" 'The orders of Lord Vladeran are final in regard to the child. Let none aid or give her succour on pain of instant death. If it is found that his Lieutenant shall have dev . . . deviated from his instructions, his position, freedom, and life are forfeit. Let him do his work then and take his reward for carrying the girl, known by the mark here above, beyond the borders of Castelu, and for her disposal, for if he serves us faithfully, he shall always have our protection.' "

Alina fell silent. Castelu—Lord Vladeran's lands. A girl. A traitor to Lord Vladeran, known by the eagle mark on her own arm.

"It means you, Alina," said Mia softly.

"Yes, Mia."

"Then the story of how you came here," cried the little girl, wrestling with the horrible thought, "of how Uncle found and saved you, is . . ."

"A lie."

"Oh, Alina. Then you're not a changeling at all."

Four
HUNTED

A lina's head was spinning and the room had begun to sway before her hazel eyes. This news that she was no changeling was in part a wonderful thing for Alina Sculcuvant. She was not the daughter of goblins, after all, but a real girl.

Yet the truth that had come to replace the story of a changeling past was also far more terrible than being nestled in the arms of wood sprites or born in the bowl of an oak tree. A girl child, somehow linked to Lord Vladeran, and the distant region of Castelu. A child that Vladeran had wanted dead.

What could it all mean? Had Malduk and Ranna been protecting her from Lord Vladeran all along, even though the parchment threatened death to any who did so? If they had, and she was no changeling, it was still like a terrible fairy tale. Suddenly the light in the room seemed to flicker, and Mia rushed over to the window.

"I can see burning torches on the hill, Alina."

"Perhaps they know of the Turks already," said the older girl, although she felt in her gut that something far graver was happening, and she remembered her strange apprehension that morning. She was still wondering where Ranna and Malduk had gone, when they heard their voices outside, close by. They were returning to the house.

Alina hardly knew what to do. She still didn't know what the parchment really meant, and she had promised the soldier to warn Ranna and Malduk of the Turks, but she certainly didn't want to be caught like this with the parchment, and she realised she was wearing Malduk's stolen coat.

"Quickly, Mia," she hissed, throwing the paper back in the chest and closing the lid. "Hide."

"Behind the pelts," said the little girl, plunging for the sheepskins piled up nearby, where she had often hidden in her games about the house. Alina didn't need to be told twice, and she squeezed into the cramped space next to little Mia, as the door to the cottage burst open. They heard the sound of stamping boots through the curling wind and Malduk's heavy cough, then Ranna's voice behind him.

"That's good at least. Mia must still be in the forest. But where can that damned changeling have gone?"

Mia looked at Alina. The couple must have checked the barn. The terrified children could see through a gap in the snowy pelts, straight towards the pair. "Perhaps she overheard us," said Malduk, "and fled into the night."

"Well, it don't matter now," said Ranna. "It'll be done with soon enough."

"If it works," said Malduk, handing his wife something that she put down on the milking stool. It was a dagger, rather fine and long, curved like a Muselman blade and the handle wrought with etched silver. Alina wondered where a shepherd as poor as Malduk could have got such a wonderful thing, so much finer than her own, and where her own knife was too.

"It'll work all right," said Ranna. "With word of these Turks, the villagers are already in a frenzy. Their blood's up."

Malduk turned to look at his wife admiringly.

"And you were right, wife. We couldn't have done it in her sleep. Not in our barn anyway, with soldiers abroad and the elders warier than ever with the raids. As you said, she might be too strong for us now. And kill her here and Mia would know of it."

Mia and Alina turned to look at each other in utter horror. Kill her? What were they saying? Malduk stared out of the window.

"And it couldn't have worked more perfectly if the witch had cast us a real spell," he said with satisfaction.

"Only because I had the stomach for it, husband," said Rana angrily. "Unlike you, with your precious conscience. But it's not over yet."

The old woman had just picked up a piece of rag and started to wipe her hands, and Alina went icy cold, as she saw that Ranna's wrinkled old hands were covered in blood. Mia had noticed it too and begun to shake.

"A stroke of genius though—Bogdan," said Malduk.

Ranna's eyes narrowed like a crow's, and Alina wondered why Malduk was talking about the shepherd Bogdan. What had they done?

"Such a filthy, black night to be out, husband," Ranna growled. "I'll make you some broth, while you clean yourself up."

"Good, woman. My feet are cold enough to freeze brandy."

Ranna walked towards the kitchen, as the children huddled in terror in the shadows.

"I still say you should have done for her there in the snows," she said, "and saved me all this bother."

Malduk sat down on the chest. He was suddenly remembering that strange morning, seven years before, when he had been walking in the mountains and stumbled on the soldier and girl in the gully, next to their dead horse. From the rockfall around them, he had realised immediately that the animal must have slipped and sent them both over the edge, killing the soldier and the horse and knocking Alina unconscious. As the little girl had lain there, he had tried to rouse her, and when she had finally opened her eyes, he had asked her who she was.

"Alina, I think" was all she had managed to say, before she swooned again.

Then the old shepherd had searched the soldier's body and found that heavy bag of gold and Vladeran's parchment. He had taken ages to decipher the strange words written there, but at last he had realised that it was the man's letter of instruction, his orders to take the little girl far away in secret, and murder her.

"We shouldn't have meddled in her fate," said Ranna in the hovel.

"Perhaps I was getting soft in my old age," said Malduk, with a half chuckle, surprising himself with the thought. "And she would have been taken soon enough with the fury of that winter, it's true. She was frightened out of her wits as it was when she woke fully.

Kept mumbling that she was sorry. About what I've still no idea."

"She's a weak nature, that's why, even for a feeble girl."

In her own childhood old Ranna had wanted to be a boy, and she had been furiously jealous of her brothers and the freedom they had around the home.

"No doubt, Ranna," grunted Malduk, "but it was when she was lying there in the snow that I . . ."

"Took pity on her," hissed Ranna scornfully. "Why, husband? There's no pity in the wild. No pity for poor shepherds, neither."

"Then I had the idea, proper, to steal the soldier's gold, and get us a servant into the bargain."

Malduk was hiding his old pain too though, his longing for a son of his own. For a time the old witch's plan to conceal Alina with strange stories of changelings had even made him feel he had been given one by magic. But that had faded.

"But when it's finally over, at least I won't have to make the witch's brew again, to make her forget," said Ranna, holding up her little bundle of herbs. "She won't have anything to forget at all, let alone the lie that this ever protected her from the fairies. Stupid child."

When the old witch on the mountain had first given Alina Sculcuvant the herb soup to protect her from the goblins, she had whispered strange words to her too, as she looked deep into her little eyes, winking at Malduk over her shoulder. A spell, Malduk and Ranna called it, and they had paid the witch handsomely in mutton for her magic, as they had for the tale she had brewed up too. But the power, which men in later days would come to call hypnotism, helped by those potent herbs, had not been hard for the old woman to conjure. Not with the state Alina had been in.

Post-traumatic amnesia it would be called, in the far distant days when science would learn to name everything.

Ranna and Malduk both laughed, and Mia swung her head to Alina again, her eyes like a frightened cat's. The older girl's whole body was trembling with fury and bitterness at the dawning revelation.

"I still don't know why the great Vladeran didn't just do away with her himself," said Ranna irritably from the kitchen, "if he wanted her dead."

"Great ones always like others to do their dirty work, don't they?" answered Malduk. "Besides, you know how superstitious they say his lordship is. He clearly wanted the soldier to take her beyond the borders of Castelu."

In their hiding place, Alina's heart was beating harder than she had ever known.

"But it doesn't matter now," said Malduk. "She'll be dead before dawn. Serves her right for opening the chest today and poking in her nose where it don't belong."

Mia looked guiltily at Alina as the shepherd got up again and stared out the window.

"Ranna. There are men coming down the track already," he said, "I can see their lights over the palisade."

"Then go and meet them, man, at the end of the path. We must appear as normal as possible tonight. I'll go around the back and pretend to be chopping wood, or looking for Mia. While I get this off my hands properly."

Malduk looked suddenly nervous, but he nodded.

"Very well, wife."

"And husband," said Ranna, "we're innocents, remember."

"Yes, wife," answered Malduk, "but it's all very well the villagers hunting her down, but what if the authorities capture her first, and she tells them what she knows?"

Ranna stared at her husband as Alina wondered why they were talking of hunting her down. For all Ranna's clever plotting, she had not calculated this.

"Then she must never speak again," she growled. "Make sure of it, man. Silence her."

Malduk nodded again and snatched up the dagger on the milking stool. The door to the house banged violently, and Alina could hardly breathe with the horror of it, while little Mia was shivering furiously. Ranna finished in the kitchen and went outside to the back of the house.

"Quick," cried Alina, appearing from the sheepskins. "We can slip away and hide in the barn to think. They won't realise I'm there, and at least she won't see you, Mia."

"Oh, Alina. What they said. It's terrible." Mia's teeth were chattering almost uncontrollably. "They want to kill you. Lord Vladeran tried before. But they've done something. They're plotting. And my aunt had blood on her hands."

"Perhaps they went to slaughter a sheep. Come, Mia, take my hand."

Alina was nearly twice Mia's height, and as they held hands, she felt as protective as an elder sister. She opened the chest and grabbed the parchment again, slipping it into her pocket as the children hurried through the door together into the snow, and heard Ranna swearing and cursing behind the house. The two girls crossed noiselessly to the barn and slipped inside. They were safe, for a while at least.

"Oh, Mia," said Alina bitterly amongst the freezing shadows, as they shut the barn doors fast behind them and the girl noticed that Elak had gone. "If I'm no changeling, then what am I really?"

"It said Castelu," answered Mia. "Do you think . . . Do you think you could really be some powerful . . ."

"A girl?" said Alina quickly. "No, Mia, don't be foolish. But what am I going to do now?"

The little girl's eyes were full of tears, but she answered her friend with all the firmness she could muster.

"You've got to go, Alina. You've got to run away, like you said. Before Malduk comes back."

Alina knew her friend was right, but she felt sick to her stomach.

"And you'll come with me, Mia?"

The little girl gulped, but shook her head firmly.

"No. It'll only make it worse. You're bigger than me, and can run faster. Much faster than any of the village children. I've seen you. Run, Alina. Now. Up into the mountains. Anywhere you can be safe."

Alina shuddered, for now the thought of the mountains didn't make her feel safe at all, yet there was a strange excitement in the girl's heart too.

"But I promised never to leave you, Mia."

"Promises only matter if you try to keep them, Mother told me. Sometimes you can't, that's all," the little girl said with the strength and practicality of a born peasant. "I'm safe with my aunt and uncle, at least, but you've got to go, and quick."

Alina nodded, finding courage in her little friend's brave words, then started moving about the barn, gathering up her few humble possessions. The little girl helped her pick up her bits of clothing, a pack, and the parcel of food she had brought her earlier, and at last Alina was ready.

But with that they heard two more voices outside. The children peered through a crack in the barn door and saw Malduk running back into the yard and, trotting alongside him, one of the soldiers they had met earlier. The one who had spoken of Achil.

"You're safe from the Turk, for now at least," said the soldier, bringing his horse to a stop. "And Stefan's men are roused. But you must look to your loved ones."

Malduk was regarding the man very nervously, for he hadn't expected to meet him on the track at all.

"Yes, sir," he said.

There were shouts and the group of villagers from neighbouring Moldov, the men Malduk had spied before, came crowding down the path, and into the yard. They had burning tapers in their hands and their mood was ugly. They were hunting. At their head was a shepherd Alina recognised, called Barbat.

"What's wrong, men?" cried the soldier.

"Sculcuvant," answered Barbat, "the changeling. Where is he?"

Alina's heart was suddenly pounding fast enough to burst. What now?

"I . . . I don't know," answered Malduk. "He was sleeping in the barn, but now he's gone. Perhaps into the fields. Why, man, has he stolen something?"

The villagers had often accused Alin of stealing things.

"Stolen?" cried Barbat scornfully. "What do we care about theft, Malduk, when this is murder?"

In the darkness of the barn, Alina's knees went weak.

"Murder?" hissed Malduk, with glittering eyes. Ranna's plan was coming good.

"We found Bogdan on the edge of the village, facedown in the snow," said Barbat, "with this in his back."

Barbat reached into his pocket and pulled out a knife with an antler-handled dagger—Alina's own dagger. In the barn the girl felt as if a thousand furies were suddenly rushing at her, and she clutched at Mia's arm. Ranna and Malduk had murdered Bogdan.

"It'll break his wife's heart," said Barbat. "It's his, ain't it, Malduk? Alin's."

"It looks like his, yes," answered Malduk slowly, feigning reluctance and shock, "but he was using a different one today, Barbat. He left it in the barn."

Malduk reached into his pocket and pulled out the curving Turkic blade Alina and Mia had seen in the house, before Ranna had wiped that blood off her hands. He held it up innocently.

"That's Bogdan's!" cried Barbat. "I'd know it anywhere. The changeling's the killer, all right. He must have murdered Bogdan for his knife, or simply because the changeling hates humans."

Alina couldn't believe her ears—or her eyes. The villagers began to shout and curse, and the soldier put his hand to his sword and in the barn Mia could see that Alina wanted to go outside, to confront the injustice of it all and speak up for herself. The little girl grabbed Alina's hand and shook her head furiously.

"I can't believe it," whispered Malduk outside. "After all our kindness, and with my little niece Mia in our home too. We'll hunt him down all right."

"No," cried a voice suddenly. "It can't be Alin. He wouldn't. I know him too well."

Alina's heart leapt. It was her friend, the old shepherd Ivan, who had pressed forwards from the throng. Ivan had a wise, open face, which although kind was not soft, and was heavily lined by his years in the open. He was much respected by the other shepherds, but the murderous villagers began to shout even Ivan down.

"We know how you favour the lad, Ivan," growled Barbat angrily, "but none of us know where he really came from. Don't thieves and murderers creep out of the snows, like witches' children? We ought to have driven the changeling out long since. A Jonah, that's what he is. Ill luck for us all."

"Yes," said Malduk sadly. "Now I think you're right, Barbat. Poor Bogdan."

"You!" said Barbat, glaring at the soldier. "What are you going to do about it?"

"Sculcuvant, you say?" answered the soldier, thinking of the children he had met earlier. "A changeling?"

"That's right. And in league with the devil."

Suddenly there was a great howl in the night and the villagers turned, as Malduk lifted the dagger. One of them pointed up the mountainside, and they could see it but faintly in the icy air, a shape etched against the night sky, like a dark shadow. A wolf was high above them.

"It's that black loner," growled Barbat, with a shudder, "the one they spotted last moon, near the stream. The man-eater."

As she listened, Alina thought of that face she had seen in her dream.

"I should get home," grunted another villager immediately. "They say that one spends all its time stalking humans. With the winter everything's fighting harder to survive."

"Perhaps the black wolf comes from the Helgra," said a third villager nervously, and the others started muttering.

"The Helgra?" said Barbat. "What are you talking about?"

"That Magyar-Dacian tribe that lives below the great castle," answered the man. "Fearsome warriors, they say, who pay allegiance to none, not even Lord Vladeran, Tepesh, or King Stefan. The Helgra worship the wild wolf as the devil, and wear their coats as talismans."

"It's not the Helgra," said Malduk suddenly, worried that the villagers would turn from the task at hand. "Changelings serve the devil too. Alin must have summoned it to aid him in his wickedness. We must raise all the villagers."

They could all see the sense in this, all except Ivan, and they started nodding and muttering again.

"He'll not escape," cried the soldier, "and he'll hang for this. Or burn."

Suddenly the door to the cottage opened and old Ranna came outside. The lurid glow of firelight shimmered across the snow between the evil old couple, as Ranna hobbled forwards. She had slipped back into the house as the men arrived, and now she was holding a handkerchief to her face and she looked as if she had been crying.

"You've heard then, wife?" whispered Malduk, as she saw her.

Ranna sniffed bitterly.

"Yes, husband, and my heart's broken. How could he? I loved Alin so."

The villagers murmured sympathetically at the old couple's bitter plight. In their hard lives they despised little as much as ingratitude.

"We must find him soon, men," said the soldier, convinced now. "Hunt down the changeling, like a wild animal."

There were cries and grunts of approval all around.

"We'll get the dogs," said Barbat.

"Come up to the house first," said Malduk, "and we'll divide you into groups. Some to search the farm, others to scour the southern fields."

"We've men searching the South already," said one of the villagers, "and others posted right along the path. The changeling won't escape us. Unless he's already in the mountains."

"Very well then," said Malduk, "come quickly. But be careful of him. With his lies and his stories, he could enchant the devil. If you find him, don't listen to a word he says. Stop the child's throat."

"Wait, husband," growled Ranna. "He won't escape us."

"Why not, my dear?"

Ranna held out Alina's handkerchief, with a stifled sob.

"What's that?" asked the soldier stupidly, and Ranna's eyes sparked furiously.

"It's the changeling's, and carries his scent. For the hounds."

"Baba Yaga," hissed Alina in the barn, glaring at Ranna through the crack in the door. Mia was staring at her aunt in disbelief.

"I'll go outside, Alina," she said suddenly, "and tell them everything."

It seemed a chance, but as the children looked through the crack at the furious mob, they knew it was madness.

"No, Mia. They'll never believe you. They've always wanted to drive me out."

Alina had forgotten the parchment in her pocket, and seemed at a loss for what to do, but Mia was already tugging at her sleeve, pulling her to the back of the barn and a broken slat of wood in the wall. Alina found it strange that the younger child had taken charge, but the terrible revelation in the house, and then the false charge of theft and murder, had dazed Alina completely. She was petrified.

"Go, Alina, now."

"But where, Mia? I can't make it across the open fields. The only path to the mountains is across the stream, through that break in the fence by the copse. But you heard what the villager said. They've men posted along the path."

"You've got to try, Alina. Please. If they find you here . . . If they get the dogs . . ."

Little Mia was holding back the large piece of broken slatting with all her strength, and Alina peered outside into the snow. The wind was catching the surface, lifting it in angry curls of icy cold.

"Hurry, dear Alina."

Alina began to squeeze through the opening, pulling her pack after her, her breath smoking furiously in the freezing air. The little girl followed her through easily, and then they were both standing outside again, looking out across open ground towards the fields, and the high fencing that ran along the track. In the distance, to the south, they could just make out moving shapes and little red specks of torchlight, while the sounds of the villagers were loud on the other side of the barn.

"They won't see you from the house," whispered Mia, staring out towards the copse near the break in the palisade, where they often played. It led to the track, across to the verge, and down to the stream beyond. It was a good way off.

"Go, Alina."

The older girl rose, and she was about to run when she suddenly stopped and turned. Alina slipped her hand into her pocket and pulled out a little carving, a cross between a ram and a wolf, that she had whittled in the fields, watching the sheep.

"I'll never forget you, Mia," Alina whispered tenderly, thrusting it into Mia's little hand. "Take this and think of me. Then one day perhaps . . ."

"There's no time. Oh, Alina. Good-bye."

Alina leaned forwards and kissed Mia on the cheek, then turned and began to run, but she heard Mia hiss behind her. "Look, Alina."

Mia was pointing at the snow and the marks Alina's boots had made, which were leaving a clear, deep trail behind her that could easily be followed when the hunt began for real.

"There's no help for it now," called Alina, in a fearful whisper. "Pray for more snow, Mia. Just pray."

"Yes, Alina. And Alina . . ."

"What?"

"In the forests. If you ever find the goblins and the elves. If you meet Baba Yaga. Tell them to make a spell to protect me too."

With a nod, and a terrible ache in her heart, the young woman turned again and was gone. Alina made straight for the copse behind the barn and then in the direction of the stream, but as she reached the copse, she saw villagers moving down the track, their flaming torches glaring garishly against the perfect white, and Malduk leading them. Then Alina heard a yelp behind her.

"Elak," she whispered, as the sheepdog came bounding towards her across the snow and jumped up to lick her face, whining and wagging his tail foolishly. "Hush, Elak, you must be quiet."

The dog didn't understand and in his excitement kept whining loudly. Alina gave one of the low whistles she used at pasture, pointing her finger at the ground.

"Down, boy."

Elak sank on his forepaws and fell quiet. Just in time too, for the villagers were almost parallel with Alina and the gap in the palisade, and just then another wolf howl came down from the mountains.

"That loner again," cried one of the men, and his voice came clear and cold across the snow. "Do you think the changeling's really made a pact with the devil, Malduk?"

"I'm sure of it," answered Malduk. "Maybe SkeinTale's really a werewolf. I should have known it."

"Werewolf?" said the first.

"A human turned every full moon from a man into a snarling, murderous wolf," said Malduk, his gaze dancing amongst the villagers, "as he drops down onto all fours to join his wicked kin and feast on blood and gaze animal flesh. A changeling indeed."

Alina shuddered, but something else had come over her as she crouched there with Elak. The potion was still in her blood, and it was working on her again, making her body feel heavy, and her eyes droop.

All the villagers were listening attentively to Malduk's words, rapt with interest and fear too. Malduk spoke like a natural teller of tales himself, for he had often listened to Alina, touching something deep and instinctive in them all. Something angry too. He looked about and spoke again.

"They say that the bite of a lone black wolf is enough to put the spell in a man's blood, so that he changes," he whispered, with a growl in his throat. "That he can't be killed with ordinary arrows neither, but only with an arrow tip, which has been hammered out of a silver cross, blessed by a patriarch."

Alina heard the mesmerising words and pressed her hand into the cold snow to shrug off the weariness. Not now, she thought, Wake up, Alina.

Alina found herself listening again. She had heard many bizarre tales and legends from the village children, even more fanciful than her own clever stories, but just as she thought a shepherd's life strangely ignorant, so she had thought them mostly silly and too fantastical. But at Malduk's words she was shuddering.

"And they say that the werewolf can talk with animals," hissed Malduk, stoking the flames of fear and hate flickering around the little group. "See into their minds and very souls."

Alina was appalled that these men might think that she was such a thing, yet she suddenly found herself wanting to know what Elak was thinking and feeling, and the wolf that had cried out too. But Alina had just discovered that she wasn't from the fairies after all, and had no such power. She faced real life now, and all alone. An icy wind licked up the snow around her.

"Well, where's he got to?" said the first villager.

"No tracks here," answered Malduk. "We'll split up. Some to where the valley opens, others near the village gate. You two men, stay here."

Elak had lifted his head and started to growl, but Alina clamped her hand around the dog's muzzle.

"Come on then," growled Malduk. "Hurry."

The party broke apart, leaving only two of their number guarding the break in the fencing. They were both carrying clubs, and Alina tried to shake off the weariness and think clearly. It was now or never. She took the beautiful sheepdog's face tenderly in her hands.

"Elak," she whispered, "I need you to do something for me, dear Elak. I know you don't really understand, but please try. I need you to run to Teela. Make as much noise as you like, but don't stop."

The dog looked stupidly at the girl and she released her grip. Elak licked her hand and whined softly. There were tears in Alina's pretty hazel eyes.

"Now, Elak," she said, pointing towards the path, "Teela."

Elak's ears were up immediately.

"Go Elak. Find Teela."

Driven by the urgency in the girl's voice, her pointing arm, and the thought of Teela, Elak sprang forwards. The dog began to race round the far side of the copse, streaking through the gap, out onto the path, and away. But he wasn't making any noise and, hating herself, Alina picked up a stone and hurled it at his haunches. The sheepdog yelped painfully and sprang forwards.

"Hey, what's that?" cried one of the two men.

They turned and rushed in the direction of the moving shape, raising their flaming torches and shouting loudly. But by the time they had come to a halt again, muttering about blasted dogs, and turning back towards their guard post, Alina Sculcuvant had broken from her covering and slipped silently through the gap in the palisade. She trailed her pack behind her to mask her footprints in the snow as she went, but because this was where the men had all gathered, and there were many prints already, in the darkness the two villagers noticed nothing.

Alina pulled her pack over her shoulder as she went racing through the second break in the fence and tumbling down the snowy verge on the other side. In no time at all she had reached the little stream. She knew enough of living in the open to take off her boots as she crossed the shallow water, still unfrozen by the coming winter, and felt it burn like fire against her skin. Then she sat for a while on a large rock on the other side, drying and rubbing her feet, then sliding them once more into her warm boots. At least the cold river had driven back the effect of the horrid potion.

She opened her pack and took out some bread, blessing Mia for the timely gift, and looked out beyond the fields. The night was pitch black, but a moon was rising, giving an eerie blue wash to the white, and Alina realised again that she was still wearing Malduk's coat, and blessed its warmth.

In the distance the young woman saw the shadow of the forests and rising behind them the foothills of the great Carpathian Mountains. When she had thought of running away before, tired of hiding, she had made up pictures of goblin forests and fairy caverns, but as she looked out there she knew that real nature waited for her now, a whole world, unknown and forbidding to the girl, yet her only hope. Alina the storyteller was accused of theft and murder, while those who had pretended to save and value her had wanted to kill her to conceal their terrible secret. They had wanted her life.

It was a life she hardly knew anything of, one mixed with sadness and fear, and yet, somewhere, the feeling of love and safety beyond. Now Alina Sculcuvant wished more than ever that she had a friend to aid her in her journey, wherever it might take her. She thought bitterly of Mia and Elak and Teela, and around the foothills she noticed great flames of orange light begin to burn and blaze and lick into the night air. They were lighting the beacon fires. Then the changeling, hunted and alone, rose and was running as fast as her young legs could carry her, out into the wild world towards the mountains beyond, and in the heavens once more it had started to snow.

FIVE

BAVARIAN BLUSTER

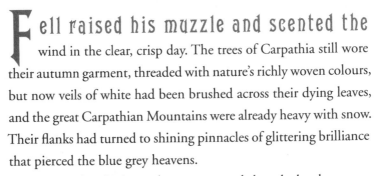

Fell raised his muzzle and scented the
wind in the clear, crisp day. The trees of Carpathia still wore
their autumn garment, threaded with nature's richly woven colours,
but now veils of white had been brushed across their dying leaves,
and the great Carpathian Mountains were already heavy with snow.
Their flanks had turned to shining pinnacles of glittering brilliance
that pierced the blue grey heavens.

The snow lay thick as a heavy coat, and though the sky was as
blue as new spring flowers, Fell was troubled and deep in thought.
Since leaving the cave he had drifted closer and closer to a human
village, thinking of the voice and the boy he had seen in the water.
Had Larka really sent her spirit from beyond to tell him of the
child's importance to nature itself? And what of those words
about the Helpers and a Guardian? The ghostly visitation was still
haunting the wolf, but in truth he wanted nothing to do with this
strange burden.

Fell caught a delicious smell on the breeze, the smell of
cooking meat. To any ordinary Varg it might have meant very
little, or been disgusting compared with the scent of a fresh kill,
but Fell knew of the humans and their strange red flowers—
their fires.

Fell knew how humans would chase and kill wild animals too, but not nourish themselves with the food straight from the bone like the wolf, but chop the carcass with their knives and put the bounty on a stick of wood over the flames that rose from the fire. They would even place it in a metal pot and add water and roots and plants to it, and let it stew horribly.

At first the unnaturalness of it had appalled the prowling black wolf, but with time, as he watched their encampments and smelt their kitchens, Fell had begun to accept that perhaps these Lera, these strange human animals, needed to do such a thing in order to eat. He pitied them for it, but Fell had grown accustomed to it too, and even come to like and recognise the scents and flavours given off by their concoctions.

Now the wolf could smell cooking rabbit and winter rosemary, and it made his stomach grumble and his mouth slaver. Three days after his strange visitation, Fell had been hunting without success and he was desperately hungry. With the heavy snowfall many of the Lera, rabbit and hare, fox and squirrel and hedgehog, had gone to ground, snuggling themselves safely away, warm and secret in their hides and burrows, hidden deep in the secret earth.

It was as if the land were going into a deep sleep, instilled by some magic potion, and was beginning to dream, or had been emptied of its rightful inhabitants by a mysterious spell. Fell had seen tracks and could sense that creatures, and thus food, were around him, but the contours of the land had changed completely, and with no natural cover anymore to hide the Putnar's approach, it was easy for prey to see a wolf and escape.

THE FUTURE

Fell padded from the cover of the trees and looked down the slope. Near a circle of rocks, he could see a little plume of grey smoke rising from a birchwood fire beneath a bubbling cooking pot. The wolf could scent horse dung too, but there was no one about, and Fell padded farther into the open. The wolf was wary, but hunger was getting the better of him, and the smells from the pot were drawing him towards the fire.

Closer Fell drew, and the wolf smiled as he saw that a coney, a baby hare that had not made it into the pot, was hanging tantalisingly on a stick, left for the morrow. As Fell approached the free breakfast, a shape stirred on the ground and he stopped dead. A man was lying fast asleep beyond the fire. An empty bottle of tsuika lay beside him and next to it one of the human's metal sticks. A sword.

Fell's muzzle curled upwards a little and he gave a nervous growl. He should have scented the human immediately, but the smell of horse and of cooking rabbit had masked him. As he stood there, he thought of that voice and its words about a human child, a boy who was close and needed his help. But how could a boy be important to nature itself? Fell wondered if it was the child's destiny to grow into a great and powerful Dragga. He had a thought then that he often had in his wanderings—that the real strength and fight of nature lay with the Dragga, the male. Fell wanted answers today as much as a meal.

The wolf raised his tail and wondered what to do.

As Fell stood there, something strange happened. Fell knew that the Sight was touching him again, even before the vision came. It was as if his eyes were misting over, and a sudden darkness surrounded him. Then Fell was seeing images in his mind's eye.

"No," he growled, trying to stop them coming. "No."

Fell was looking on a human homestead and in the doorway a human Drappa was smiling and waving, while two human cubs, a little Dragga and Drappa, held their mother by the waist, laughing and giggling happily.

Fell's eyes cleared and he was looking on the sleeping man once more, but now it was as if the very will had been sucked from him, and he felt weak and ashamed.

"What's happening to me?" Fell whispered, thinking of how he had understood those squirrels, but still the wolf couldn't move. Then there was a shout and Fell saw two horsemen galloping towards him. The soldiers, the Turks from the East, had spied him from the brow of the hill and were racing to save their companion. Their shouts and the whinny of horses woke the sleeper too, and seeing the black wolf, he cried out and grabbed his sword. The horses had almost reached the fire now, and as Fell saw the riders raise their spears, he gave a snarl and turned and leapt away.

Straight for the trees the wolf ran, his tail streaking behind him, but the horses were after him and his trail was clear in the snow. Fell knew all too well how quickly the hunter may become the hunted in the wild, and he was terrified. But the fear was made worse by the confusion that the vision had brought on him, and the sense of shame that he had not been able to strike the man. Fell had seen how humans could fight and kill, with the violence of the wild Putnar, and felt no pity for the creatures. Yet the Sight had drawn him into the man's mind, only to bring this strange confusion of purpose.

On Fell ran through the forest, with the chasing horses drawing closer. He saw the ground dip and heard the sound of water. Below him was a little river, snaking off through the forest, and Fell heard that warning voice in his mind again: Fear it, Fell. Fear death by water. But he swerved towards it this time and, just as the horses reached him, sprang onto a rock and leapt for the drop.

He sailed across the gulf, as the riders pulled hard on their reins and brought their mounts to a halt. Fell landed on the far side of the bank, his hindquarters splashing into the still-unfrozen water, as a spear landed in the soft snow beside him.

In truth the horses could have leapt the river too, but a wolf is dangerous prey, especially in the early winter months, when the savagery of survival is so strong in his blood, and the Turks had other matters to attend to. They were scouting, far from their Southeastern homelands, and had no time to lose. They had an army to take their messages to.

On the other side of the river Fell began to pad far down the bank, angry and startled, and still desperately hungry. The calm winter white was so beautiful around him, and yet all Fell's knowledge of the world, all the knowledge that had been passed to him from his father, Huttser, and his mother, Palla, from their own parents too and theirs before them, was working through his muscles and mind and being, telling him how dangerous such beauty could really be. For if Fell didn't eat soon he would weaken and then start to make mistakes. Then, if something befell him and he hurt himself in his journey, the Kerl would have no pack to aid him at all.

His five long years alone had already taught the wolf hardiness and self-sufficiency, taught him to swallow his loneliness and go on. But it had brought the pang of isolation too, and a strange resentment that he had to rely on himself entirely. Fell growled and pushed away the feelings of self-pity threatening to overwhelm him. It had been his choice to become what he was, his choice to walk the world alone.

The wolf stopped and looked up at the harsh mountain peaks above him. Had it really been his choice though? Fell hadn't chosen to be born with Larka, the white wolf, in the den, nor to be cursed with the powers of the Sight. Then there was all that his aunt Morgra had told him. The darkness and anger that engulfed him through her manipulations had taught him that his very nature was evil, and that all there was in life was the search for power and survival. Why did it all end in death too, as he had seen so often? Nothing really chose its path, thought Fell sadly, for every living creature, from Lera to man, was swept up in the great river of being, and borne along like leaves on a windy sea, to what destiny none of them really knew, or controlled at all.

Fell padded on. No, he told himself sternly, there is choice. That's what Larka's journey had taught them all. For though they were all made by nature, man and animal could have freedom if they truly chose it. As Larka had chosen to throw off the power she had been given when her mind had touched the human's—the power of the Man Varg, the greatest Putnar in the world.

Or is it only man that has real freedom, thought the wolf mournfully, only man that can really choose a path, with his clever mind? The ever forgetful Lera were ruled so much by the daily needs of survival, by the land and the animals they hunted, and that hunted them. Compared to man they were like sheep, lost blindly in a snowstorm.

Is that why Fell had carried the human child on his back down from Harja and returned it safely to its mother five years before? The little baby had become almost feral living with the wolves, but Fell had given it back to its own, in the village below the Stone Den on the mountaintop. To live and grow amongst its kind, perhaps into one of those very soldiers who hunted and killed the wild wolf. Why? Because, as Larka had taught, all things must be free and be true to their nature. Yet Fell had tried to make a pact too, a pact that the boy child had seemed to understand—the pact of the Putnar—a pact that said while his cries would remind man of the freedom and beauty of the wild, man's power must protect the wild too, in exchange.

Had man understood him, the wolf wondered now, or was Fell's pact just a hopeless dream? Fell had seen little in his journeying that had reassured him that man understood anything at all, with his relentless hunting of the wolf, his destruction of tree and forest, and his endless wars. Was it the Lera then who still had something to teach man instead? Fell's thoughts went back to the strange visitation in the cave, and that voice's insistence that a changeling was important to nature itself. Again the old fortune-teller Tsinga's words came back to the wolf, words in a different journey but perhaps just as relevant—*You must survive . . . for life itself!* How could it really be?

The wolf stopped and the fur rose on his back. He had come to a section of the river where the banks narrowed and the water dropped downwards. But instead of a gushing, laughing torrent, Fell saw a still pool that was beginning to freeze in the cold. Right across the narrow river a dam had been built, a lattice of branch and tree trunk, sodden with water. Fell's tail came up and he bared his teeth. Man must be close once more.

However, as Fell scented the air, the wolf caught nothing human on the breeze. Instead, around the strange construction, which so reminded him of men's dark dens and their wooden churches, a pungent, musky scent filled the air that made the wolf's mouth water.

Fell heard a splash and a swishing sound, and to his amazement, saw a heavy branch moving straight towards him across the water. It wasn't floating or drifting along aimlessly, it was moving as if it had a mind of its own, and it suddenly changed course and swung right, towards the dam. Fell blinked in absolute astonishment, and wondered if he was still haunted, or if all things in life, even the trees and stones, were really alive.

But no, a shape emerged on the edge of the dam. It was a dusky grey colour, tinged with brown, and as furry as a rabbit. It came backing out of the dripping water, pulling at the branch with its huge teeth. Fell could see whiskers and little ears now, and for a moment thought it was one of the otters he had hunted in his travels, until he saw the creature's strange tail—the oddest tail Fell had ever seen. It was flattened like the end of the branches that men used to row their boats across their waters, while the creature's hind legs were webbed like a duck's.

Fell had a startling thought. Could this creature be the Guardian the voice had spoken of? Perhaps it was odd that a wolf like Fell had never seen a beaver before in the wild, but in truth they were more common to the northwest, and this one had strayed very far from home. It was still completely unaware of Fell, so keen was it to finish its work, for its mate and kits were waiting deep below the lodge it was building for them. Now the beaver began to pull the log across the ground towards it, twisting and turning its powerful little body, dragging the heavy thing into place.

As Fell watched, he felt a strange wonder, for after his thoughts about man and the power of their minds, here was this amazingly clever and purposeful little animal. Then the beaver stopped and began talking to itself and Fell realised that he could understand it, just like the squirrels. "Vork, vork, vork," it said, "on, on, on."

Fell paused, thinking of those words about a Guardian, but hunger was wrestling inside the wolf, his own instincts for survival. The black wolf padded closer.

"Survive," Fell whispered to himself as he had often done. "I must survive. That is the law of the untamed wolf."

With that, the beaver sensed him and swung round. It didn't flinch or startle though, nor dive back into the water. It just stood staring back defiantly at Fell, with enormous brown eyes and shining, quivering whiskers. Then the beaver cocked its head and opened its dripping mouth, to show a set of quite gigantic square teeth. But rather than speak, it just yawned. Fell was amazed at the creature's reaction in the face of a wolf. His tail came down slowly.

"Aren't you frightened of me?" he growled.

At that the beaver tilted its head, and Fell could see the surprise in its eyes.

"Not *of* you," it answered in a strange accent, "but zat I can understand you, yah."

"It is the Sight," whispered Fell. "Something is happening; something in nature, I think."

The beaver nodded.

"And vat doo you vant?" he asked.

"What do you think I want?" growled Fell.

"To kill and eat me," answered the beaver coldly. "Zen vat are you vaiting for?"

Fell was even more surprised at this remark. The beaver didn't seem frightened of him at all.

"Vell?" he went on scornfully. "You expect me to give you permission, perhaps? Try or don't try, but don't vaste my time looking at me like zat."

Fell was struck dumb. As a wolf, his instincts were trained to two basic responses in the wild—fight or flight—but Fell had never met a creature before that seemed to take the attitude of talk or be rude.

"But aren't . . . aren't you afraid of me at all?" he whispered.

At Fell's question the beaver sat back on his haunches, propped himself up on his bizarre tail, and pulled his little front paws through his whiskers.

"Afraid of vat?" he almost snorted. "Of being eaten? Every day a creature like me faces zat threat. If I spent all my time vorrying about all zee zings zat could happen to me in life, I'd never leave zee hide, let alone finish my lodge."

"Oh," said Fell, almost ashamed that he had failed so miserably to make any impression on the beaver whatsoever.

"Father told me never to vaste time on fear," said the beaver. "Get on vith it and don't complain, zat vas Father's motto. Mates to care for, and hungry kits to feed. Zat's real life, and have zum fun doing it, I zay. It all ends zee zame vay in zee end, anyhow, vether it's in a stomach or in zee ground. Besides, I have zings to guard."

Fell suddenly wondered if he was in a dream—a beaver talking to him so philosophically like this about life and death. But it was the last thing that the beaver had said that had stuck in his mind, and again he thought of that voice and Larka's face.

"Tell me," he said, "you seem to know much. Then what do you know of the Guardian?"

"Zee Guardian!" said the beaver immediately, looking frightened despite all he had said. "Doesn't one vith zee Zight know of him already?"

"No, tell me."

"Zee Guardian is a great and terrible myth," said the beaver with a shiver, "and in legend is zaid to know all zee deepest zecrets of zee Zight."

Fell's yellow gold eyes narrowed. Perhaps this Guardian could tell him how a child could be important to all of nature. Besides, when he had become a Kerl had he not promised himself to hunt for meaning and track down lies? "Who is this Guardian?" he asked. "Where is he? What is his name?"

"None know zat grave zecret," answered the beaver, "except if he is real, zee Guardian valks alone, shielding his identity from all, zey zay, and zpeaks with a mouth of stone."

Fell had never heard anything so ridiculous in all his days. He felt rather embarrassed for having asked. But the beaver went on.

"Zey zay zome pretend to be him. Zome of zee Lera. For zere are many tricksters in zee lands beyond zee forest!"

Fell had relaxed, for the black wolf had decided not to eat the impudent animal after all, and he rather liked the twinkle in its cheeky eyes. The beaver had caught the meaning in Fell's body too, but he didn't relax quite so much as the wolf.

"And who are you then?" asked Fell.

"Ottol," answered the beaver, lifting his head boldly, "from zee great black forests to zee vest."

Fell knew his own country as the lands beyond the forest, and he had no way of knowing that the beaver meant the region that one day men would call Bavaria.

"And you?" asked Ottol abruptly.

"Fell," answered the wolf.

Ottol dropped his paws immediately.

"Ah yes, zee lone black voolf," he said rather more warily. "Vee have heard rumours of you, Fell, though I zought zem stories. You are almost a legend, roaming zee forests and scaring zee Lera vith your cries. Vy do you do it?"

Fell was strangely pleased by his own reputation, but his lips curled up.

"You wouldn't understand," he answered darkly. "You're no Putnar, Ottol the beaver."

"And zat I'm not, zanking zee Great One," said the beaver. "I eat zee bark and delicious berries. Having to hunt and kill all zee time, and to eat varm meat, it's deeeeesgusting."

"Is it?" growled Fell, getting his appetite back almost immediately. "Perhaps I should teach you just how disgusting it can be."

"Spring and jump at me, vould you?" cried the beaver sharply. "Vell, doo it. Go on, zen, and zee just vat happens, you fool."

This was too much for Fell. Almost faster than you can say "river beaver," he sprang at the creature with a snarl, but Ottol launched himself off his powerful tail and dived back into the water to safety. On land his little feet made him slow, but in the water he was master of his own world.

Fell, on the other hand, landed on the spot on the lodge where Ottol had been perched, and as soon as he reached the slippery logs, he felt his paws scrabbling hopelessly and the ground beneath him moving. The logs in the dam wall had begun to slide, and it was all the wolf could do to stop himself being hurled into the river, or pulled down between the powerful branches.

Two logs caught his front right paw, so painfully that it felt like a human trap—the metal teeth they left in the forest—and part of the lodge wall fell away in a noisy cascade. Fell thought he would be caught and crushed, but as they went on rolling, his injured paw was released again, and the wolf managed to get purchase with his back legs. He gave another leap, and just as a part of the lodge fell in on itself with an almighty crash, landed on the bank, safely.

He felt a bad pain in his right paw though, and as he looked down he saw blood staining the snow. Fell whimpered bitterly and began to lick at the deep cut on his leg.

"Now zee vat you've done," came an angry, scornful voice, and Fell looked up to see Ottol glaring at him from the far bank. "I knew zat vood happen. It vill take me two whole days to rebuild it."

Fell snarled, but the beaver, far out of reach now, held his ground.

"Vy do you zink I didn't run ven I first zaw you? I knew you'd spring and damage my lodge."

"I thought you zed you veren't frightened," snorted Fell angrily, mocking Ottol, and licking his paw again.

"No, zo I'm not," said Ottol proudly, "for vee are from a family of vorriors, and one zing my father alvays zaid to me, 'Don't be afraid, Ottol, courage my boy. And remember, strike upwards. Strike upwards, if you strike at zee stars.' But I'm not stupid, and I'm not ready yet to be zee meal for a zilly voolf, legend or not."

"If the river weren't so cold, you'd be a meal soon enough, bold beaver," growled Fell dangerously, his breath smoking in the air, and hiding the fact that he feared the water too.

"And how vood you catch me with a voonded paw?" asked Ottol scornfully.

The beaver paused though, and something kindly came into his intelligent eyes. "Yet vee are even now, are vee not, Fell?" he said. "You damaged my lodge and it damaged your paw. You'd better doo zumthing for it. It vill be dangerous in zis vether."

Fell eyed him slyly. It was absurd for a beaver in the wild to be trying to help a wolf like this, and the Putnar suspected some ulterior motive. In fact Ottol did have an ulterior motive, for quite apart from wanting to protect the new lodge, of which he was so extremely proud, his hide was deep below it and inside it was the beloved family he was guarding. He wanted Fell's focus away from his home.

Yet Ottol, for all his Bavarian beaver bluster, was not an unkind animal, and he had seen something in Fell that he liked too.

"I can bring you zum plants I know to help it heal."

Fell looked up.

"I'm all right," he growled proudly, "and I don't need any help from you."

"Don't you indeed?" said Ottol. "And vere are you going?"

Fell's eyes narrowed. How could he tell the beaver of the voice, and his vision of a human with a mark on his arm, that he had been told he must help. In truth Fell had still not accepted the mad injunction, and although the voice had said the child was close, he had no idea where he was going at all.

"I wander," he answered sullenly.

"And all alone, vithout a mate and a family of little ones to care for?" said Ottol. "I can't zink of anyzing more terrible."

"A family?" said Fell softly, thinking of Huttser and Palla, and their cubs—his brothers and sisters—Khaz and Kipcha, Skop and little Larka, whom his parents had named after *her*. "What point in a family, Ottol? They grow to face the same pain and darkness as everything else, and then to die too."

At this the beaver dived into the water again and swam back towards Fell, who marvelled at the creature's lack of fear of the water. He pulled himself out on the lodge once more and shook his coat.

"You're dark indeed, voolf," he said. "Why zo, Fell ZlipPaw?"

"Because I'm a Kerl and have seen much darkness. Because it's my nature."

"Is it indeed?" said Ottol, "and vould you doo zomething for me, Fell?"

"What?" asked the wolf in surprise.

"Vould you turn zat log for me vith your good paw? Zee one on top of zee smaller, over zere. It vill free zee first, and help me get back to vork."

Fell was surprised by the request, but for some reason he got up and limped over to the log. He began to nudge it with his muzzle towards the lodge, but as he did so felt something warm and pleasant on his back. A shaft of hot sunlight had come slanting through the winter trees, and after sitting in icy shade, he now felt warmth on his back. It was exactly as the clever beaver had intended.

"Zere," cried Ottol, "you zee?"

"See?" said Fell, rolling the log and looking back.

"You know zee zunlight too, voolf, and you like it."

"I didn't mean that," snapped Fell coldly, but very much liking the sunlight on his back. "I meant . . ."

"Zee darkness of zee world," said Ottol, "I know. Zee darkness of zee wild Putnar and zee fighter. Zee darkness of dreams and nightmares."

"Yes," growled Fell.

"I too know zee darkness, I know zee warm, zafe darkness of an earthy hide and zee misty, curling darkness of zee endless flowing vorters, and a vorld of strangling veeds beneath. I know zee darkness of leaves and zee musty, zecret places of zee forest."

"But that's not . . ."

"Not?" snapped the beaver, "not zee zunlight, no. Not vot you zink is black in your nature either. But it is zee darkness, as zee zun on your back, or zee glitter of corn in a field, is zee light. But is one any better zan zee other?"

"What do you mean?" growled Fell.

"Look at mushrooms of zee forest," said Ottol thoughtfully. "Beds of fungus and lichen. Fields of gorse and bracken, vere a million living zings breed and grow in zecret. Do not zee other Lera feed on zem to live? Has darkness not a power too?"

Fell was silent.

"But if you zink it zee only power, you're wrong," said the philosophical beaver, "for it is zunlight zat draws zee dark power from zee earth, and zo makes zee trees grow tall. Zo from vere doo you draw your power, voolf, zee darkness or zee light? And can't you hear it, Fell?"

"Hear it?"

"Zomething is happening, as you zaid. Zee voice of zee Great One, my kind call it. Talking through all nature."

Fell blinked. Was that what the squirrels had meant? Did a mysterious Guardian really exist, to give him an answer to this madness?

"Zee miracle comes again, as does zee spring. And if you zink darkness your only power, vill you not stay in zee shadows like a guilty zing, hiding away forever?"

"I . . ."

"Zere," said the beaver smugly, "perhaps you have been too long in zee dark, Fell ShadowTail. Look to zee light."

Fell took a step forwards.

"You don't understand," he growled again. "Besides, you build your dam, and hunt for your mate and cubs, but you do not have what I have. The freedom of the untamed wolf."

The beaver cocked his head questioningly.

"Freedom without responsibility? What freedom is zat? None at all."

With that there was the most extraordinary sound, a kind of barking and then a swishing and two tiny heads popped out of the water, followed by a third, as large and handsome as Ottol's. It was his mate and her kits.

"What's zee racket, Ottol?" the female beaver snapped irritably.

"Stay back, children," cried Ottol to his kits, for the little baby beavers were scrabbling up the bank towards their father, and thus closer to the wolf.

Ottol suddenly wished with all his heart that they had waited till early summer to have children, but the journey to this strange land had disrupted their natural rhythms. The look of terror from Ottol's mate was evident too, as she rose from the water and saw the black wolf on the riverbank. She started to slap her huge tail on the surface of the water in desperate warning.

"It is all right, Ottol," growled Fell softly, feeling rather amused. "I'll not harm you, or your family. I swear it."

The female beaver blinked in astonishment that she understood Fell, then stopped slapping the water, for she realised there was no one else to warn anyway. Fell was suddenly surprised at himself for making so many promises.

"Zen I zank you indeed," said Ottol graciously, dipping his head politely.

"And now I must be gone," cried Fell, startling the little ones with the power of his growling voice, "for if I do not hunt soon, it is I that'll be dead. And I am a wolf."

"Ah yes, your freedom," said Ottol, his eyes twinkling like

dewdrops. "Zen perhaps you should go zat vay, to zee clearing beyond. I zaw deer tracks zere, zis morning."

"And have you no sadness for a deer?" asked Fell a little coldly. "Just because your own kits are safe?"

"Oh, yes, yes indeed," answered Ottol, "but as you zay, zey are mine. And I love life, Fell, and a fair chase too. Nature is nature, as zee Great One decrees, in all its harshness, or zelfishness. But tell me, Fell," added Ottol, watching the wolf as he began to pad away, "you have your freedom perhaps, but have you nothing to protect? To care for."

Fell did not answer and felt a strange sorrow in his belly.

"Well, good hunting zen, Fell of zee Riverbank," cried Ottol, as his family gathered nervously around him.

Fell began to run, his right paw stinging furiously. He realised that he was sad to leave the beaver, and his pretty little family, for it had been good to talk with Ottol, almost like a friend. But then he came to the clearing and saw the slots of a sika deer in the snow. Fell's head went down immediately and his pace grew faster, and in a moment the wolf had spotted it. It was a small deer, grazing on its own, and although it looked thin and scrawny, at least it was a meal.

The excitement coursing through Fell's body protected him from the pain of his wound, and his pace didn't slacken. The little deer was young and inexperienced, and within a moment the black wolf had sprung.

Fell missed the kill. The thing that had happened to Larka long ago, and to Fell many times, was happening again. In his mind's eye the Sight had already given Fell a vision of what might have been, and of the stricken deer's pain, which Fell experienced in his own body, while in reality he missed the leap and the deer ran free.

"The light or the darkness?" growled Fell as he licked his still hungry lips and looked mournfully at the animal vanishing into the distance. Fell realised that his path had taken him towards the edge of the trees, and as he looked out, he saw the valley and, far below, the village of Moldov he had been skirting now for three days, despite his reluctance to follow the voice. Fell's heart beat faster, as he thought of his vision in the pool and wondered if the child was really sleeping somewhere below. Was he not sworn to hunt for meaning and to track down lies? But he shook his head. Ottol's words of the Guardian had been utter madness and he wanted nothing to do with it. He threw back his sleek black muzzle and howled.

SIX

BLUE ICE

Alina Sculcuvant heard the savage voice on the wind, and it made the young woman start and turn fearfully. She was in the open and far below her she could see the valley where her flight had begun, laid out like a picture book. She shivered bitterly and stamped her booted feet in the snow. They were so cold they felt like blocks of ice, but her shirt was damp with sweat, and Alina knew that if she stopped too long the air might chill it to her back.

Alina had halted for a moment to sit on a large rock, and around her the air was filled with chattering cries, as three magpies scavenged in the snow behind her. The late afternoon sun was pressing through drifting clouds, and she suddenly pulled up the sleeve on her right arm to look at the mark. Then she got up and scrambled on up the slope.

Just that morning, along the edge of the tree line, Alina had seen a group of villagers from Moldov and amongst them Malduk. Now she hated him with all her heart. They had almost caught her with their dogs, but Alina had managed to pull herself down into a large abandoned badger's set, and the scent had masked her own.

The scent had made the hunting dogs so wild that their masters had begun to drive them back down the mountain. Alina had waited almost two hours in that tiny, cramped space, curled up like a ball, but at least it had been warmer in there, and the girl had almost fallen asleep.

Alina had known that she had to keep moving, to get as far away as possible from her home, or that terrible place she had had to call home. They would never stop hunting her now, and the chase could not end in a trial, or any kind of justice. It had only one possible end, if they caught her—Alina's death.

The terrified girl felt darkness swamp her thoughts as she scrambled on. Any friends she had in the world, and they were few enough, she had had to leave behind her, and she was bound she knew not where. Her world had changed entirely with the discovery of that parchment, and the revelation that she was not a changeling, but somehow connected to the great Lord Vladeran in the region of Castelu.

But how? She had always known that she was not destined to be a mere shepherdess, dressed as a boy. Yet when she recalled her dreams, they were of a household where she slept in a bare room and was treated little better than a servant. Her past seemed no better than her life in Moldov. Alina had understood from the parchment that she had been given over as a little girl to be murdered. But how could someone so great as a Carpathian lord want the death of a child, and a girl child too? Was she really a traitor? Alina strained to remember but could not.

Something else had changed for Alina, in these three days of her flight. Each night she had managed to take shelter from the bitter weather, first in the hollow of a great oak like a fairy child, then in a drift of leaves, kept warm by the snow itself, and finally in a narrow cave in the mountain. She had felt like a goblin as she had done so, but each night her strange dreams had grown stronger and stronger.

Alina had dreamt of that child again, lying in its cot, the baby she had felt was her brother, smiling up happily at her. And of that beautiful woman with curling black hair again—Roma, Roman, or something like it—yet who had ordered her about as roughly as Ranna had, and who had entrusted her with some grave duty. Then Alina had been looking down at that wooden cot, and it had been empty, and suddenly she had heard a cry, a low, searching howl. Wolves. Why was it that so many times in recent days Alina Sculcuvant had dreamt of wolves, who seemed to be summoning her to some deeper understanding?

The guilt connected to the fate of that sleeping infant was more terrible than ever though, and Alina realised that the herbs that for so long Malduk and Ranna had tried to control her with had worn off, and that the dreams, or memories, could only get stronger.

The night before, in that stony shelter, the dream had been the most real—of the great black wolf with fearsome, piercing eyes. It had been standing before her, its ears pressed forwards as though listening. Was it hunting her too, or had she somehow really summoned it?

Alina pushed away the horrible thoughts, and stumbled on through the forest she had just entered. She was desperately hungry, for Mia's food had been finished on the second day, and although she knew it had saved her life, and she had managed to slake her thirst with handfuls of snow, it was not like a real drink and her belly was grumbling. Her climb into the mountains was taking her away from the streams and rivers, and Alina wondered now if her stomach would ever feel full again, or her tongue refreshed.

Although she had had to kill a sheep once with Malduk, and had hated doing it, she had no experience of hunting, and knew only a little of the berries or plants of the land, what few remained with the growing winter. She had tried gathering some that morning, berries as dark as ink, and although at first they had tasted fine, they had made her sick in the snow. Even if Alina had known how to set a snare, or to chase the wild creatures like a man, with the loss of her knife she had no tools or weapons, and besides, apart from birds flying south, Alina had seen no animals at all.

She looked up at the trees around her and felt fear whispering in their branches. Night was coming, and the forest was a place she had always associated with fairies and spirits. Now she realised how exposed she was. *Without the witch's charm to protect me, perhaps the goblins really will come and snatch me back.* The thought lasted only a second, and Alina realised suddenly how foolish she was being. She wasn't a changeling at all, the parchment proved it, she was a real girl now, and she was suddenly sure fairies and goblins didn't exist at all.

Alina stopped in the wood. She had come to a clearing and sensed that there were people about before she reached its edge. Alina spotted a fire, blazing in the snowy twilight, and eight or nine men and women crouched around it in the clearing, warming their hands and feet.

She heard a strange, haunting melody—the sound of a fiddle whining softly through the coming night. Alina wondered in amazement if she had stumbled on the fairies after all, until she realised from these people's colourful clothes and their dark faces that they must be Tsingani—gypsies.

The sight was almost as mysterious and magical as coming on a real fairy encampment, and Alina crept behind a tree to watch. They were talking and laughing loudly, as they passed around a bottle of rough wine and plucked spitting chestnuts from the flames, or munched on goat meat around their fire. One of the gypsies, a tough, handsome man with coal black hair, suddenly spoke.

"What will the winter bring this time?" he said. "It looks like it'll be a bad one."

"Perhaps I should look into the flames," said a gypsy woman at his side, "or read the cards."

"Why?" said the man. "You have the Gift?"

"The Gift, Father?" said a voice at his side, and Alina noticed a little boy with curly chestnut hair, sitting beside him on the ground.

"A true gypsy power," said his father. "A gift to see things, beyond the ordinary insights of people. They say that you're either born with it, or not, and it comes through here."

The gypsy touched a finger to his dark forehead in the firelight.

"A gift of seeing further, and of knowing more," said the woman with a kindly smile at the little boy. "A gift to predict, and to understand too, although there are those that might call it a curse. They say changelings have it above all, so let's hope the fairies didn't drop you here amongst us, boy."

The others laughed, but Alina's ears had pricked up, and she wondered if she herself was a gypsy.

"A gift to look into the minds of wild animals too," the woman went on, and the boy's eyes boggled in his head. Alina remembered Malduk's words.

"Wild animals," he whispered, peering nervously around at the forest and almost spotting Alina behind the tree.

"It's not any animal that we gypsies have to fear, son," said his father with a laugh, ruffling his hair fondly. "It's those damned villagers. They're hunting something again. I've seen them on the mountain."

"It's wolves," said the woman. "They think they're demons."

Some of the gypsies chuckled loudly around the fire, and shook their heads at such foolishness.

"You're brave on such a night to laugh at demons," said another man, "when they say Lord Tepesh rides out again."

Nine pairs of eyes were suddenly regarding one another through the firelight, like nervous wolves themselves. There was no more terrible name in the lands beyond the forest than Vlad Tepesh, even to the Tsingani, who tried to live outside the laws of men. The name itself meant the "Impaler," after the Wallachian warlord's custom of impaling the bodies of his enemies on wooden stakes. He had used the practice to suppress his own people, and collect taxes too, but also to strike terror in the hearts of his Turkish enemies in the Ottoman lands.

He was the son of that great Prince of Wallachia, Vlad Dracul, who had been murdered by the Hungarians years before, and whose name signified that he was a member of one of the secret Orders, the Order of the Dragon. Dracul itself meant "Dragon," but in those dark days of fear and symbols, if such things have ever lessened their grip on man, it had another meaning too, for it was a name for the devil himself. This Vlad Tepesh then, because he was the son of Vlad Dracul, carried another title, which has lit fear and horror in the hearts of humans to this day—Draculea. Dracula.

"We'd better not be heard saying it though," muttered the gypsy woman, in the growing darkness, "if we value our hides. Not of a great overlord like Draculea."

"What have the Tsingani to fear of overlords, woman?" said a third man scornfully. "Lord Tepesh's palace is more leagues away than I can count. If I could count."

The others laughed again, but the gypsy who had spoken first was shaking his head.

"They rumour that Draculea drinks human blood," he said angrily, "and that in his castle he invokes spirits and talks with the very dead."

"Old wives' tales," said the gypsy woman, trying to calm the frightened boy, "stories for Baba Yaga. We Tsingani shouldn't trouble ourselves with such lofty matters anyhow."

"Know our place, eh?" said the boy's father, raising an eyebrow.

"Perhaps. And isn't it Tepesh who, like King Stefan, keeps the lands at peace and the Turk at bay? Besides, I've heard of the kindnesses Draculea does. His charities. The Orders are sworn to protect the land, and the Tsingani too."

"That they may be, but he's a wolf in sheep's clothing, all right," murmured the man, with a look of deep suspicion. "And the Orders are not what they were."

"You know Draculea seeks alliance with his cousin in Castelu, Lord Vladeran," said the second man, "some say against the King."

Alina's eyes flickered at all this high talk. She had never heard before that the terrible Lord Tepesh was the cousin of Lord Vladeran, and it filled her with fear.

"Because, like Draculea, Vladeran walks the left-hand path," said the first gypsy. "They say the fathers in their holy church have heard of it. It would be the flames even for grand lords if they found them guilty."

Alina was attracted by these people and their haunting tunes. She was bitterly hungry too and could have done with some of their food or the warmth of their fire, but with this news of Vladeran walking the left-hand path, and plots against King Stefan Cel Mare himself, the poor girl suddenly felt more terrified and alone than she had ever felt.

She had feared fairies once, but now the real world seemed far more frightening than anything she had dreamt of in her powerful imagination. Alina Sculcuvant turned and crept away into the night.

She slept fitfully again and woke with the dawn, continuing her flight from Moldov, and thinking for a time she had escaped. But by late afternoon she heard the sounds of the dogs on the slopes below her again and quickened her pace. Alina had come to the beginning of a col, rising up through a narrow ravine, and because it was out of the wind, and the trees on the sides of the slopes hung outwards, shielding it from snowfall, much of the jagged rock was bare, and glistened in the damp like knives.

It was a cold, forbidding place, but Alina could hear the delicious sound of mountain water somewhere above her, and at the thought of a drink hurried on. She stopped to refresh her parched lips in an icy rivulet that flowed from the slope, but as she was bending down, and twilight began to fall, Alina heard the sharp snap of a branch and swung round. Someone was coming straight towards her.

The path behind her was shielded by a twist in the mountain, but as she looked back Alina realised that there was nowhere to hide, and that she could not possibly climb the steep slopes around her quickly enough. If the men and their dogs had picked up her tracks or her scent again, she was cornered. Alina crouched down and clasped two large rocks in her hands to hurl at them. But as she stood again, she saw a single figure appear, struggling wearily along and panting as he came on up the slope with his staff.

"Ivan!" cried Alina delightedly.

"Thank God," whispered the old shepherd warmly as soon as he saw the boy. "I thought I'd never catch up with you, child." He gasped for breath and stopped to lean on his crook. Its top was carved finely into the shape of a ram, and Alina had often admired the thing.

Alina dropped the stones and ran over to Ivan, helping the old man towards a boulder, where they both sat down heavily. Alina remembered gratefully how he had spoken up for her amongst the villagers.

"Your legs are strong, WovenWord," he panted, sucking at the air and looking at his young friend admiringly, "and your lungs able to cope with this thinning air. It's good. Though not for an old fool like me. I've been following you since you escaped."

"But what are you doing here, Ivan?" said Alina.

"No time," answered the shepherd, between his strained breaths. "They're close again. I've been using my tracks to lead them astray these last three days, but they've split into two, Barbat and Malduk, and there's only one way up the mountain now. Half the group are set on this course too. Malduk's."

"But Ivan . . ."

"Hush, child, and listen carefully. I know you didn't do it, but I've never seen Malduk so intent on anything in all his life, nor the villagers as thick as thieves. There's been a skirmish in the valley with Turks, which has distracted many of the soldiers, but the villagers hunt you ceaselessly, with cries of changeling on their lips. Driven on by Malduk."

"If they're so close, I'll never make it up there," said Alina desperately, looking towards the col.

"No, you won't. But go that way and you might have a chance. See that little path?" The old shepherd pointed up between two rocks on the side of the culvert. "It's an old deer track I used to take often in my youth, when I roamed these hills without a care in the world. It leads straight up, and then out onto the ice field."

"Ice field?" gulped Alina.

"That's the only way you'll be able to escape them," said Ivan, his face darkening with the very thought of it. "On the ice field above, though it can be slippery, you'll leave no tracks, and I doubt they'd follow you there anyway. It's full of fissures and pitfalls, so you must be very careful. Night is coming, but don't stop, and whatever you do, don't fall asleep. Sleep is the bitter accomplice of the cold."

Old Ivan stood and handed Alina his crook, with its fine carved top.

"Take this," he said gravely, "and use it to prod and test the ground before you. There are many places to fall, so keep your eyes and your senses open. But trust too, in His power."

Ivan crossed himself and Alina clasped the crook almost proudly, although she wished it had been given to her in happier circumstances.

"If you can cross the ice field safely," said Ivan, "you'll be able to get down into the next valley, and then over the mountains proper. There's a village far beyond them to the north, over three mountain passes, if I recall, at the end of a wide valley. They call it the valley of Baba Yaga."

Alina's eyes opened in amazement at the name. A name to conjure within a fairy tale.

"A great cairn crowns the mountain at the valley entrance and below it a wooden church by a little lake. A blacksmith I know lives near there. His name is Lescu and he was once a great soldier—the Warrior Smith, they called him in his day. That man will help you, I know it, if you tell him Ivan sent you."

"Thank you, Ivan."

"But be honest with him. Tell him only the truth, WovenWord. The truth is your greatest ally now. No more lies, eh, girl?"

"Girl?" gasped Alina, stepping back and steadying herself with the crook. "Then, you know? You've known all along I'm a girl."

"Not all along, Alina," answered the old man softly. "It's a pretty name. But I began to suspect when your voice didn't change, and no hair grew on your chin. The others thought it was because you are younger than your years, as you tell them, but I remember Malduk saying you were eight when they found you, and I did the calculation from the time you came here. I've noticed other things too about the changes in you."

Alina blushed.

"And many times when the others have been on the point of guessing, I've protected your secret. A changeling secret, stranger than any tale of goblins. I told them that you wouldn't wash with us because of a scar you had, and that you are thin because Malduk and Ranna starved you, though heaven knows that's true enough."

"Oh, Ivan," said Alina gratefully, realising there was no time to tell him the truth of who she now suspected she might really be. "I wish I could have shared my secret with you all along. Yet so many secrets surround me now."

"There are many strange things about you indeed," said Ivan, nodding thoughtfully. "I've always known it. It's not just what you've been hiding from the shepherds, or that mark on your arm. It's some quality you have, whether changeling or not. May God protect you, my girl, but you must protect yourself too. They hunt you like a man now, and in some things you must learn to act like one, but never forget your true nature, and use your wits and cunning too. It's not just Malduk and the villagers you have to fear, now that your hiding is at an end."

Alina thought her hiding was only just beginning.

"What do you mean, Ivan?"

"The winter begins, and the wild animals are hungry and frightened. There are other hunters than people out there. Bear and mountain lynx. Wolves."

Alina looked back nervously.

"A wolf," she whispered. "I've dreamt of a black wolf recently, like the one they were talking about that night. Though I didn't summon it, I swear."

The old shepherd looked into her face and his eyes shone.

"Have you indeed? Well, perhaps it has some meaning. They say dreams can have deep meanings, though I don't know the truth of such magic."

"Magic?" whispered Alina sadly, thinking of all the powers she had wanted as a changeling, and feeling very vulnerable. "There isn't any magic in the world, Ivan. Only cruelty and hate."

"Isn't there, WovenWord?" said Ivan. "Well, perhaps we'll see." Ivan smiled. "Here," he added suddenly, thrusting his pack at the girl. "There's food and water in there, a knife and a good, warm woollen shirt. My own shirt. And something else you may need."

Alina took it gratefully and looked sadly at her old friend, as she transferred her meagre things from her own pack into his, and he watched like a father sending a child out into the world.

"Now go, Alina. I'll take your pack and cover your tracks. When they come, I'll say that I saw you lower down the mountain."

"Will they believe you? Isn't it dangerous, Ivan?"

"Many respect me," answered the brave old shepherd. "And the last thing they'd dare to call me is a liar."

Ivan winked.

"Now go, girl."

Alina had slung the pack over her shoulder in the moonlight.

"And, Alina, don't believe that the whole world is like this. It isn't."

Her heart was full to bursting, and she hated to leave Ivan, but Alina knew this was her last chance to escape. She thanked him with all her heart and turned away. Already in the foothills below, they could hear the voices of barking dogs coming closer and closer. Malduk and the hunters were near.

"Go, Alina. Hurry."

So she began to climb, hard, up the deer track, higher and higher towards the heavens, and although the path was as thin and winding as a skein of drawn wool, made naturally over the years by the endless movement of red deer, following one another's slots through the hard landscape, to the changeling it was like a magic carpet in the coming night, through the snow and stone.

Alina felt the air about her grow thinner and colder as the darkness came in, and above her head great swagging mountains of storm-laden cloud began to gather in the sky. A mist came in with the darkness, wisping about her head like a ghost, but shielding her too from any watchers below.

Alina felt as if she were rising towards heaven itself, and wondered if she were already dead, murdered by Malduk and Ranna in her humble manger, and was being carried away on a ghastly dream. But then she heard the hungry voices of the dogs below, pursuing her still, and felt the cold air draw her skin like the covering of a drum, sending pricks of pain into her lungs as she breathed. Alina knew only too well then that this was real and she was not dead at all, but that wherever she was going, it was death indeed that was facing her now.

At last the thin deer track brought her to the top of the steep slope though, and as she crested the summit, she gasped in utter astonishment. Before Alina Sculcuvant, in the shining moonlight breaking through the mist, lay a great sweeping island of white. Except that through the covering of snow, strange colours flashed in the landscape, and the ground before her seemed in places rucked like a folded sheepskin. It was the ice field.

Alina felt a blast of cold come off it that nearly knocked her over, for beneath its snowy shroud the ground before her was pure ice, a frozen river, two hundred feet deep in places and far deeper in the places where the mountain fissured. By the action of its bitter cold, it hardened any snow falling on top of the glacier, and as soon as Alina reached its edge, the girl realised that Ivan had been right, for her footprints made no impression on the surface at all, and thus would leave no trace for her hunters.

Alina stopped to open Ivan's pack. She was deeply glad of the shirt that she now put on under Malduk's coat; it warmed her immensely, and she was delighted to find four apples, a little haunch of venison wrapped in a cloth, and a little leather bag filled with water. But along with a sharp knife there was something else of great use in the pack: a pointed stick and, tied to it with string, another flat bit of wood, with a half hole in it. They were the tools that Ivan used to rub together carefully with kindling, to make sparks to light his fires in the fields.

Alina looked around and noticed a little log nearby. There was just room enough in the pack to add it too, which she did, then Alina drank some water in the darkness and, hearing the dogs again, wasted no time, but walked up and out onto that brilliant expanse of ice.

It was with a terrified awe that she did so, not only because the girl found herself so small in the gigantic landscape, dwarfed by the icy immensity of the glacier, or because she was being hunted like a hare and the sounds told her that her pursuers were hard on her heels, but because she seemed to have entered a kingdom of strangely brutal beauty, and one that called instantly to some older and deeper instincts in the girl.

Alina realised that her strength and wit alone would help her to survive out here, and somehow it connected her to a power, or a force, she felt far greater than herself. Although she had little time for churchgoing in Moldov, Alina found herself making the sign of the cross too, just as Ivan had done.

But if Alina had hoped to invoke the almighty himself to her aid, she soon found that no one was on her side. For in the heavens the clouds were massing, and a bitter wind came up over the glacier, screeching in her ears like a night witch and grabbing the hardened snow in great fistfuls and hurling it in her face.

Time and again she was nearly blown over by the icy blasts, and she quickly found herself stumbling, her hands turning red and then blue as they met the snow. Alina soon wished she had not picked up the log at all, for it made her pack far heavier to carry.

Her eyes began to water, then sting like firebrands in the blast, but the worst of it was listening to the dreadful sounds wrapped up inside the hunting wind, for the storm that had come up seemed to have a thousand voices in it. Some called like evil demons; others wailed like lost and anguished souls; some seemed to cry out a terrible warning, like goblins indeed, or the voice of an ancient god demanding vengeance. "Traitor!" the raging wind seemed to cry after her. "Traitor!"

Alina wished she could drink that potion again, if not to hide her from the fairies, then at least to give her warmth, and as she pressed on she remembered Ivan's words about the ice field and began to imagine endless unseen pitfalls in the ground ahead of her.

With nearly every step she prodded the ground with Ivan's great crook. Mostly it hit the hard snow and ice, and Alina went on safely, but more and more, as she climbed higher up the huge glacier, she found the crook suddenly sinking into the snow, and she would have to skirt the sudden drift, testing and poking to find its edge with the staff, to be sure of not disappearing inside.

It made Alina's progress painfully slow, as did the cruel wind and the fact that she could hardly see anything around her in the blizzard. She was soon exhausted, and every muscle in her body seemed to ache with the searching cold. As Alina shuddered and went on, the voices in the wind seemed to be inside her head.

She had just managed to skirt another deep drift, when Ivan's staff plunged straight downwards and, to Alina's horror, a great slab of snow vanished right in front of her. There seemed to be a hole in the ground itself, for as the girl peered down she was looking at a great well of ice, which caught the voice of the wind and threw it back at her in a mournful bellow that seemed to call her name. "Aleeeeenaaaah."

Alina swung up her head and cried out furiously, turning her face into the angry wind.

"Stop it," she screamed. "Leave me alone. Why won't you leave me alone?"

But the storm wouldn't leave her alone, and as she turned her head and looked back, a sudden break in the mist showed her not only how slow her progress had been, but what she was sure were figures on the edge of the glacier. Then on the air, as the break in the blizzard closed again like a trap, she caught another note on the wind, a kind of howling.

Alina told herself it was the wind, skirted the hole, and scrambled on, then tripped and fell on her face in the darkness, picked herself up and fell again. She cursed bitterly and started to cry, and she kept jabbing angrily at the snow with the crook, as if trying to harm the monstrous white itself. But Alina soon realised the futility of such an act, and how it was tiring her out even more. With that she heard a clear howl through the storm.

"What's that?" she whispered, turning her head in the blizzard.

Alina saw a shape through the snow, darting by to her right. She screwed up her eyes, but shook her head. It must have been a rock, seemingly made to move by the swirling snowflakes or the drifting moonlit clouds, and now it was gone again. The howl had been nothing but the storm. On Alina went, and then she thought she saw the shape again, ahead of her this time. A moving smudge of black.

"Who's there?" Alina cried angrily, thinking of her dream, but her weary, piping voice was swallowed by the wind.

She shook her head, as if trying to shake off a nightmare. Nothing could be out here with her on the ice field, Alina told herself, and even her pursuers must have given up the chase in this terrible weather and bitter cold. She wondered now, with the intensity of prayer, when morning would come to her aid.

Suddenly there it was again, and Alina swung round. She was sure of it this time. A shape, like a huge black dog, and close.

In Alina's terror and distraction, she had forgotten to keep testing the snow, and suddenly she lurched forwards, her arms and the crook flailing out in front of her, as she heard a loud crack. It was breaking ice, and Alina dropped violently. One hand was holding Ivan's crook in its middle, and as she plummeted, she felt the stick catch on the ground above, and her other hand grabbed at it instinctively.

Alina was swinging in midair from Ivan's crook now, which was spanning the top of the hole she had just fallen through. She looked down in terror as she hung there. The drop beneath her seemed to disappear into a plunging black chasm, falling away forever.

"This is the world," whispered Alina Sculcuvant bitterly, through gritted teeth. "This is the real world."

The girl pulled with her arms and her shoulders, with all her might, and with some effort she had begun slowly to rise, when suddenly there was a terrible snap. Ivan's staff broke in two and the girl was falling, dropping into the fatal gulf.

Great walls of blue green ice rose around her, as she fell into the glacier. The shock of it was bad enough, but nothing compared to her landing, for her right foot buckled under her and she felt an agonising pain shoot through her whole body. Her head struck something hard and cold, and within the moaning belly of the storm-driven mountain, everything went black.

Fell's ears came up. The wolf had turned away from Moldov and thoughts of a child and now was scenting a storm on the wind. But amongst the shadowy trees in the darkness, it was something else that set fear running like poison through the Varg's veins—dogs. They were close, somewhere below amongst the thinning forest, and Fell knew by the tones of the cries— hunger mixed with fear—that they had scented him too. In a straight fight between a wolf and a dog, even a large hunting dog, Fell had very little to worry about. But, by the sounds of it, this was a large pack, and besides, Fell had injured his paw on the beaver's lodge.

The black wolf saw them break from the trees, and behind them came a group of ten or fifteen humans. Fell's lips curled up to show his teeth. A human was already pointing up the slope in the darkness towards him, and Fell was suddenly furious that his thoughts of a child had brought him so close to man again.

"There. Not a wasted journey," cried Barbat on the slope, although he was tired and angry, after his group had split from Malduk's. "The boy may have slipped our clutches, but that wolf has been haunting the valleys for far too long. Its pelt will fetch real gold, and besides, the dogs need to taste blood."

The others agreed and were already unleashing their animals. Fell turned and fled. The wolf slipped several times, and because of the cut to his paw, and not having eaten anything substantial in so long, he found his natural vigour failing him. But Fell reached the top of a steep slope and the edge of the ice field, just as the wind rose furiously and the blizzard began.

Fell was used to the higher mountains, far more so than tame dogs were, no matter how they were starved and beaten to make them ferocious and keen for pursuit, and he could see well in the dark. But not even Fell had encountered country like this before. He could feel the ice sheet below him, and it reminded him of that fateful day, long ago, when he had fallen into the waters through the river, when his family had been fleeing Morgra and her Balkar fighters. Ice, he thought grimly, what had they called it then? "The still element that holds all in potential."

The path of a springing wolf is light compared to many though, and Fell did not fall foul of the fissures and cracks before him; nor was he even aware how much danger he was in.

It was not for a good while that the fleeing animal spotted the shape ahead of him. At first he thought it was another Lera and he wondered if a wild lynx was abroad. But his eyes were accustomed to blizzards, and the black wolf soon realised in astonishment that it was a young human. The creature was faring badly in the storm, and though the wolf could not imagine what it was doing out here, Fell smiled inwardly as he thought how vulnerable these talking Lera were, when away from their dangerous packs.

Animals weakened in the wild were easy to hunt and so provided food for a wolf, but in their sacrifice also helped to keep the rest of a herd and the wild Lera of the land strong and healthy. That was the harsh law that had shaped Fell's life, and now he thanked the wolf gods Tor and Fenris for the gift, for in his furious hunger Fell realised what easy prey lay ahead of him.

Once again the balance of nature had turned. The sound of the dogs had faded and now the hunted was suddenly the hunter again, and it restored the wolf's courage and pride, sending warm jets of adrenaline coursing through his powerful being. His quarry had already begun to turn, clearly aware of the hunting wolf now, but Fell was long used to stalking and worrying a prey, sometimes for days on end, and he began to circle it.

Yet even as he did so Fell felt a sharp pain right in the centre of his forehead, and then, as he watched his prey through the terrible storm, his eyes opened wide. Like a ghost the human had just vanished into thin air.

SEVEN

THE GIRL AND THE WOLF

Alina WovenWord opened her hazel eyes, with that fleck of green in the left pupil. The very effort was painful, for it felt as if the lids were frozen together, and as she stirred, she felt an agonising pain in her leg and cried out. Her voice surrounded her in a hollow echo, and she sensed immediately that she had fallen into some kind of cave. For now though she couldn't see if this was so, for she was blinded by the sunlight shining straight down on her face, from somewhere high above.

Alina managed to move her head a little, out of the glare, and caught a hint of clear blue sky above her. The dawn had come, and it had stopped snowing. She wondered how long she had lain here. In truth it had been no more than half a day.

Alina's hazel eyes were clearing, and she managed to turn on her side painfully, and looked around in utter amazement. She was inside a cave, although not a cave made of rock or stone, but of pure ice. It was about half the size of Malduk's hovel, and the rounded ice walls were a deep turquoise blue, ribbed with green, that shimmered and sparked in the brilliant daylight about her, warming her weary being.

The sunlit cave was far warmer than it had been up on the glacier in the open, but Alina felt awe and fear to be in that place, a place as ancient as the glacier itself, and as pristine as the forming of the world. She had dreamt of fairies kingdoms or elven dales in the past, but this seemed far, far stranger.

She raised herself on her elbows, but as she tried to move, the pain came in her right leg again. She had sprained her ankle badly, and now she could hardly move. As she looked up, her heart sank too. She would never be able to climb those sheer ice walls to freedom. They rose straight up, broken only by the presence of a wide ice ledge about halfway up, but too high to reach. Alina was trapped in the ice cave.

She closed her eyes and laid her head back bitterly. Alina realised how much danger she was in, and she was thirsty and desperately hungry. She thought of how Ivan had warned her against falling asleep in the cold and then, more hopefully, of the food in Ivan's pack. But when she opened her eyes to look for the pack, she saw that it had slid to the far corner of the ice cave and she would have to crawl across to retrieve it.

She tried and slid hopelessly on the ice, unable to get any hold. For the moment Alina was simply too exhausted, and she slumped again. Although she fought it, sleep came quickly, in a whirl of frightening dream images, and the girl lay there groaning and muttering in the ice cave, bathed in sweat that froze to her body and made her red hair spikey.

The dream that came when she closed her eyes was so real that Alina Sculcuvant felt that she wasn't sleeping at all. She was standing in that room she had often been in in her sleep, and next to her in a cot lay that baby she thought her brother. Not a goblin, but a human child. But whereas before it had always been just a ghostly shadow, now its handsome little features were perfectly defined, and she could see its little stomach, with a thin line of hair on its belly. Alina knew then that she was not only dreaming, but remembering.

The woman with the curling black hair, her mother, was suddenly standing next to her—Roma, Roman—and she was telling her sternly to watch the crib. Alina felt confusion, for she wanted to hug her mother, yet she had talked to her so coldly. How proudly the young girl had answered though, and how proudly she had begun to stand guard over that baby boy, with his charming face and that strange little line of fur that threaded up to his belly button. But then, in the night, Alina had felt hungry and gone to the kitchen nearby, to fetch some food.

On her return Alina had found the doors to the chamber open, and to her horror, the child was gone. Suddenly Alina's dream memories were filled with rushing figures, carrying burning tapers, and the air was torn with cries and fearful shouts, and little Alina heard the mournful cry of wolf song. Then her mother was shouting and accusing her, and the girl realised with horror that a wolf had crept into the chamber and snatched the baby away. Her own baby brother.

That awful feeling of guilt that had dogged her for so long consumed Alina entirely. Now Alina knew why guilt had hung in her heart for years, and she almost wished she were dead. Her own brother had become the food for wild animals, for wolves, because Alina had failed in her duty. She wondered suddenly if all her thoughts of a fairy past, of goblins and spirits, had been because of more than the witch's story of a changeling, and if she had clung to them somehow to avoid confronting this terrible reality, for stories often conceal a bitter truth of life. The thought seemed to call a howl out of the shadows themselves. "Traitor!"

Alina opened her eyes with a start. Something was above her, looking down.

The great shaft of sunlight was still shining into the cave, making everything glitter and glow eerily, and as Alina peered up, her heart nearly froze. That pair of yellow gold eyes from her dreams was watching her hungrily, through a cloud of smoking breath. Yet they were real.

Alina could just see a muzzle too, and the hard glint of vicious white teeth. Her dream was coming true, and suddenly the shadow moved. The creature sprung down to the ledge above her. It was the black wolf.

Alina backed against the ice wall in horror. She knew enough of hungry dogs to know that it was hunting, and she realised in that instant that there was no escape. Alina had the knife, but it was in Ivan's pack, and she would never reach it in time.

Alina began to shout and scream. "Go away! Get away from me!" she cried, and in return the wolf let out a furious growl. She started to kick at the floor of the ice cave with her boot in her terror, sending up shards of frozen water to try and frighten the animal away. It seemed to inflame the hunter even more, and with a dreadful growl, it suddenly jumped again.

"No!" cried Alina, lifting an arm to shield her throat, as Fell sailed towards her. For years the girl had been made to hide from danger, and now the world had caught up with her at last. To Alina's surprise though the animal landed noisily on the floor of the cave near her, like a huge cat testing its balance on the slippery surface, and stood there with its tail raised, only a few feet away.

Fell did not strike. It had gone against all his instincts to enter that strange place at all. For hours he had watched Alina from above, and at last his hunger had got the better of him. Yet something extraordinary had happened as soon as he had landed on the ledge and seen Alina's face properly. Fell had recognised the face he had seen before in his own vision. The boy in the water.

His heart was filled with wonder and fear, and he thought of the voice's words about destiny. But now he was near the human, he saw that this was no boy. It was a human Drappa. And something else had come upon Fell. It was that throbbing ache in his head again, that he had first felt above, and his sight seemed to mist over. Opposite him Alina was feeling it too—a dreadful pain through her mind, like looking too long into direct sunlight.

The girl and the black wolf stared at each other in the glittering ice cave. Fell looked around at those walls of ice, and it was as if he were under a river, but although an ancient voice was telling him once again to fear a watery death, he suddenly realised that this frozen element could not drown him, or pull him down into its depths. The wolf felt less afraid.

Then to Alina's relief and astonishment, Fell simply lowered his tail, turned, padded over to the far corner of the ice cave, and lay down, though he swung his muzzle, still watching the girl intently.

Alina realised that he might change his mind at any moment and attack, and that she was now the prisoner of this dread creature. If she did one thing wrong, it could be the end of her.

The girl could see every aspect of the wild animal. The silky delicacy of his thick, black coat, the great paws and the curling claws, the thin, spindly vigour of his legs. He was at once a dog and not a dog, because Fell was much more than a dog. Mist wreathed out of his panting muzzle, and Alina felt as if she had been reborn suddenly amongst the wild beasts, in a womb made by pure cold.

She thought of the animals she had encountered on Malduk's farm. Alina liked them far more than many of the people she had met, and from what she knew of some of the villagers, especially the men, or from stories of war, she always thought of them as far less dangerous than people. Yet even tame dogs could suddenly turn, and here was something she had never encountered, a real wild wolf. Alina shuddered as she thought of what Malduk had said of the bite of a lone black wolf under a full moon, turning a human into a vicious beast—a werewolf.

It seemed like hours that they stared at each other, the wolf and the girl, in that mysterious cave in the heart of the glacier. Fell remembered playing a game of stares as a cub by the riverbank, near their den. If Alina moved faintly, or made a sound, Fell would growl or snarl and lift his tail in warning. Their eyes watched each other, fascinated, appalled, yet drawn together by more than fate, by the ache in their heads, by the secret knowledge that these ancient enemies were not here by mere chance at all, and that they had seen each other before. It was the dreams they had shared. It was Fell's obsession with man since he had become a Kerl, and what that voice had told him in the cave. It was Alina's fascination with the wild. It was the Sight.

But as they looked at each other, Alina Sculcuvant noticed that although the wolf could hold her gaze far longer than Elak or Teela, he would soon have to look away too, if only for a moment. The girl realised then that her very will was grappling with his, and since she could see that the strength of her eyes made the wolf angry and nervous, she too would look away, so as not to challenge the wild creature into anger and attack. If she had been in the open, she would simply have run for her life, but here she could do nothing.

With time the ice cave began to grow darker and colder and a full moon rose in the heavens above them, while the light travelling from the stars across millions of miles of as yet uncomprehended space, began to pick out tiny specks in the failing glare of the setting sun.

Then hunger, fear, and sheer exhaustion got the better of the girl and the wolf, and they began to grow desperately tired. Alina found her eyes drooping, and thinking of the danger of sleep, and of the wolf, she had to fight to keep herself awake. Fell had begun licking his injured paw and whimpering slightly, and Alina could tell that the animal was hungry too.

"What are you, wolf?" she whispered nervously. "What are you doing here?"

Fell looked up at the echoing voice and his ears rose with a snarl.

"Why haven't you eaten me?" asked Alina softly, trying to smile at him, but thinking herself utterly foolish.

Fell heard the strange human sounds, and although no comprehension came to him of the meaning of Alina's words, he could sense from their tone that there was no threat in her voice, only a desire to understand.

"I'm Fell," whispered the black wolf's thoughts, amongst his growls. "Who are you, human Drappa? I've seen you before in my dream. No. I've seen you with the power of the Sight. But I thought you a Dragga. The boy I once . . ."

All Alina heard with her human ears was a deep, rumbling growl from the black wolf's throat, but as she lay there she shivered, for it was as if some thought had just jumped into her mind, like a voice whispering to her from far away. Almost a name—Fell.

"We're both injured," said Alina quietly, wondering if she was somehow being enchanted, "and you're starving like me, by the look of you."

Then Alina remembered the food in Ivan's pack and his knife too.

"If you let me closer to my pack, perhaps I can help you," she said softly, looking towards it.

Fell just licked his paw again, and slowly Alina stirred. She was pleased to find that the pain in her leg had lessened and some of her strength had returned. She shifted towards him and Fell gave a warning growl, but Alina raised her hand slowly.

"It's all right, wolf. I mean you no harm."

Fell growled again, but he wasn't frightened of a wounded

Drappa, and his golden eyes were lit with interest. Could this vulnerable creature really have something to do with the survival of nature itself?

Alina began to pull herself slowly across the ice floor towards the black wolf and the pack nearby. She could smell the creature now, and the scent was something like a fox, but far stronger. On Fell's icy breath she caught the odour of his last kill, and it made her recoil instantly. Alina sensed the power of the animal too, held in the living vigour of his body and muzzle and teeth, and she knew that if she moved too fast she would be dead.

But Fell let her come and open the pack, pulling out Ivan's knife and the meat. It was a fine piece of deer, smoked into tenderness by Ivan's loving wife, and Alina quickly pulled it apart with her hands. There was a small piece in her left hand and a much larger in her right, and with a smile she threw the larger towards the wolf.

It landed just in front of Fell's snout and his eyes opened wide. Though it was cooked, Fell was far too hungry to resist the gift of meat from this strange Drappa. Alina nibbled at her own piece of venison, feeling the life-giving juices begin to churn in her stomach. It was oddly embarrassing to be eating in front of the wolf, but Fell opened his jaws and snapped up the venison, whole. In three or four powerful bites, it was chewed enough to disappear in a gulp down his hungry throat.

Fell licked his lips and looked once more at the human. There was gratitude in the wolf's strange eyes, but Alina drew her legs up to her chest and huddled back against the cave wall. As it grew darker and colder in the ice cave, gloom fell on the two of them, for now they felt as if they were being frozen into statues in the heart of the mountain, and it grew so cold that soon Alina could no longer move. "Wolf," she kept whispering. "We must stay awake, wolf."

She fought off the dream sleep, from which she might never awaken again, although weariness had seized her very blood. She pinched herself and could no longer feel the pain. She knew that if she closed her eyes she would never open them again. Then Alina remembered Ivan's little tools in the pack. How could she have been so stupid? Fire.

Clasping the pack again, she just managed to open it and pull out the little sticks that Ivan had used to make his sparks, though her hands ached with cold. She saw the remnants of the broken staff on the cave floor and realised that she could use it for fuel, and the log that she had picked up on the edge of the glacier. Alina was furiously grateful now that she had not discarded it in her exhaustion, and began rubbing her legs hard to make them work again, then pulled herself over to the bits of crook. She managed to snap them into several pieces and made a little pile, as Fell watched her with a tilted muzzle and growled softly.

Alina took Ivan's two little fire sticks and, balancing the top one between her freezing hands, began to rub furiously, although she could hardly hold them straight. Fell whimpered a little beside her, uncomprehending of what the Drappa was doing, but fascinated too. As Alina worked, she could feel the wood growing hotter and hotter, but she suddenly realised with despair that she had no kindling to make the tiny sparks ignite.

She was at her wits' end and ready to give in totally, when she remembered the parchment. It was still in her pocket. It was the only proof of her strange story, and one day she might need it badly, yet there was no choice now. She pulled it out and crumpled it up angrily, then set to work again. Fell snorted, as he saw little puffs of smoke begin to rise between Alina's shivering hands, and his voice turned to a growl.

The parchment suddenly caught and Fell whimpered. A flame lit in the ice cave, like fire from heaven, and the paper flared brilliantly, and with it the evidence of who Alina really was, sending light and sudden warmth flickering around their little ice prison. The girl hurried the bits of crook onto it, and blowing hard, soon she had a good fire going on the cave floor. Piece by piece she added the broken crook and then perched the log against them happily, as it all began to catch and burn.

A deep wonder had woken in the black wolf as he watched this miracle. A wonder and a fear too, as he felt the warming heat against his fur. Fell had seen many human fires, like the fire by the cooking pot, and had watched a conflagration burn in the forests after a lightning strike, like a bolt of heavenly power, but he had never seen how man mastered the flaming red flowers before.

He whimpered again, and when Alina looked at him once more, he dropped his eyes immediately. If the structure of a wolf pack is made in the hierarchy of relations between dominant individuals and their weaker relations, then Alina WovenWord had suddenly become a Drappa indeed.

The girl felt a pride flame in her too, almost as warm as the flames that the healing fire was now giving off. Life seemed to move through her being like a hot wind, and it was like breathing again. Alina let out a great, relieved sigh. She knew that the fire could not last forever, but if it kept them going until the sun rose once more, then perhaps they would have a slim chance. For another day at least.

So they sat there, the young woman and the injured black wolf, their thoughts rippling with the firelight dancing in the ice cave, mesmerised by its heat and brilliance, and the shadow images it seemed to summon from their minds too, as it flickered around those walls. Their fearful breaths stopped smoking with cold, and a sort of cheer settled over them both. With his thick winter coat, Fell would naturally have survived longer than Alina in the ice cave, but he too was grateful for the heat and light.

The comfort of the fire brought memories to Fell of his time as a cub in the den, with his old nurse Brassa and his sister Larka. Memories of his adopted brother, Kar, too, who had survived his own parents' murder at the hands of the Balkar packs and had become part of their family. Poor Kar, who had spent so long in his own cave on a mountaintop, wrestling with loss and pain and the madness of isolation.

What was Kar doing now? wondered Fell. *Is he growing old and weak, at seven years in the wild? What of my parents?* Alina was remembering too, as she looked into the firelight. Remembering things that had lurked like shadows in the back of her troubled mind, and it felt like nourishment. She remembered her mother's once tender arms about her, as she sat at home by a fire, until something had caused a change in her. She remembered that red-haired man, strong yet aloof. Her father. She remembered too the birth of her baby brother and the jealousy that it had brought. Had Alina betrayed her duty on purpose, that terrible night?

"Who am I?" she whispered to herself, as she sat at that impossible little camp fire, opposite a wild wolf. And what had occurred after that evening? The reason Alina had been driven from her home to be murdered still eluded her.

The fire saved them. Fire which Prometheus, in the myths that the ancient forebears of this land—the Romans—had told around their own campfires more than a thousand years before, had stolen from the gods and given to man. The god Zeus had punished Prometheus, chaining him to a rock, to have his liver eaten out each day by an eagle.

The log was heavy and damp, and it burnt very slowly, but now the embers had crumbled into a hot grey dust. Alina's spirits were flagging again, when the two prisoners caught the first sensations of returning sunlight steal across their faces. It came like a breath of hope, the daylight high above them, and Alina looked at Fell as a companion in arms might after a terrible battle.

Yet the warm light of day brought a bitter revelation too. The fire may have saved them, but they were still in exactly the same predicament as before, and now Alina felt hungrier and weaker than ever.

"Wolf," she said, "I'm going to try and stand up."

The girl's hand hurt as she pressed it against the ice floor, and as soon as she pushed herself upwards Fell rose too, his tail lifting, his front legs set in attack. "Down," Alina nearly said, until she realised that this was not Elak, and not a creature to be tested so lightly.

Alina took all her weight on her good leg and then gingerly pressed down on her right. It was too painful to stand on properly, and she hopped backwards to the edge of the cave and propped herself up against the ice wall. The knife was in her right hand, and Alina looked around properly. To her horror she saw that the cave floor fell away completely on one side, the drop she had seen when she had been hanging from Ivan's staff.

"It's a dark place we're in, wolf," said Alina gravely. "And it's time we got out again. Both of us."

She looked up. Even standing, she couldn't reach the ledge Fell had sprung from. She had an idea though, and she turned to the ice wall and, with a sudden swing that made Fell growl, struck the ice with the knife. It sank in deep, and grasping at a small outcrop of ice with her other hand, Alina pulled herself up a little way, as Fell watched her warily.

There was another small outcrop that she managed to get purchase on with her left foot, and pulling the dagger free and swinging it again into the ice above, she pulled herself even higher. Alina was wobbling precariously though, and she realised that if she fell she could tumble over the edge of the chasm. But the lip of the ledge above was almost in reach now, and Alina swung her arm and managed to get her fingers over the edge. It was wet and slippery, where the sunlight from above had melted the ice, and as Alina pulled, her hand slipped completely.

The girl went sailing backwards and, to her horror, found that she was falling, not towards the drop, but towards the wolf. Her body struck Fell's, and with a furious snarl, he turned and sprang at her, as she landed on her back on the ice.

His jaws were open, and Alina didn't feel fear as such, just a kind of grim resignation, yet as the wolf stood over her, something new stirred in her too, the anger of a fighter. Her eyes blazed.

In that moment Fell remembered the powers of the Sight to control wills. Could he control this human? His thoughts, directed by the Sight, began to reach out towards her consciousness, as they had once reached out to the Balkar.

"Give in, Drappa," whispered his angry mind. "Obey me. I, who have been darkness. I, who shared the vision with Larka and all the Lera. The secret of what man is and what sorrow he can bring. I command you."

As Fell wrestled there, he realised that it was as if, in all his journeying, he had reached the borders of a strange new land, and that no curse or blessing would ever let him pass. He could not reach Alina's will. Fell felt strangely foolish.

They both sensed the energy though in each other's being, moving through their bodies like a secret language, and as their eyes locked again, so close this time it was as if they might meld into each other, Alina saw the strange sliver of green in Fell's right eye and the wolf the green splinter in Alina's left.

It brought something like wonder and recognition to them, and although all Fell's wild instincts were telling him to strike, he couldn't attack this Drappa. The wolf remembered wrestling long ago with his sister Larka in the Red Meadow, the field of spirits that lies before the journey beyond, and the words about destiny and a Guardian, and then the ache in his head came again. Suddenly Fell was thrown sideways in the cave.

Alina had not moved, or done anything at all. It was like the force that two lodestones make when brought together, that men in later days would call a magnetic field, and somehow both the girl and the wolf knew then they could not harm each other. Ever.

A voice came sounding and echoing through their heads, as if from the cave itself. "What is happening to us?"

The wolf and the girl looked at each other in utter amazement, and suddenly they were talking. Not in words or in growls, but with their thoughts.

"You are Fell, are you not?" asked Alina's frightened, wondering mind. "The lone black wolf."

"A Kerl, my kind call it, man cub. And you are Alina, I think. I've dreamt of you, with that mark on your arm. Though I thought you a Dragga."

"But how can this be? Are the shepherd's stories of werewolves and transformations true? How are we talking like this? Is there really such magic in the world?"

Alina thought of goblins and sprites and fairies. This was far more miraculous.

"It's the Sight, child. The gift that comes through the forehead. Only a very few possess it. My sister Larka looked into the mind of the Man Varg once. The Man Wolf. It brought the animals a terrible vision of the past and future. And I have the power too.

The power to look into minds and control wills entered the world when my aunt Morgra summoned the spectres from one of the worlds beyond, with her Summoning Howl."

"But what do you want of me, Fell?"

Fell remembered that voice in the cave, the voice he had tried to resist.

"I don't know. To aid you perhaps? To learn from you and understand? Before I met you, my dead sister told me to help you, I think. Told me you may have a great destiny, child."

Alina's pretty eyes opened wide in the ice cave. She, have a great destiny? Alina had wanted to believe that she was better than a shepherd, even if she wasn't a goblin princess, and to see more of the world than the environs of Moldov, but that was not the same as having a great destiny.

She thought of the parchment and the link to Lord Vladeran, and of the way she had usually felt with Ranna and Malduk. Alina had thought so little of herself in Moldov, and now the gulf between these two worlds seemed quite impossible. Fell's thoughts filled the girl with one emotion alone: fear.

Fell could feel this, and he thought again of trying to control her will, but as the wolf looked into her strong, bold eyes he knew that that was a thing he could never do. Yet as he lay there he was not angry at that powerlessness. Indeed, he felt a strange calm. He suddenly wanted to help this child.

Like a snapping rope, the link between them both broke and there they were again in the ice cave, as Alina spoke with human words now.

"Did I . . . did I really know your thoughts, Fell? But it can't be. Animals don't think like us."

Fell growled. The human sounds were incomprehensible to him.

"The Sight," whispered Alina, remembering the gypsy's words about a gift. "What is the Sight, Fell? Where does it really come from?"

The wolf did not answer her. Alina had raised herself again, but as she did so she felt something on her cheeks that made her shiver furiously. Both creatures felt an icy gasp of air breathe into the cave, as if from a tomb, and surround them. They had to escape soon.

Alina noticed something else then. Her clothes were wet. Next to where the fire had burnt, the ice had melted, creating a little pool of water in a dip in the ground, but the water was trickling now to the back of the cave. Alina expected it to form another little pool where it hit the wall, but instead it just vanished. There was some kind of hole.

She scrambled over to it and, with the hilt of Ivan's knife, began to bash away at the ice wall. A section of it crumbled away and Alina could see an opening beyond. She turned the knife and started to scrape and cut more purposefully, and after a while, a passageway was revealed through the ice. Alina's heart leapt, as she saw the glow of daylight somewhere beyond.

"Fell," she cried happily, finding it strange to use his name aloud. "I think there's a way out."

Fell had already got to his feet and come padding over.

"I'm going to try and crawl through, Fell. Come after me."

The girl knew that her words meant nothing to the wolf, but she grabbed Ivan's pack and, without looking back, began to pull herself through the opening. She found herself in an ice tunnel that slopped downwards at first, wet with water from the fire, and then rose again and seemed to open into another chamber beyond. Alina scrambled up the passage and gasped in utter amazement as she reached the end.

It was a chamber, fifty times larger than the first. It dropped before her like a great frozen waterfall, a gigantic ice cathedral, shimmering with greens and brilliant blues and plunging downwards towards a field of jagged white spikes far below. As Alina looked down, she felt like a fairy queen, but her heart was in her mouth, and when she looked up it soared like an eagle, for the chamber ceiling was almost transparent, and through it Alina caught the faint impression of sky and moving cloud above. The top of the chamber lay on an exposed part of the glacier, where the wind constantly cleared away the falling covering of snow.

She sensed immediately the breath of freedom above, and then she saw it, to the left of the chasm. A kind of gallery ran along the edge of the ice cathedral to a natural bridge that spanned the vast gulf itself and rose almost to the ceiling. It was a dangerous path, for it looked as if a god five miles tall had descended from the very heavens and sculpted that bridge in secret, with brilliant, immortal hands.

"Fell!" cried Alina happily, her voice dwarfed in the echoing immensity of that place. "Come on. There's a way up."

THE LEAP

Alina began to inch to the left and crawl along the ice gallery, her head dizzy with the plunging drop to her right. She heard a whimper, and then a growl, and turned to see the black wolf standing there, on the edge of the giant chamber, his tail shaking furiously, looking out on the beetling void.

"Don't look down, Fell. Follow me."

The girl surprised herself with her confidence and rose now, clutching at the wall on the left to keep her balance and tottering as she crept towards the bridge. Then she was standing before it, and her heart felt like stone. She could not tell how thick the ice was, and neither could she see any support below it: no natural arches or buttresses that might hold it up.

In that moment her courage failed her and she wanted to turn and run. Yet there was nowhere to go. Hopeless and afraid, she wanted to be in the barn, curled up in a ball, listening to Mia tell her a story. Alina wanted what all children want, and adults too, to be safe. As she stood frozen to the spot, she heard the wolf growling, and a thought came to her that freed her from her fear, the realisation of what she had achieved over the past few days, more than she had ever thought possible.

After years of mistreatment and loneliness, after swallowing for so long the criticisms of Ranna and Malduk, and the lies about her changeling past, she had taken control of her fate, and escaped being murdered and survived on her own in the open, despite being hounded by dogs and chased by a terrible storm. This knowledge gave her a sense of pride she had never known before, and courage too.

Alina hurled Ivan's pack forwards, and it landed on the bridge with a thud, sending a shower of snow crystals into the gulf, but the span held.

A growl came from behind her, low and deep and angry, and there was the black wolf almost at her back. Fell's ears were pressed forwards, quivering, and his eyes glowed with the intensity of a vision. Fell was remembering Larka on a similar bridge.

With the power of the Sight his sister had foreseen her own death, but Larka had gone on anyway, to save her brother and rescue the man child. So she had faced Morgra. Was Fell facing his own death now too? he wondered. Did life move in strange patterns that simply reflected one another, like sunlight on water, moving always towards one end alone—death? Yet if Fell died here, on this icy bridge, it would not be for any purpose, as Larka's death had been, but a lonely end, in the secret heart of the mountain.

Alina was already moving out onto the span. One step after the other the brave girl took, feeling the ice arch tremble beneath her and testing its strength with her weight. Then the black wolf came too, following slowly in her paw marks, giving himself up to what he already knew was a greater intelligence than his own. Soon they were halfway across, and the whole ice bridge seemed to shake beneath them.

"Quickly, Fell!" cried Alina as she felt the ice start to give under her feet, and flung herself forwards desperately. Fell felt it too, and with a fearful whimper, as if he had been caught in a trap, he veered to his left and sprung backwards.

Then the bridge was gone, tumbling and crashing down with Ivan's pack towards those bitter spikes, nearly a quarter of a mile below. The whole centre of the mighty ice bridge had disappeared into the gulf, leaving Alina on one side of it, near the ceiling of the chamber, and Fell on the other.

They looked at each other across that huge chasm, the girl and the wolf, and a void, both real and imagined, opened between them. Fell raised his tail and lifted his throat. His great mouth let out a howl that seemed to come from the belly of the world. It filled that mighty chamber with frustration and despair—"Aaaooww." All his life Fell had longed for freedom, and now it had brought him to this.

Alina had not given up yet though, on herself or the strange wolf, a creature she had touched with her mind. In that moment she learnt one of the greatest secrets of life: It is often easier to fight for others than it is for yourself.

"Fell!" she cried. "You must jump."

Alina could see that the black wolf did not understand her, and she stood, speaking urgently.

"Listen to me, Fell. You must listen. We spoke before. Why not now?"

Then suddenly their eyes were locked, those slivers of green, and that pain had come in their foreheads.

"Fell. It's me, Fell. Understand me now, before it's too late. Jump towards me, before the rest of the bridge goes."

"No, human. I can't. It's too far. I'll fall."

"You must, Fell. It's your only hope. Have faith. Please. Do it now, Fell. I order you."

Fell looked back at her, and it was as if her thoughts were controlling his. He felt the remaining edge of the bridge rock below him, and with a furious spring, the black wolf leapt towards her across the giant gulf.

A dog would never have made the jump, but a wolf's legs are far more powerful, honed by nature and evolution, by the survival and success of the fittest, and the black wolf was sailing through the air, springing across the void. His front paws made the distance and landed on Alina's side of the chasm, and his back paws too, but only just, for they were slipping backwards, scrambling desperately on the edge. Fell would have fallen, if Alina hadn't reached out and grabbed at the wolf's coat. She felt the loose folds of fur and skin around his neck and tugged as hard as she could.

She saved Fell, but the black wolf felt such anger at the human's touch that he could not help himself. He turned and snapped at Alina's arm, and would have sliced it in two if their momentum, as they fell backwards to safety, had not made him miss.

"Don't ever touch me, human," snarled Fell's angry mind. "I'm wild, unlike you, tame man cub. You may be a Drappa, but I will kill you if needs be. Do not forget the freedom of the untamed wolf."

Even Fell was surprised by his own ferocity, and the instincts that had sprung uncontrollably from his being, and for a moment he dropped his eyes guiltily. Then, as they lay there staring at each other, both shocked by what had just happened, Fell's thoughts began to calm.

Alina gave the wolf a cold, resentful look, then rose silently and turned towards the top of the chamber. She scrambled up and, still bitterly angry at what Fell had nearly done, began to bash at the ceiling of the ice cave. Her fist went through on the third try, and Alina felt a rush of fresh clean air on her face. They were almost free.

It took her a little time to make a good-sized opening, and she pushed her shoulders up and out. Another blizzard was coming up over the mountain, borne on the bitter wind, made in the heart of lowering clouds. It rose around the mountain like the ancient furies, raging perhaps at the child who had made fire for a wolf in an ice cave, like a goblin, or perhaps with no purpose at all, except the natural movement of hot and cold, and of the elements.

Alina crept back inside, under the howling sky, and felt a new emotion, long lurking beneath the surface of her gentle being: bitterness. The pride at her own escape, and the leap across the void, was pushed back into the shadows by thoughts of a world that had done her nothing but harm. It was all so unfair. For some reason it was a world that had named her changeling and wanted her death, and now the elements themselves, perhaps God himself, seemed to be conspiring in her destruction.

Alina turned back to Fell with a sinking heart. For hours that blizzard raged and the temperature sank so low that soon Alina's teeth chattered furiously, and she could no longer move her hands. If she had lived with knowledge freed by science, she might have known to cover her head, for there the heat and energy of the body leaks out most quickly in the cold, but she did not have such knowledge.

Alina and Fell sat apart, still smarting with resentment and unable to communicate anymore. And so Fell did not sense the life beginning to ebb from this strange human, as the hours wore on. Being far larger than the previous cave, and close to the top of the mountain, where little tunnels made by meltwater had created air channels to the outside world that let in jets of icy wind, the place was also far, far colder than their little ice cell. And now the wood and food were gone.

Alina was young, but with her injured leg and the effort of mind and will that she had expended to bring them to where they were, she was finally succumbing to the bitter cold. But even as the cold attacked her from without, dark feelings attacked her from within: bitterness about Malduk and Ranna, guilt about her baby brother, and a terrible sense of her own worthlessness. Alina WovenWord wanted to die.

Other creatures had died there long before, and lay buried in the ice around them. Not fifty yards from where Fell sat panting in the cave, the body of a deer was still perfectly preserved. It had become lost in a storm more than a hundred years before and had eventually succumbed to a sleepy death. Then by the action of the glacier, seemingly solid but in fact a slowly moving river, it had been pulled downwards and squeezed tight within ribs of ice, but preserved too, so that if something had come to thaw it out, its body would have been perfectly edible, and almost as fresh as the day it had died.

But there were far, far older things within the mountain too. A man, a Stone Age warrior, was held in its unforgiving grasp. He had been hunting on the mountain some two thousand years before and had died at the hands of neighbouring villagers, murdered as Vladeran and Malduk and Ranna had tried to murder Alina. Although his features had been crushed flat, and the organs of life had perished within him, he was preserved like the deer. As were the myriad insects and microbes that had lived in the ancient waters that once swelled the river that had flowed freely down these mountains. The strange history of the world, of the earth and the animals that inhabited it, was piled up and frozen in this place, footprints in time that only insight, understanding, and imagination could ever hope to unlock.

Alina huddled up to try to stay warm, but it was hopeless, and at last she could battle tiredness and sorrow no more, and she fell asleep. When the storm finally ceased and the skies opened once more in their tranquil, blue immensity, Fell rose and managed to push his snout through the hole Alina had made into the friendly, sun-washed air.

But as the black wolf turned to the girl again, he whimpered. She was lying on the icy ground, overcome by cold. Her very spirit had been leaking out of her, and now Fell gave a loud growl to rouse her. Alina opened her eyes and saw him dimly. She tried to move her lips, and the wolf drew closer and sniffed at the air.

"Go, Fell," said Alina faintly. "Go, my strange friend. I'm so terribly cold."

The black wolf stared at Alina and whined. He still felt guilty at how he had snapped at her, and remembered those words about helping a child, as his sister Larka had once helped a baby in the snows. It was his turn to save a human, yet Fell, so long used to fending for himself, had no idea what to do.

He dipped his head and licked Alina's hand. She felt the warmth of it and smiled a little, remembering Elak and thinking herself back in the barn. But then her thoughts grew dizzy and dark again with all that had happened. This wasn't Elak, this was a wild animal. Perhaps she *was* a fairy child.

Fell stretched himself next to her and Alina felt the heat of his fur. Gently she reached out a trembling hand and placed it on his back. She felt Fell twitch slightly, but he did not move or growl at her this time, and her hand was soon warm in his fur. Alina could feel the power and the life of the wolf directly, and she pulled herself over to him and, very softly, laid her freezing head on his moving flank.

Fell gave a low growl, but it was to reassure her, and there Alina lay, her head on the black wolf's side, rising gently up and down with his breathing. She could comprehend nothing of its meaning. How she could understand a wild wolf, or how and why the Sight had touched them both, but now Alina would never know. It was over.

The wolf whined again.

"It's all right, Fell," she whispered, in a voice so small it vanished into the vastness. "Some curse touches my life. But tell me, Fell, what was this great destiny that might have joined us?"

Fell thought of those strange words about it being linked to the very survival of nature, but in that place, it felt like almost a sacrilege to say it, and it filled him with fear. He held his wolf tongue.

"Go from here then, wolf. Be free. I shall never know."

The wolf did not stir, and as he felt the girl drift to sleep once more against his flank, in the quiet stillness, a sense of peace came over Fell. Then something strange and wondrous began to happen. The cavern walls flickered with light and then images began to appear in the ice. They were of man and his journey out of nature, and Fell recognised them as the same vision that Larka and all the animals had seen at the citadel of Harja. The Great Secret.

Fell saw fish crawling from the seas and that strange furred creature again, a human ape, rise up on its haunches and clasp a flaming taper in its grip, as he and the Lera had seen it years before—man.

Civilisations rose and fell, and wars gripped the land. Nature and the Lera were being turned to man's hungry purposes. The wolf growled as he watched, and in her sleep Alina cried out too, for the same vision had appeared in her dream. They saw the future and a huge metal sphere fall, and then a mushroom cloud of flame and fire, followed by a terrible warming of the world, and melting ice caps that in turn brought a winter of ice. Wolfbane's Winter, the wolves had called it, after the Evil One.

Yet as Alina slept at Fell's side, the vision changed to fields and gardens and orchards, well tended to by laughing men and women. The wolf's growls became calmer, as did Alina's breathing, and Fell thought of a story of long ago, about the clever wolf Fren, the hero of all young wolves, and of his best friend, the red girl. The story had told of how Fren had saved the child from his brother Barl, and how he had killed Barl and so been marked by Tor forever, in the centre of his forehead, with a difficult power. The power of the Sight.

Fell looked at Alina's short red hair and wondered if her very presence had turned the vision to one of beauty and peace. Then Fell remembered something Kar had spoken of long ago, a vision of man that Larka had given him alone. Not man humbled into meekness or despair, by the anguish of his sensitivity, and not man as just a violent, fighting animal destroying all before him. But man as a Guardian. A Guardian of being and nature itself, as strong and healthy as the wolf that chases the wild deer, unashamed, yet as wise, heroic, and loving as a god. That vision had been of men and women, but men and women with the eyes of wolves. Now Fell helped a human. Perhaps it was a vision both could live up to.

Yet the images seemed to change back again, and the wolf started to snarl as he began to see deserts and dry water beds, the earth cracked and broken and dying.

He swung his head suddenly towards the human, with an angry growl. Was it because of her kind that this might come to pass in the world? If it was to be so, why should the wolf help the human child? The wind howled and suddenly Fell blinked. That voice he had heard in his cave seemed to be there again.

"Fell."

As Fell listened, he heard no more words, but he thought once more of a Guardian, who knew the deepest mysteries of the Sight. Could such a being really exist outside Kar's vision, like some secret god, in the lands beyond the forests? Even as he thought it, Fell looked on in amazement.

There was Larka again, in the ice, but now her face was gigantic in the cavern, a hundred feet high, and she seemed to be looking down kindly on them both. Larka's image lasted only for a moment, before melting back into the bluey white, but her fleeting presence had awed her brother, and made him guilty for his thoughts about the child.

When Alina opened her eyes again, woken by the sound of a

stalactite falling from the ice ceiling above, the wolf was gone. She felt the sting of loneliness and sorrow, but the swirl of dreams took her once more. Her short young life had been so full of pain and mystery already, so full of the anger and hate of people, that she hardly cared anymore. She wanted it to end at last, and the sleep of eternity to enfold a changeling in its tender arms.

The girl felt it near her face first, then smelt something sweet and sickly fill her nostrils. Alina had smelt that sickening smell before, when she had slaughtered the sheep with Malduk outside the house at the Christ Mass. It was the smell of blood and raw meat. A kill.

Her senses recoiled in disgust and she opened her eyes to see Fell standing before her again. His tail was raised and his black muzzle was red with blood. Fell looked strong and powerful with the kill, and beside Alina lay a haunch of meat. It was part of a mountain goat that the wolf had found and hunted on the very edge of the glacier. Alina blinked in horror as she looked at it. She knew what the wolf intended her to do, but something deep inside her refused. Then Alina felt the familiar sensation in her forehead.

"Eat, man cub."

"I cannot, Fell."

"Would you give up so casily, little woman?" growled the wolf angrily. "It'll bring you strength and life."

Alina blinked slowly. The meat was warm and wet with blood.

"Take it down, Drappa, or you will go to join Tor and Fenris sooner than you should."

Alina was human indeed and no changeling, and thus, as Larka had shown the animals up at Harja, her instincts for survival were just as strong, perhaps even stronger than Fell's. Or would have been if she'd had an easier journey of it. Should she fight? Could she? She thought of little Mia urging her on and sat up a little.

Alina pulled a thin sliver of flesh from the prize and she blanched and curled up her face in disgust as she raised the raw goat to her freezing lips.

"How fragile you are, man cub. Take it. It's good."

Alina put the bloody meat to her lips, and tearing away a little piece with her teeth, she started to chew. She almost retched, but held it down, and felt strength returning. Alina was loath to eat the raw meat though, and she suddenly saw something else on the ground beside her. It was a large root, of the kind that Fell had once seen deer digging for, and which he had scented near where the goat had been. He had had to scrabble through the snow to get to it.

"Oh, Fell."

Alina picked it up and, touched by the wolf's determination to help her, felt a new determination in her own mind. She bit into it hungrily, and though it tasted acrid, she felt even stronger. She sat up a little more and persisted.

"Good, man child. You may prefer roots, but one sun I shall teach you the ways of the wild hunter. The true power and freedom of the Putnar. Of nature."

Fell lay down beside her again and watched like a Dragga guarding a cub in the den, as the young woman took that primitive meal, and soon life was flowing once more through Alina's warming veins, making her cheeks glow.

"There," came Fell's pleased mind. "You've done well, human. Like that man cub long ago."

Alina turned her head questioningly. Her lips were mouthing silently now as she ate.

"Man cub?"

"You could not know the story, human. I almost think it a fable myself. It was a child, a baby Dragga, stolen by the Varg to protect it from the she-wolf Morgra. My aunt. It was part of a legend."

Alina looked at Fell in astonishment.

"Stolen? From where, Fell?"

"From a human village, below a castle on a mountaintop. The Stone Den, we call it. The empty place, whose hundreds of steps my aunt Morgra once climbed. Though there was nothing at the top."

Alina's eyes opened even wider. The fairy castle of her dreams and nightmares, floating amongst the clouds. Could it have something to do with her?

"But why? Why was it taken?"

"As I said, it was part of the legend of the Sight. It was marked, like you. A wolf called Tsarr found it first."

"Marked? How?"

"A natural mark. A little strip of fur on its belly. Like wolf fur."

Alina's thoughts flamed into clarity.

"My brother," she cried. "I think it was my baby brother, Fell."

Fell looked back hard at Alina.

"Your brother? How can this be, human? I carried it on my own back."

As they stared at each other once more, and caught the flicker in each other's eyes, with those shards of green, they both knew it was true. Their fates had always been bound together by the Sight.

"Yes," thought the wolf. "And you have the Sight too, human. You asked me of your destiny, and now you are stronger, I shall tell you."

Alina blinked and shivered nervously.

"If the words I heard are true, you are somehow connected to the survival of nature itself."

Alina Sculcuvant's eyes opened in utter disbelief. It couldn't be. What was the wolf saying?

"How?" she whispered fearfully, staring helplessly about the chasm. "Why?"

"That I don't know, Alina. There is one who might know though, if he exists. The Guardian."

"Guardian?"

Alina thought she remembered a giant face in her dreams, and she felt as if the wolf was suddenly talking of God himself.

"The Guardian of the mysteries of the Sight," said Fell, though doubting himself. "I would find him and reveal your destiny."

But Alina was thinking of a different destiny to her own now.

"What happened to him, Fell? My brother."

"Bran we called him, after the Sikla of our pack. He brought the Lera a vision, a vision I just saw again."

Alina stirred. She had seen such strange things herself as she slept in the cave.

"But the child was returned, by me, safely to the village beneath the Stone Den, to its own kind. To its mother with the curling black mane."

The curling black mane. Alina knew that it was the woman of her dreams, and so that the woman must be her mother. There was confusion at that, but Alina felt as if a weight had been lifted from her shoulders too. The child, her brother, who she herself had failed to protect in its cot, wasn't dead. He hadn't been eaten by wolves after all. Suddenly the feeling that she was a traitor, that she had been sent justly into exile, seemed to leave her.

"Oh, Fell," came Alina's grateful mind, "I don't know how this is, or how I've met you and can understand you, but I know now that I have to find him. And my mother too. Not goblins or fairies, but real people. Find them and remember."

"Where, human?"

"What was it like," Alina asked suddenly, "this village where you left my brother?"

"Simple enough. Like many I've seen in my travels. With a wooden stockade and wooden dens."

Alina shook her head. That was strange. It sounded like Moldov, and hardly connected to a great lord like Vladeran in Castelu, or some high destiny.

"I must go that way, Fell."

"Then I shall come with you, human, and we shall learn together and seek out the Guardian. A Drappa alone in the wild always goes in danger."

"This Stone Den, is it far?"

Fell licked his black wolf lips, cleaning the goat blood from his jaws, and wondered what the root had tasted like.

"Many paw marks, across the mountains. It will take us half the winter."

Alina was already pushing on her elbows, struggling to get up.

"Peace, human," growled Fell. "Don't waste your strength. You know nothing of moving in the wild. You must be neither hasty nor foolish."

But Alina was standing. She swayed slightly.

"Very well, Fell. But now I must be in the sun again and heal."

Fell suddenly remembered that Larka had once said that the greatest power of the Sight was to heal, as Alina punched through the hole and rose from that icy tomb once more. The day opened before her, a sweeping vision of rocky crags and clear white mountains, bounded by the bright blue sky. The storm was over.

A bird was winging through the distance, a beautiful snow hawk, and Alina felt a sudden, glorious sense of freedom and elation, as someone would who has walked through darkness to discover only the light, and the marvellous beauty of being. She must have stood there for a good hour, her spiky red hair thrown back to the brilliant sunlight, drawing it into her skin and being, like a flower opening to the summer. She swallowed in the fresh clean breeze, as if gulping water, and wanted to laugh and shout with pure joy.

Fell stayed in the giant cave, pondering in his shadowy mind their strange meeting and this news of the child's link to another baby, but feeling an odd foreboding in that ice cathedral, as he finished the goat and left Alina alone on the glacier.

The girl did not notice the men coming over the brow of the mountain. Their path was silent across the snowy ice, and by the time she turned, they were already on her. There stood six villagers, carrying staves and knives.

Barbat was there and another shepherd Alina knew called

Fermin, who had always been kind enough to her. But in their middle stood Malduk, holding his back painfully. It had been a bitter struggle for the old shepherd to maintain that pursuit, but his hate and will had driven him on. And his fear of Ranna too.

"So, changeling," cried Malduk, "you survived the storm by some witchcraft. But you'll not escape us now."

Alina could not believe her eyes, but, though stunned, she noticed how wary the other men seemed of her.

"What have you to say, murderer?" hissed Barbat. "After Ranna and Malduk gave you succour for so long. Traitor."

"Lies," Alina WovenWord cried furiously, and her eyes glittered contemptuously. All the fear that she had felt for Malduk had suddenly vanished. "Ranna's the murderer. Stabbing Bogdan in the back with my stolen knife and stealing his dagger."

The other men looked at each other questioningly and turned to Malduk, but Barbat spoke again.

"And why should she do such a thing?"

"So you would think it was me, of course, and hunt me."

Malduk smiled thinly. "Those are the lies, changeling. And you're good at lies, indeed, SkeinTale. I saved your life, you ungrateful brute. Why should we want you dead?"

Alina slipped her hand to her pocket, but realised the parchment was no longer there. She had consigned it to the flames. All proof had gone.

"Because of Lord Vladeran's secret. That he tried to kill me once too."

The other shepherds were looking at one another wonderingly now.

"Lord Vladeran?" whispered Fermin.

"Wicked boy," cried Malduk, feeling a terror that Alina should mention the lord at all. "Talking of high lords. You besmirch even the name of Vladeran." Malduk was smiling at the others and spoke loudly and with scorn to cover his fear.

Barbat had stepped forwards.

"What's this talk of Vladeran, boy?" he hissed. "What have such high folk as Vladeran to do with you?"

"Yes," said Fermin. "Do you speak of it because Vladeran's soldiers have been in these parts again? You heard them outside the church, didn't you, when that man was talking of Vladeran and the Lady Romana?"

As soon as Fermin mentioned the name "Romana," Alina went deathly cold.

"The Lady Romana?"

"Lord Vladeran's wife," said Fermin. "That's how this got into your head, isn't it?"

Alina felt a yawning despair, and she wanted the ice field to open again beneath her and swallow her up, or goblins to fly down and snatch her away. That was it. Not Roma, a Tsingani name, not Roman, but Romana. The name she associated with that woman with a curling black mane. Her own mother. This woman Romana was Lord Vladeran's wife. Could it really be? Then Vladeran was her father, and her own parents, human parents, had tried to have her murdered. Alina's legs went weak.

"Come back with us now, Alin," said Fermin suddenly, "and you'll be judged fairly, boy. We'll see if there's truth in what you say."

Alina thought of her time with Malduk and Ranna. She had known little fairness amongst the humans, and she suddenly realised that one of the most terrible things in the world is not to be believed. Yet this bitter revelation about her parents had robbed her of all will. Alina felt as meek as a lamb to the slaughter.

"No," she whispered. "Please. It's not lies, Fermin. Ivan will speak for me."

Malduk smiled again and shook his head.

"Oh no, Alin. Ivan will speak for no one ever again."

Alina's hazel eyes opened in horror.

"You killed Ivan?" she snarled.

"Not at all. His heart took him when I . . . questioned him."

Malduk's eyes glinted, and Alina felt real tears scalding her cheeks. Dear Ivan.

"We'll not harm you though, Alin, as Fermin says," lied Malduk coldly. "I give you my word. The word of a human being."

Alina felt an ache in her forehead and heard a growling voice in her mind.

"Beware, Alina. Don't trust the Dragga."

The wolf was speaking to her from his hiding place below.

"Fell?"

"You'll not get down the mountain alive, Alina," came the black wolf's growling thoughts. "I've touched his mind. It is filled with shadows. The human has a horn dagger in his pocket and intends to use it on you soon, when the others are not watching perhaps. To silence you forever. You must fight them, child."

Just then Alina saw Malduk's hand hovering at his pocket. As she looked at the old man she had worked so hard for, as she thought of all he and his wife had done, she felt a fury bubble up inside her that was like the fire flaming in the ice cave.

"So, old man," she cried, "you'd murder me with your own hand, with that dagger you're hiding, as Ranna murdered Bogdan. Murder me before I ever returned to tell the truth."

Malduk blanched, and the others saw it. How had this girl known exactly what he was thinking and what was in his pocket? How had she known about Ranna? Was she a changeling and a servant of the devil after all? The others were looking at him, and Malduk realised that his face had revealed the truth of it.

"Witchcraft," cried the old shepherd angrily, drawing the blade. "He has witchcraft in him, and must be silenced before he does more evil."

The others were so startled that they did nothing, and Malduk lunged for Alina. Before he could strike her though, he heard a snarl and the old shepherd was knocked sideways in the snow by a leaping black shape.

Malduk just had time to look up and see the glint of savage white teeth, before the wolf snapped his mouth shut on Malduk's throat, stifling his scream. The pain was not great, for Malduk died almost instantly, but for the watchers in the snow the horror of it was terrible.

There they stood, Alin the changeling shepherd boy and a great black wolf, who seemed to have risen like a dark vision out of the pure white snows, to defend the child. Malduk's words of a wolf had been true then, but his blood was staining the ground, and the shepherds were powerless to act. There was a sudden break in the storm and the air seemed to clear.

"So, you came to hunt me down like a wild beast," said Alina bitterly. "Even you, Fermin? Go back to Moldov. Tell them I'm innocent of this crime, but that I'll have nothing more of humans, until I find my own people again. And the truth."

The hunters were trembling and backing away, their thoughts more filled with amazement and confusion at a shepherd moving through the world with a wolf at his side, than any sense of Alin's innocence, or any need for justice. Alina's hand came down, and she felt the top of Fell's sleek head, warm under her palm.

"Come, my friend," she said in human words, although her mind was talking to the wolf too. "Let's be gone from this place. I've a destiny to follow, and we've a long journey to make."

With that Alina WovenWord and Fell the wild black wolf turned and began to walk away across the snow. They limped at first, but as they went, their pace grew stronger and they started to run. They realised that their hurt was already beginning to heal, and their pace quickened even more. Side by side they went, the young woman and the black wolf, and as they began to run through the snows towards the wild winter, and Alina's destiny, a destiny that somehow involved the survival of nature itself, in the minds of Barbat and the shepherds, they were already running into legend.

PART TWO
THE PAST

NINE

THE FONT

The great Lord Vladeran sat in a rich fur cape, on a chair of carved oak, by a stone fireplace, listening to his soldier's report in the flickering firelight. An old hunting dog lay at his feet, and Vladeran's face, hard, cunning, and handsome, was propped on a large gloved fist, as his deep black eyes flared at his soldier's words.

"Alive?" he whispered angrily. "You're sure, Vlascan?"

The captain of Lord Vladeran's Shield Guard was wary, for he knew his overlord's flashes of anger, and he looked nervously at the dagger at Vladeran's belt. Messengers had suffered for their messages in these halls. His eyes wandered to an ornate insignia in the centre of his master's leather tunic: a red cross, with tongues of yellow, like flames or golden wings, at the four points.

"Your lieutenant did not manage to kill the little girl," answered Vlascan, "when you ordered her beyond these borders. He died in a fall, and she was saved by a shepherd."

Vladeran had often wondered why his lieutenant had never returned, and now he knew.

"What shepherd?"

"An old man called Malduk. He kept her as a servant, dressed as a boy. That's why she went unnoticed until the rumours began."

They had come to Vladeran like a bad memory from his spies, the rumours of a girl concealed as a boy, near the distant village of Moldov, with red hair and about the age Alina would have been by now. It was said that the redhead was a changeling, and had come out of the snows six or seven years before.

Lord Vladeran rose now. His great furs flowed about him, and his heavy soldier's frame, six foot two, swayed in his boots. At his feet the hunting dog growled softly as he spoke again.

"The shepherd knew who she was?"

"I think so, my lord. Or something of it."

"He'll be impaled for it, as cousin Draculea impales the Turks. No doubt he planned to blackmail me later."

"Malduk's already dead, my lord," said Vlascan softly. "And when I sent our soldiers to question his wife, Ranna, and their little niece, they had vanished into the snows."

In a glove of deerskin, dyed red, Lord Vladeran's hand closed into a fist, as if snatching at something that had already eluded his grasp.

"Damn it, man," he hissed, and his eyes narrowed. "But Alina. She spoke to anyone of Castelu?"

"No, my lord. We found an old woman, a witch skilled in herb law, and questioned her for her tale."

At the word "questioned" the soldier's eyes flickered, just as Malduk's had when he had spoken of Ivan. The witch was dead too.

"She had long given the couple a potion to hold the girl's thoughts, and together they invented a tale of goblins and changelings. Alina had lost her memories."

Vladeran seemed to relax a little.

"Strange. And now?"

"I don't know, except the villagers are still hunting her. Or a changeling boy, as the shepherds still think her to be. Alin WovenWord is accused of murder. It seems that Malduk repented his kindness and was trying to do away with her."

Vladeran's eyes glittered.

"Alin WovenWord, eh? Perhaps this Malduk had a change of heart because she has remembered who she really is, or discovered it somehow. Where is the damned child now?"

The soldier's eyes flickered again. "My lord. There's a tale that the changeling walks the mountains." Vlascan paused fearfully, and his hand came up and fingered the livid scar on his right cheek. He was one of the soldiers who had warned the children of the Turks that night, and Vlascan felt bitterly guilty that he had come so close to the child and missed her. His master must never know it.

"But not alone, my lord."

"Someone aids the girl? Are there traitors everywhere?"

Vlascan struggled with the words. "Not someone, my lord. Something. A wild animal."

Vladeran's hard, blank eyes turned on Vlascan in utter disbelief.

"What fairy stories are you talking now? What animal?"

"A wolf, my lord, a lone black wolf."

The look that suddenly gripped Vladeran's face was dark and strange, a mix of wonder and fear, but almost foreknowledge too. The soldier thought that the lord might draw his dagger and strike him down.

"I think it nothing but peasant superstition, my lord, like goblin tales, but the wolf's said to have torn out Malduk's throat in defence of Alina."

Dark thoughts were racing through Vladeran's cunning mind now, but used to living his life and hatching his plots in secret, trained in the subtle ways of a politician and a soldier, he knew above all how to keep his own counsel, and how to shield those thoughts too.

"Very well. You've done well to bring me this news, Vlascan, and shall be rewarded for it, I promise you that. Now tell me of the Turk, and Stefan Cel Mare."

"The Turk comes again, my lord. The land is ringed with fire, and blood soaks the soil in the lands beyond the forest. The Ottomans press on the borders once more, and the armies of King Stefan are gathering again. Your cousin Tepesh summons his men too, to raise the banners of Wallachia."

"And so shall I. These battles shall serve our plans indeed. We shall rise by it in the King's eyes, or in my cousin Draculea's reckoning, if Stefan fails his people in the face of the Turk. We must play them off, the one against the other."

Vladeran felt angry as he spoke of Stefan Cel Mare, a king who would one day be known both as Stefan the Great and Stefan the Holy. He knew that if the King ever discovered what had happened in these halls, there would be a terrible price to pay. And though Draculea was his cousin, and ruled in Wallachia with such terrible cruelty, he had no more trust of him than of King Stefan. This despite Vlad Tepesh's membership in the holy Order of the Griffin, the insignia of which Vladeran bore on his tunic.

The Order of the Knights of the Griffin had been established under the High Court of Budapest seventy years before, like another Order that the Impaler also cleaved to, the Order of the Dragon. Both bound their acolytes to defending the West against the infidel, and to upholding both King and Church.

Vladeran thought nervously now of the holy oaths he had taken when he had been admitted to the secret Order, and the five great principles that above all else he had sworn to defend—the protection of the earth, the nurturing of peace and the support of the downtrodden, the defence of the feminine and the pursuit of knowledge. Sacred ideals indeed, but ones that both he and Draculea had steeped and mired in blood.

"And your immediate orders, my lord?" asked Vlascan.

"Hunt the girl down. WovenWord must not survive. If any hear of it, or discover who she really is, you shall die by my own hand, Vlascan. Bring me her head."

Vlascan listened gravely.

"None must know of this. What would Stefan do if he ever discovered the plot? He may value my strength, even if Castelu is not a kingdom to rival Wallachia or Moldova, but he knows the need for law in this land. A law we have broken."

The nervous soldier nodded in the flickering firelight.

"And keep your counsel in all this, Vlascan. Now get out."

Vlascan bowed deeply, turned, and marched from the great chamber. As Lord Vladeran watched his captain go, he rose. He was already thinking of the reward he would give Vlascan when the work was done, and it had the shape of a knife in his captain's back.

None connected with that day could live to tell the secret, not even the captain of his Shield Guard, and Vlascan knew far too much already. Malduk's wife, Ranna, and her niece must be found and silenced too. But Vladeran's thoughts turned to wolves again, and he looked towards a great tapestry hanging on the wall to the left, wrought with mythical hunting scenes.

"Vladeran, my dearest lord."

The lord started and turned at the soft, feminine voice. A beautiful woman was standing before him, with long, black, curling hair and glittering, smiling eyes. It was the woman Alina had often seen dimly in her dreams. She was at the side of the room and seemed to have appeared from nowhere, although another tapestry swayed gently against the wall behind her.

A handsome blond boy was with her, wearing a huge, mischievous grin. The worry in Vladeran's face vanished and his features became a mask of charm and warmth.

"Romana. Elu. You startled me."

"We crept up the secret stairs, my love," said Romana, with an artless smile. "We heard that soldier's footsteps leaving, as we slipped into the recess beyond the arras, and so knew it was all right to approach."

Vladeran smiled too. "I see, my love. Well, you mustn't sneak up on me like that again. I'll have it sealed."

Romana's lovely dark eyes grew a little sad.

"But don't you want us to visit you?" she whispered warmly. "In secret or not."

"Of course, Romana, but there are others who might use the

stair for darker purposes. That's all I meant. It's a dangerous world."

The beautiful lady's eyes darkened. She knew just how dangerous.

"Vladeran," she said, a little reproachfully, putting her arm around her boy's shoulder. "You said you would come and visit us this morning."

"Forgive me again, Romana. There's been much to do. War comes and Stefan and Tepesh raise their armies. The King shall build more of his churches in the land, if he secures his victories against the Turk."

Elu grinned. "Shall there be fighting then, Father?" the little boy asked happily. "Oh, I hope so."

"Elu misses your visits so," said Romana. "He said you promised to teach him how to use a sword properly."

Vladeran looked down and smiled at the boy.

"And so I shall, Elu, so I shall," he whispered. "Soon enough."

Elu pulled himself from his mother's grasp, looking nervously at the hunting dog for a moment, then ran towards his father. He caught hold of the lord's arm with his hands, hands that the man could have crushed in a single fist.

"I'll be lord below the castle soon, won't I, Father?" he said. "And fight alongside King Stefan, or Draculea?"

Vladeran forced a smile this time. "That's right, my son. Although not at so young as seven. Don't hurry towards the future, lad, for why should you wish for such cares, when your mother and I keep your inheritance safe for you, until you become a man?"

The dark thought seized Vladeran again, the thought he had first had when Vlascan had spoken of a black wolf. His son had once been snatched away by wolves, and now Alina, alive and well and thought a changeling, had been seen with a wolf too. How could it all be? A strange destiny was working itself out in the lands beyond the forest, and it was time to talk with *her* again. Vladeran looked back to the tapestry, with its hunting scenes, and pulled his furs about him in the cold, then swung his strong head towards his beautiful wife.

"Go, my darling," he whispered. "Take Elu back to our chamber. I'll visit you both soon enough, but now I must pray."

Romana walked up and took her boy by the hand, but Elu pulled it away again. When his mother turned to go, though, kissing Vladeran lovingly on the lips, the little boy followed her as she swept out of the room. As soon as they were gone, Vladeran looked down at the dozing dog.

"Stay, Vlag," he ordered, striding across to the heavy wall tapestry woven with hunting scenes and sweeping it aside to reveal a stone recess, like a kind of little chapel. In this ancient palace, where there were so many passageways and secret places, like the stairway behind the arras up which Romana and Elu had come, this was the most secret of all.

Vladeran paused almost fearfully. Candles flickered at the back, and in the centre was a stone font, half-filled with water. He stepped inside and pulled the tapestry behind him. Vladeran often came in here to think and plan, but now as he gazed into the water, he remembered how he had stood here years before.

He wondered if the rite he had observed so long ago would work again.

He pulled off a glove and held up his right hand. In the centre of the palm was a deep scar that had long healed. Now Vladeran plucked the dagger from his belt, held his hand out over the font and hesitated again, fearful of what might come; then, in a single draw, he made a second cut with the knife across his palm, opening the skin.

Vladeran lifted his palm to his lips and sucked it, and then, squeezing hard to make a painful fist above the unholy font, he watched coldly as his blood began to drip into the water. Vladeran, the cousin of Draculea, had learnt many dark arts in the lands beyond the forest, and now he was praying that the power would come once more. With the first red drop the water went murky, with the second it seemed to move, and with the third it changed altogether.

"Come," hissed Vladeran, like a fallen priest, as an image seemed to be trying to form itself in the water, "by the powers that live beyond the sight of men, come to me. I summon you once again."

As Vladeran looked down into the font, he smiled as he saw a face appearing in the water. Not a human face but an animal's. A she-wolf. Although she looked old, her eyes glittered brightly. Her right ear was missing, and her muzzle had strange tufts of hair that had sprouted under her deep facial scars. She was growling, but her true words came into Vladeran's mind.

"Why have you summoned me once again, human? Summoned me from the misty, anguished regions in the Red Meadow?" hissed the she-wolf. "Where we wait to journey finally towards the Land of the Dead? We searchers. We echoes of the Past."

Vladeran craned forwards, as if the closeness might carry his speaking thoughts more quickly into the world beyond.

"I woke you once, she-wolf, when we learnt that my son had been amongst your kind," answered his thoughts, "and so learnt of the strange events on the mountain of Harja. Learnt too that through animals the pathway to beyond is closer than for man. And now another comes to meddle in the affairs of humans."

"Another?" said the she-wolf's thoughts, and her left ear twitched.

"Another wolf. A black loner."

The she-wolf's dark, impenetrable eyes grew like moons. For so long now she had lain amongst the spectres in the Red Meadow. Only once before had she been woken by this man, with the dark arts Vladeran had learnt of the secret power of blood and water and words to summon visions.

"Fell," hissed Morgra in the water, for that was the she-wolf that looked back at Vladeran now. Fell's hated aunt and the cause of so much darkness and death years ago. "It's Fell, I'm sure of it."

"Fell?"

"My little nephew," said the she-wolf, "and the brother of Larka, the white Varg that you . . . that I told you of. He too has the powers of the Sight, and I commanded him once."

"But what can a wolf want with a human?" asked Vladeran's wondering mind. "The human he travels with now. A girl."

"By the shadows in your eyes, Dragga, I see it's more than just any human, is it not?" murmured Morgra's cunning thoughts. "Has it not some great destiny, this child?"

Vladeran was silent, but his eyes narrowed angrily.

"But how should I know what he wants?" the wolf went on. "What do I really see in the Red Meadow, but visions of eternity? I'm not flesh and blood, human, but the stuff of dreams and of nightmares. Of myth."

"But when you lived, you said that you communicated with the dead," thought Vladeran angrily, for even though he was a brave, ruthless warrior, Vladeran feared death above all things, and even more so, what came after it, "summoned them from beyond."

"The Searchers," hissed Morgra's thoughts, remembering that terrible night when she had used the powers of the Sight and a Summoning Howl to open the Pathways of the Dead, and call an army of spectral Varg from the Red Meadow to help her fight the rebel wolves. "Yes. They came at my howling, indeed."

"Then the two worlds may communicate physically, even as we do now. Could you not send out these Searchers to . . ."

"No," snapped Morgra. "I was a living wolf then, touched by the Sight, and a legend was being fulfilled. But Larka's power closed that doorway, and there are none to call us from your side."

"But I must find this black wolf, for if I find him I will find the girl he travels with. The girl they call changeling."

"What's this to me, human? I can see nothing from here of the warm, hot life of the world, unless you call to me with the blood in the water. I'm like one blinded forever."

"But I reside in the world of the living," answered Vladeran. "Teach me then of the Gift. The Sight."

Morgra gave a low, snarling growl and, in the water, a shape seemed to wing past her head. A raven.

"The Sight is the gift of animals, human." The she-wolf paused. "Yet, as Larka showed us all on the mountaintop, when she became the Man Varg up at Harja, man too is a Lera. An animal."

Vladeran nodded gravely, remembering the strange dream he had had all those years ago. He had been standing amongst ancient Roman stones, and it had felt to him as if he had been able to see the history of the whole world, and all about him there had been wild animals. But amongst them was a strange humanlike creature climbing down from the trees. In that moment he had known, more certainly than he had ever known anything in his life, that the stories of his childhood, read from the great Bible, were as false as tales of fairies and changelings, and that man too was like these creatures around him. An animal.

Vladeran nodded coldly.

"Yes, Morgra. Man is an animal too, and so man must act like a wild beast."

Morgra's eyes narrowed. "Very well," came the she-wolf's thoughts. "We will see what I may teach you, human. You summon my spectre in the water with the gift of blood again, to warm the veins of the lost for a time, and make me remember what I'm not. So this time I shall instruct you."

Vladeran smiled grimly.

"And in return you shall tell me of the world. Of the hot sun on a tumbling mountain river, and the smell of cornflowers in the open spring meadows. Of the eagle and the falcon swooping for a kill down the clean, bright air, and the taste of new flesh in the morning."

For a moment the she-wolf had an expression that, if she were human, could be described as a smile.

"Larka has long passed to a place beyond even the Red Meadow, where I wait and suffer in purgatory," she said, wondering at the mystery of it, like one tormented who was speaking of some mythical good that she could never understand. "She who taught that all must be free, and stopped me controlling the world through a human's mind, and the child's power. Very well then, Larka, my dear, once more perhaps we'll see."

Even as she said it, Morgra's thoughts seemed to grow faint in Vladeran's mind, and her image began to fade. It was as if she was helpless against the very name of Larka.

Vladeran raised his fist again and squeezed hard, breaking the seal of congealing blood on his palm and muttering dark words. As soon as the red drops hit the surface, Morgra was sharp and clear again in the font.

"And Fell. Her dark brother, Fell," came Morgra's struggling mind. "He was mine once, human, and lived in shadows. I tormented his heart and mind and made him kill at my command. So he's closer to the shadows than he ever knows. Closer to you, my lord, than this child, I think."

Vladeran's heart was beating furiously and he smiled.

"We must hunt the girl and the wolf," he growled. "Must track them down and kill them both."

"You ask much of spectres," whispered Morgra's mind. "But I shall tell you then of Fell's true nature, human, to trap him with, and together perhaps we shall teach the world of the real power of myths."

"Myths?" whispered Vladeran.

"Not stories told by wolf or man to frighten children, of Wolfbane and of werewolves, of grasht and goblins and of silly vampires, fables to frighten cowards with the threat of evil and of sin. But the power that lives beyond those stories, and makes them strong indeed, that lives in nightmares and in sleep. That is ribbed into the very fabric of conscious being. The power of love and of hate."

Vladeran shuddered, and even he wished to be away from this stony place of death, back in Romana's arms, touching and loving the living.

"We've a pact then, she-wolf," he said softly. "And I shall bring you more blood."

"A pact?" said Morgra's angry mind, remembering how she herself, a barren she-wolf who could never raise and love a family of her own, had once so longed to make a pact with Larka's little family, to join them and protect them too. "A pact we have indeed then. So be warned, human, never to break it."

Far away, a face, hidden in shadow, stared out through a high window at the mountains beyond. His eyes were filled with sadness and longing, and he clutched his left arm painfully, like one who had long been ill. He had a kingly bearing, but he was thinking now how he had failed in his duty in the lands beyond the forest.

"Is there any more news?" he asked sadly. His voice was as deep and passionate as water rushing over shiny pebbles.

The armoured knight he was addressing dipped his head respectfully, as he stood behind him in the great hall.

"We're sending out riders."

"And you believe the rumours?" came that powerful voice.

"Some," said the knight.

"Search for any who might know of it." His master felt a sharp pain in his arm. "And this strange story?" he added. "The wolf."

"That I don't know. That sounds like a tale made by children."

"Yes. And yet . . ."

The story of a wolf was a strange one, indeed. Like Vladeran the man suddenly remembered that vision that had come to him years before. He turned and walked back to the throne in the hall and sat down wearily.

"What will you do?" asked the knight respectfully.

"Do? We must keep looking."

The soldier was looking at his master's finely worked jerkin as he said this last. It was emblazoned as Vladeran's had been, yet unlike Vladeran's tunic, beneath the red cross and yellow flames lay the image of a golden animal, part lion, part eagle, curled about itself, so that its tail was in its mouth and its wings folded. Only the secret leader of the Order wore such a thing. The Griffin.

TEN
A WOLF TRAIL

We're close," said Alina WovenWord,
"to the valley Ivan told me of. Baba Yaga's valley."

Alina poked at the fading embers, by the mouth of the cave where they had both just spent the night. Two cold months had passed since their escape from the ice field, and together the girl and the black wolf had climbed higher into the Carpathian Mountains, fighting through the swelling snows, but enjoying too the peace of clear, crisp days and winter sunshine. Now they could see the cairn on the mountain above, and with luck beyond was the valley.

The trail had been difficult at times, and Alina had often looked out across the sweeping white mountains and the great lonely expanses of Transylvania and gulped with the sense of her own minuteness in nature.

"Are you sure we must visit this blacksmith?" asked the wolf.

Fell growled at the strangeness of the conversation. He had always known that he could peer into humans' minds with the Sight, but to communicate with the girl like this, to actually talk to her, as if Alina were a growling wolf herself, or Fell a chattering human, had astounded his thoughts and frightened his soul. It was like one of the cub's stories. And now he knew the voice on the wind had been real.

Fell had already learnt how the power only came at moments of great pressure and intensity though, and how it did not seem to work at any distance. Perhaps being sealed together in that ice den had brought it on them, but Fell knew in his heart that it was more than that.

"I think so," answered Alina. "If we are to journey to Castelu, I need help, and better clothes. This winter is too dangerous."

Alina was far from sure of their journey, as she fed kindling into the rising flames, and felt a desperate pang in her heart. If Vladeran and Romana were really her parents, why had they wanted her dead, and was her little brother still alive? Yet an even darker mystery surrounded her now, if all this was to be believed: the very survival of nature itself. What could it all mean?

Alina looked for reassurance into the catching flames. Fire had kept her alive in these freezing weeks, and had brought the wolf comfort too. She had lost Ivan's pack, but she still had his knife and, with her skill at carving, had made more of those clever little tools to light the kindling.

As the girl had cooked the meat Fell had brought after his hunts, the wolf had grown used to its heat and flames, and although he did not really understand its nature, he had come to fear it less and less. It sometimes made Fell almost guilty sitting there though, for the wild wolf sensed that he was being touched by the tameness that visited men's dogs and, to the Varg, made them weak and lazy, or robbed them of their freedom.

Yet out here in the snows, travelling with the human was not the same as living in their strange homes, Fell kept reassuring himself. Their nights were lit by starlight and the great moon, the wolf goddess Tor, not the oil lamps that burned in the villages. They drank not from human cups, but from pools and mountain streams, and ate meat fresh from the kill, even if Alina WovenWord always insisted on cooking her own. The roof of their home was the endless sky, their walls the trees and rock slopes, and the bed where they laid their heads was the living earth itself.

"And we must be wary as we travel now, Alina," came Fell's thoughts suddenly. "The humans we saw yesterday were marching, like your kind always do. They were warriors, I think, Drappa, and I've seen what they can do to one another. It's terrible when the bloodlust takes them."

"Yes," answered Alina, but another thought came to the girl. What a thing it would be to be a warrior, free of fear. Did those who had to face a great destiny not have soldiers at their back? Alina had nothing, except Malduk's coat, a knife, and a strange wolf at her side.

Although she was desperately grateful to Fell and owed him her life, Alina had not forgotten how he had snapped at her on the ice bridge and killed Malduk on the glacier, and often in the nights she had woken fearfully to see the wolf lying near her, and wondered if he might suddenly turn on her too with his teeth. Whenever she was with him, she felt the power and anger lurking beneath the surface of the wolf's being, a spirit at once vital and impetuous.

At times as they journeyed, Fell had sensed his own wild instincts begin to rise almost uncontrollably too, until he had recalled his vision of the young woman in the water and remembered that this was no ordinary human. She was the sister of the little baby that Larka had tended to in the snows and who Fell himself had carried on his back five years before. Some deep destiny was working itself out.

"So we go, human?" asked Fell, half rising.

Alina hesitated and went on gazing out into the distant, snowy expanses.

"After breakfast, perhaps."

Fell's eyes glinted and the wolf began to lick his paw cheerlessly, although his wound from the dam was healed. Three nights after the glacier, Alina had approached Fell to examine the cut. He had let her, and Alina had fetched herbs, as she had once seen Ranna do for Malduk, and made a poultice to bind to the wound with a piece of cloth torn from her shirt. In the days to come it had fallen from the wolf's leg again, but the poultice had soothed Fell's cut, helping it heal, and made him wonder again at the power of man.

"We're united by the Sight, human," he said suddenly, "but I cannot walk amongst your kind. I am wild."

In that moment, Alina thought of how the villagers had feared her as a changeling, and how she had concealed herself from goblins, and realised then that they both knew what it was like to be an outsider, but a sudden fear flickered in her eyes.

"But you'll stay near me, Fell?"

"I will, human."

Alina sighed gratefully. Mia was gone and Ivan dead, and all her life she had been alone. Whoever the people in her dream were, they had failed to protect and care for her, and it had made poor Alina feel worthless. But at least Fell was at her side.

"Then we'll find Lescu after breakfast, Fell," she said firmly, "and ask him what he knows of the world. Of Lord Vladeran too."

Alina looked at Fell.

"Besides," she added almost guiltily, "it would be good to sleep in a warm barn for a while, and it'll be easier to journey to the castle when the snows melt, I think."

Fell felt sick at the idea of the human dens. "Very well then, Drappa, although it will be dangerous for me, let us be finding your human. Then I must stay in the shadows."

The two of them breakfasted on a pheasant Fell hunted down, and then set off once more.

But the cairn was farther than it looked and a blizzard came up, so they were forced to shelter in a cave. Fell had gone hunting when Alina woke and in the ravishing day the girl decided to walk out into the snows. She soon found herself in a small forest of lovely silver birch trees, on the slope of the mountain. As the light sparkled in the snow about her and glittered on the strange silvery bark, Alina felt as if she were wandering through a wonderful dream, or one of her own stories, and for the first time in her life she felt like a real changeling child.

She seemed to walk for an age, confident that her tracks in the snow would lead her easily back to the cave and Fell, but as she went on, she heard the guttering of water, and then the most extraordinary sound. A furious snarling and a snapping, mixed with loud, delighted yelps.

Alina broke into a clearing and there stood Fell. The black wolf was on top of a dead boar, tearing at it furiously, sating his hunger and growling with pleasure. The snow was spattered red with blood, and Alina looked on in horror. She backed away again, hoping the wild beast wouldn't see her, but she broke a branch beneath her foot and Fell swung his head immediately and his eyes glittered savagely.

Alina gasped. For a moment the girl thought there was blood in them, and Fell seemed so different from the creature she had laid her head on in the cave.

"Beware, human," growled Fell's mind, and Alina felt that pain to her forehead again, "for the bloodlust grips me."

Alina backed away even farther, up against a silver birch that stopped her retreat, and Fell jumped off the boar and padded towards her. Alina was looking beyond the wolf at the dead animal, lying in the snow.

"But it's so ugly," she whispered, shuddering.

Fell stopped in front of her and growled.

"Ugly, human? Why? I am Varg, and live by the chase. I must eat, must I not? It is natural."

"Yes."

The savagery that had gripped Fell seemed to leave his staring gaze. He whimpered softly, and then rubbed his muzzle in the snow to clean it and looked up again and yawned.

"You're horrified, Drappa?"

"I . . ."

There was a sudden sadness in the wolf's mind, as there was in the girl's. She thought of goblins and witches, and found these real facts of nature far more terrible.

181

"Is this the wild then, Fell?" she whispered, trembling against the beautiful tree, and almost wishing she was back in the barn. "Is this what nature really is?"

Fell blinked at her, but the wolf did not answer. He could sense the girl's disgust, and her fear too. Animals sense nothing so quickly as fear.

"You're Putnar too, Alina WovenWord. Man is."

"What do you mean, Putnar?"

"Man is a predator, like the wolf. You eat animals, do you not? To live."

"Yes, Fell. But . . . but not like this. I could not do this. I . . ."

"Could you not?" growled Fell angrily. "I wonder, Alina. For I have seen many of the works of man, far worse than the fighting wolf, since we learned the Great Secret on the mountain."

"What Great Secret?"

"The secret that a vision brought us, Alina, when man and wolf's thoughts were united. Larka and your baby brother. The secret of man."

"Tell me."

"That man too is an animal."

Alina WovenWord's eyes opened in amazement almost as great as when the wolf had spoken of her destiny. What was it that was moving through her mind now? Alina loved animals dearly, and had always wanted to know of the wild, thinking it part of her changeling power, but she had never really thought of herself as one of them.

Why was that? she asked herself, as she cowered against the tree. Was it because of the story she had heard in the wooden church in

Moldov, of a fabled garden where the first man, Adam, had been placed by God himself? There, woman, Eve, fashioned from Adam's rib, had joined him, and together they had lived with the animals. Until they had eaten from the fruit of the tree of knowledge, and been banished from paradise forever.

That story placed man above the animals, until man's fall at Eve's hand, and linked humans to God himself, fashioned in his image. But now a black wolf was telling the girl a grave secret. That man was an animal too.

Alina remembered her dream in the ice cathedral when she had slept on the wolf's side, of that creature that had looked so human, climbing down from the trees and rising on its legs. It had been like that dancing monkey that travelling players had brought one festival to the village of Moldov.

Could it be true? Was Alina herself, were Malduk and Mia, Ivan and Ranna all just animals, like Fell? There might be no goblins, but the world was suddenly filled with changelings again. Alina gazed at the dead boar and thought of how Malduk had taught her to butcher that sheep at festival. She ate meat like Fell. She was a Putnar, as he had said.

"Yes, Fell."

Fell could see that Alina's hazel eyes were glistening with tears.

"Alina. Come with me. There's something I must show you."

The black wolf turned slowly, then with a yelp began to bound down the snowy slope towards the stream below. He stopped and looked back.

"Come and see, Drappa."

Alina hesitated and then walked nervously past the dead boar.

Fell was waiting for her by a small thicket, and as Alina neared him, he spoke again.

"You must stay concealed, human. Must not disturb them."

There was a tenderness in Fell's mind, and the girl crouched down by him, wondering what he wanted to show her. His muzzle was pointed towards the far bank of the stream. Alina's heart quickened as she saw what Fell was looking at. Two large grey shapes were lying in the snow beyond, several little bundles of fur bounding around them, squealing and yelping, tumbling over one another and fighting with their little paws. It was a small wolf pack, just two adults and their four cubs.

"Why don't you approach them, Fell?" whispered Alina, but the wolf simply gave a sad little whine.

As Alina asked it in her thoughts, one of the cubs set off boldly from the others, and reaching the verge above the water, he gave a spring and found himself skittering and tumbling down the bank. He landed in a painless heap, then picked himself up and padded towards the water. It was the most beautiful little animal, about the size of a large puppy, with huge paws and enormous eyes, and its tail wagged happily as it stood there. Its bright young gaze seemed mesmerised by the glittering water, as its little tongue lolled from its tiny furry muzzle.

In that moment it looked up and saw Alina. There was no fear in the look, just a fascinated questioning, and as Alina gazed back at the lovely little thing across the water, a sudden awe enfolded her. The day was so bright and clear, the air so wonderfully fresh, the cub so pretty and artless, that, as the strangers looked at each other, Alina Sculcuvant felt then the deep, grave wonder of being, and the power and mystery of nature, all around her.

"You see," whispered Fell. "And you say it's ugly?"

Alina put her hand gently on her friend's back.

"No, Fell. It's beautiful."

"Yet perhaps it's true that you're more than Lera, Alina," growled the wolf softly. "I've often thought it. In the ice cave I could not control your mind, as I can those of other animals."

The two wolf parents had got up now, and although Alina didn't understand the growls, Fell listened as the Drappa called down the bank.

"Be careful, Brag. That mad Kerl might still be about, asking questions of a Guardian."

The little cub wasn't listening. He was too caught up in his adventure.

"And it's dangerous by the water, Brag. Varg fear nothing so much as—"

"Hush," growled the Dragga beside her. "Don't fill the cub with fear. Teach him to be strong."

Alina and Fell went on together that evening and, just before dawn, they came to the cairn and across the brow of the mountain, and looked down over a wide valley.

Alina's heart lightened as they spotted a small wooden church on the hill below them, above a frozen lake. It looked just like the place Ivan had described—Baba Yaga's valley.

Alina felt something strange stir in her, as she thought not of stories of the witch, but of going amongst people again, especially after seeing that little cub and its family. But at her side Fell was not looking down the valley at all. His sleek black head was raised to the sky, and his golden yellow eyes were sparkling. The Varg was gazing up at the millions of little lights, still twinkling and glowing like dust clouds in the darkness above them. Alina felt dizzy too and very small, as she stood by Fell and threw back her head to look up at the gigantic sweep of the Milky Way.

"We call it the Wolf Trail, human. The pathway between heaven and the earth."

Fell wondered at the story. He had already discovered in his travels how dangerous stories can be. He had seen that the fear amongst the Varg of the mythical Wolfbane, the Evil One, had filled them with anger and hate. Indeed, under the power of Morgra's mind Fell had, for a time, come to believe that he himself was evil, and the very conviction had inspired his actions. Yet Fell liked this tale.

"Heaven," thought Alina at his side, remembering when she and Mia had crept into the wooden church in Moldov and listened to the priest's sermons with half an ear. She thought again of a Garden of Eden, and of how many lies had already surrounded her changeling life. "Isn't heaven just a story, Fell?"

The black wolf nodded.

"Perhaps, Drappa. Perhaps Sita never really came down to earth at all, I've often thought it."

"Sita?"

"In the tales of the Varg, the holy she-wolf Sita was sent down by the wolf gods Tor and Fenris, but was reviled by the Varg, who would not believe what she was. Her death was prophesied and they let it happen, let her be killed. But Sita rose again, to prove to the Varg the power of love. My sister Larka believed that story. It drove her on to her death, I sometimes think, and her sacrifice."

"The Christ," thought Alina's wondering mind. "It's the tale of the Christ, Fell. Humans have the same story."

The girl and the black wolf stood wondering on the mountaintop, feeling the chill air on their faces, seemingly lost in a dream, as they gazed into the immensity of the heavens. How could it be that wolf and man shared the same story? Or were they just in a story themselves, lost in a fable, as they hunted through the world for meaning?

The friends began to walk, side by side, down the slope towards the humans, as the Wolf Trail faded above them and dawn broke around them. As they went Alina WovenWord noticed that the wooden church was abandoned.

Light had come when they reached the edge of the forest below the church and stopped by a big freestanding oak. They saw a little homely house not far in the distance, with a corral for horses and a large barn.

The air was suddenly filled with human sounds. The "tink, tink, tink," of hammering metal and of a man at work in the wooden barn beyond, where the glow of hot firelight warmed the freezing morning. It was a blacksmith all right. Fell hung back in the darkness of the trees, his black muzzle pressed forwards nervously, his ears cocked sharply for any sign of danger, as he scented the air. He felt torn by the girl's imminent departure.

"Good-bye, Fell. I will spend a couple of days with them," whispered Alina. "Then come and tell you of what we do next. Stay close, wolf."

"I shall human, I swear it. And while you're gone I shall start searching for the Guardian in these parts. But do not let these others know of my presence in the forest. They fear me."

Again Alina remembered how they had feared and hunted her as a changeling. "I promise,"she said.

She looked down at her friend and smiled, then she stepped resolutely from the trees. For a moment the black wolf wanted to follow her, but he knew that he could not. He was wild. As Alina walked away, he growled and swung his head. He felt the sensation that somebody or something was watching him, and as he turned his head slightly, he thought he caught a movement in the trees behind him. Fell was sure now. Something was following them in the forest.

Alina was already well out in the open. Nervously she approached the blacksmith's forge and felt self-conscious, realising that after so long in the mountains she must look terrible. She tried to think of a story to tell, a half lie at least, to explain how she had survived in the snows on her own and crossed the mountains in such weather.

She was inventing quickly, as she stopped in the doorway of the forge to see a powerful man with long black hair standing in a leather apron, hammering at a piece of metal. He was in his middle years, but still had a fighter's form, strong and sinewy, and his sleeves were rolled up around his forearms. The sturdy blacksmith looked up, and seeing Alina, he smiled.

"Hello, lad. How can I help you?"

Alina opened her mouth to answer, but she felt caught, and realised that she had hardly spoken a human word in a whole month. She remembered too her promise to Ivan.

"You mistake me, sir, I'm no lad," she answered, "although it's safer sometimes to dress as a boy, when you travel the world alone."

The blacksmith's eyes sparkled with interest, and he put down the blade and hammer. He stepped forwards, picking up a cloth and cleaning his hands of coke and soot.

"A pretty girl too, if I may say, though you clothe yourself like a vagabond. This is a strange day indeed, yet what you say of safety is true in these times. Who do you seek here?"

"You, sir. If you're the blacksmith Lescu."

"I am."

"Ivan sent me."

The blacksmith hurled the cloth away and strode straight up to Alina, smiling delightedly.

"My dear friend Ivan. How is the old rogue?"

"Ivan . . . Ivan is dead," answered Alina sadly.

The blacksmith's head dropped and he sighed bitterly, although his handsome, intelligent face held the wise resignation of one for whom such news was not entirely unexpected. Ivan had been old, and life in this country was desperately difficult, and on their last parting Lescu had not expected to see Ivan again. He looked up now and smiled.

"Well, let me clean up here," he said, "and over a good breakfast, you'll tell me more of this strange meeting and what a young woman does, wandering alone out of the forests. Of poor Ivan too."

"Oh, thank you, sir."

Alina could think of nothing better than a good breakfast.

Lescu was already plunging his grimey hands into a barrel of water, but as he washed, he looked quickly towards the trees, as if he had just seen something there.

"You travel alone, you say?" he asked curtly.

Alina reddened a little.

"Yes, sir," she lied. "Yes, I do. Why?"

Lescu's keen eyes were still searching the trees, but he spotted nothing.

"Very well," he said. "There are many strange things in Baba Yaga's forests. Come then."

He led her towards the nearby farmhouse, and as they approached, the door opened and a boy with long brown hair that tumbled around his shoulders stepped outside. He had a strong, open face, with bold, blue green eyes and was humming to himself happily, but as soon as he saw Alina, he stopped with surprise and embarrassment. Alina thought him tall and very fine. Suddenly a shape came tearing out of the house behind him. A large brown hunting dog, larger than any Alina had seen, bounded straight at her, barking furiously.

"No, Gwell!" cried the young man. The wolfhound seemed possessed though and came leaping at Alina, snapping and snarling.

"Down, Gwell!" shouted the blacksmith, who had just stepped in front of Alina. The dog stopped dead, but his wary eyes were locked on Alina's, and he was still snarling.

"Has the devil got into you, Gwell?" snapped Lescu angrily. "Or a demon? Stop it!"

Alina held her ground. She knew dogs of course, and had had a powerful bond with Elak and Teela, but she had never caused a reaction like this before. Alina found herself shaking all over. The boy had run towards them, and grabbed hold of Gwell's fur, crouching down and looking up guiltily at the stranger.

"I'm sorry," he panted. "I don't know what's got into him today. He thinks you a threat."

"Are you?" whispered the blacksmith, turning to look at Alina sharply, and then back towards the trees.

"No, sir."

Gwell had calmed a little, seeing the two people he most loved in the world protecting the stranger, and now he stopped barking altogether, although he was still glaring at Alina. She realised that both he and the blacksmith were sniffing the air.

"Where on earth have you been, girl?" asked Lescu, with a laugh. "You smell like a badger's set. Doesn't she, Catalin?"

Alina blushed, especially in front of the handsome lad, but not as deeply as Catalin. His cheeks had gone bright red, from the realisation that this was no boy at all, but a pretty young woman, the prettiest he had ever seen in fact. He felt his stomach knot.

"I . . . I slept in caves and in the open," answered Alina, stuttering, "crossing the mountains."

"Wonders never cease," said Lescu, looking deeply impressed. "Well, you must tell us of that, indeed. But first it's a good hot bath for you, girl, to get that stench off you, and out of poor Gwell's nose."

"Yes," said Alina gratefully, suddenly feeling weary. She looked down more kindly at the dog, then up at the man. "Thank you, Lescu."

"If you come from Ivan, then you have nothing to thank us for," said Lescu softly. "Now come, lass, let's get you safely inside."

TARLAR

Fell's footfalls in the forest were as silent as the noiseless air as he padded through the trees. When Alina had left him alone, the wolf had watched her meeting with the blacksmith and felt a jealousy he hadn't known since he was a cub. Like the time when Kar had arrived in their pack and befriended his sister, or when Fell had first learned that Larka possessed the Sight. But then hunger had overcome emotion and the wolf had decided to hunt.

The black Varg was scenting now, looking for signs of deer or rabbit in the wood. Fell heard a chattering up ahead. The wolf knew instantly what it meant. It was the sound of feeding ravens, and thus the chance of a meal. Only the power of the Sight bestowed communion with birds, the Helpers, but in the wild, in real nature, a wolf had a far more basic bond with birds. It was one of fact and necessity.

When wolves hunted and made their kills, the smell of blood would bring those hooded black wings hurrying to join the feast. Equally, when a Lera stumbled and died naturally in the wild, ravens and other birds might find its body, and their cries alert the wolf. So part of the wild wolf's nature, of Fell's nature, was not the role of the "mighty" Putnar at all, but that of the mere scavenger. It brought Fell a kind of humility, as he ran towards the sound.

He growled hungrily as he spotted these flying scavengers up ahead. A dead stag lay on its side on the edge of the river, its stiffened grey back touching three large rocks. It was a young deer, a two pointer, and its antlers, as hard as tree bark, curled around like human daggers. Its staring eyes were open, as if it were still seeing out into the world, but its gaze was cold and dead, and on its back stood three feeding ravens, where a wound was already touched by the busy movement of insects. Two had their angry beaks at work in the carcass and one stood sentinel, while other cawing Corvidae winged their looming shapes towards the prize.

Fell was in no mood to share with anyone though, and with a snarl he leapt towards the carcass, and in a great flurry of beating wings and indignant cawing, the ravens rose like a black cloud and flew away.

Normally, in the almost endless and seemingly insistent struggle of nature, Fell's meal would have been interrupted by the pecking birds, as they grew confident again at having a wolf in their midst, knowing a raven was hardly a prize for a Varg. But these scavengers had fed well already, and there were other morsels in the wintry forest that day.

So Fell found himself alone with the dead deer, and sank in his teeth with satisfaction at such an easy gift, pulling at the meat unashamedly. The wolf did not fear now that the Sight would suddenly show him a vision of its own being, its anguish, for the thing was long since dead. Fell ate peacefully, not with the bloodlust on him, but a measured intent.

When Fell had sated his hunger on the delicious deer, he turned to the river, and where the ice at the edge had frozen solid, he broke it with his paw and snout and began to lap away at the chilly water. Then he lay down. With a soft whine that turned into a long, delighted yawn, Fell closed his tired eyes and laid his black head on the frozen earth to rest.

If the ravens had stayed, they would have noticed that as the sleep came on Fell, his whole body began to twitch, and the ripples of life worked on his muzzle, revealing that he was dreaming powerfully. It brought a low growl from his belly, as one talking in sleep, or a Lera facing a danger he could not escape.

Before Fell's dreaming vision was a human face—a man with brutal head and searching black eyes.

He stood in a great fur cloak and his lips were curled into a cruel smile. He was in a kind of stone den, and at his side was a raised water pool. He opened his mouth and began to speak, but human words did not come out at all. Instead Fell heard the yelps and growls of a wild wolf. The man was addressing the sleeper in his own language, yet the voice sounded female.

"Fell. Listen to me carefully, Fell. We have been searching for you."

Fell felt as small as a young cub again and shuddered furiously, for he knew that voice.

"It's been so long, Fell my dear. Where are you wandering, my friend?"

"Morgra?" Fell growled in horror.

"Yes, Fell. You thought of me as your mother once. Will you not heed me again, my dear?"

"Never," growled Fell's sleeping thoughts as he shook uncontrollably. "This is just a dream. You're dead, Morgra."

"So I am, Fell DarkEyes, as is your beloved sister Larka, or was her voice just a dream too?"

Fell twitched. How had his aunt known of it?

"As you shall be dead too, one day, for all things die. That is the fate and destiny that nothing may escape. But the past may return, and I would help prepare you for the shadows."

"That's all you know, Morgra, with your hate. Shadows and darkness."

In Fell's dream, or his vision, Lord Vladeran smiled at the wolf and spoke again with Morgra's voice.

"That is all there is, Fell, beyond the seeming of life. You know it now, above all the struggling Lera. Why do you pretend to be what you're not? I know the power and glory you felt in the shadows."

"The anger and hate," growled Fell. "It was power, but it was also evil and lies. Like the lie that Wolfbane, the Evil One, exists."

Lord Vladeran's eyes flickered and he smiled knowingly, as Morgra's voice came again.

"Don't be foolish, Fell. Of course Wolfbane exists. The Evil One is everywhere. Just look around you."

The sleeping wolf whimpered softly on the ground.

"And you're a wolf, Fell, black and powerful and strong, gifted above even Larka with the Sight. So take your rightful place in the world. You journey too, searching and alone, as I did once in life, looking for a meaning to it all. But there is no meaning, Fell, except power. No purpose and no heroism, and thus no despair. Life is simply what it is, and only the strong and the ruthless prevail. Children learn that as they grow, learn to throw off the lies they were taught nestled in the bosom of their family."

Fell began to struggle in the dream.

"You lie, Morgra. You always lied to me. And now I hunt down lies."

"And do you not lie now, Fell, walking with a human and turning against your true nature?"

At that Fell growled. The man's eyes seemed to be looking deep into him, searching something out, as if asking a question. He was looking for Alina.

"You know of it?" asked the dreaming wolf.

Lord Vladeran's eyes flickered and Morgra's mind spoke again.

"We know of it, yes. So where are you now, Fell? There's blood on your lips. Have you killed this changeling already and left her for dead in the forests, as she should be?"

"Never. She is   "

Fell stopped his thoughts.

"Go, Morgra," he snarled furiously instead. "Or whatever you are. Get out of my mind. You're nothing but a phantom, and you're dead."

"Yes, my dear, but we saw together how the mind is shaped by phantoms, did we not? You guard her, I see. Very touching. But you do not love man, Fell HateThroat. You cannot."

Fell twitched in his sleep and thought of words of nature and the child's destiny.

"You know what they are, and what they will do to the wild world. You do not love the Lera, either. You alone see life as it really is, Fell. And if you do love the Lera, or care for their future in the wild, then do it for them. Go to her in the night and kill her. End this foolishness."

The wolf snapped his jaws in his sleep. "Leave me be, witch."

Again Lord Vladeran was smiling, filled with Morgra's darkness.

"It will be so, Fell LoneTail. You know you will strike her. It is only a matter of time."

"Never."

A sparrow turned on a branch, as it heard Fell's helpless cries, and fluttered nervously.

"You've sensed it already, have you not? The desire to kill her. To express the only nature that really matters. Your own."

Fell's growls turned into a guilty whimper, as he remembered pouncing at Alina in the ice cave.

"Of course you have, my dear. It's only your instincts, nothing more. Accept it. Why should anything blame itself for its nature?"

Fell moaned as he tried to wake himself.

"Well, then, wake now and look into the water, Fell. Use the power of the Sight to see the future."

"No, Morgra."

"You must, Fell. I command you with the Sight."

In his sleep the wolf rose and turned towards the frozen river. As he reached it, although still dreaming, Fell opened his eyes, and looked out in startled horror. On the far bank stood a huge black raven, watching him with its beady eyes. Fell thought for a moment that it must be Kraar, Morgra's faithful servant and helper, until he remembered that Kraar too was dead. It was just a raven, and it suddenly took wing. Although Fell's eyes were open, he could still hear that terrible voice in his mind. His aunt's voice.

"Look down, Fell, and use the Sight to see the truth."

Fell lowered his muzzle. In front of him was ice, sprinkled lightly with snow, but on the surface was a moving image, like the pictures in the glacier. It was Alina WovenWord and she seemed stronger than before. The girl carried a bow and a sword, topped with an animal carving, and she turned suddenly and smiled at him. How could she have changed so fast? He knew this was the future.

To Fell's horror he saw himself in the ice too, with the powers of the Sight, saw himself jumping at his friend, his great claws prone, his jaws closing about her throat. Alina had no time to draw the sword, or defend herself from her friend. Fell knew as he watched himself that the bloodlust was on him, and although he felt horror, fascination came too, and a kind of grim triumph, as he struck down the human creature, and raised his muzzle and howled in the vision.

"No!" cried Fell, trembling bitterly on the bank, and closing his eyes to stop the vision. The wolf backed away. But the voice came again.

"Yes, my dear. The Sight does not lie. You know that it did not lie to Larka, and that she could not escape the destiny she saw. You shall kill the girl anyway, so why not now, Fell DarkHeart, there where you are hiding. Bring on your destiny sooner, for it shall come in the end."

"Never, Morgra. Get away from me. You're a liar. A dead liar, and nothing but a dream."

Fell growled furiously and shook his whole body, as if he had just emerged dripping from a river. He swung his head left and right, and snapped at the empty air. The wolf was fully awake now, and blinked stupidly as he looked about him. There was no one there. No human or she-wolf speaking to him. Just the busy, eager silence of the forest. It had all been a terrible dream.

Fell's legs were still shaking, and he felt a dreadful sorrow in his heart, almost as great as the one he had felt when he watched his sister fall to her death.

"Alina," he whispered desperately. "What shall I do? I'm a danger to you, I know it now."

Then Fell realised something appalling. If the child's survival was linked somehow to the survival of nature, wasn't Fell a danger to all around him? He turned and began to run like one hunted, and as he ran he thought of those eyes that he had sensed watching him. Was his wicked aunt Morgra really alive? Or if not alive, had she returned to the land beyond the forest from the Red Meadow, to spread her hate and cruelty once more amongst the Varg, like the spectral Searchers had once done? It couldn't all be beginning again, thought Fell bitterly. As if the journey of being simply took you in circles, from darkness into light, and back again into the shadows.

Fell suddenly remembered Ottol's question, *Where do you draw your power from, Wolf, the darkness or the light?* As he thought of what he had just seen in the ice, he knew now, with all the strength of his being. "The darkness," the wolf whispered bitterly, "only the darkness."

Fell howled as he ran, and in the blacksmith's home Alina heard him and looked up, but others heard Fell too in the forest and turned to follow the call.

Fell must have run for an hour, and when he finally stopped, panting for breath, the very effort had cleared his mind a little. But as he stood there he thought he could see a she-wolf approaching him through the trees. Could it be Morgra's spirit? He set his teeth hard and waited, but he suddenly saw two wolves bounding towards the clearing where he was standing. His heart fluttered like a newborn chick, and his eyes widened in absolute amazement, as he looked at that wonderful face.

"Kar!" he cried delightedly.

Before him, panting and sucking in breaths, stood his adopted brother Kar. The wolf was about the same size as Fell, only he had the natural colouring of a grey. The whitening fur around his long, intelligent muzzle showed the advance of age, but Kar's clever eyes were as bright and kind as ever. Fell wondered with an aching heart where all those years had gone.

Another wolf was standing behind Kar, a sleek she-wolf, whom Fell did not know. She was a beautiful grey, with bright, healthy eyes and a lovely, bristling tail.

Suddenly the two males ran towards each other, circling and scenting and wagging their tails delightedly, their nostrils filled with recognition, transformed into passionate memory. Kar and Fell were reunited.

"At last I've found you, brother," cried Kar happily. "It is good to see you again. So good."

"And you, Kar," said Fell. "It's been a long time."

"Much too long, Fell. Often we've heard of you amongst the Varg, though. You seem so young, still."

"And you heard of me in dark stories, no doubt?" said Fell, with glittering eyes that looked beyond Kar to the pretty she-wolf. Kar did not demur. Instead he turned his head.

"This is Tarlar, brother. She has joined our pack."

The she-wolf made no sound, but instead she cocked her pretty head and stepped further into the clearing. Fell took her in with his eyes, and for a moment, since he was a Dragga, and one whose territory she was approaching, he kept his tail raised in dominance.

"I ask you Larka's Blessing," said the lovely she-wolf, with smiling eyes, and Fell lowered his tail.

"Then you're welcome indeed, Tarlar. Especially if you come with Kar."

Kar's tail was wagging. From all he had heard of Fell, he had feared that he might not allow them to approach, and Kar remembered his own time as a Kerl, in a high, lonely cave, and how it had almost sent him mad. Yet Fell seemed well, and so youthful too. But then Kar himself already suspected that the Sight had some power to extend life.

"You spoke of the pack," said Fell softly. "How are they?"

Kar's eyes flickered.

"Well, my brother. The cubs . . . how foolish it is to call them that now. Kipcha and Khaz, Skop and . . ." Kar paused, "and the other Larka. They've all grown strong and healthy. The pack thrives."

"And Slavka?"

It was the rebel wolf who had thrown off the bitter struggle she had once engaged in to live with the family, and Kar's eyes saddened.

"No, Fell, Slavka's gone. Though it was a peaceful end. When Palla . . ."

Fell felt a jolt. So his mother, Palla, was still alive too.

"Mother," he whispered with a soft growl. "Is she well?"

"Yes, Fell. Though very old now."

"And my father, Huttser?"

It felt strange for the black wolf to speak his father's name. Huttser was a faded memory to Fell. Kar's tail had come down, and a dark look crept into his eyes. Almost of sorrow.

"What's wrong, Kar? Is Huttser . . ."

"He's fine," said Kar quickly, sensing Fell's question, "but something has happened, Fell. A moon ago. A wild pack. They call themselves the Vengerid."

Fell's tail came up and he growled. He knew the Varg word. It meant "vengeance."

"Tell me."

"They are led by a wolf called Jalgan. They're like the Balkar, Morgra's slaves, only their strength is not made up of male Varg alone. Drappa and Dragga fight and kill side by side, with no purpose but fighting itself. They are as wild and free as the sea. They came down on us in the night, last full moon, although Jalgan was not with them. With Huttser at our front, we fought them off, but the pack is in danger. They'll return."

Fell felt his heart stir.

"Skop has the strength of a Dragga in him, Fell," said Kar, "but the others are not used to attack, and have not yet even taken mates. Larka does not take to fighting much, and the strength of our pack is nothing against these Vengerid."

"What does this Jalgan want?" growled Fell angrily. "Why does he call his pack the Vengerid? What revenge does he seek?"

"Nothing but vengeance on life itself, or so he says," answered Kar grimly. "He teaches that because all things die, the only way to conquer suffering is to make others suffer. Although Huttser warned them off, Jalgan has sworn to return himself and destroy our pack one day. Huttser is still strong, for a wolf of his years, but I do not think he can fight Jalgan openly."

"But why, Kar, why do they come?"

"Jalgan challenges all the Varg to face him, and says that he will admit he is wrong only if one is bold enough to fight and defeat him. But there is another reason . . ."

Kar swung his head now, and was looking at Tarlar. The she-wolf stepped closer.

"Let me speak, Kar," she said. Tarlar lowered her tail to show respect, although there was nothing frightened in her being. Fell thought how bold and fine her voice sounded, and how lovely were her eyes.

"Fell LoneTail," began Tarlar softly, "I've heard much of your journeying, and something from Kar of the darkness and sorrow you've seen. Well, I too have known it. For I was once of the Vengerid."

"You," said Fell in surprise, wondering what the she-wolf was doing here.

"I once thought them so fine and strong, and Jalgan the bravest of all wolves," said Tarlar bitterly. "Until I saw the cruelty and hate they're breeding. Until Jalgan murdered my brother."

Fell blinked slowly. "Your brother?"

"Kenkur was his name. He was always more of the Sikla than the Dragga," said Tarlar sadly, and Fell felt his heart stir for her. "At first, when they took us, he hid his hatred for fighting, but at last they spotted it."

Tarlar lowered her beautiful eyes.

"How I blame myself. I was young and idealistic, or just foolish perhaps, and caught up in the adventure of it all. How I loved the chase, and the strength and freedom of the Vengerid. All my life I had been wrestling with what it is to be a wolf, and this seemed an answer. And then there was him."

Tarlar's huge eyes blinked.

"Jalgan," she said. "Oh, he was so handsome and powerful to me once, with his streak of silver grey right along the centre of his back. He noticed me too, and I knew that he was admiring me. So I would listen to nothing of Kenkur's doubts, and told my brother he was being weak and cowardly, and that this was the way of the true wolf. To glory in the bloodlust and to marvel at the kill. To be free."

Fell nodded slowly. He had often thought it himself.

"I was angry at him too, when he said anything against Jalgan. And speak he did, because Kenkur feared for me. Jalgan was beginning to court me, and Kenkur saw that it was drawing me closer and closer to the Vengerid."

Fell could see that Tarlar was trembling.

"So one day, when we had argued, Jalgan singled my brother out before the whole Vengerid. He called him Sikla and traitor and took out his throat."

Tarlar's beautiful bushy tale had come down behind her and she whimpered.

"You must not blame your . . . ," began Fell softly, but Tarlar interrupted him with a loud growl that surprised Fell with its ferocity and pride.

"Must not blame myself?" she cried, and her eyes showed not guilt, but clarity. "Yes, Fell, I must. Not only because I did not stand up for him, but because Jalgan called on me to swear allegiance to him, and to the Vengerid. And I did it. Because I was a fool and I wanted him. Even though my own brother was lying dead before my eyes."

"I'm sorry," whispered Fell, feeling bitterly sad for the beautiful, remorseful she-wolf. "It's sometimes hard to stand outside a pack. And are you your brother's keeper?"

"A pack?" snorted Tarlar scornfully. "A bold, brave pack? What is a true wolf pack, and the strength of the Dragga and the Drappa— the right to lead and feel the power—unless it is to guard and protect the Sikla, too, the weakest of our kind, as we protect our very cubs? That is the law of the untamed wolf. Only that makes us truly beautiful in the wild. That is the truth."

Fell thought of Ottol and that he himself had nothing to protect, until he suddenly thought of Alina.

"For does not nature put enough troubles in our way?" Tarlar went on passionately. "And kill us with illness and hunger and time too, without our having to turn on each other, with anger and blindness and hate?"

Fell was listening closely to Tarlar, and he realised that he had listened to no wolf so carefully in all his life.

"And although it's a fine thing to be a Dragga and Drappa, the finest thing in the world perhaps," said Tarlar with glittering eyes, "does not all the pack work for the future, and who knows what each may carry in his heart, or bring into the light, Dragga or Sikla? Who knows what secret truths their lives may hold for all of us?"

Secret truths? Both Fell and Kar remembered the secret then that the Sikla of their old pack had entrusted to Fell's mother, Palla, on his death. The death that came because he had fought so heroically against his own fear and cowardice to aid the family. It was the secret that, after all the fighting they had witnessed, seemed as simple as a sigh: It's not so bad to be the Sikla.

Tarlar raised her beautiful head and looked straight at Fell. Long enough for him to feel her moving in his heart.

"When at last I saw the truth, I left Jalgan and the Vengerid," she said, "and went out into the world."

"To become a Kerl?" asked Fell, almost hopefully.

"No, Fell. That path was never for me," answered Tarlar softly.

"For why wrestle with the world alone, when two pairs of eyes may see better than one, and four better than two?" Something stirred in Fell's stomach. "Another's eyes may always temper the arrogance of the triumphant heart, while when the sadness and the weariness come, happier eyes can renew the world again with their vision. So I went in search of a real pack."

"My family?" said Fell, feeling strange indeed to use the word.

"Yes, Fell," answered Tarlar softly. "They welcomed me in, and I knew I had found a home, and so I must ask your forgiveness."

"Mine?"

"All things must ask forgiveness. It was I that brought the Vengerid and Jalgan down on their dear muzzles. He sees me as his true mate, and would have me back at all costs."

Fell was not surprised by Jalgan's determination. He fixed his eyes on Kar's now, and suddenly knew why his adopted brother had come.

"You want my help, Kar, against the Vengerid?"

Kar seemed caught between pride and purpose, but he nodded.

"Yes, Fell. Although Huttser said your journey is your own, he cannot fight Jalgan openly, and your mother told me to find you. Palla said that you would want to know at least. That it was your right to know. Do you have it still, Fell? The power to look into minds and . . ."

"Control wills?" Fell nodded slowly and shivered. He remembered how he had once used it to blind and torment the Balkar, but he feared to ever use it again. "I still have the power, brother, amongst the Lera at least."

Fell grew silent, thinking of his family. They bore his blood, but were no longer his family. He had been away so long. Not just the five, hard years since he had climbed into the mountains, but truly since that terrible night on the river when he had almost drowned and been captured by Morgra. Perhaps even longer, perhaps since his very birth in the den below the abandoned castle. Perhaps Fell had always been alone. Perhaps we all are.

"I cannot, Kar," he whispered at last, looking guiltily at Tarlar. "I travel on a different path now. "

"With man?" said Kar, though not disapprovingly. Fell thought of that vision he had had of his teeth tearing into Alina.

"Yes, Kar, with man. Or woman. She has a great destiny. One that involves us all, I think. That involves the survival of nature itself."

"Then it's true what Skart said," whispered Kar.

"Skart," said Fell, remembering the steppe eagle who had aided Larka, one of the Helpers. "You've seen him?"

"Yes, Fell. He came to us before he died."

Fell growled. Then Skart too was dead. But it did not matter. Everything dies. That was the law of life—the bitter, unchangeable law. "What did he say, Kar?"

"He was very old and weak. He said something of a human. A child."

"Yes?"

"Then he began to ramble and talk in strange words. Like a prophecy. 'Before it's done,' he said, 'everything must be turned about. The Dragga must become the Drappa and the nature of opposites must be revealed in ice and fire.'"

Fell shivered and remembered the ice cave.

"He said a wolf must rise from the earth, and the water, too, to be reborn, before he hears the Great Secret on the air, and becomes a voice of power in the world."

Fell's eyes narrowed.

"I think he was mad before the end," Kar added. "He said the clawed Putnar must open its wings too, and the wild wolf talk through man and woman, then sprout two heads, even as the dead are restored."

"Sprout two heads?" growled Fell. "It's impossible."

"Yes," agreed Kar. "But how did you learn of the child, Fell?"

"I heard a voice, Kar, on the wind," answered Fell, feeling rather foolish. "I think it was Larka."

"Then perhaps it's true," whispered Kar, and for a moment he was lost in wonder, but he spoke again. "The Sight still has you in its grip, and you've made a pact."

Kar was searching Fell with his intelligent, philosophical eyes, but not with any judgement in them, but simply the desire to know and to understand.

Fell recalled the pact that he and Kar and Larka had once made as cubs, when they had travelled together in the face of so much fear and sorrow, to aid one another in all they did. The pact that had brought Kar out of the shadows of his own mind, to help Larka, and that had led Larka up to Harja, to save Fell and the human child.

Fell nodded at his adopted brother.

"And I would not ask you to break such a pact," said Kar gravely. "For Larka gave me a vision of man too. One filled with hope."

Fell nodded.

"At least I've delivered my message, and Skart's, if it was for you," said Kar softly, "and now I must return and help them. That is where my heart lies, brother."

"And mine," said Tarlar proudly.

Fell felt another desperate sting of loneliness and thought of Ottol's family.

"Can you not stay awhile?" he asked.

Kar looked at Tarlar and then Fell. The black wolf realised that his brother was almost frightened of him, but Kar nodded slowly.

"Yes, Fell. A night perhaps. We will talk and maybe hunt together, as we did when we were young, and when the sun rises we will leave you alone once more."

The black wolf growled, pleased that Kar had not tried to force or persuade him in any way. So Fell and Kar and Tarlar spent the night talking in the forest, pressing away the shadows with their memories and their stories, and Kar learnt of all that Fell had done and seen since that day that he had lifted his head with a howl and gone into the wild. So much more than Kar had seen, bound as he remained to the daily care of a wolf pack, or could ever really know.

Fell, in turn, heard of his parents, Huttser and Palla, who had survived longer than any wild wolves in those parts, and the cubs that had been given the names of lost members of the old pack. He felt odd as he listened, for at Kar's words about these grown Varg, he almost felt the stirrings of tenderness.

But it was like a story for Fell, rather than real events, and he felt a wall of resistance, almost darkness, between himself and this little family. Although he knew their names, he could not see or sense them in his mind's eye, and he knew that he was blocking his own heart.

Why had Fell really gone away and left them? Was it simply because he had to find his own meaning amongst man? Or was it because of what he himself had done when he had thought that he was evil, and how he had betrayed them, what he was capable of doing and thinking and feeling, which meant he was a danger to his family. So in a way Fell had gone out, a lone Kerl, to protect them from himself.

The wolves heard the approach of morning in the chattering of waking birds, and Kar said, "We must be gone now, brother. I shall tell them that you are . . . are well."

"And tell them . . ." Fell looked hard at Kar. "Tell them that I'm sorry too. It's not because I fear it."

"I know it, Fell. And you're always welcome amongst us," said his brother softly. "The pack lives now in the valley beyond the Great Waterfall near the Stone Den. It would be easy to find us."

"It shall not be, Kar," growled Fell, looking at Tarlar again.

"I'm sad," whispered Kar, "for I have not the strength to save them from Jalgan, or to accept his challenge. But we give you Larka's Blessing."

With that Kar and the beautiful grey wolf Tarlar were gone, although as they left Tarlar turned just once and looked back fondly at Fell.

Fell began to run, and felt loneliness about him again, but strangely it was Tarlar more than Kar that he missed. But he began to think of Skart's strange words. The Helpers had the gift of prophecy, and some things Skart had said seemed to echo Fell's journey. He had touched fire and ice and risen from the earth to kill Malduk. Things had been turned about indeed. But the rest seemed mad. How could a wolf sprout two heads?

For two days and nights Fell roamed through the trees, torn between two calls now, the call of his old family, somewhere in the mountains, threatened by the Vengerid, and the pact that he had made with the human, now sleeping safe in a human den. It brought Fell pain and confusion.

Part of him wanted to help Alina, part to help his family, and part to go as far away as possible, to be free of it all, of any ties or responsibilities, and live, alone and wild again, away from wolf and man, away from the Sight. As he ran, his pace quickened and he gloried once more in the feeling of the ground beneath his pads and the scent of game on the air. But Fell came to a clearing and sensed the danger almost before it happened. He saw the strangely mounded leaves before him, and smelt the presence of man.

Suddenly, with a startled yelp, Fell was falling. His body twisted with an angry howl and leaves rose in a swirl into the air, as earth walls and darkness swallowed him up.

TWELVE

THE WARRIOR SMITH

I t's a miraculous escape," said Lescu the
blacksmith cheerfully, yet with doubt sparking in his eyes.
"A wonder too that such a blizzard didn't finish you off completely
on that ice field, WovenWord."

Alina had just told father and son something of her life near
Moldov, and then the story of the cave, where she had fallen and
sprained her leg, walking on the mountain. She had mentioned
nothing of the reason she had been up there though, or of Fell and
the Sight, saying that she had simply escaped through a tunnel in
the ice. She had hardly known where to start her story, certainly
not until she knew she could trust them.

She looked a deal better as she sat at the simple table—her
now clean red hair shining—and plunged a great spoon into the
bowl of delicious stew in front of her. Alina felt almost human
again. Lescu sat opposite and Catalin stood gawping at her in utter
astonishment.

It was as if a whole world, new and brave, had opened before
Catalin's blue green eyes. He was a handsome lad, strong and tall,
a great teller of stories himself and much feted amongst the village
girls in the district. He had often walked with them and kissed
them too, but most he found rather silly and foolish, and in his

heart he was much more interested in riding and swimming, and learning the arts of the blacksmith. He kept looking across at Alina now. She had come out of the wild, dressed as a boy, and had survived so many terrible dangers already. Catalin had never seen anything so extraordinary in his life.

"It must have been freezing down there, Alina," he whispered, with warmth and sympathy in his eyes, thinking of the cave, "and you must have been horribly hungry."

Alina remembered the raw goat meat that Fell had brought her with the root, but she just smiled.

"But why did you try to cross the ice field in winter?" asked Catalin.

Alina paused and shrugged again.

"It wasn't much of a life in Moldov. It was time to set out."

"Then you've been trapping all the way across the mountains?" asked Lescu, fixing Alina with his steady eyes. The blacksmith already knew that the girl was lying about something, or leaving a part of her tale out, and now Lescu wanted to know what.

"Yes," answered Alina quickly, looking away, "and eating berries."

"Then you've a skill indeed, Alina, but whatever the truth of it, if you're a friend of Ivan's, you're welcome here. Isn't she, Catalin?"

"Of course, Father," answered the boy warmly. "It'll be so good to have company."

The blacksmith smiled at his son. They had a good life together, but after his wife's death a few years before, and with the isolation of the place, so far from the village, and no other children in the house, he knew how lonely Catalin would often get.

"What do you mean 'the truth of it?'" asked Alina nervously, realising she had no reason to feel indignant at the challenge.

The blacksmith leaned forwards gravely across the table.

"You can't fool me, WovenWord, as you've fooled many," he said, although not unkindly. "A good name they gave you in that village—Sculcuvant. But by the sounds of your story, you were running away from something."

Alina felt her cheeks flush. Instantly she began to weave another lie in her head, but then remembered what Ivan had told her about truth being her greatest ally. Lescu was staring hard at her, and something else made her tell the truth. Fell had been able to look into her thoughts. Perhaps the blacksmith could too.

"Who really goes for a stroll on an ice field?" he said. "Tell us the rest of it."

Suddenly, like water breaching a dam, it all came out, as Alina told them her true tale. Almost all of it. The blacksmith and his son listened in even greater amazement as she told them of the life she remembered, from the day she had been found by Malduk as a changeling in the snows, to that terrible night that Mia had shown her the parchment and they had overheard Malduk and Ranna plotting her death. As she spoke, she wondered if they believed her. Father and son didn't say a single word until she had finished.

"Ivan helped me escape Malduk," she concluded, "and told me to find you. So here I am."

Alina sat back and smiled awkwardly. It had been marvellous to tell the truth. Or most of it anyway. She still hadn't mentioned Fell, or Malduk's death.

"And I'm glad you did, changeling," said Lescu, looking warily at his son. Catalin's mouth was hanging open, thinking the whole thing like one of his own stories. "The winter turns our valleys and villages into little islands, and no news has come to us yet of this, but if you'd approached some of the others with tales of Lord Vladeran, I doubt you would be sitting eating stew with friends."

Alina smiled meekly. She was desperately relieved the adult believed her.

"But it's a strange tale to take in, and you must be careful to whom you tell it, Alina WovenWord."

"Yes, Lescu. I will."

"But you think your own parents wanted you dead?" said Catalin in horror, sitting down heavily at the table.

"I . . . yes . . . I don't know. I have dreams."

"The mark you saw on the parchment," said Lescu, "show it to me."

Alina rolled up her sleeve. They saw that little eagle there, with opening wings.

"Well, it's no mark of Castelu," said the blacksmith.

Alina was surprised and her heart beat faster. She had already begun to associate that bird and the parchment with Vladeran and Castelu, and suddenly wondered if she had been wrong and perhaps Vladeran and his wife really weren't her parents at all. Perhaps she didn't belong to Castelu at all.

"Stay here with us awhile," said the blacksmith kindly, "until I can find out about this mark, and whether they're still hunting for a changeling."

"Thank you," said Alina, shivering. "But what does Vladeran look like, Lescu?"

"Look like? I've never seen him, child."

"But he lives in a village, below a great castle on the mountaintop?"

The blacksmith laughed out loud.

"Heavens, no. The likes of Vladeran live in a village, Alina? You'll have King Stefan living in a manger next, or Draculea in a church. Good Lord Vladeran clothes himself in rich furs, and shields his power with high walls."

"The castle then? I once thought it floated in the clouds."

The blacksmith shook his head.

"That empty place, if it's the one I think it is, is the home of the grasht, or so they say," answered Lescu. "Vladeran's great palace and fortress lie beyond, across another mountain, and approached by a narrow pass, defended by a mighty river. That's the distant region of Castelu, although the hand of Vladeran extends much further."

Alina felt something stir in her. Castelu. It sounded a fearful place. Was that where her destiny really lay? And were Vladeran and Romana her parents? Yet if it was, and they were, then why had Alina been in a village with her baby brother that night the wolves had come? It didn't make sense. But then very little did.

"We can find out more of this when the snows thaw," said Lescu, seeing the changing emotions on the pretty girl's face. "Let's speak now of your own story. You say Ranna killed Bogdan? Alina, are you listening to me?"

"What?" Alina looked up sharply from her own dark thoughts. "Oh. Yes, yes, she did. I know it."

"And Malduk wants your death, too, more badly than ever?"

"Wanted," sputtered Alina, and she wished she hadn't. She blushed furiously.

"What do you mean 'wanted'?" asked Lescu sternly, his eyes narrowing as he leaned forwards again. Alina didn't know what to do. It had to come out at last, what had happened on the ice field, yet the girl suddenly feared that it would turn Lescu and Catalin against her, and she felt as if she was walking into a trap.

"Malduk's dead," she whispered, dropping her eyes.

"Dead? How, girl?"

"He . . . I . . . I killed him," lied Alina. "With my knife, up there on the mountain."

Alina sat there trembling and Catalin stepped forwards, and Lescu's eyebrows knitted as he stood up.

"And how did you escape them after that?" asked the blacksmith quietly.

Alina felt her heart pounding, but something told her that even though she was lying, and dear Ivan had told her not to lie to Lescu, she was still doing the right thing not to betray Fell's presence, or her promise to the wolf.

"I don't know," she stammered. "I must have been more used to running across that kind of ground. They were slow and eventually they gave up."

"With an injured leg?

Alina simply shrugged again. Lescu looked long and hard at Alina

WovenWord, as did Catalin, whose pleasure at seeing such a pretty girl in their home was suddenly overshadowed by the thought that a man had died at her hands. Yet it made him regard Alina with a kind of grim respect too, and at last the blacksmith spoke.

"And what should we do with you now, Sculcuvant? You've killed a man, by your own admission. Do you not think this a matter for the Courts?"

"The Courts?" gulped Alina, recalling tales she'd heard in Moldov of the cruel punishments of the Courts, in the lands beyond the forest. Both Alina and Catalin stared at the blacksmith, and Lescu suddenly shook his head and smiled.

"Don't worry, child, I'll not hand you over to the authorities. If all you say is true, then this Malduk has had his just deserts, all right. By the sounds of him, the world won't miss his passing either, although he did save your life once. Besides, real justice has long been in danger in these lands."

"Why, Lescu?" asked Alina, feeling greatly relieved, but smarting bitterly at all the injustice she had suffered already.

"Perhaps because men don't know what true justice is anymore, and think might alone the right," answered Lescu sadly. "Perhaps because the King cannot impose his authority easily, with lords like Tepesh in the land and your . . . Lord Vladeran. They engender fear and greed everywhere, and those hateful twins breed lies. When there's no truth, Alina WovenWord, how can there be any justice, and what can grow fine and strong without that?"

Alina felt something stir in her heart. She thought of old

Ranna's plot to kill Bogdan and blame her, and how easily it might have worked, but she realised that Lescu was still looking closely at her. Much she had said had been true, but she hadn't spoken of the strangest part of her story, and had just confessed to a crime she hadn't even committed. Alina felt as if she were weaving a dangerous web about herself and she almost determined never to lie again.

"Well," said Lescu at last, "you're welcome for now in Baba Yaga's valley."

The girl's eyes flickered.

"Why is it called that, Lescu?" she asked.

"Because they say that something lives in the forest," said Catalin. "I'll tell you the story if you like."

"Not now, son," said his father. "There's been enough talk, and it's time Alina was in bed, and resting."

"Bed?" said Alina wearily, "but it's the middle of the day."

"And Catalin and I have work. With war coming, King Stefan calls for more swords to be sent daily, although they never know how to use such fine things properly. But you, young woman, look tired enough to sleep for a week. So you shall, under a roof where people care for you. Then perhaps we'll put you to work about the place."

Alina tried to argue, but the kind blacksmith would hear nothing of it, and soon the girl found herself in a neat little room, with snow flowers in a jug in the corner. She looked about in amazement, for until now she had thought a barn good enough for a changeling girl like her, and this was like heaven.

"Sleep well, child," whispered Lescu, as he and his son stood attentively in the doorway. "Perhaps when you're recovered, you can earn your keep by telling us some of your stories."

Alina smiled and nodded.

"But will it be safe to sleep in our beds tonight, Catalin," added the blacksmith with a wink to his son, "with one such as you in our home, Alina WovenWord?"

They smiled and Alina felt a rush of gratitude to these two men, as they closed the door softly. She climbed into bed happily, and as soon as her head hit the pillow, her weary body gave in completely. Alina could not remember sleeping in a proper bed before, and she remembered Lescu's words about a house where people cared for her.

She found herself thinking of Fell, as she drifted off to sleep in her lovely warm bedding, wondering if he was all right in the forest, and if Baba Yaga was really out there too. But then she reassured herself with a smile that those were just stories, and that Fell was wild and certainly knew how to protect himself in the open, even from a witch, as dreams carried her away.

Alina was so tired that she slept for three whole days. Her sleep was interrupted only by the gentle knocks of Catalin, who would bring her food, and water to wash herself. She tried to get up several times, but each time the young man insisted that she stay and restore her strength. She had dark, fitful imaginings in her sleep, and it was the evening of the third night when Alina had her clearest dream. It was of that creature she had dreamt of in the ice cave, that human ape, and man's role in the world. She woke feeling sad and terribly guilty, yet stronger than ever too.

A full moon was shining through the little window in her room, and Alina got up to dress. She saw that they had placed new clothes on a chair beside her bed. There was a plain white dress and a little shawl, and Alina felt strange as she slipped into it. Her hair was short like a boy's, badly cut with the shears and rather spikey, but in the dress Alina suddenly wondered if she looked pretty.

She opened the door to her room quietly and crept outside in her bare feet, only to hear voices coming from below. Lescu and his son were talking softly together.

"No one in the villages has heard anything, Catalin," the blacksmith was saying. "I've asked around, and all they talk of now are Turks and Stefan's fight. They'll pay no heed to another around the house, changeling or not."

"Then she can stay here, Father?"

Lescu paused, and Alina felt her heart beating faster.

"It's a dark thing that she's killed a man, Catalin, but darker still the reasons why. I fear for her indeed if Vladeran and Romana are her parents. Yet why they should want her dead I cannot fathom. She's only a girl and can be no political threat. Yes, she can stay, my boy. She needs our help, and I like her spirit. Perhaps she'll share some of her stories."

"Oh, Father. Thank you."

"But we must keep her story secret from the villagers. A strange destiny follows this child."

"Yes, Father."

"You like her, don't you?" asked Lescu.

The boy was silent for a while, and Alina found herself hanging on his answer. Lescu had got up and was fumbling with something at the table.

"Such eyes she has, father," said Catalin at last. "There's something special about her, I think."

"And the least of it is that mark on her arm, or talk of changelings. But take this, Catalin. Put my bag in the dresser."

"More gold, father?"

"Yes, boy. At least the threat of war pays a blacksmith well. Gold is one certain thing in the world, when men and the Courts are so uncertain. Though it's sad that gold seems to move men's hearts entirely."

With that they heard a creak on the stair and looked up to see Alina standing there. She pretended she hadn't heard, but she suddenly felt embarrassed and ran her hands through her hair and grinned foolishly at the men. Lescu nodded approvingly as he saw her in the dress.

"You look restored, Alina," he said. "Well enough to help us around the farm, tomorrow, perhaps."

"Oh, gladly, Lescu, and anything else that I may do to repay your kindness. Both of you."

Catalin was blushing as she reached the bottom of the stair and he noticed her pretty bare feet.

"Come, Alina," said Lescu warmly, "sit at the table with us. Catalin's promised to tell me another story of Baba Yaga. You can listen too."

"I'd like that," said Alina, smiling and sitting down.

Catalin felt awkward in front of a changeling child, famed

for her stories, but he was used to spinning yarns to entertain his father, so he began.

"I bet you know all the tales of the witch, Alina," he said. "How she lives in a log cabin that walks around on dancing chicken feet, with a fence made of human bones, with skulls on top."

"Except for one piece of fence," said Alina, "reserved for the hero of the story."

Catalin nodded and his eyes glittered.

"Yes, Alina. And how the keyhole of her front door is really a mouth, filled with sharp wolf's teeth."

"Which only appears when you tell it a magic phrase," said Alina, *"Turn your back to the forest . . ."*

"But your front to me," said Catalin quickly.

Lescu laughed.

"Well," he cried happily, "we've a brace of storytellers here indeed."

Catalin smiled and went on. "Some say old Baba Yaga was always so angry because each time someone asked her a question she aged a whole year," he said, keen to impress both his father and the pretty girl, "and so Baba Yaga would have to drink tea made from blue roses to restore herself. So if you bring her a gift of blue roses, she'll grant you a wish. But the truth is she's just an evil old hag, who steals children and threatens to eat them up."

Alina shivered a little.

"Baba Yaga has many servants of course," Catalin said eagerly, "and three riders visit her house. One white . . ."

"For the day," said Alina.

"One red."

"For the sun," said Lescu, joining in.

"And one black, for the black, black night," said Catalin, nodding sagely. "And on such a black night, a girl was sent on an errand to see her, named Vasilissa the beautiful."

Alina's eyes opened appreciatively, for she had heard many stories of Baba Yaga, but none of a beautiful girl called Vasilissa.

"Now, Vasilissa was terrified of Baba Yaga, of course," said Catalin, "and she had been warned that, although she could ask Baba Yaga about the three riders, she could say nothing of her servants, for then the old hag would kill her instantly. She also knew that to approach Baba Yaga was always a dangerous thing, and that what would protect her most was her own purity of spirit, her careful preparation, and showing the old woman the greatest politeness. So with humility in her heart, lovely Vasilissa reached the terrifying hut, and heard it squawking like a chicken."

Alina and Lescu smiled and sat back appreciatively.

"Now, Baba Yaga was in a good mood that day," said Catalin, "and so Vasilissa completed her errand unharmed, but as she was about to leave through the gate to that wicked fence, the old hag looked into the tea she was making, and saw her own reflection there. It made her think of how young and beautiful Vasilissa was in comparison.

"At that she flew into such a terrible rage that she jumped into her mortar and raced after the girl. 'Look out Vasilissa,' cried a voice near the fence of bones, although the girl could not see who had spoken. 'She's coming,' cried another voice, but it was too late, because the old hag scooped her up and imprisoned her inside her walking house.

"But Vasilissa was not alone in the house of the witch, for two of Baba Yaga's servants appeared, a cat and a dog. Now, Vasilissa loved animals with all her heart."

Alina looked up at that and thought of Fell.

"And she was so kind to them both, so gentle and tender, that they decided they must help her escape. So one day, when the black rider had come again, they opened a window in the house, and told her to climb out and hide in a tree. 'Thank you, Vasilissa,' they said. 'We love you.'

"Vasilissa was sorry to leave them, but she was so gentle as she climbed into the branches, making sure not to damage any, that she heard one of the voices she had heard before. 'Thank you, Vasilissa,' said the tree, which was one of Baba Yaga's servants too, 'I'll help you as well.' 'But how?' whispered the beautiful girl wonderingly, 'Baba Yaga has many spells, and I fear she'll follow me, tree, if I try to escape.' The tree thought for a while and then said, 'We must ask the gate.'

"Suddenly the gate started talking too," whispered Catalin. "'Dear Vasilissa,' it said warmly, 'You were so gentle and polite when you first opened me, that though I am only a servant, I will help you too. You must hide in the . . .' But the gate stopped, for being a swinging gate, he was used to changing his mind. 'No, Vasilissa, you must run as fast and far as you can, as soon as the red rider appears, and not stop until you see the white rider. Baba Yaga will follow, but if you reach the white rider before her, her spell will be broken forever.'

"'Look,' said Vasilissa, trembling, for the red rider had just appeared on the hill. 'Run then, Vasilissa,' boomed the tree, bending down and placing her carefully on the ground, beyond the fence of skulls and human bones. 'Run, beautiful Vasilissa,' cried all the servants together. Vasilissa started to run, as fast as she could as the sun rose, and there was a terrible screech behind her. The old hag Baba Yaga was in pursuit, in her giant mortar, steering through the air with her pestle and beating the poor clouds with her broom."

Alina shuddered as she listened, and as he spoke, Catalin seemed to hear a voice in his own head. *Wake up, Catalin,* it seemed to say.

"Vasilissa the beautiful was so terrified of the old woman that she ran faster than she had ever run before, as the red rider beat the ground with his hooves. She ran west over fields and hills and at last she came to a valley. Baba Yaga was nearly on her, but just as she was about to pounce, Vasilissa saw the white horseman before her, on his fine white horse. The spell was broken, and suddenly, because of the old hag's cruelty to her animals, she was transformed into a great black crow."

"And the valley was this valley?" said Alina softly.

"Yes," answered Catalin, with a grin. "Of course. But that wasn't the end of the story, Alina. For Vasilissa was so kind that she asked the horseman to take pity on the old hag. So he summoned her house and changed her back again, saying though that Baba Yaga could never leave our valley, or she would be changed into a crow once more."

Lescu nodded with satisfaction, but something strange had come into Alina's face. It had been a wonderful tale, and yet she realised suddenly that that was all it was, a story, and in that moment Alina suddenly felt too old for stories. With that they heard a cry outside, a single howl in the night, that filled the air. Alina started and looked anxiously through the window. It was Fell.

Lescu noticed the look immediately, and his clever eyes narrowed.

"A wolf," he whispered gravely. "I think it's fallen into one of the pits. It's been howling for a day."

"Pits?" said Alina, trying to hide the concern in her face, and suddenly wanting to be in her own clothes.

"Before the winter, we dig wolf pits in the forest to protect out livestock," said Lescu. "It's an old tradition around here, Alina. Most of the villagers put stakes in the bottom, but I think it a cruel custom and leave mine empty. The fall's usually enough to kill them, but if they escape again, well good luck to them."

Alina was trembling, and Lescu saw it.

"What's wrong, child? By the warmth with which you talked of Elak and Teela, I know you love animals as much as Vasilissa, but you can't care for a wild wolf," Lescu smiled. "They take our animals, and so threaten our lives."

Alina thought of the shepherds round Moldov.

"Why, I almost think you do care," cried Lescu, with a laugh. "Your heart's big indeed. But come. Perhaps I should open some wine or tsuika, to toast your recovery."

"No," said Alina, jumping up. "Thank you, Lescu, but I think I'm still wearier than I thought. I'm up too soon, I fear."

Lescu raised an eyebrow, but he didn't argue, as Alina thanked Catalin for his wonderful story, wished them good night again, and went straight back to her room. As soon as she closed the door, she started to look around. At last she found her own clothes in a chest in the corner, cleaned and neatly folded.

She changed quickly, but then stood listening for a good while to the noises of the house. When she was sure that Lescu and Catalin had gone to bed, she pushed open the window onto the freezing air and climbed outside, slipping down onto the little roof below her window and jumping lightly down to the snowy ground below.

All was dark and silent in the house, but Alina spotted Gwell lying there on the porch. The hunting dog looked up at her, but Alina no longer smelt of wolf and he didn't react. She bent down and stroked his head.

"Good, boy," she whispered. "Stay there now, Gwell."

Gwell growled contentedly, and he closed his eyes and let her stroke him. Then Alina rose and crept away. As soon as she reached the trees, she began to run fast through the cold forest, and as she got farther and farther from Lescu's home, she started to call.

"Fell. Where are you, Fell?"

Alina could see very little amongst the looming branches, and hear nothing at all, but soon her eyes grew accustomed to the forest in the moonlight. It made her going easier, but she had little idea of what she was looking for, except that she scoured the ground for a hunting pit. Alina wondered now a little fearfully if there could be any truth in the tale of Baba Yaga, and she searched for what seemed an age, but could find nothing at all. She was almost at her wits' end, when she felt that ache in her forehead and her vision began to cloud.

"Fell, is it you?"

"Yes, Alina."

"Where are you, Fell?"

"In some kind of trap. It smells of man."

"You're hurt?"

"No, Alina. Though hungry enough."

"What can you see, dear Fell?"

"Leaves and broken branches. Earth too."

"Above I mean. Look up, Fell."

"I see a great elm. It stands on its own. And the stars. The Wolf Trail. And there's water near. I can hear it."

"You must be in a clearing. There."

Alina had just spotted the clearing and a single elm tree, and heard the faint guttering of water under the ice. She rushed forwards, her heart pounding, and was delighted to see the edge of a wide hole, and there was her friend again, peering up at her.

Fell was badly shaken, more by the shock than the fall, but he was unharmed. The wolf looked up at her and noticed how much better she looked, but he slunk back in the pit, as he remembered the horrible vision he had had on the river. Had it really been the future? Would he really kill her?

"What's wrong, Fell?"

"Nothing, human," he growled bitterly, "nothing at all. Can you help me?"

"I'll try."

Alina looked around and spotted a small, fallen trunk. It took her a long time to drag it to the top of the pit, and Fell growled in exasperation. She managed to drop it down though, to make a kind of ramp, and Fell sprang up it and out. The wolf licked the girl's hand gratefully.

"Thank you, friend. That's the second time you've saved my life, though it was your kind that made that trap."

"And it's your kind that takes our sheep and animals to live," the girl found herself saying cheerfully. The wolf and the girl stared at each other. It was true what they had both thought, and there was no answer to it. No moral to it either. It was just how things were.

"Fell," thought Alina suddenly, "this great destiny you talk of. You say it involves nature itself?"

"Yes."

"I saw it again in my dreams, Fell, that vision of what man's success will do to the world."

"Yes, human. Or what you might do. Yet I asked your brother once, five years ago, to make a pact. To be strong, but to protect us too."

Alina nodded slowly, looking thoughtfully at Lescu's trap and feeling guilty again. Fell suddenly growled.

"Don't look sad, Alina. You mustn't blame yourself for the whole world."

Alina looked down at the wolf in surprise.

"No, Fell, perhaps I mustn't."

"How goes it with the humans?"

"They're kind and I . . . I can trust them, I think. I've told them something of my story."

Fell growled warily.

"It's all right, Fell. They know nothing of you. But I must stay with them awhile, as the winter worsens, and learn from the blacksmith."

"The one working with metal and the red flowers? I watched when you met him and that filthy dog nearly attacked you. I looked into the human's thoughts. He has good thoughts. Better than mine, sometimes."

Alina placed her hand on the wild wolf's head. It felt right to touch the animal again.

"Yes, Fell, and I like him," Alina paused. "His son, Catalin, too. He's a fine storyteller. I think they can help us. The snows are still thick, but Lescu knows much that will aid us. I must learn from them all I can."

"And they'll miss you with the dawn, so you'd better be getting back. Learn from them indeed, human, and grow, but know that my eyes will be guarding you from the forests. But I'll seek out the Guardian too."

Alina suddenly felt desperately grateful to the wolf.

"And I'll bring you food from the house, Fell, when I can," she said eagerly. "I don't want to steal, but it will be my own, and they'll not miss it. I'll leave it by that big oak, where we first saw their house."

"No," growled the wolf immediately. "It's in sight of the human den."

"Then further in the wood."

"Leave it out in the open, and the other Lera will steal it. All are hungry now."

"Then I'll hide it under something."

"How will I find it?"

Alina WovenWord pondered for a moment, and thought of Catalin's tale of Baba Yaga, then thought of a story she had told Mia.

"Stones. I'll leave a trail of little stones, leading from the big oak to the food."

"Good, Alina. Staying in one place will make it hard for me to hunt, when the Lera in these parts know of my presence."

"And be careful, Fell. There are more pits in the forest, and many are sewn with stakes."

Fell nodded his black muzzle, and his yellow gold eyes flashed.

"I'll find you when the snows thaw then, human cub. Until we meet again, Drappa. May it be soon . . ."

With a growl Fell turned and began to run. Like a panther he went, streaking through the forest, jumping log and stone, and glorying in his freedom once more, as Alina Sculcuvant watched her friend with relief, feeling the same pangs as Fell had, but also gratitude in her heart that he was safe again. Then the girl turned back towards her human home, thinking of one thing alone: the strange tale of Baba Yaga and Vasilissa the beautiful.

THIRTEEN

Balance

Lescu was at work in his forge and Alina WovenWord stood behind him, marvelling at his skill. She was in a much finer dress now, another that had belonged to Lescu's wife, and her red hair had started to grow out. The young woman had already begun to help with the chores: milking and baking, chopping wood and making food. But she had found herself drawn to what the blacksmith and Catalin did in the forge—men's work.

As the wintery days had worsened, Alina Sculcuvant had been true to her word to Fell. She would hide away food at meals, as Mia had done for her, leaving it for her friend at the end of a trail of pebbles from the oak tree. Sometimes, she would go to Gwell's kennel and, apologising to the dog, take some fresh meat for the wolf. She had not seen Fell at all, but when she saw the food gone, or his paw prints in the snow, and heard his calls in the night, Alina knew that he was still at her side, and she was glad.

As for Fell, he still ranged those hills, skirting the abandoned church and worrying for the human, wondering about Morgra and the horrible vision he had seen, as he sought out word of the Guardian. Often in the night he would look down though, and see orange firelight flickering in the windows of the blacksmith's house, and wonder what it would be like to be nothing more than a tame dog, sleeping peacefully at Alina Sculcuvant's side.

The blacksmith was standing now in a shaft of wintery sunlight slanting through the window, and there was a growing pile of new swords on the ground.

"So what will you do, Alina?" he asked, as he swung the hammer. "Journey to Castelu to find the truth about who your parents are?"

It was freezing outside, but with this heat, Alina thought it a wonder that all the snow on the mountains outside had not melted already.

"Yes," she answered, with a heavy sigh. "When the spring comes, Lescu."

Lescu's kind eyes were suddenly filled with worry.

"Why, Alina? In crossing the mountains you've proved yourself as good as any boy, it's true, but it's madness what you plan. If Vladeran is your father he has broken every natural law. Anyway, he tried to kill you, and there must be some dark reason for it. They say he has sworn himself to upholding the Salic law throughout the lands beyond the forest. Perhaps that's the reason."

Alina's hazel eyes flickered. "Salic law?"

"That women should have no rights equal to men."

"Why?"

Lescu smiled.

"In seeing Eve as the cause of man's fall from paradise," he answered, "lords like Vladeran and the elders of the Church have long taught that you are inferior to men. Perhaps you do have noble blood. You've a fine quality about you."

Alina was silent as she wondered.

"Yet that mark isn't of Castelu," the blacksmith went on. "It's strange, and I beg you to forget this path, girl. Can you not let sleeping dogs lie? Vladeran would be a fearful opponent, and that road takes you through Helgra country."

"Helgra?" said Alina, remembering the name from that last terrible night in Moldov.

"Magyar tribesmen, from the lands of Hungary, Alina," said the blacksmith, "although united it's said with a Dacian people in those parts. A wild, savage people. Their cult is nature, and they're said to worship animals and the wild wolf. Their territory lies in Castelu's domain. You'd have to cross it."

Alina's heart stirred, but at this talk of a cult of nature a question came into her mind.

"Will you tell me something, Lescu?" she asked suddenly. "Do you think people are . . . well, do you think we're the same as animals?"

He stopped hammering and looked up in surprise.

"What a strange question, child. Don't say things like that around the holy fathers."

Lescu paused to think, though, holding the sword he was making in the air. "No, of course not," he answered at last. "Yet I've seen men act like wild beasts."

"Why?" asked Alina sadly, yet suddenly feeling it a childish question.

"That's difficult to answer, Alina. Hate and fear? The search for power, and land and gold? Sometimes because of beliefs they're brought up with. I often wonder."

"What do you mean beliefs they're brought up with?"

Lescu turned to look at Alina intently.

"Why should we accept the beliefs we're born into, Alina?" he said. "Christians believe that God came amongst us as a man, do they not? Yet the Muselmen say he was only a prophet, and that God has no name. We paint our churches with images of man and beast, of angels and judgement, while in the East it is forbidden to show images of God's creatures. We fight and kill each other so readily, yet if I had been born in the East, would I not believe the stories they believe, and if they had been born here, would they not be Christians?"

"I suppose so," answered Alina Sculcuvant. It all seemed so strange. "Do you believe in God, Lescu?"

Lescu's eyes flickered.

"God the Father? Well, my own father did, Alina, but I don't know. I'd not make a fool of myself spending a lifetime searching for something that isn't even there."

Lescu suddenly lifted his hammer and looked at it.

"Did you know blacksmiths were once believed to be great magicians?" he whispered. "By those who did not have their knowledge."

"No."

"But the blacksmith's true magic is mastering the nature of heat and metals, and of firing and blending. It's a great scientia, and I think it is scientia that will one day free man from the fables he grows up with, Alina. But we stray from the matter at hand. You believe you must travel to Castelu along a dark path?"

Alina straightened her back.

"I must find out if they are my parents or not, and why Vladeran wanted me dead. And if my brother lives," she answered firmly, "and what this mark means too."

Alina was also thinking of what Fell had said of her destiny, and of nature itself. It suddenly seemed a terrible, impossible burden.

"Perhaps Vladeran still wants you dead, Alina. War comes, and the King is already on the march. The land will be dangerous to cross."

"I thought you might help me."

The blacksmith paused with his hammer arm.

"Help you? Indeed, but I'd rather you turned away from this road. If it's my advice you seek, that's my counsel."

"But Ivan told me that you were more than a blacksmith once," said Alina slowly, "that you were a soldier and a warrior. The Warrior Smith."

Lescu brought the hammer down again, so hard that it made the metal sing angrily.

"I fought against the Turk, it's true, and found some fame fighting and killing men." A dark look came into Lescu's sweating face. "There's nothing uglier and more terrible than war, Alina. Why do you mention this, child?"

"I thought that you might . . ." The young woman hesitated. "Might teach me something of your skill."

"As a blacksmith, and to earn a living as a Fierar?" said Lescu. "I can do that indeed, as can Catalin, although the people in these parts would not think it woman's work. You'd fare better in the marketplaces as a storyteller."

"No, Lescu. I meant teach me to be a warrior."

The blacksmith swung round in amazement.

"A warrior!" he cried incredulously. "Teach a girl? A child?"

"I'm not a child," said Alina indignantly, lifting her chin proudly. "Why won't you teach me?"

"Why won't I? Teach you how to wield a heavy metal sword, and march fifty miles in thick mud and pouring rain? Teach you to camp without sleep or food, then meet men trained since the cot to fight and kill?"

Lescu laughed, but he seemed angry at the memories, and he began hammering once more, and turned his face away from Alina Sculcuvant.

"You're a girl, Alina, and growing into a young woman, but you've spent too long wearing clothes not your own, and it makes you foolish. Life isn't a fairy tale, WovenWord, even if we live in Baba Yaga's valley."

Alina felt her cheeks burn, but she stood her ground.

"It's because life isn't a fairy tale," she said hotly, "that I need to learn about the real world. Because there are no changelings, or goblins, or walking houses. Because I have no parents worth the name."

The blacksmith shook his head angrily and was silent.

"If not to be a warrior, Lescu, then at least teach me how to defend myself," begged Alina. "You could make me a sword of my own."

The blacksmith turned and smiled coldly.

"Defend yourself? If you don't put yourself in danger, you will not need to defend yourself," he answered simply. "You look pretty indeed in that dress; my wife wore it the day she first came to this house, and your hair is growing. One day you'll be married, and find your happiness. Know your nature then, and don't try to step beyond what you are, or can be."

Alina thought darkly of nature. For the first time since they had met, she felt furious with the blacksmith. In touching the powers of the Sight, and in the link with the black wolf, had she not already stepped beyond her own nature? Yet it didn't feel unnatural, her friendship with the wolf.

"I didn't put myself in danger," she said. "They did. I've been in danger ever since I was a stupid child."

"And you're right to shout out the injustice loud and clear," said the blacksmith. "But why do you talk so scornfully of being a child? Children want to grow up so badly, but it takes time and care and love, and it's a thing that should be guarded and enjoyed. While the greatest duty of an adult is to protect the young. To teach them the borders of the world. To help them make the future."

"Adults need to teach children to grow up too," said Alina angrily. "And that stories of magic are all a pack of lies."

Lescu's eyes flamed. "Silence!" he cried. "What you ask I shall never do. I do not even teach Catalin the arts of war. War's not a game for silly children."

"But Lescu . . ."

"Enough. Don't raise my anger further, SkeinTale. What you ask's unnatural, and foolish too. There's milking to be done."

Alina glared at Lescu, and turned and stomped from the forge. As the blacksmith watched her go, and thought of Alina's dark, lonely history, he felt sorry for her, but he went on hammering at the metal with renewed urgency, and shook his head.

Alina's request set a rift between the girl and the blacksmith that did not heal for some time. Alina would grow silent and sullen in his presence, often stilling her storytelling in the house, but whenever Catalin asked her what was wrong, she would shake her head and tell him angrily it was nothing.

The girl was smarting deeply inside though, and she realised now that it was because of a feeling that had long been locked within her. A feeling that made her as angry and bitterly resentful as Baba Yaga had been of Vasilissa in the story. She would wake suddenly, feeling a dreadful rage inside her, and then she would think of Fell, and want to strike out, and harm the world about her, for all the harm and injustice that had been done to her. For what her own parents had done, perhaps.

Sometimes it was so painful that it was as if she were locked in chains, and wrestling to throw them off, but the young woman felt that she had not the strength, yet she fought nonetheless, feeding only on anger and hurt, and really fighting with herself. She grew sharp and brittle in the presence of the men, thinking of the shepherds and Malduk, and at times almost hating Lescu and Catalin as much as they.

She had not the experience to realise that there was a deep hole in her heart. For all things need the nurturing love of strong protectors, to grow happily and well, like the sunlight drawing flowers from the earth.

There was other resentment inside her, too. In order to enter the tough world of men, so she could work tirelessly for Malduk and Ranna, Alina had already had to dissemble, and hide her true nature. But now, when she had asked her new friend openly about the world of men, he had denied her. Alina had felt his scorn, and amusement too, at the very idea that she could be as good or as strong as a man.

Yet what was her true nature? Alina wondered, as she wondered what nature really meant, or if she could have anything to do with its survival. Like the children of Moldov, Alina had grown up believing many things about how men and women are, and about the world around her, yet what she was learning now was telling her that those things hadn't been true at all. Something else was eating at the young woman's heart though. As she looked out into the snows, and listened to the sounds of the forest, wondering what Fell was doing in the wild and if he had found the Guardian, Alina was afraid of the future.

On several evenings Lescu saw in her eyes the anger and fear that she held for her journey, mixed with her determination, as she gazed fixedly through the window in the blacksmith's house or she sat at table. But the blacksmith had known blood and terror in the East, and seen grown men break down and cry like little children, before their thankless deaths. That was no fate for the girl. Concealment was a far better ally in her journey.

Then one day, as the snows grew thinner, a man came riding through in search of new shoes for his horse. As Lescu worked away on the nervous animal, calming him with his strength and precision, the cheerful stranger began to tell him more of the wars that were coming to the lands beyond the forest.

"They say Stefan and his nobles already fight the Turk," he

said, "although why he asks for the aid of Vladeran and Draculea, I'll never know. The King's too trusting, I think. They rumour Vladeran has other ambitions for the lands that lie about his own, while Draculea is a law unto himself."

Lescu grunted, but went on filing down the horseshoe he had just attached to the stranger's animal. Lescu did not want to hear anything of the world beyond the forge.

"Vladeran's savagery is legendary now. His persecution of the Helgra grows worse by the day."

Lescu snorted and scraped harder.

"You'd have thought the Order of the Griffin would rise up in their defence. They're sworn to protecting the earth, and the people in it. Or were, at least."

The man, seeing the blacksmith didn't want to talk, changed tack.

"It's good, strong shoes you make," he said admiringly, "and we all need strong armour nowadays. I trust you've prepared your son to fight properly," he added, looking over to Catalin, who was setting out more nails for his father. "You live out of the way, it's true, but I doubt any will be able to avoid the fighting, even here."

Lescu stopped working and looked up guiltily at his boy. Tenderness, and fear for Catalin, pierced his heart. Lescu wanted nothing for his son but happiness and peace, but he suddenly thought that we may wish all the peace and love we can on the world, and for the people in it whom we care for, but what if the world changes suddenly? Isn't it our duty then to prepare them for what might be? To prepare them to fight. Yet as he stood there, the blacksmith wasn't thinking just of Catalin.

The shoeing was done, and the stranger paid Lescu in silver and mounted his horse.

"I wish you well, Fierar," he cried. "Perhaps finer lords will bring you better pay than I can afford. I met two riding a fortnight back, who would bring you much gold. They served the Order of the Griffin."

Catalin looked up with interest, but Lescu hardly reacted at all.

"They were on some strange mission too, but then that Order is always cloaked in plots and secrecy. Their leader's identity is as well hidden as the Old Man of the Mountain. Yet I heard them talking. They seek out a girl."

Catalin looked sharply at his father, and Lescu's brow furrowed, though only slightly.

"Some redheaded child," said the garrulous fellow, "and very important by the sounds of it."

The blacksmith was silent, but the hammer in his hand was trembling.

"Important?"

"So they said. I don't envy her, if what they rumour now of the Order is true," said the man, pulling on the reins and turning his horse's head. "You know Lord Vladeran cleaves to the Griffin. Perhaps he leads it. Yet if he does, why should he persecute the Helgra?"

As the stranger rode away, a figure stepped from the shadow of the forge. Alina had heard everything. Lescu saw the fear and resentment in her clever eyes. Then Alina Sculcuvant simply turned, her thick red hair swinging about her shoulders, and walked scornfully away.

Three mornings later she was in the forge, cleaning out the coke from the bottom of the fire, and trying not to get it on her dress, when she heard a clanking beside her and turned to see a pair of shears clattering across the stone lip of the fire. Lescu was standing behind her.

"What are those for?" she asked sullenly.

"To cut your hair again, of course," answered the blacksmith, looking at the pretty young woman and shaking his head. "It's grown too long for a lad who journeys into such danger, and one who would wield a sword, I think."

Alina's hazel eyes opened wide and her heart began to beat faster.

"Then . . . then you'll make me a sword, Lescu?"

"I'll do more than that," answered Lescu reluctantly. "I'll teach you the skills of a warrior, as you asked. Or start to anyway."

Alina wanted to hug him, but something held her back. Perhaps the very arts he was talking of.

"Thank you, dear Lescu."

"Don't thank me, Alina," said Lescu gruffly. "Simply learn and prepare, as carefully as for a visit to Baba Yaga."

Alina smiled.

"I will. I promise."

She didn't pick up the shears though, and instead grasped her hair and began to bind it in a knot behind her head.

"If the Order of the Griffin is searching, we may not be able to hide you here, Alina," said Lescu. "But they look for a girl, so you may hide as a boy again. And if you're set on your course to Castelu, I must help you indeed. Now calm yourself and listen," added the blacksmith, striding forwards and picking up a piece of metal and his hammer. "Bring me my apron and light the fire."

Soon a blaze was burning in the forge, as Lescu worked the bellows, and when it was hot enough, he plunged the metal roughly into the flames.

"When metal has not been hammered out properly," said Lescu, as he lifted his hammer and started his lessons, "it will be brittle and break easily, and so it is with a man's heart. Or a woman's, perhaps. We'll see, but a warrior must be tempered like good steel."

Alina nodded enthusiastically.

"So temper both warrior and blade, I say, before you send her into battle. I'll not have you going into the Griffin's lair unarmed."

"The Griffin's lair?"

"Perhaps Vladeran does lead the Griffin Order. Perhaps he is your father. Whatever the truth of it, we must prepare you to face him."

"How?" asked Alina, wondering now what it really meant to be a warrior. Lescu put down the sword and pulled the apron from his chest, uncovering his leather jerkin. He leaned forwards suddenly and gave Alina such a shove that the girl went flying backwards and fell over in the dirt, startled and winded.

"Get up, silly child," cried Lescu furiously, "and if you have the guts for it, learn to defend yourself to the death."

Lescu's eyes were blazing, and Alina was so startled by the change in the man that she felt sick and terrified. She just sat there, staring back in amazement, and Lescu kicked some dirt towards her.

"Up, child. Or are you really just a thief and a murderer?" he hissed. "You say you killed Malduk in defence, but I say you're a liar, a word weaver, or else put a knife in his back. It seems you're a coward too."

"I'm not a—"

Lescu kicked more dirt.

"Fool. Coward and liar. I say you didn't cross the mountains without help. Have you allies in the hills? But I'll tell you my truth. To me you're nothing, whelp, and it's time I showed you."

Alina felt that furious, bristling anger inside her again, that almost lifted her to her feet on its own. She remembered Ranna and Malduk's constant insults and petty punishments, and how she had always hated herself for feeling so guilty in their presence, and for not fighting back.

Somewhere Alina realised that Lescu was simply goading her on, but her anger flared up like the forge, with the injustice of it all. With a cry of fury, Alina WovenWord hurled herself at the blacksmith.

"No. Stop it. I hate you."

Lescu simply stepped to the side and brought a hand down heavily on her back, not intending to injure her, but to add to the momentum that was already carrying Alina on.

The girl went sailing past him and crashed into a bag of corn in the far corner of the forge, in a painful heap. She struggled round to face Lescu. Alina was furious and ashamed. Her hair had tumbled down about her shoulders again, and she felt scalding tears on her cheeks. Lescu strode over to her, put a hand on her arm, and helped her gently to her feet.

"Peace now, Alina. I'm sorry."

Months and years of fear, frustration, and confusion were welling up inside her, and suddenly the tears came gushing down her face, as they had often done in the barn on Malduk's farm when she had been alone.

"No," she sniffed miserably, "you're right, Lescu. What I ask is foolish and stupid. I'm just a girl."

Alina dropped her head.

"Perhaps," said Lescu, with a kindly smile, "but know yourself, girl. You've other things than a man's strength. You've wit and intelligence, heart and instinct. And you have great courage too, that has brought you this far, against the odds. Brute strength is far from everything."

Alina looked up hopefully and tried to smile. No one had called her brave before, and she felt proud.

"There, Alina, I was too strong on you, too soon," said Lescu softly. "That's the bully's way, and it'll not happen again. But it was good to see the anger flow from you at last, Sculcuvant, and self-respect too. Come here."

He led Alina over to the water bucket by the forge and stared into it.

"Look there, Alina. My father always taught me that although, as we grow, we desperately seek others' approval—our friends', our parents', the world's—what really matters is what we see when we look there, and see ourselves. That's the true judge we always wake to in the morning. The mirror of ourselves."

Alina looked down too.

"I've watched you many times at work, Alina, and in the house telling your stories. So thoughtful and melancholy, so timid often, when you're not consumed with anger. You feel deeply, and it's bad for you to hold in your feelings too much. You've a right to them."

Alina was surprised by the idea that she had a right to her feelings, but by something else too. She looked pretty in the water.

"Yes," she sniffed, wiping her face on her sleeve and trying to smile, "I suppose I have."

"Don't suppose, Alina. Be yourself."

"Yes, Lescu, I'll try, I promise."

Alina wondered what that meant though. What does it really mean to be oneself?

She looked back at the water, and suddenly a jolt of fear went through her. There she could see herself, but not in reflection. She was sitting at a great oak table, and Catalin was next to her, and the table was heaped with rare meats and beakers of blood red wine.

Alina blinked in astonishment at the magic of it. Tales of changelings and Baba Yaga may have been false, but this seemed a deep power indeed. What's happening to me? she wondered, and almost immediately the picture changed.

Alina trembled. There was Ranna, and her face was rapt with fury, as she ran through the snows. She was moving through the night, and at her side was Mia. The little child looked frightened and lost, and Alina suddenly felt a terrible guilt that she had found no fairies or goblins to cast a spell to protect her friend. But Mia kept stopping and seemed to be helping her angry old aunt. Then the picture changed again.

There was Alina again, not in a fine hall but sitting on a stone floor, surrounded by filthy straw, her hands chained. The place looked terrible and Alina felt a shudder of terror. Was this her future? It was a prison.

"Alina. What's wrong?"

The pictures in the water vanished, and Alina shook her head.

"Nothing, Lescu."

"You must listen carefully to what I tell you now, Alina. It's how you control and direct your anger and the force inside that matters," the smith went on. "Discipline's everything, especially for a girl, naturally weaker than a man. Though not all men, it's true."

Alina's tears had dried and she realised that Lescu was saying something very important. She stepped towards him.

"You stumbled at me in a blind rage," said Lescu. "So I turned your own power against you with the brush of a hand. Calm and purposeful. As *you* must be. To master the art of fighting, a true warrior must first master himself. Or herself."

Lescu again picked up the sword he had been making. It had begun to cool, and he swung it cleanly through the air.

"To know a true threat," said Lescu, looking at her keenly, "and then to let the anger come like a directed flame, that's the skill. To control it and strike with a calm, clear mind, like the blacksmith wielding his hammer, turning another's force against him."

Lescu swung again, jabbed, and then turned and struck at

Alina's face. But he brought the blade to a stop just short of the young woman's forehead, and smiled again.

"And do you know what the best skill that I could ever teach you is?" he asked.

Alina raised a hand slowly and pushed the blade away from her face. It was cold to the touch now. The gesture made Lescu look at her admiringly, for it had pride and dignity and strength.

"A cut, Lescu? A thrust? How to parry?"

"Oh, no," answered the blacksmith softly, lowering the sword completely, "how to stand on one leg. Perhaps for an hour at time."

Alina almost laughed at her friend. "One leg?"

Lescu sank slightly and lifted his right leg completely off the ground, as he held the sword. "Balance is everything. Balance of body and mind and spirit."

Standing there in this strange way, Lescu was perfectly still, but he suddenly moved the sword and swung it over his right shoulder. He brought it to a halt at a perfect right angle, like a compass needle reaching a meridian, and hardly swayed at all.

"With balance and control comes clarity and power," said Lescu, "and the ability to move at will, and to be aware of all around you. Always come back to the centre then, and be connected."

"Connected?"

Lescu brought his foot down heavily on the ground.

"With the earth," he said loudly, "for it is that which saves the warrior. The earth is the stage on which all our arts are played out. Like a flower, or a plant taking nurture from the soil, the warrior connected to the force of the ground will find life and power flowing through him."

Alina thought of the ice field and the wild power she had felt out there, and of the black wolf too. Were humans really connected to that power? The power of nature?

"But I see that I'm telling you things you think silly, or do not yet understand. Well, we'll see. My own teacher, who travelled far to the East, taught me things our brutal Western knights do not know," said the blacksmith. "How to turn an attacker's own force against him, how to shift a hundred pounds with three ounces, and how everything begins in here."

Lescu touched a finger to his forehead, as the gypsy woman had done by the fire, when she had spoken of the Gift.

"In the mind, Alina. A real battle is all won here first. Or lost. And sometimes it's as if a fight is all played out here first, before it even happens. Your true enemies are not only the soldiers waiting to face you, but fear and uncontrolled anger, lack of precision and self-doubt. For all the natural paradoxes and confusions of life, for all the times we long for the instincts of the wild animal, never forget what lies here. Higher mind."

Alina was deeply impressed with Lescu's strange words. No man had ever talked to her like this before, except perhaps a voice she had lost touch with long ago. That man with dark red hair. She suddenly had a memory of a voice, calm and encouraging, and it seemed to say, *I'll always protect you, Alina.*

"If you truly wish the warrior's way," said the blacksmith.

"I do," said Alina WovenWord gravely.

"Then we have work to do, my girl."

FOURTEEN

BABA YAGA

The Warrior Smith was true to his word, and Alina Sculcuvant did learn to balance on one leg, if not for an hour, then for a very long time indeed. It hurt badly at first, but with time she grew stronger, and as supple as a mountain goat, and felt something inside her strengthening too, not only in her heart but in her whole being and spirit.

Alina learnt to climb trees and run fearlessly across the narrowest of ledges. She learnt to take a fall, and defend against hurt by fighting the fear tightening in her body and telling her mind to let go of it. She learnt the art of breathing deeply as she moved, and of deepening the way she swallowed at the air, so that her breaths were not shallow and uncontrolled as they had been, but calm and purposeful, giving her strength. Alina wished now that Fell could see her.

She hadn't cut her hair yet, for she had liked how she looked in the water, and a few days after Lescu had agreed to teach her, they had learnt from a tinker that the soldiers of the Order of the Griffin who had been looking for a girl had ridden east. As Alina trained, she bound her hair back in a ponytail instead.

It was only after these many lessons in the open that Lescu took her to the forge one day. From a hook by the door, next to a long bow and a quiver of arrows she had often seen there, hung a leather jerkin. He asked Alina to buckle it on, and then put leather guards on her arms. At last, he gave the young woman one of the swords he had forged for Stefan's armies.

So, the man and the beautiful young woman, with her red hair bound back on her head, began to work at sword fighting. Although it was happy, playful training, in their strokes and thrusts, in their blocks and parries, Alina realised that this was far more than play. It was like animals, who in their youthful gambols, are learning to grow and testing their strength. Like the wolf cubs by the river.

Alina often thought of Fell. In the days and weeks that had passed in the blacksmith's home, she had heard Fell's call many times. The lone black wolf had been seen by the neighbouring villagers too, as he hunted for the Guardian, but although they had sent trappers to catch him in the night, Alina knew from the vanishing food at the end of her pebble trail that he was still free.

She was deeply relieved, but the more she had looked out from the window of her little room, and thought of the journey she had to make with Fell when the spring came, the gloomier it made her. She thought of what she had seen in the water, and if it had been a premonition of the future. If so, the end of her journey was a miserable prison.

But the fact was that Alina had never been so happy in her life. Lescu was teaching her new things every day, yet without any of the horrible bullying she had suffered at Malduk's hands, and not long into her training with a sword, he had stopped her one morning and nodded his head approvingly.

"You've a skill that I've seen in few men," he whispered.

Alina felt her heart fill with pride, and learnt in that moment that one of the surest antidotes to all the fears and anguishes of the complex heart is achievement.

But it wasn't only the training that was making her happy. It was Catalin. As she worked about the tidy little farm, and they competed in their storytelling, Catalin was so attentive to her that it sometimes even made Alina a little embarrassed. They often walked together in the snows, when Catalin wasn't off on his own in the mountains, or wandered down to the stream with Gwell, to break the ice and fetch water, and their bond was growing every day. They could sense it in each other's awakening bodies and opening hearts.

Lescu could see it too, and it only made him pleased, for he knew the loneliness his son had felt growing up without his mother. As the young storyteller watched Alina train, he was sometimes pleased by how she seemed to be coming out of herself, and how fine and strong she looked too, as she swung bravely at Lescu with a sword. As bold as Vasilissa the beautiful.

Yet something sad and resentful also came into his thoughtful, blue green eyes. Catalin would shake his head then and sigh bitterly, and often when they practised he would suddenly turn and stride off angrily towards the house. One day Alina chased after him, and undoing her hair and letting it fall freely about her shoulders, she asked Catalin what was wrong.

"Nothing," the lad answered sullenly.

"Please tell me, Catalin. We're friends, aren't we?"

Catalin was shaking, and he rounded on her furiously.

"It's you, Alina. You're what's wrong. What do you think you're doing, behaving like a man and a soldier?"

Alina reddened.

"Don't snap at me like that."

"It's just not right. Father always says that soldiers bring such trouble to the world."

"Your father's teaching me to defend myself, Catalin."

"Teaching you something he refuses to teach me," said Catalin indignantly. "And for what? To learn how to be killed?"

"No, Catalin. I hope not, anyway. But I've got to go on a journey. You don't."

Catalin was staring into Alina's lovely hazel eyes, and he saw there was pain in them.

"Does it really matter what happened, Alina?" he said passionately. "Why does everyone think of the past? If I thought of the past all the time, and Mother's death, I'd be sad every day. You're here with us now, aren't you?"

Alina nodded slowly. "But I have a right to know, don't I? Especially if Vladeran is my father. To know if I have a high destiny."

"And you've a right to be happy too."

Alina looked back at the handsome young man and felt a great tenderness for him.

"I suppose I do."

"Then stay with us, Alina. Father looks on you now as the daughter he never had. And I . . ."

Catalin blushed, despite himself, and dropped his eyes.

"Oh, Alina, please don't go out there. You can live here, and when the spring comes again you can help us turn the land and plant for the summer. All there is out there is fighting and sorrow and death."

Alina looked away. What Catalin was saying was so tempting, that in that moment she almost wanted to give up her quest altogether. She suddenly realised too that, although she desperately longed for a family and missed the presence of loving parents, something could come to replace them that was just as important—friends.

Alina felt a rush of gratitude to the friends who had helped her already. To Catalin and Lescu. To Ivan and Mia. To Fell. It was the thought of Fell that made her think of her journey again.

"But, Catalin, can I really be happy here without finding out who I am?"

"Don't you see?" cried Catalin furiously. "This noble lord—perhaps your father—tried to murder you, for whatever reason, and if he finds out you're alive, he'll try again. I think you're mad."

Catalin was about to break away, but Alina stopped him.

"Don't be angry," she said softly, "not like I've been. Not like Baba Yaga."

Catalin looked back at her, and though he shook his head, he smiled. "Think about staying at least," he said.

"I will, I promise."

Alina did think about it, deep and hard, and the more she sat with Lescu and Catalin at the table, eating their food and talking and laughing with them, working at the men's side, or telling great stories with Catalin, the more the prospect of journeying across the mountains to face what danger she knew not, loomed like a black cloud in her mind, or like Baba Yaga chasing Vasilissa through the wood.

She felt herself almost ready for the journey now, or as ready as she would ever be, yet it was one which, when she sat with quietness and calm and looked out at the beautiful forests around Lescu's home, she no longer wanted to make. And with this thought, she felt she was betraying Fell, and perhaps even the wild itself. Betraying nature.

Not once since Alina's training began did Lescu try to argue with her about the future. And one day, when he barred Alina from the forge, the girl realised that Lescu was making something.

For three days and three nights the blacksmith worked, in a blaze of fiery light, hammering away, and still when it seemed to be finished Lescu kept whatever it was he had made a secret. He continued to train Alina too, but made it clear, in everything he said and did, that she was welcome to stay.

So by the time the long, bitter winter finally turned, by the time the snows began to melt and water rushed down from the mountains to swell the rushing streams, by the time the young crocuses began to push their heads from the sleeping earth and stretch their tender leaves to the friendly sunlight, Alina's fifteen-year-old heart was almost set on staying with her friends forever.

The melting snows opened the valley like a flower and brought travellers and villagers thronging to market nearby. One brilliant morning Catalin and Alina set off to buy provisions, telling each other spring tales, and they were soon caught up in the sheer glory of the day.

The handsome youngsters were in a delighted mood, glorying in the warm sunshine and the silky air, the smell of flowers and each other's company, without a care in the world. Alina looked so pretty that Catalin wanted to kiss her, and they kept flirting with each other as they walked. For a while they sat on a tree stump, watching a shepherd with his flock, as the brilliant sun pressed through drifting clouds.

The young people wandered on, but as they came down the narrow track that led to the fair, they paused and Alina pulled up the hood on the coat Lescu had lent her. There was a man on a cart, surrounded by a noisy throng.

"It's true, I tell you," he was insisting angrily. "The road to the South's open again, and I heard it myself."

"Go on with you," shouted an old woman in the crowd. "You're just trying to earn coin with your silly fables."

"It's no fable," said the man angrily. "They saw him on the mountaintop, as real as day. A boy and a lone black wolf."

Alina felt a chill, as if winter had just returned. A single stranger had pressed through the throng nearby, also in a hood, and he was listening intently, as the crowd murmured.

"I heard the rumour," shouted another man, "but I'd heard it was a girl."

Alina was suddenly tugging at Catalin's arm.

"Come on, Catalin, let's get back. This is silly nonsense."

"Wait, Alina."

"And I saw a black wolf ferreting around the farms and homesteads," said another woman. "It seemed to be looking for something, and I've often heard it howl."

"It's witchcraft," said a frightened voice, "the devil's work."

"They say the changeling's a murderer," insisted the man on the cart, "and that his wolf tore out a man's throat. A shepherd called Malduk."

Catalin turned to look at his friend in horror. They were talking about Alina. And a wolf.

"Don't listen, Catalin," said Alina desperately, as she tried to pull him away again and blushed deeply. "It's just a stupid story, nothing more."

Catalin was searching her eyes intently though.

"Don't be silly, Catalin," said Alina. "You can't believe it, can you? A black wolf."

The young man's blue green eyes flickered with confusion.

"No, no, I suppose not."

"It's like Baba Yaga's house, Catalin, or the lies Malduk and Ranna made up about me," said Alina, and Catalin suddenly remembered that by her own report this pretty young woman had killed a man—Malduk. "But it means that they're still hunting for me, Catalin. We must tell your father."

As they hurried back to the farm, they did not notice the hooded figure watching them intently, or how hurriedly he mounted his horse and rode away. Nor did they see the vicious scar on his right cheek.

That afternoon, as Catalin told his father what they had heard, and Alina insisted furiously that it was mere fairy tales, as false as Baba Yaga or all that had followed her, Lescu listened gravely. When it was finished, the blacksmith asked Catalin to chop some wood behind the house, then took Alina outside onto the porch.

"Now then, FalseTale," he grunted, as they stood outside, "why don't you tell me the truth at last? No more stories, eh?"

Gwell, who was lying on the porch, whimpered quietly and licked his paws.

"The truth? What do you mean, Lescu, I always—"

"Damn you, Sculcuvant!" cried Lescu furiously. "Don't you trust me even now? Can't you trust anyone? I know it's true. It's why Gwell snarled at you when you first arrived, because you smelt of wolf."

"I . . ."

"It's how you made it over the mountains. It was with you in that ice cave, wasn't it? I've often seen you gazing out into the forest and known that something waits out there, but not witches. I saw you that night, leaving the house, after I spoke of traps, and food has often gone missing. I found a strange trail of stones in the forest."

Alina blushed and bowed her head shamefully. She hadn't realised that clever Lescu had noticed her thefts, as he noticed everything on the farm.

"I'm not angry for the theft of food," said the blacksmith, more softly, "not if your intention was good. Tell me then, Alina, at last. You're not a killer at all."

So the rest of it came out. The true story of Alina's meeting with the black wolf, of the miracle of their communication and of the strange events of their journey. When it was finished, Lescu nodded soberly, but not without fear in his eyes for the strange young woman.

"It's wondrous," he whispered, thinking of how Alina had asked him if people were the same as animals, "truly miraculous. Enchantment seems to follow you wherever you go, changeling. But I've heard of such things before. Of children lost in the forest being reared by wolves. As for this power, this Sight, there are stranger things in the world, and some have deeper bonds with the animals than others. This wolf killed Malduk, didn't it?"

"Yes, Lescu."

"Then perhaps it's your friend, and I realise now you've been protecting him too. But others will see it only as evil and witchcraft, and hunt you for it. As they will hate you too for trying to show the strength and skill of a man. And Catalin must never know of such a thing. He can be superstitious, and it would unsettle him deeply."

"No, Lescu. I promise it."

"What are you going to do, Alina WovenWord?" asked the blacksmith gravely.

"Go, and go quickly," answered Alina firmly, feeling sick to her stomach. "I'm only a danger to you and Catalin now. Wherever I go I'm nothing but a curse."

Alina was already knotting the hair on her head.

"Don't say that, child. Ever."

"It's true!" cried the young woman in anguish. "Disaster and sorrow seem to follow me everywhere I go. I must begin my journey."

"There's another way," said Lescu, looking towards the forests. "Make this wolf understand that you're happy here, and that you've found a real home. The rumour will fade like a dream, and become just another fairy tale, peddled in the markets around Baba Yaga's valley. The villagers from Moldov are looking for a boy now anyway, not a girl, and we keep ourselves far enough apart to stop people meddling in our affairs."

Alina wanted nothing more desperately in all her life, but she thought of Fell and what she would say to him. She thought of the danger to Lescu and Catalin too.

"I . . . I must think, Lescu. Must walk awhile."

"Of course, Alina."

She turned and walked past the barn and the forge. She made for the stream and the edge of the forest, and as soon as she neared the great oak, she stood looking deep into the tangled trees and began to call.

"Fell. Are you there, Fell? I must talk to you, dear friend."

Only the whispering of the breeze came back to answer the troubled young woman. Alina must have stood there for hours, wrestling with her desire to stay with Catalin and Lescu, and her duty to safeguard them, by leaving their home forever. She looked out into the wild and listened to the whispering voices in the trees. She thought of her meeting with Fell in the cave and the great destiny that awaited her. Alina thought too of what she had seen of Fell, and how hard it had been out there in the mountains.

She began to walk, calling in her mind to Fell, wrapped in confusion. The parchment had proven she wasn't a changeling, but a real girl, but her meeting with Fell had been as strange as any witchcraft. If the Sight was a real power, a power greater than common magic, then perhaps this destiny she faced was true, and she was somehow important. Yet Alina doubted now even the tales that she and Catalin told, growing up as she had to face the true harshness of life.

Alina stopped suddenly. She had come to a part of the wood where the trees ended abruptly, and the ground suddenly sloped down towards a shallow ravine. Alina heard a strange sound, and what she saw stole her breath away. There, lurching across the grass, was a wooden house. Alina felt fear lock her to the ground, and as she realised that the noise was the clucking of a chicken, although she could see none about, a wonder and terror came to her greater than she had ever felt before.

"Baba Yaga," she gasped. "It's Baba Yaga's house. Then this really is her valley. Magic does exist. It's true, all of it."

Even as she said it, fearful of arousing the old hag's interest, or sending her rushing for her mortar and pestel, Alina noticed that the moving house didn't have chicken legs at all. Instead, underneath it were rolling logs, carrying it along the gully, and behind it she now saw men, pushing it along.

It wasn't a witch's cottage at all, but one of the little wooden churches in the lands beyond the forest, that were built so small and light and compact that in times of danger from the Turk they might be lifted entire onto logs and taken to a safer place. For man will try to guard his faith more preciously even than his gold.

With that a rooster appeared behind a tree, crowing and darting its head haughtily, and Alina might have laughed, if she hadn't felt so foolish. As she watched the funny male chicken, she wondered to herself again if this great secret of man and animals was really true. Then she remembered Lescu's words of war and death, and she realised that it didn't matter to her. Fell's face was in her mind's eye too, and she knew she cared greatly for the wild creature, but that other faces had come to her now, and they belonged to Catalin and Lescu. To her own.

As Alina thought of how her mind had suddenly tricked her into believing a church was Baba Yaga's house, as she thought of Ivan's words of being true to herself too, to her own nature, she suddenly made a decision. It was growing dark as she turned back to the house, and a three-quarter moon was peering through the skies, but there was a wonderful lightness in her tread.

"Lescu!" she cried happily, as she neared the oak again. "Catalin! I will stay with you. I don't want a great destiny. I don't care if they are my real parents. I'll go into the mountains, until they've stopped looking, but then I'll come back. I'll come home."

Alina was filled with joy as she ran, and the wonderful lightness of resolve, but as soon as she passed the forge, she knew something was desperately wrong. It was the strange silence that hung about, and the absence of smoke curling from the little chimney. Alina heard a nervous whinny and saw a group of horses corralled at the back of the house.

She rushed up to the porch and saw the front door broken in, and then the blood. It stained the entire front porch, and Alina recoiled. Poor Gwell was lying there, a silent, unmoving shape, for the hunting dog's throat had been cut. Alina burst through the door with an angry shout, but she stopped in her tracks in horror.

"No!"

There sat Lescu, in a wooden chair. He looked as if he were asleep, but the blacksmith's heavy arms were bound fast to the chair, and his head was slumped forwards. His jerkin was bloodstained and a dagger was poking from his chest, near his heart.

"No, Lescu. Please, no."

Alina rushed towards him, but as soon as she touched him she knew that he was dead. She felt sick and heartbroken, and winced as she pulled the dagger out of the dead man. Alina sensed that she wasn't alone in the room and swung round.

"So the hare's taken the bait?" said a soft, cold voice in the shadows.

She recognised the man in the hood from the market. He stepped from the corner of the room, and as he lowered his hood slowly, Alina saw the vicious scar on his right cheek and gasped. "You!" It was the soldier who had warned her and Mia of the Turks that terrible night.

"What have you done?" she snarled. "Murderer. Assassin."

The girl had never felt such terrible hatred in all her life, not even for Malduk and Ranna.

"You're the murderer, are you not, Alin SkeinTale?" answered Vlascan, the captain of Vladeran's Shield Guard. "By reputation at least. And we're just soldiers, defending ourselves. He would not have died if he had not grabbed for the dagger, and he would have suffered far less if he had told us where you were."

Alina felt salt tears burn her eyes, and hate churn in her stomach. She wondered where Catalin was. Perhaps he was safe. She was wrestling with the terrible fury inside her, a fury that brought a strange helplessness, and remembered what Lescu had said of control and balance. Alina tried to clear her mind, and calm her heart. To breathe.

"By what right do you do this?" she whispered coldly.

"Put the knife down, girl."

Alina stepped forwards with the knife raised, but another soldier emerged from the shadows, clasping Catalin by the neck and holding a blade to the lad's throat. Catalin's eyes were burning and his cheeks were stained with tears.

"Alina."

From his right stepped another soldier, as two more appeared with drawn swords on either side of Vlascan. The captain smiled contentedly.

"I missed you once, but your flight's over, girl," he said. "Now put down the dagger, or the boy dies."

Alina's mind was in turmoil, but slowly she placed the dagger on the table.

"Now roll up your sleeve," ordered Vlascan, who nodded as she did so and he saw the little eagle on her arm.

"Long and hard we've searched for that through the winter snows, and now we have you, like a partridge for the pot."

"What does it mean?" whispered the young woman, staring down at the eagle. "This mark."

Alina Sculcuvant felt she was nearing the truth of who she was at last.

"That you should be dead already. For your noble blood."

Alina felt something stiffen in her spine. Catalin was staring at Alina, and the young woman felt as if Vlascan's words had just answered her prophetic heart.

"Then I do have noble blood. The mark means that I'm of the house of Castelu."

"I know nothing of the mark," answered Vlascan with a scowl, "except that it leads me to you, and though not of Castelu, it's the same as your mother Romana bears."

Alina was trembling. Her mother. She still feared to hear the truth.

"Then Romana is my mother?"

Vlascan nodded.

"And Lord Vladeran my father?" Alina asked, not wanting to believe.

Vlascan looked at Alina in amazement. "Vladeran your father?" he cried. "Of course not. You are Lord Dragomir's child."

Alina blinked. *Dragomir*. The name instantly brought an image to Alina's mind, one she'd never been able to conjure when she thought of Vladeran—of the man in her dreams with the dark red hair. Aloof, yet kindly. *Dragomir*. A strange hope lit in the girl's heart. Yet how could it be if Romana was her mother?

"Then who is . . ."

"Lord Vladeran? Your father's best friend and lieutenant, of course, until Dragomir's death."

"Death?" said Alina in horror.

"On the battlefield, fighting the Turk."

There were tears stinging Alina's eyes.

"How the Lady Romana grieved then, until Vladeran wooed her. She didn't heal fully though, until she bore him a fine son of his own. Your half brother, Elu."

Suddenly Alina understood. The little baby she had been guarding was not her brother, but her half brother.

"How Vladeran hated you when his son was taken by wolves in the village below the castle where Romana bore him." The castle that had towered over the dreams and nightmares of a wild wolf pack, whose destiny had been touched by the Legend of the Sight. Fell's pack.

"That's why he wanted me dead," cried Alina, "because I didn't protect Elu?"

Vlascan smiled. "Yes. He was filled with thoughts of revenge when Elu vanished. You had always opposed Vladeran's love for your mother too, and stood in the way of his ambition."

"Why? I'm only a girl."

"Only a girl? Perhaps you are, child, but the true heir to Castelu."

Alina WovenWord stepped back in amazement, and Catalin's eyes were locked on hers. It couldn't be. Not only was Alina the Lady Romana's daughter, but she was the heir to Castelu. A destiny indeed.

"But how?" she whispered, trembling furiously, and feeling a horrible weakness.

"Don't you know anything of it?" grunted Vlascan. "Well, it won't hurt to tell you now. The line of descent in Castelu stands, by ancient custom that stretches back to Roman times, outside the common Salic laws in the lands beyond the forest, and is one of absolute primogeniture."

Vlascan was scowling scornfully.

"I don't understand," whispered Alina.

"It means, girl, that unlike the true law, the Salic law, which always excludes female children from inheritance, it passes naturally to the eldest child, whatever their sex. As it once passed to your mother, Romana."

Alina was trembling.

"Then why didn't Vladeran just kill me himself?" cried Alina bitterly, remembering also how coldly her mother had treated her.

"Perhaps he tried," answered Vlascan, "but my lord is deeply superstitious, like his cousin Draculea."

Tried Lord Vladeran had indeed. When Romana had returned in mourning for Elu from the Helgra village, Vladeran had crept into Alina's chamber to kill her himself. Vladeran had never liked the little girl. She was an impetuous, difficult child, full of will and instinct, and more like a boy than her feminine mother. She had always loved to pick up swords and fight the boys, to argue and to learn things he thought the natural right of men.

Yet fear and superstition had stayed Vladeran's hand. He felt suddenly that a curse might fall if he did such a terrible thing within the realms of Castelu. It seemed also a betrayal too far of those holy principles he had once sworn to protect in his inauguration into the Order of the Griffin.

So Vladeran had found a man, a soldier, to drug Alina and take her beyond the borders of his land, in a world that guarded its borders as keenly as it fought for power and position against the threat of the Ottoman.

There his lieutenant was told to slay the girl. He would have done it too, if a pack of wolves had not called in the night as he rode with little Alina and startled his horse so badly that it had shied and slipped over a ledge.

Vladeran had often regretted that he hadn't made sure of the thing himself, now more than ever.

"It's a strange tale," said Vlascan, "and grew stranger with the howls that rose when your mother returned to the village."

"What do you mean?" said Alina, feeling a deep pain in her heart.

"She had gone there again, perhaps to mourn for your half brother, for she adored him."

Alina's heart tightened.

"Imagine your mother's surprise, when a great chorus of wolf song went up, and rushing to investigate, she found that there in the snows was the boy child again, Vladeran's son. Elu was alive and well, and although he had the scent of wolf on him, and even seemed to growl strangely as they approached—or so they say—he was unharmed."

Catalin's eyes were filled with shock, for he was learning that real life could be far stranger than stories, but his heart felt only the bitterness of his father's murder.

"That sealed Romana's joy. And Vladeran's too," said Vlascan. "Their son was restored."

Alina felt a fury at this woman from her dreams, who had treated her as a servant, and who had married her father's best friend. Had

Romana been happy because she could only really love a boy child? Vladeran's son. Had Romana hated her own daughter all along, and let Vladeran try to kill her?

"Where is my half brother now?" she whispered, suddenly feeling far less tender towards him.

"Safe in the palace, of course. But tell me, was it the memory of that night when he was taken that made you invent your clever story of a wolf companion? Some call you the changeling storyteller."

Alina stared back coldly. Her heart was burning with all she had heard, and aching for Lescu too, and her own dead father, but in that moment she remembered all that the blacksmith had taught her. She took in a gulp of air and tried to calm her breathing and her churning thoughts. Words came back to her. *A fight is won and lost in here.* Something else was happening in Alina's mind too. She was reaching out, searching in the darkness, calling for help.

"Fell, come to me, Fell. I beg of you."

There was no answer, and Alina's eyes moved slowly around the room. The revelation of who she really was had made the other soldiers pause, for they had known nothing of it.

Alina noticed that the soldier to Catalin's right had not drawn his sword and that it was hanging loosely in the sheath at his belt. If only Alina could rush him and draw it herself, the young woman might have a chance. But no. A single move of the second soldier's arm, and Catalin's throat would be cut.

Unless she could turn and swing in time. Then one or both of the soldiers by Vlascan might strike at her back. As Alina weighed all this in a split second, seeing the very movements in her inner mind and playing them out, the soldiers about her still didn't move, for they thought a girl no real threat.

"Let's be done with it," said Vlascan suddenly. "The others'll be here soon, and we've wasted enough time on a woman."

Vlascan stepped forwards, but in that moment Alina unleashed the will that she was channelling through her body. She sprang forwards, and as her left hand gave the freestanding soldier a sharp shove in his chest, her right grasped his sword hilt.

The blade rose cleanly from its sheath, as the soldier toppled backwards and crashed to the floor, and Alina turned on one leg and swung the blade down towards the soldier holding Catalin. It cut his knife arm, and with a cry, he dropped his dagger and Catalin broke from his grasp, throwing himself on his dead father and clasping his dear face.

Alina sensed one of the soldiers by Vlascan moving to strike, and felt his sword above her head. She had no time to turn. Instead she swivelled her sword in her wrist and brought it up and back behind her, under her own right arm. The soldier's movement impaled him on the sword, and Alina let go for a moment, turned, and, striking the wounded soldier in the chest with a cry, pulled the blade from his body and raised it to check the advance of Vlascan and the other.

They had stopped anyway, amazed by the girl's speed and skill. The two of them, and the soldier clutching his arm, too, were suddenly filled with fear and wonder, but not as much as Alina now had for herself.

"Impressive," hissed Vlascan. "Did you learn it off the blacksmith? Well, these skills shall die with him, as they do with you."

There was a groan from the chair, and Lescu half raised his head, his bloodied lips suddenly mouthing. The blacksmith was still alive.

"Father," whispered Catalin bitterly. "I'm sorry, Father."

"Catalin," gasped Lescu faintly. "The girl, help the girl."

Catalin was looking about for a weapon, and the others were watching Alina warily. Alina swung her head left and right, calculating who to fight next. They did not dare advance on her, but Alina saw Vlascan look up momentarily, towards the stairs. Was another soldier up there? Before she could turn, she heard a swishing sound, and felt a horrible pain in her right shoulder.

A knife had been thrown from the stair by a soldier who had been searching above. The pain of it entering her body made Alina cry out and drop her arm for a moment, and her guard too. The soldier she had pushed to the floor struck from below, knocking the sword from her hand, and in a sudden drawing of blades, Alina WovenWord was surrounded again.

"Do it now," cried Vlascan angrily, as the soldier on the ground rose. "And make her pay dearly."

It was the shattering of glass that made them turn, and the huge black shape that came flying through the window. The wolf knocked one soldier to the ground. For a moment, all the others were aware of was a snarling black muzzle and angry, pointed teeth. The soldier beside Vlascan struck out in horror, but Fell went for his throat next, and stopped him in the instant. The powerful wolf turned and growled viciously at the others.

"Stand back, Alina," came his angry thoughts. "I can't control them with my mind, but still these weaklings are mine."

Alina reached up and pulled the dagger from her back with a cry, as Vlascan cowered there. He could not believe what he was seeing, and nor could Catalin, who just thought that Baba Yaga herself had come crashing through the window.

"Then it's true," gasped Vlascan. "The wolf story's true."

"Yes," cried Alina furiously, "I walk with the wolf, so beware, little man."

Catalin was looking at Alina WovenWord in terror, as Fell growled furiously at her side. The boy was utterly horrified, and his fear and confusion were blending with his agony for his dying father.

"Very well," hissed Vlascan, rallying and raising his sword. "Then we've a man's fight after all."

Fell took Vlascan in a snarl, as Alina turned and used the dagger to put an end to the wounded soldier, who had just thrown himself towards her. She felt tears burning her cheeks as she did so, but she held her resolve. Her story of killing Malduk had been a lie, but now she had just killed two men, and she felt little glory in it.

There was only the soldier on the stair, and the one whom Alina had struck first, but seeing the strange fighting girl and the black wolf amongst their dead companions, they both raced for the door.

"Witchcraft!" cried the one who had thrown the knife. "The Evil One is here."

Fell swung round and snarled again.

"Leave them, Fell," cried Alina in disgust.

They ran for their horses and galloped away into the growing night, driving the riderless animals before them. In the house, Alina lowered her dagger again and turned sadly towards Catalin and his father.

"It's all right, Catalin, we're safe now. For a while."

Suddenly there was another groan, and Lescu had raised his head again. He was reaching out a hand towards Alina, like a father to a daughter. She rushed forwards and grasped it tenderly, and Fell growled as he watched the strange humans. He didn't like their scent at all.

"Alina," gasped Lescu. "Then this is your wolf. And your journey too, dear Alina. You know it now. I heard what they said of your birthright. You've noble blood in you indeed, and thus a dangerous road, amongst people who seek power alone."

"Perhaps, Lescu."

"But beware, daughter," whispered Lescu faintly, "above all beware of bitterness and hate that kill the mind and soul. I've taught you well, but see clearly, and know that nothing anyone ever does to you can be as terrible as what you do yourself. Remember that. And know too what 'Alina' means in our tongue—'to comfort.' "

Alina could feel the strength leaving the blacksmith.

"Take my son into the mountains with your wolf. Protect each other—two great storytellers, together. Swear it. Make a pact. Love each other."

"I swear it, Lescu. On my life."

Tears were flowing down Alina's lovely face, and she felt as if her passionate heart were breaking. This was one of the only people she had ever loved, apart from those dream shapes she had so desperately wanted to love and feel love from, and already he was being taken from her. As Ivan had been. As her father had been too. Alina had never felt such a terrible pain in all her life.

"Go now. Hurry. And may the gods speed you in your journey. But first, look in the forge."

"The forge?"

"In a box by the bellows," said Lescu faintly. "I made it for you with all my skill, Alina Sculcuvant, now you're becoming a woman and a warrior, and I finished it this very day. When I knew what to carve on the top. May it serve the heir to Castelu well."

Lescu's hand closed hard on Alina's and he slumped completely. The kind blacksmith was dead. Catalin groaned and sank to his knees, but Alina fought back the scalding tears and, with a bitter pain in her heart, prised her hand from dear Lescu's. She rose and felt that ache in her forehead again, though far less than the terrible pain inside her.

"We go, Alina?" came Fell's angry thoughts. "I don't like this place."

"Yes, Fell," answered Alina aloud, "into the mountains, towards the castle and the palace beyond. The region of Castelu. My home."

Alina turned to Catalin, who was still cowering from the wolf by his father's side, to see him glaring at her angrily.

"Come, Catalin," she said firmly. "Quickly."

Catalin looked into her eyes and she could see fear in the blue green, as the lad shook his head furiously.

"Catalin, please. I swore to Lescu."

"No. Get away from here. Leave me to my father. He's dead."

"Please."

"Go away. Get out of our house."

Alina paused. She saw the horror in his eyes.

"Very well," she whispered.

She turned proudly and, with Fell padding after her, walked silently outside, hurt by Catalin's fear, but with the thought to leave him alone with his father awhile, before asking him to leave once more.

Catalin rose slowly. His mind was in turmoil as he stood looking down at his father. He had never been happier than in these last few months, because of the strange, beautiful young storyteller, and now, because of her too, his father was dead and he was all alone. Because of this noble lady, the heir to Castelu, a devil in the shape of a wolf now stood outside his home.

Yet as Catalin stood there, feeling terrified, he realised bitterly that there was nothing to be done but to go with her for now. There was nothing left here. The girl, this witch child, had been right; the soldiers would return. Catalin turned and walked to the dresser to retrieve his father's store of gold, and then with a last bitter look at Lescu, he walked outside.

As he reached the forge, he saw Fell standing in the moonlight, but the wolf let him pass inside. Alina was standing by the bellows, and as he entered she put down the shears. Her beautiful red hair was cut short once more and lay in curls about her feet.

Alina looked down now at a long wooden box, and as she opened it, her amazement almost drove out her misery at Lescu's death. There was the most beautiful sword Alina Sculcuvant had ever seen. It was almost half the young woman's height, and hammered out of the finest folded metal, but as the heir to Castelu lifted it in her hands, she found it light and perfectly balanced. Its handle was carved from antler horn, and at the top it was worked into the shape of a wolf's head. Finest of all was the engraving in the middle of the sword, just below the hilt. It was the mark of the eagle.

Alina raised it in its sheath, draped with a cord of leather to hang it from, and slung it over her shoulder like a magic blade. Then she turned proudly and walked back towards Catalin. She peered into his eyes, and realised from the confusion she saw there that she had to take the lead.

She took two hooded coats from the back of the door to the forge, giving one to Catalin and putting one on herself, and picked up two horse blankets laying in the barn. Then, almost as an afterthought, she unslung the bow that hung by the door, and a quiver of arrows, then clasped Catalin by the arm and pushed him out into the moonlight.

Fell was waiting, staring up towards the star-flecked skies—the Wolf Trail. With that the three of them—the boy, the wolf, and the heir to Castelu—began to walk towards the mountains and the future.

FIFTEEN

TO CASTELU

But how, Sculcuvant?" whispered Catalin,
glaring at the wolf in disgust. "It's witchcraft, darker than
any of the tales we tell."

The young man sat on a tree stump, as the black wolf tore into a
snow rabbit. The ground was flecked with specks of red, and Alina
sat opposite, with her jerkin half open, rearranging the poultice
she had made for her injured shoulder.

For two days Catalin had followed Fell and Alina SkeinTale
without talking, and now they had almost come to the far end of
Baba Yaga's valley.

Although Catalin had not been able to hear their thoughts, he
knew now that there was some special power that worked between
the girl and the wolf, and it had made the young man retreat into
himself, almost as much as Lescu's murder had. He looked on the
wild creature as a kind of demon, and on his former friend as a
being wrapped in witchcraft—a very sorceress.

"I . . . I don't know, Catalin," answered Alina, glad at least that
he was speaking. She closed her jerkin again. "It just happened.
And we're linked by fate, and a power called the Sight. The Gift
some call it. You heard what that soldier said of my half brother,
Elu, how he was stolen as a baby and returned by wolves."

Catalin glared at Alina with something close to hatred in his eyes.

"It's you," he whispered. "It's because of you and that . . . that wicked thing that my father's dead."

Alina hated Catalin for saying it, but it was just.

"I . . . I would have done anything to save Lescu, Catalin," Alina whispered desperately.

Another name was in her head though, and one that brought sorrow too. Dragomir. Her own father was dead as well. Catalin snapped the stick he was holding and jumped up.

"Damn you, SkeinTale. Damn you both to hell."

Fell rose immediately and snarled, but Alina cried out. "No, Fell. This is between us."

The wolf lay down again and whined. He felt almost jealous seeing them talking together.

"You speak to that thing as if it were a person," said the young man with disgust, slumping down dispiritedly again.

"We've a bond, as I said," said Alina simply, "as you did with Gwell."

Catalin felt sick as he thought of his own dog, lying there with his throat cut. He had loved Gwell deeply. He loved animals as much as Alina.

"That's not a dog, it's a wolf. They're killers, SkeinTale. Wild beasts."

"You don't understand," said Alina coldly. "And don't call me SkeinTale."

"Understand what?" snapped Catalin scornfully. "Understand

that this stinks to heaven? Understand that it's unnatural, and what a wicked thing is happening?"

"Fell, come here awhile," whispered Alina, turning to the wolf.

Fell looked up, but he did not move. He didn't trust Catalin at all, and if his instincts and his thoughts of the vision had sometimes made him want to strike at Alina, he felt it tenfold with the young man.

"Why don't you order it?" asked Catalin mockingly.

"I can't order him," answered Alina sharply. "The wolf does as he pleases. He's wild and free."

"He's under a spell, don't you mean? Your spell."

"Don't speak like that, Catalin. It's a lie. Like magic is a lie. And fairy tales."

"So many lies, since you arrived, anyway."

Although Fell had not understood Alina's spoken words, he suddenly rose again and, lifting his tail, took a step towards them. Catalin saw it, and it made him recoil immediately. He nearly slipped backwards off the log he was sitting on.

"Get it away from me!" he cried. "I don't want that devil anywhere near me."

Alina felt scorn for her friend.

"You're frightened of him, Sikla?" she said coldly, her hazel eyes glittering.

"So what if I am?" answered Catalin angrily. "A wolf that appears from nowhere, whatever your history? A killer. Wouldn't any man fear that? It seems like sense to me."

Alina looked into his eyes. "Yes," she said softly. "And I know how hard it is to be a man."

Alina was thinking of the shepherds, and the bullying she had often seen amongst the village boys, the bullying she had felt herself, and she had meant the remark kindly, to reassure Catalin, but he misunderstood her and thought she was mocking him.

"And wouldn't any man be frightened of a girl who wants to be a soldier?"

Alina jumped up now.

"Wants?" shouted the young woman furiously. "Did I want to be taken from my home? Did I want to be hunted, or your father to be killed? Did I want my own father to be dead? Or want my mother . . ." Alina paused and tears rose in her flashing eyes. "I haven't wanted any of this."

She wanted to cry, but the heir to Castelu straightened her back. "Yet it seems to me that life just happens sometimes, and when what happens is bad, you can either give in, or you can do something about it."

Alina had her sword slung across her back, and despite himself, Catalin thought how fine she looked, but he could still see Fell behind her and it made him nervous and angry.

The wolf sensed the emotions coming off the lad, the male aggression, and it made him deeply unsettled. He wanted to react with snarls and teeth, but Fell had realised that the boy and the girl were not enemies, and it caused a painful confusion in him. Suddenly Fell growled and sprang away into the trees. He wanted to be in the wild.

"Fell, come back."

The wolf was gone.

"He'll return," said Alina to herself, "probably by nightfall. But we'd better get moving again, Catalin. The soldiers will be on our trail by now."

"Is that an order, from such a fine noblewoman?" Catalin said resentfully, sitting still on the stump. "One with such a great destiny."

Catalin blinked at his own words. In truth, all that had happened had made Catalin revise his feelings for the girl. But so too had Vlascan's revelation in the house that she was the heir to Castelu.

She had thought Vladeran and Romana her parents for a long time, but Catalin had seen the lovely girl as an equal, of ordinary stock like himself, and a fellow storyteller, who he had begun to hope might walk at his side. Suddenly it was if she lived in a world entirely apart from a blacksmith's son, as if she had been hurled into the stars and now was looking down on him. Catalin did resent her for it, and feared her too.

"Of course it's not an order," answered Alina, deeply stung. "We're good friends, aren't we? I swore to your father that we'd protect each other. Perhaps more than that," she added softly.

The pretty young woman's heart was reaching out to Catalin, but he turned it away coldly.

"You," he sneered. "Why would you need protecting, with a demon at your back? And mastery of a sword, like a man? Surely the Evil One himself watches over you both, my fine Lady Baba Yaga."

Alina glared at Catalin, then reached slowly up to her back and drew the sword Lescu had forged her. She pointed it straight at him.

"If you fear the Evil One, or the heir to Castelu," she said coldly, with a sneer on her own lips, "then don't worry, Catalin Fierar. I alone shall protect you, boy, with my sword."

"No, thank you," said Catalin, stung by the insult.

"It's dangerous in the mountains and the wild," said Alina, and her tone was truly mocking. "Perhaps if you'd learnt to use a sword when your father trained me, I wouldn't need to worry about you so much."

Catalin stood and his cheeks were burning.

"What's that supposed to mean, girl?"

"It means . . ." Alina paused, seeing how badly she'd hurt him, and pulled back from her anger. She began to stammer. "I . . . I know your father didn't want to teach you how to fight, Catalin. Wanted to protect you. But . . ."

"But what?"

"You might have joined us, and learned about a sword. About courage."

Catalin said nothing. He looked ashamed, and Alina suddenly felt ashamed of herself too.

"I'm sorry, Catalin, sorry for everything," she said bitterly, sheathing the sword again. "It'll be all right, somehow, I promise you. But it's too dangerous to stay here."

The young woman had bent to pick up the bow and the quiver that lay at her feet, and Catalin was looking at it strangely.

"Are you coming, Catalin?"

"No."

Alina stared hard at him and saw that nothing she could say would sway him.

Her eyes grew sad. "Very well then. We go that way, Fell and I. To the northeast, towards the empty castle. It's a long journey, Fell says, and you can change your mind and come, if you like, but if you don't, stay out of the open. The best game is lower down the mountain, where the grass is richer. You'll find them easiest where the Lera—where animals need to drink."

Catalin said nothing, although as Alina began to walk away, he felt as miserable as she. Yet as soon as she was out of sight, Catalin's spirits lightened a little and he told himself that he was well rid of the witch, and the beast that walked at her side. Catalin had grown up in nature and he knew many of the arts of hunting and trapping for himself. He knew things that Alina did not know, and he loved the wild, although he had not got as close to it as Alina.

Yet as he sat there, wondering what to do, he suddenly felt dreadfully alone. The light faded, and as the shadows grew in the trees on the edge of Baba Yaga's valley, an owl started hooting in the blackness. Catalin jumped, as he heard a cry on the evening air, a wolf howl. It might have been Fell, or it might not, but it reminded him of the many dangers that lurked in the mountains. He suddenly stood up.

"Alina," he called nervously, and the young storyteller started to walk quickly in the direction they had both gone, "wait for me."

• • •

Fell was running fast through the trees. It was so good to be on the move again, and with a sense of purpose. The girl's journey had begun in earnest and he was bound to her, but the presence of the Sikla, the human male, had unsettled him deeply. The young man's eyes had always looked at him so accusingly, and Fell had known that Catalin did not like having a wild wolf as company.

But there was something else. With many of the other humans Fell had been able, for snatches of time at least, to look suddenly into their minds and see their thoughts with the Sight. Yet he had tried to do it with Catalin on the first night they had left the blacksmith's den and been quite unable.

It was as if Catalin was blocking him somehow, and it had made Fell angry and frustrated, for he'd had a reason to want to search the lad's mind. He wanted to find out what kind of human the boy really was. If he was more than a Sikla, a Dragga even, and what he knew of the world. If they should trust him in the wild.

Fell swung his head and spotted a familiar silhouette running ahead of him at a distance.

"Alina."

Alina was bearing her sword at her back and carrying that bow as she jogged swiftly through the undergrowth, trying to make it above the tree line before the night thickened. She was still smarting at some of the things Catalin had said, and hated his fear and distrust, but she was also bitterly guilty at all that had happened—that old, consuming guilt that was almost a friend.

She felt Fell's presence at her side, twenty yards away, and looked across to see the black wolf running parallel with her. She smiled warmly, and they both quickened their pace in the forest. Alina breathed deeply and steadily, and both of them sprang over logs and jumped ditches as they ran, ran as fast as Vasilissa.

"Alina," came Fell's searching thoughts, "we go to the Stone Den now?"

"That way at least, Fell. To a palace beyond the castle and to this human lord I spoke of, and his Drappa. I am connected to her, Fell, by blood. They are my lands."

"Blood connects us all, human, like the rivers that flow through the wild."

"But I fear it," came Alina's honest thoughts. "I know now that my father is dead, and that my mother has married the man who tried to kill me. I think she tried to kill me, too, after my half brother disappeared."

The wolf was thinking of how often the Varg tried to usurp one another in their fights to mate in the wild.

"And the human lord knows of your presence now, and hunts you?" he asked.

Fell could still remember the taste of human blood on his lips, the soldier's blood, and it sent strange thoughts dancing through his mind and suddenly made him think nervously again of his vision of killing Alina.

"Yes, Fell. And something happened in the forge. I looked into water and saw visions there. I think of the future."

"You have the Sight, Alina."

Alina nodded gravely. "Did you find your Guardian?" she said.

The wolf shook his head. Fell had learned nothing more from the Lera of the Guardian.

"Whatever our destiny is, Fell, I must not be frightened. And I have nowhere else to go. I've learnt some skills at least, with the dear blacksmith."

"I see it, Alina. Feel it, too. And I've been sharpening my teeth on stone and bone. But if you mean to do this thing, perhaps you need some help."

"Help?"

"From a human pack. We hunt better in packs, I've learnt that now."

"There's no help for it, Fell. I'm alone, though I have you."

"This boy though, he comes too? He makes me nervous."

"I don't know, Fell."

Fell suddenly had the feeling that the link between them, the link made by the Sight, was straining apart. It was as if Alina was suddenly shielding her own feelings for Catalin from him, and it startled Fell, and made him question, jealously.

"It's good to be with you again, human cub."

"And to be with you, Fell FastPaw," answered Alina's racing mind.

It was good, for as they ran together through the forest Alina suddenly felt more alive than she had ever before. It was as if her eyes were as strong as Fell's in the twilight, and she could smell everything about her. Leaf and fern, the richness of the swelling spring earth, the moss and lichen on the rocks in their streams. They broke from the tree line at speed, the wolf and the bold young woman, and came to a hill above a little valley. As they both stopped, panting but happy, and looked down, they saw a small roe deer, grazing on the sward.

"I'll hunt it for us, Alina."

"No, Fell. Let me."

"What, Drappa?" came Fell's amused yet questioning thoughts. "Will you chase it down, then take it with your teeth?"

Alina had slipped the bow from her shoulder and drawn an arrow.

"No, wolf. Watch and learn. This is the power of the human. The art of his mind. His scientia."

The girl strung the arrow on the bowstring, but Lescu had not had time to teach her any skill with the thing, and although Alina thought herself something of a warrior already, she soon got a sharp shock. The bow gave an awkward twang, the arrow, neither true nor straight, fell far short of the roe buck, though close enough to send it darting away in fright, and Alina felt a violent jolt on her hand from the string, that cut her skin and made her thumb bleed.

"Aggh."

"Why do you try these foolish human tools, Alina? We should trust to stealth, and speed, to tooth and claw. To nature."

"Perhaps because I do not have them at my beck and call, like you," thought the young woman almost sadly, wondering again what nature really was. "Perhaps because I am only what I am. I might have taken it with my sword though."

"If you had ever got close enough, yes. And you would not have got close enough, human, for animals have powerful instincts. But do not lose heart, Alina WovenWord. I'll chase it down for us, with nature's power."

Fell was gone in a flash of streaking black, and in the distance he took the deer. On his way back though, carrying the creature's limp body in his mouth like a gift from a huge cat, he spotted the red flowers on the hill—a fire—near to where he had left Alina, and two humans sitting by it. Catalin had found Alina on the mountain again, and for the time being they had made peace.

So they began their march in earnest, that strange little triumvirate, sensing that Vladeran's soldiers were following them into the wild, but going to meet the lord himself in his halls of stone. Often Catalin walked apart from the other two, still fearing and distrusting this bond between human and wolf. Often Fell walked alone too, guarding them from the mountaintops like a wild sentry, although he prowled their fires in the night, at once distrustful of the young man and fearful for the girl, and watching for wild Putnar amongst the trees.

As they went, not once did Catalin and Alina tell each other a story, but instead they looked out from the mountains, and like a flickering dream, those wayfarers saw evidence of what was happening in the real world of men, and the wars that had indeed lit the lands beyond the forest once more, like a furious flame.

In the valleys they saw soldiers on the march, raising high the waving banners of Moldova and Wallachia and Castelu, woven with the crests of King Stefan or Draculea, or the symbol of a castle on a mountaintop. On the hills they saw flames licking about wooden churches, and in the foothills they found the bodies of men; of Turk, of Vladeran's soldiers, or Draculea's and King Stefan's armies, left alone beneath the thoughtless skies, to feed the Lera and the earth. If this was the world of men, then its magic was a terrible thing.

They crossed rivers and streams, they skirted wide mountain lakes, they scrambled into rocky caves and crept along high, narrow passes, and as they went they felt the spring beginning to swell towards summer, and Lera return in abundance to the land. Rabbit and hare, deer and boar, otter and badger crept out of their hides and their holes and walked once more unafraid of the winter, as the trees opened their buds and rustled, and birds filled the thronging skies. All the while Fell asked of the Guardian, but the animals just shook their heads in fear at a wolf who could talk to them.

Still Catalin watched the heir to Castelu and the wolf with a wary eye. Many times Alina would suggest that Catalin draw closer to Fell, and try to understand him, for she felt that he too might have the Sight, but Catalin would always shake his head angrily. Alina, on the other hand, seemed to grow closer and closer to the wolf, and often Catalin would wake by their fire and see her standing alone by the black wolf's side and looking out on the land. Sometimes the wolf would creep down to where she lay and wake her, by growling softly or licking her face. Sometimes he would shake his tail so happily when he returned from a hunt and saw Alina, that he would remind the lad of Gwell.

One sun Catalin drifted away and became separated from the other two. They had been walking up ahead, and he found himself thinking bitterly of Lescu and his home. His time with Fell had dulled his own instincts for danger in the wild, and as he was walking down a narrow gorge, he heard a furious growl.

At first Catalin thought it was Fell, but to his horror he saw a gigantic grey wolf, his front paws up on a stone, watching him coldly. He did not move, but around him a small wolf pack was suddenly springing down on Catalin with the bloodlust in their eyes.

The young man turned and began to run, but he stumbled on a branch and fell badly, grazing his hands and face. He picked himself up again and ran on, pushing away the pain, but the ravening wolves had almost closed on him. Then Catalin saw a shape coming towards him. Fell's tail was up, but there was no fear in his yellow gold eyes. He ran straight past him at the newcomers, and suddenly the air was filled with the growls and snarls of fighting wolves. Fell was driving them back.

Catalin cowered in horror. It was as if the wolves were all around and Fell was in the centre, fighting for his life, and Catalin's too. Fell swung left and right, growling and snarling and snapping, here catching skin and fur with his powerful teeth, there dragging his claws across a throat. One of the attackers he caught in the eye, blinding it, and another he bit so hard in the tail that it let out such a yelp that it sounded as if it were dying.

Two things helped Fell against so many attackers: the strength and vigour that the black wolf had earned alone in the wild, and his own dark reputation. For this group of Vengerid, for so they were, had heard of Fell of the Mountaintops, and it had made them fight with far more fear and far less tenacity than they would normally have done. So at last Fell saw all six of the attacking wolves cower back before his fury.

"Bravo," said the big wolf who was still watching from the rock. He raised his great grey tail, as grey and shiny as the strange shock of raised fur that ran right up the length of his rippling spine. It ran towards a neck as thick as an oxen's, and a muzzle both brutal and primitive.

"Who are you?" growled Fell.

"They call me Jalgan, Dragga. And I commend you on your skill."

Jalgan. The leader of the Vengerid.

"What do you want?" said Fell warily.

"Nothing. We go to increase our pack and like a fight to entertain us. Though I am not in the mood today. You should join us."

Fell said nothing. He was thinking of Tarlar.

"What is your name?" asked Jalgan.

"Fell."

Jalgan smiled and nodded. "I have heard of you. As one alone who might be worthy to take my challenge. Will you, Fell?"

Fell looked back at Catalin and then Jalgan. "The fights of the Varg do not concern me," he answered.

"A pity," said Jalgan, smiling. "I think it would be a better fight than the old fool who has taken it. Huttser."

Fell's ears came up immediately, and he almost snarled.

"Huttser?"

"You know of him?" said Jalgan. "He was not a bad fighter, I'll give him that, for one of such age. Twice he fought off my scouts and now has taken the challenge. The only wolf ever to do so."

The others were growling scornfully, and Fell felt pride through his muscles as he heard that his father had shown his power again.

"It won't be much of a fight though, and I fear the old dog will be dead before I reach him, with the wound he has already."

"Wound?" whispered Fell dangerously.

"My scouts wounded him badly. And he's old, the oldest Varg in the lands beyond the forest, so they say, so it will not heal well. I fear I will be deprived of my glory. They say this Huttser is dying."

Fell felt a terrible weakness enter him. His father was dying, and the others were in danger too. Tarlar.

"I don't think I shall take his challenge. I have pack members to seek out," said Jalgan. "But when he goes, I will fall on his pack like a ravening vulture and take back my rightful mate."

Fell felt a pang in his heart, but he knew that now was not the time to show weakness, and he had to maintain his dominance.

"Then why don't you go, Jalgan?" he cried. "And leave others in peace."

The leader glared at him, but Jalgan turned and led the Vengerid away, with swinging muzzles and angry growls. Fell shook himself and turned towards Catalin.

The lad was picking himself up and Fell walked towards him and lifted his tail, but he stopped and did not go any closer. If Catalin had had the Gift, he might have been able to read the black wolf's scornful, angry thoughts.

"Don't look grateful, human," Fell thought coldly. "I did this because I could and for her, not for you, although the Dragga of a true pack protects all. Even a Sikla like you."

With that Fell turned scornfully and went bounding back towards Alina, who had no knowledge of what had happened at all as she walked far up ahead, her eyes ever fixed on Castelu and her home.

That night Catalin sat by their fire, watching the black wolf strangely, and for the first time, he felt grateful to the creature. Just for a moment he wished that he had Alina's power to reach him and thank him in some way. Yet the young man was frightened too.

Fell's thoughts, meanwhile, were consumed with what he had heard of Huttser. It made the wolf growl and whimper in his sleep, and when he woke his mind was turning towards that valley beyond the Great Waterfall. The valley where Kar had said his father and mother were. And Tarlar too.

As they travelled on, Alina had the sense that they were getting closer to their goal, a sense far stronger than her youthful feelings of things about to happen, and she tried to talk to Fell in her mind, but the black wolf was distant and preoccupied now. By evening, twelve days later, he had not hunted, and they had not eaten more than a rabbit that Alina had managed to snare.

They made a simple camp on the edge of an elm forest, near a stream, and Catalin lit a fire. Alina had taught him the technique with the sticks, and the young man and woman both wondered if Fell would hunt, but he sat above them on a slope, wrapped in his thoughts. Catalin got up and wandered towards the stream to drink, but as he cupped his hands, he found the water strangely discoloured, and when he sipped it, he suddenly spat it out again. It tasted foul, and they slept that night with hungry bellies.

THE PAST

It was Fell who woke first. Dawn was breaking all around them, sending shards of brilliant pink splintering through the mauve. Fell got up and yawned, a huge wolf yawn, and stretched himself. Then, with a great shake of his coat, thinning again now to a sleek spring gleam, he lifted his black tail and padded down the slope towards the two young people, to wake his friend.

Alina was wrapped in her blanket by the smoking embers of the fire, her sword and bow by her side. She was calm and peaceful in her sleep, and the wolf noticed her pretty nose twitching slightly, as the dreams passed through her mind. Fell swung his head. Catalin had stretched and turned over in his own sleep. The wolf did not like the young man, but he was suddenly not sorry that he had protected Alina's friend from the Vengerid.

Fell's stomach rumbled though and he realised how hungry he was, and just then the oddest thing happened. He caught a powerful scent on the breeze, filling his nostrils. He knew immediately what it was, and that it shouldn't have been there. It was fresh meat. Not the normal smell of a living animal, which would have raised Fell's instincts for the hunt, but the smell of new blood.

Fell's ears came up, but he did not wake Alina. Instead he turned towards the trees, where the scent was coming from. The wolf was still sleepy, and exhausted with worrying all night about his father. Perhaps it was that which made him sloppy and careless as he reached the edge of the wood. The scent of meat masked the smell of man that lurked behind it.

The blood scent was very powerful now, irresistible to a hungry wolf, and as Fell looked into the shadows of the wood he saw the carcass hanging in the crook of a tree. It was a dead deer, and it was just possible that a lynx had taken it and left it there to return to later and feed.

Fell knew that this was not so as soon as he stepped towards it. Suddenly he felt the cords beneath his pads, before they moved under him and around his back legs. Two humans had emerged from the trees ahead, holding in their hands the end of the rope that they were pulling at violently. Fell found himself spinning round, and he was lifted into the air by his back paws. The black wolf let out a cry, half bark, half howl, as much to alert Alina and Catalin as to frighten the attackers.

The wolf was suddenly hanging in midair from the lasso, hidden in the grass. Alina heard the desperate snarls and yelps in her sleep and woke with a start. Instinctively, she grabbed for her sword and sprang up and towards the sound. She saw Fell hanging there and three more men racing towards her from the cover of the forest.

"Quick, Catalin," she cried, "an ambush."

As Alina swung round, she was startled to see that where Catalin had been lying there was just his blanket. The young man had bolted. Alina felt a sword tip at her back, between her shoulder blades, and she heard a familiar voice.

"Put down your weapon, changeling."

Thinking of Fell as much as herself, Alina lowered her sword slowly and heavy arms grasped her, binding her wrists behind her back.

"So we have you again," said the soldier—one of the soldiers from Lescu's cottage—and smiled as they spun her round. "And no wolf demon to help you now?"

Alina glared at this human, but felt that ache and heard Fell's thoughts.

"Alina, forgive me. I should have sensed the trap."

"Hush, Fell. Don't struggle. It will hurt you."

"There's nothing for it now, human cub. No one to help. And that boy, that cowardly Sikla. He's run for his life. Perhaps this has all been a trap."

Alina felt an awful sadness, and a shame for Catalin too.

"But, Fell, can't you try and get to the soldiers? Control them with the Sight."

"I can't, Alina. I've told you, I can't control humans."

"What are you looking at, witch?" cried the soldier, clasping Alina's chin. "Your familiar? The devil in the shape of a wolf, eh."

"If my hands were free, you wouldn't touch me like this," hissed Alina angrily.

"That I've seen, changeling," said the soldier, "so your hands shall never be free again. And as for this beast, take a good, long look at him. Your last, Baba Yaga."

They began dragging Alina towards Fell, hanging hopelessly from that rope like a living trophy.

Alina wondered were Catalin was, but realised that Fell had been right. The frightened boy had probably run far away by now, even faster than Vasilissa. She was glad at least that Catalin was free and safe. It had been her fault that Lescu had died and that poor Catalin had been drawn into a story that he wanted nothing to do with.

"What do you want with us now?" she whispered.

"Only your deaths," answered the soldier coldly, "here in the forest, and long overdue. Say farewell then to your friend. He goes first, but you'll follow the wolf into the darkness."

"Oh, Fell, I'm sorry I've brought you to this."

Fell was growling and his body twisting and struggling in the air.

"Kill the demon. Now."

The soldier was looking at one of his men, but the other seemed frightened and hesitant.

"What's wrong, man?"

"The Helgra," answered the man timidly. "We're in their territory now, and they revere wolves. Their elder lives in the village below the castle to the south, where the baby was stolen."

Alina looked up. He was talking about the village from where her half brother had been taken. Then it was a Helgra village.

"It might go hard for us if they knew we'd killed a wolf in their lands."

"Don't be foolish," said the leader scornfully. "Vladeran broke the Helgra's power long ago. These are no longer their lands, and they'd not turn a hand against us."

Still the soldier hesitated, for in truth he was just as frightened at getting anywhere near Fell, and the leader turned to another.

"You do it then," he grunted. "Cut the wolf's throat. Take out his entrails."

The other man had few reservations, and Alina dropped her eyes as his sword came swinging round towards the black wolf. Fell had no escape. It was finished.

She heard it before she saw it, a strange swishing through the air. Alina looked up and saw the arrow pass straight through the soldier's throat and out through his neck. His eyes never even closed as he hit the ground and his sword fell from his grasp.

As quick as lightning another arrow took the soldier who had mentioned the Helgra, straight in the heart. He died without even knowing who had finished him. The others were turning right and left, twisting their swords, looking in vain for their invisible assailants.

"The wolf," hissed the leader. "Finish it. If it's the Helgra, this devil summons them to its aid."

As the archer heard the order, from just behind the brow of the verge, he tried to calm his breathing and, with an expert hand, strung another arrow. He raised the bow and took aim once more.

The streaking arrow bolt took the soldier holding Fell's rope deep in the gut, and although it would be a slow death, it ended his fighting forever. He let go of the rope, and Fell came crashing to the ground, just safe of a slicing blade. But before Fell could struggle up and launch himself at the closest soldier, the man was dead, too. The archer's arrow had searched out the hard red muscle of another angry heart.

There were only two soldiers left now, the leader and the last of his men, who was killed by an arrow through his neck. The leader grabbed a sword and raced at Alina. She was defenceless, her hands bound, but the soldier never reached her. The hidden archer had released a last arrow, which grazed Alina's cheek in its flight. She froze and felt the leader stiffen behind her, then crash to the ground too, the arrow in his face.

Alina's heart was thundering, and all she could think was that the mysterious Helgra had saved them.

"Who are you?" she called. "Show yourselves!"

As the figure rose on the brow of the little hill, Alina Sculcuvant gasped in utter astonishment.

"Catalin!" she cried. The young man stood there, her bow in his hand.

Catalin began to walk slowly towards them, as Fell gave a low, approving growl. The young man bent down wordlessly and took the sword from the dead leader's hand, then, with decision, cut Alina's bonds. She was free too.

"Catalin," she whispered, rubbing her wrists painfully. "But how? I thought you'd . . ."

"Run away?" said the young man, thrusting the sword into the ground. "Because you think me a coward, Alina WovenWord?"

"I . . . I'm sorry. But the bow. Why didn't you tell me?"

"Tell you what? That I've a skill too? Or that for years I've honed it on my own in the hills?"

"Of course. Why didn't you join your father and me in the training?"

"So as not to encourage this path you've taken," answered Catalin sadly. "Perhaps I would have thought differently if I'd known you are the heir to Castelu. But Father never wanted me to be a warrior, Alina. I think it would have broken his heart. He hated what he'd seen."

"But all these weeks in the wild. You could have hunted for us."

"I didn't want to touch my bow," said Catalin.

"Your bow?"

"I made that bow myself, but these past weeks I've been too angry at Father's death to use it."

Alina remembered Lescu's warning about hate. She thought how much taller Catalin looked, and how fine and intelligent were his blue green eyes.

"Besides," said Catalin, shrugging, "you had your wolf to hunt for you, didn't you?"

He was staring at Fell. He held the wolf's gaze now, and Fell suddenly looked away.

"Fell saved my life too," he whispered, "and for that I'll always thank him."

Fell began walking towards the young man, his tail lowered. He padded straight up to Catalin Fierar, and then, very gently, the wolf licked his hand, just as he had done to Alina in the forest. Here were a Dragga and a Drappa indeed.

"You say you're no changeling," said Catalin, as Fell padded away and lay down at a distance, watching them both, "but you're surrounded by a kind of magic. Although now I know that there is none of Baba Yaga's witchcraft in it."

"No," said Alina softly. "When I touch the wolf's mind, I realise that Fell thinks his own heart black, yet he struggles towards the light too. His heart has been wounded badly by life."

"Then the three of us have something in common, Alina," said

Catalin. Alina gave a little cry of gratitude and compassion, and threw herself on his neck, kissing him on the lips.

Catalin held her, and in that moment he felt prouder and happier than he ever had in his life. He looked into her beautiful hazel eyes and felt the fear of it and the excitement too, as if he were travelling to another country.

The young man had often walked out in the dewy mornings, with the soft, fresh grass wet under his bare feet. He had watched the morning mists kiss the mountaintops and the sun glitter on dancing rivers, and felt the wild mystery of the forest. He had seen horses drop their fowls at dawn, and watched them struggle into painful life, and held newborn chicks fluttering in his tender hands. He had hunted the Lera too with his bow, though always with respect for the animals he took. But none of it did he think as rare and beautiful a magic as the creature that he now held in his arms.

"Thank you, dear Catalin," she said as he stood back. She held his hand.

"Don't thank me for anything, Alina," Catalin said softly, feeling that they walked as equals again. "And I'm sorry, Alina, about your parents. We have much to face still, and I've been thinking we need some help."

"Yes, that's what Fell thinks. But from who?"

"The Helgra, Alina. I heard what that soldier said and they must hate Vladeran as much as you. Perhaps we should go to this village below the castle on the mountaintop."

"Yes," said Alina, stroking Catalin's hand, "the village where it all began."

"My father told me about the Helgra. He said they're mercenaries, so perhaps we can buy their assistance."

"Buy it with what?" said Alina in surprise.

Catalin was reaching into his pocket, and suddenly he pulled out the bag of gold he had taken from the dresser before he left.

"There's this. If it helps you, Alina WovenWord, you're welcome to it."

Alina smiled and nodded gratefully, but her fear returned.

"When they spoke of them in Moldov, they said terrible things, Catalin. That they worship the dark one too."

Catalin had been emboldened by what he had done, but his eyes flickered fearfully, and as Fell watched them there together, these strange humans, he whimpered and laid his head on his paws and sighed.

Sixteen

THE HELGRA

Fell saw them below him in the coming light, Alina WovenWord and Catalin Fierar, walking down a narrow gorge. He growled softly, and not without jealousy, for they looked very fine together, but he was glad that his human friends were safe, as he shadowed them on the mountain. They had travelled far together, trying to keep their spirits up by telling each other stories again, and now they were nearly at the Stone Den.

The sun was rising as he reached their side, and Alina's sword was strung across her back, Catalin's bow on his arm, as they saw it high on the craggy precipice opposite them—the outline of a vast, ruined castle. The castle that had become the very symbol of Castelu, for it lay in Castelu's domain.

Dawn was spreading around its sombre walls and the great stone stairway, which rose up and up towards it through the vaulting pines. The huge weathered steps sparkled in the sunlight, and the splinters of light that were reaching out from the forest below it wrapped themselves around a little village, nestling just beneath the cliffs.

"At last, Alina," growled Fell proudly, "the Stone Den."

"Yes, Fell. We're nearing my home."

The wolf's black muzzle dropped to the sight far below them—a group of wooden dens with smoke curling from rooftops.

"That village, Alina. The Varg took your brother from there, and there I returned him too."

Fell was suddenly thinking of something else. The cave where he and Larka had been born. It was nearby too, and he wondered if he could remember where it was.

"It's the Helgra village," said Alina aloud, almost remembering herself.

Fell growled as he thought of his long connection with humans, and how he had led Alina and Catalin back to this place. And as he realised that everything Skart had told Kar seemed to be coming true, the worries that had begun to consume him returned. Fell seemed to be on a path that was guided by more than his own will, and if he trusted the visions of the Sight, it was a path he already feared the end of. A path that led to Alina's death at his own jaws.

Fell looked up again at the castle high above, and felt desperately small. At least he knew that the tales that had been told of that fearful place, tales filled with darkness and superstition, that had kept men's hearts in the shadows in Transylvania for generations, had been a lie. Fell knew from his own history that there was nothing up there at all, no demons or vampires, nothing but human brick and stone, and he was glad of it. He lifted his muzzle and howled, and when his song was finished, the place was no longer quite as lonely as it had been. Fell turned to Alina, and she spoke again with her thoughts.

"This Guardian, Fell. You still have not found him?"

"No, Alina."

"Then perhaps he doesn't exist."

"Perhaps not."

"Or perhaps you're the Guardian, Fell. You've guarded me."

The wolf growled at the strange thought.

"But now we must face this alone," said Alina, as boldly as she could, "and have courage together."

Fell's sleek black fur was suddenly quivering.

"Oh, dear Alina."

"What is it, Fell?"

"I've feared to tell you before, but it's time to now. Not *we*, Alina. I've brought you safely this far at least, and we've shared the wonders of the wild, but now I must leave you."

Fell's mind was filled with guilt, and Alina swung round and stared in amazement at her friend. She felt sick to her soul.

"Leave us, Fell? But why?"

Fell's shadowed thoughts gave only part of the answer, and he whimpered softly.

"My father, Huttser, is dying."

"Dying?"

Alina felt for the dear wolf. Thinking of her own dead father, she wondered again if death and misfortune surrounded her wherever she went.

"That Vengerid pack told me about his wounds," came Fell's trembling thoughts, "and he has challenged their leader. Perhaps he's gone already, but I must hurry to him now. I've kept my word at least, and brought you to the Stone Den, while the Great Waterfall where his pack are is not too far from here. Besides, Alina, perhaps a wild wolf has spent too long near your kind."

Alina felt something struggling in Fell's thoughts, something she could not see, and it frightened her as she stared at her friend.

"But without you, Fell? What will we ever . . ."

"You'll be safer now you've the Dragga to aid you."

The three of them stood there, just little specks in the immensity of that beautiful, mysterious landscape, and Alina wrestled with the loneliness that had suddenly come on her again. Darker fears were around her too, fears of where her journey would take her next, and what it would tell her of her mother. Yet the young woman stood resolute.

"The Helgra," thought Alina suddenly, shielding the sorrow in her heart. "They revere the wolf, Fell. They're friends to your kind."

"Man revere the wolf?" came Fell's growling mind. "That I'd see with my own eyes."

"Then come with us, dear Fell, just to the village at least. We may need you there to help gain the Helgra's trust, if you can wait a sun or two more to see your father."

Alina felt guilty at trying to delay him, yet it was true that she needed him to face these mysterious men.

"Perhaps your presence will help, Fell, although it may be dangerous."

Fell was torn, but at last he answered. "Very well then, human cub. One or two more suns I can spare, and so will go with you as far as this village, but no further. Then I must be gone to my own kind. I've spent too long away."

Alina was desperately relieved, but miserable too that their parting had only been delayed awhile.

It took the travellers another day to descend the mountain, and at first their path took them away from the Helgra village and down onto a stony road. It was night by the time they reached a large stone building set back from the road, with stabling for horses and smoke curling from its chimney. It was an inn. The comforting glow of firelight shone in its grimy windows, and the human sounds of song and laughter crept out into the night.

Alina and Catalin left Fell in the field beyond, by a willow tree with branches that trailed like a witch's hair, and stowed their weapons in the grass for him to guard, then drew up their hoods, approached the inn, and pushed open the door.

The shadowy room was thick with smoke and full of rowdy drinkers, as boys and serving girls carried tankards of frothing ale about the place. They all looked up warily as the two young friends entered, but seeing little threat in the hooded figures, they returned to their conversations.

Catalin bought two mugs of beer, and they sat in a corner by the window, at a low wooden table, listening to the talk and a storyteller in the corner, who was spinning a yarn rather badly, much to the anger and irritation of the others. It was strange indeed to be amongst people again. A couple of soldiers were playing at dice nearby, and one of them began to speak of the wars.

"It goes hard for the King," he said. "The Turk push him back to the borders of Moldova."

"Stefan needs more men," said the other soldier. "Draculea and Lord Vladeran ride to aid him again?"

"They send soldiers, yes, and so the King had better watch his back."

"True enough. He should call on the Helgra too."

The other soldier looked up in surprise, and let out a great roar of laughter.

"The Helgra? Vladeran's long turned them into a pack of bleating sheep."

"Wisssst," hissed the first. "Don't say it so loudly, man. This road skirts Helgra lands, and some in here may be Helgra spies."

Some of the drinkers in the tavern were indeed looking their way, but the other soldier stared challengingly around the room.

"What of it?" he said loudly. "What has a Saxon soldier to fear from Magyar scum?"

"You know the stories of them," murmured the first soldier. "Some say they eat human flesh, and torture any who enter their lands, then strip their bones and put their heads on stakes to warn off intruders. They're not Magyar alone. They've Dacian and Roman blood."

Alina's eyes were flickering nervously at Catalin. This fence sounded like the one round Baba Yaga's house. She suddenly feared the help they sought.

"Fairy tales to frighten children," said the other soldier. "The Helgra have nothing now, not even honour. Vladeran razed his vassals' homes, and burnt their villages. He stole their livestock, sent half of them to rot in his dungeons, and confiscated their weapons too. Vladeran even killed their blacksmiths, so that they can forge no more, and they're starving."

Catalin found himself staring into the flickering firelight nearby, thinking bitterly of his dead father, and the forge where they had worked so happily together. How strange and terrible life could be. But inside, Alina's emotions were mixed, for if she had hoped that their friendship with the wolf might have brought Helgra aid, it sounded as if there was little aid to be gained. Yet it made it less fearful approaching their pack.

"Well, perhaps there's some justice in it," said the first soldier, "if what they say of the Helgra has any truth."

"Justice in Vladeran and Romana's lands? You're drunk."

The heir to Castelu felt a sharp pang in her heart and with it a new emotion. Guilt for the peoples of Castelu. The soldier laughed again, taking a great draught of beer and hurling two dice into the box, which clattered against the side and came up on three.

"There's no justice in the lands beyond the forest," the soldier went on. "Stefan's too hard-pressed and his nobles too greedy. The Courts are a mockery, and all do as they please."

"Perhaps the Orders shall bring some justice," said the first soldier suddenly. "The Order of the Griffin, or the Dragon. They're sworn to protecting the world forever."

The man's voice had dropped to a whisper as he mentioned the secret Orders, and Alina turned her head sharply. The soldier had leaned forwards.

"They say the Griffin's leader has heard of Vladeran's ways, and wants accounting."

"Who is he?"

The soldiers huddled even closer over the box, and the one who had talked of accounting picked up the dice.

"Some say the Impaler himself, Draculea, but such things are not for us. His identity has always been a hard-held secret."

"Who cares if there's no justice, when there's gold to be had. This girl they hunt. The bounty's risen to a hundred gold pieces."

Catalin shot a glance at Alina immediately, and she stirred warily in her seat.

"Well, we've no time to win it. Hey, you, what are you staring at?"

The man was glaring at Alina angrily, for he had suddenly noticed her listening.

"Nothing sir," she answered as gruffly as she could, shielding her face from the firelight and taking a swig of beer.

The men went on with their game, and Catalin and Alina finished their drinks quickly and slipped outside. Fell was still by the willow, and they gathered their weapons, and were about to make camp for the night when they heard a rumble in the heavens and the lowering clouds above them broke.

The downpour was torrential, and they ran into the lee of the cliff for better shelter, but as they came to a stream, rising steadily all the time, Alina noticed that something strange had come over Fell. The wolf kept sniffing the ground and whining.

"What is it, friend?" asked her mind, as she noticed that the stream looked a sickly brown colour. "Is it the Helgra?"

Fell didn't answer her.

Suddenly Alina heard the sound of a little waterfall, and Fell went as rigid as a pointer, his tail raised and his muzzle pressed forwards. Alina was greatly relieved to see what Fell was staring at, for they were all soaked, and there in the rock face, partly obscured by a tree, was the entrance to a cave. She rushed forwards with Catalin, and they found that it was warm and dry inside, and a good place to sleep.

"What's wrong, Fell?" she asked again, as Alina saw the wolf still hanging back in the pouring rain. "There are no Lera here."

Fell blinked and padded forwards, brushing past her and standing in the cave mouth.

"No Lera, Alina," he answered sadly. "But many memories. For this is where Larka and I were born. Our birthing den."

Alina was amazed, and the three of them sat together in the cave that night, under the stone roof where Fell had been born, wondering at the strangeness of it. Fell didn't talk to Alina at first, and the mystery somehow added to the fear that the young people now had for the Helgra, despite their need for help.

"Shouldn't we make some kind of plan, Alina," asked Catalin nervously as they huddled together, "of what we tell them? From what those soldiers were saying, trust isn't strong in these parts."

When Fell had first spoken of finding a pack, Alina had clutched at the idea, as she had always wanted real friends. Then Catalin had suggested going amongst the Helgra, and it had seemed the right course. But now Alina was not so sure. She had kept moving towards Castelu, longing to know the truth of her mother, but thinking of her rightful inheritance too. She hardly knew what path she was on.

"I don't know, Catalin."

"Do we take Fell with us? If they revere the wolf."

Alina looked at her friend lying there, but Fell was lost in his own thoughts and memories.

"Not yet. I can't ask him to walk amongst humans, until we're sure of them. But he'll be ready."

"This bounty for a girl," said Catalin. "If these Helgra are as poor as they say, they may not readily turn down a hundred gold pieces, if they find out who you are."

Alina tried to smile.

"Then again I walk as a boy, Catalin," she whispered and her eyes flickered. "Or a man."

Alina had spoken in a tiny voice, a mere whisper, which outside might not have been heard at all, but here in his birthing den the wolf noticed with surprise how Alina's words bounced off the stone walls of the cave, and were magnified so greatly in the echoing chamber that they sounded loud and brave and strong.

With the dawn they crept out of Fell's birthing den, and down towards the fearful Helgra village. It was in the neck of the valley, ringed by a timber stockade that rose into the morning sky like teeth. Plumes of black wood smoke rose from its humble housetops as they approached, and Alina thought she could see spears placed in the ground near the entrance, and wondered if they were really topped with human heads.

She seemed to remember the place dimly. Fell scouted the stockade, and when he returned he nodded his muzzle.

"All seems quiet enough, Alina," he growled. "Most of the humans seem to be in their dens, and there's a strange, sad air about the place. I fear it."

"We'll go in first then, my friend. It'll be safer and look more natural that way. But come if my thoughts call you, Fell."

The black wolf's yellow gold eyes glittered in agreement. So it was that Catalin and Alina approached the fearful Helgra village, as two young men, side by side, while Fell waited warily on its outskirts, much too close to human dens for his own comfort.

The smoke seemed to rise like a funeral fire, as they set their nervous feet on the track approaching the village entrance, putting up their hoods and fighting thoughts of being flayed alive. They felt sick to their stomachs as they neared those spears.

"Perhaps there's one without a skull on its top," whispered Catalin with a grim smile. "Ready for me."

"For a hero, you mean," said Alina, thinking of the story of Baba Yaga's fence and squeezing his arm.

Their path was set, and if it was human heads they expected to see at the tops of the spears, all they found were the skulls of cow and deer. It was still a gruesome sight, and they were little reassured by the gloom that seemed to hang in the air like the smoke as they passed through the gates.

A group of Helgra children spotted them first. They looked as thin and ragged as urchins, and when they saw two armed visitors walking into the village, they stopped playing with pebbles for marbles and twigs for swords, and gathered round Catalin and Alina, pulling at their clothes. From dirty faces they stared wonderingly at the sword and the bow, their eyes as fat with fear as their bellies were thin with hunger.

"Have you an elder?" asked Catalin loudly, to a lanky boy with dirty blond hair. A nod was his only answer, and they were led by the little pack of children to the centre of the village. There was a tangible air of fear and sorrow all around, for many of the grimy houses were boarded up, and there were few animals in sight. Instead, angry adult faces peered out of darkened windows, and shutters were opened and slammed again.

"What has Vladeran done?" whispered Alina bitterly, as they walked. "It's terrible, Catalin."

As they reached a kind of square, with a well and a barn, and nearby a kind of covered conference place, strange memories flickered through Alina's mind. She was sure she'd been to this place before as a little girl.

The blond-haired lad ran to a long, thatched house on the side of the square, and was inside for some time, but at last he reemerged with three Helgra adults. As soon as the first saw the bow and sword at their backs, he gave a low whistle, and from all around the square figures appeared like trained sheepdogs, not with swords, but armed well enough with pike and hoe and staff. Catalin and Alina were suddenly surrounded by Helgra men, glaring at them suspiciously.

"A good start, SkeinTale," whispered Catalin, with another grim smile.

The three Helgra adults came forwards. One was an old man, with long white hair and a stooped back, wearing a scrawny wolf cloak around his shoulders, and by the way the second—a thick-set man with a powerful, bold face—was helping him, it soon became apparent that the old man was blind. The third figure was thin and lean, with a half beard, and hovered in the background with veiled eyes.

"You're courageous to walk so openly into our village," said the larger man coldly, as Alina and Catalin looked at the pikes around them. "There was a time when none would have dared do so. The Helgra are fallen into contempt indeed."

"Are you the elder, sir?" ventured Catalin softly.

"That I'm not," answered the man gruffly, indicating the old, white-haired man at his side. "My father Ilyan here is elder to the Helgra. The headman of this village, and thus of all the Helgra villages in these parts. I'm his son Ovidu, and this is my younger brother Cascu. Who are you?"

"Catalin Fierar and Alin Sculcuvant, sir," answered Catalin, "travellers in the world."

"What kind of travellers? Soldiers perhaps, though young ones indeed."

Catalin's eyes flickered.

"We're storytellers, sir. Travelling storytellers."

Alina smiled and felt a warmth inside her.

"And what do you do in our village, storyteller?"

Catalin looked nervously at Alina. He hardly knew how to answer, although he had tried to take the lead.

319

"We're hungry, sir, and have come a long road. We seek help, and mean no harm. We've gold."

Catalin had put his hand to his belt, but the elder's first son let go of his father's arm and stepped angrily forwards.

"You insult the elder with your filthy coin, storyteller?"

"No, sir, I only meant . . ."

"And how do we know that you're not really Lord Vladeran's spies," said his brother Cascu suddenly, "come to test our loyalty with your lies, and lead us into a trap? He sets many traps and has many spies. Even amongst our own."

He had a thin, nasal voice and a mean look, and the armed men were muttering and nodding, as Alina wondered if she should call on Fell.

"And you're hungry, you say?" snorted Cascu. "And so come to scavenge perhaps, or steal the last scraps of food from our children's bellies with your lying tales."

"My brother's right," said Ovidu. "All men are hungry, but with the 'justice' of Vladeran's and Romana's rule, we've nothing to spare, so what's your bellyaching to us?"

Alina stepped forwards now. She could see that the Helgra were none too pleased to welcome strangers, even travelling storytellers, but she thought of those soldiers playing at dice, and knew she had to take a risk on the gamble of the world. So she spoke, calmly and clearly, refusing to be intimidated by the circle of men.

She told them that they had crossed the high mountains, struggling for months through bitter weather, returning to the lands beyond, where Alina had been born, and sought to learn all they could of the house of Castelu.

She could see immediately the angry flame that lit in the men's eyes at the mention of Castelu, so she added hurriedly that they were no friends of Lord Vladeran. It was enough to set the white-haired elder's blind eyes sparking with interest, but all the while Ovidu looked sullen and suspicious, while his brother Cascu was studying their faces with new interest, and clever, darting eyes. Suddenly the old blind man hobbled forwards.

"You've a young voice, storyteller," he said, tilting his head as if listening, "for one who speaks so boldly."

Ilyan raised his shaking hands.

"Come here, lad," he whispered.

Alina hesitated, fearful of being discovered, but she saw she could not refuse and so stepped forwards. The old man put his hands to her face, and with his sensitive, spindly fingers, for years his only eyes, Ilyan began to examine Alina's features, as she flinched at his touch.

"Good cheekbones," he whispered, "and a high, intelligent forehead. I hope your heart's as strong. What colour is your hair?"

Alina paused nervously.

"Red, sir."

Ilyan stepped back at that and smiled.

"And now I do not doubt your courage, for it's brave of a girl to walk like this amongst the Helgra."

"A girl?" whispered Ovidu. "Is it true?"

There was a murmur amongst the assembled men, and Catalin

looked nervously at Alina and fingered his bow.

Alina pulled down her hood slowly.

"Yes, it's true," she answered, "but although my clothes may dissemble, I come with truth in my heart. And on my tongue." Alina felt strangely proud as she said it and remembered Ivan's words about truth being her greatest ally.

"Gold," whispered one of the Helgra suddenly. "Vladeran offers gold for a redheaded woman."

"Hush man," snapped Ilyan. "Would you take Vladeran's filthy gold? Even with a bounty set so low on the head of the heir to the lands of Castelu?"

Alina flinched and Ovidu swung round.

"What, Father?"

"A girl travelling through the wild to Castelu," said the old man, with a delighted chuckle. "A secret bounty. It's as I long suspected. She's the girl, Alina, the redheaded child, whom they said was lost in the snows, and killed by the Turk. Elu's elder sister."

"Seize them!" cried Ovidu immediately.

The men rushed forwards and, before they could react, grabbed hold of Catalin and Alina roughly. Ilyan was muttering though, and swinging round his blind eyes towards his son.

"No, Ovidu. What are you doing, boy?"

"Spies, Father. It's a trap indeed. I'll not have you end your days in Vladeran's dungeons. Cascu, her sword."

Cascu plucked the blade from Alina's back and handed it to his brother.

"We set no traps," said Alina angrily. "The rumours about my disappearance are the lies. I am Alina of Castelu, as you say, but it was Lord Vladeran, not Turks, who had me kidnapped long ago, and sent me to be murdered in the snows. I hate him with all my heart, as you do, I think."

The claim made the men pause, but Cascu glared suspiciously at Alina.

"You're a storyteller indeed. You've proof of this fable, woman?"

"There was a parchment." Alina dropped her eyes. "But it was lost."

"And in times like this, it is too dangerous to believe such nonsense, or let you live," growled Ovidu. "Even if it is true, I've no love for the children of Castelu, and none in these times will mourn the deaths of two wandering children."

As he said it, one of the Helgra cried out.

"Look there."

The elder's first son turned, as did the others, and they all gasped in utter astonishment. Through the very centre of the Helgra village, watched by those terrified children, came a lone black wolf.

Fell's bushy tail was held high, and he growled as he swung his muzzle left and right, his yellow gold eyes surveying the humans about him, although with a look that was unconcerned, and almost bored. The effect on the Helgra was instantaneous though, and an awed murmur went up amongst them, like a wind.

"What's happening?" whispered Ilyan, clutching at the air.

"The wolf comes amongst us," cried an old Helgra woman. "He walks with the children."

Ilyan found his older son's arm and grabbed at it.

"A wolf," he whispered. "It's an omen, Ovidu. A good one. She is the one."

Fell was truly delighted with the effect he was having on the superstitious Helgra. The ring around Alina and Catalin broke apart, leaving only the two men holding them. Doors had begun to open around the village, and ragged Helgra families emerged, peering in wonder and amazement at the extraordinary scene.

Fell padded on, straight past Catalin, brushing his leg with his tail, as Ilyan sniffed at the air. When he reached Alina, the black wolf stopped and looked up at the proud young woman and her now shaken captors. With a huge yawn that showed his teeth, Fell lay down at Alina WovenWord's feet, licked his lips, and laid his head softly on his paws with a sigh.

"You didn't call, Alina," came his thoughts, "but it felt wrong somehow, so I came."

"The wolf," cried Ovidu in astonishment, "the black wolf serves the lost heir to Castelu. Release them, instantly."

The two Helgra were more than pleased to release the strangers, and jumped back themselves from that black apparition. Alina was going to speak, but Ovidu had already come forwards. He dropped to a knee before the wolf and the girl, and held up Alina's sword by its wolf hilt.

"Forgive me, storyteller," he said humbly, looking nervously at Fell. "We've seen much suffering, and trust few these days. But if your tale's true, and a wolf serves you, then you've my service, willingly. And the Helgra's. For we honour the Varg as no other

324

animal in the world. Though many animals we honour indeed."

"You know the name of the Varg?" asked Alina in surprise.

The elder's son looked up at her, and his eyes were afraid.

"It's the name the Helgra have used for centuries, Alina of Castelu. Since Dacian times."

"Very well then," said Alina. "Know then that it's the name the wolf uses for their own kind too."

Ovidu's eyes were full of the mystery of it, though still doubting, but he bowed his head to the storyteller. With that, he suddenly gave a gasp.

"The mark," he hissed, staring now at that sword, and the eagle that had been wrought into the tempered metal by the clever blacksmith.

"The eagle?" said Alina, immediately. "You know what it means, Ovidu?"

Ovidu rose slowly, looking even more wonderingly at the newcomer.

"Of course. The opening wings of the steppe eagle are the ancient mark of a Helgra woman."

"Helgra?" cried Alina in astonishment. "Is this a story?"

Ilyan was listening intently, and nodding to himself.

"You've the mark too, don't you?" he asked. "On your arm. A little eagle."

"Yes, Ilyan."

"And it proves all you've said," cried old Ilyan delightedly. "For the Lady Romana bears the same mark. The mark I gave her with my own hands when her mother brought her to me as a child, to let it be remembered she has Helgra blood too. The mark I gave you as a little girl also, when Romana brought you to me. Oh, Alina. Alina of Castelu. You have returned."

Ovidu and Cascu were looking at their father in absolute amazement, while the listening Helgra villagers had begun to murmur. Fell raised his head, and his ears twitched.

"I've never told you of it, Ovidu," muttered Ilyan, "for although it may soon be time to pass on our ways to my eldest son, I thought it a sad thing, now Castelu has turned against us. But Romana has Helgra blood in her veins, like Alina. Not as much as Saxon, but enough to give them a special place in my heart, for Romana honours our ways. As did her husband, Dragomir."

"A special place, Father?" said Ovidu bitterly. "The woman who stands at Vladeran's side, to destroy her own people? To destroy the land itself. And nature."

"No," said Ilyan angrily, "I tell you again, I've never believed it of the Lady Romana."

Alina swung her head, and her heart was beating like a war drum.

"She was hurt badly when Dragomir died and led astray, but her heart is good," said Ilyan. "This evil comes from Vladeran alone, and Alina's tale of kidnap and murder at Vladeran's hands proves it to us. I think it was easy for Vladeran to turn her heart, after her husband's death."

Alina was trembling furiously, wrestling with the memory of Romana's unkind treatment of her, yet wanting with all her heart to believe what Ilyan was now saying of her own mother. The mother she so wanted and needed to love. But she didn't believe it.

"And now a great thing happens!" cried the elder happily. "A miracle. The lost heir to Castelu, the sister of the boy taken by wolves, returns, with the Helgra mark on her arm, and brings a wild wolf to honour us. There's hope in my old heart again. I've witnessed something I thought these blind old eyes would never see."

Cascu and Ovidu were blinking in wonder. Cascu's eyes were flickering strangely, but Ovidu suddenly grinned.

"These are strange tidings indeed, and we would learn more of them," he said. "But now you look hungry and tired from your journey. Would you honour the Helgra by dining at our tables this very night?"

Catalin looked up hopefully, and then he frowned.

"But you told us that your village was poor," he said, "and that you've no food."

Ovidu smiled a little slyly.

"These are dangerous, evil times, lad," he whispered, clasping his father's arm, "where men's hearts must sometimes be closed and mysterious to survive. We've learnt to hide what little food we have from Vladeran's jackals. Each homestead shall bring what they possess, and those barrels of wine and mead we have hidden in the winter earth shall be dug from their graves. We shall light tapers in the great hall, and our boys and girls shall sing once more the songs of the Helgra, in pride and honour. Cascu, see it is done."

As Alina WovenWord stood there, amongst her own once more, she was trembling furiously at the miracle of it, but inside she felt suddenly that the world was filled with magic indeed.

SEVENTEEN

GOBLIN SONG

T he feast they made for the travelling storytellers that night was rare, for in the halls of the Helgra, Alina of Castelu and Catalin Fierar sat between Ovidu and his blind father Ilyan, at the head of a huge oak table, groaning with roasted chickens and boars on wooden platters, and beakers of blood red wine, passed from hand to helping hand. It was the vision Alina had seen in the bucket in the forge so long ago.

It was not of the splendour of Helgra times of old, perhaps, but the Helgra men and women who sat there looked with marvelling eyes at the sumptuous banquet. Few of them begrudged the price of their hidden stores, or worried at the cost in times to come. Instead they kept looking at the handsome young strangers in the flaring torchlight, wondering what the arrival of the lost heir of Castelu meant for their beleaguered people, and how a girl who bore the mark of a Helgra woman could carry a sword so bravely and be served by a wolf.

"Tell me more of Vladeran, Ilyan," said Alina softly at the banquet table. "And my mother, Romana. Of their marriage."

Alina's voice was pained, and the blind old elder shook his head and pulled the wolf cloak tighter about him.

"Don't be too hard on your mother for marrying Vladeran, my

child," he whispered. "Children can be too hard on their parents, until they learn themselves how hard life can be. She loved your father, Dragomir, dearly, but when he died, I think it broke her poor heart. It's why, perhaps, she became so distant with you, for you reminded her too much of him."

Alina's piercing hazel eyes were full of memories of Romana's scolding looks and cruel words, and of the child's longing for the love they had once shared so deeply. She reddened. Perhaps they were childish thoughts now, as childish as thoughts of fairies or goblins.

"Vladeran is persuasive," said Ilyan gravely, "and Romana must have felt a deep sorrow and loneliness. So Vladeran wooed her and she bore him a son. It was in these very halls that you watched over Elu that night, after his birth, when he was snatched away by wolves. And now you come amongst the Helgra again. It's a strange destiny indeed."

Only Alina Sculcuvant knew just how strange.

"It was only really after Elu's reappearance that day that our persecution began."

"Why?" asked Alina.

"Vladeran grew obsessed with his son's return on the wolf's back, and with Helgra knowledge of the wolf and the wild. I think he sought to master it. Perhaps he believed we had something to do with Elu's disappearance."

His return on *Fell's* back, thought Alina.

"Vladeran sought out our wise men, and asked them all they knew of the Varg, while some say that he even learnt ancient

Helgra arts of how to commune with Varg spirits from beyond. Arts I have long suppressed. I cannot believe any of my people should have taught him."

Ilyan suddenly looked very sad.

"Then Vladeran fell on us like a man-eater," he whispered, "and set to destroying our power and independence. He didn't trust us and was jealous of our knowledge of the wolf. He has spread nothing but hatred and evil in the lands of Castelu, and nothing but death and humiliation for my people. How different from the days when Romana and Dragomir walked amongst us, your parents, with kindness and with love, to listen to our tales, and bring us gifts of food. They cared for my people and our ways. For nature."

"Unlike Lord Vladeran," growled Ovidu. "He claims to be of the Order of the Griffin, sworn to defend the downtrodden and protect the earth. The earth! He scorches our crops, and poisons our rivers with the bodies of rotting cattle. It shall bring him no good in the end, I swear it."

Ovidu took another swig of ale and shook his head, as Catalin remembered the foul taste of the river, and Alina thought about her destiny and the survival of nature.

"But if it's true what you say of my mother, why didn't she stop him?" asked Alina fearfully.

Ilyan's blind eyes flickered with doubt. "That I don't know," he answered. "Perhaps she knows nothing of it."

"What of King Stefan?" said Catalin suddenly. "Father always said he has justice in his heart."

Ovidu had dropped his eyes thoughtfully.

"Stefan has some affection for us, although they say he has a hard, cold head too, and little time for our ways or beliefs. But I do not think he'd approve it if he knew what Lord Vladeran has being doing to his subjects, Magyar or no."

"And now Vladeran has tried to murder the heir to Castelu," muttered Ilyan. "And a Helgra woman. Perhaps we should turn to him."

"Yes, yes, indeed, Father. But the King is busy in the lands beyond the forests," said Ovidu, "fighting the Turk, even as he tries to unite his own warring peoples, Slav and Vlak, Magyar and Saxon."

Alina was still thinking of Dragomir and Romana, though, and how Ilyan had said that they had loved the Helgra. What had turned her mother's heart?

"My parents. They did not fear your dark fame then?" she asked. Ilyan tilted his blind old head and grinned.

"Our dark fame, you say, storyteller? We are forced to tell tales to make others fear us, Alina of the Helgra, and so make strangers leave us in peace."

The clever elder suddenly reached out his wrinkled hand and clasped the young woman's.

"It's a miracle that you should return though, and bring a wolf amongst us," he whispered warmly. "And such a wolf. We try to carry that spirit with us, Alina, if we have to go into battle, as we once did so proudly, and wear their skins if we find a carcass in the wild, but we're not foolish enough to believe that real wolves could live amongst us like our dogs. Not even yours."

Alina realised that perhaps the old man was saying something important about nature and the wild. That it was not the same as this civilised gathering.

"We know too that their path is wild nature's path, unadorned by the needs and cares and fears of man," whispered Ilyan. "Untroubled by our thoughts and our stories."

Alina smiled.

"But as we listen to their songs, we know that there's pain in that wild path too, and that we are men first. We've even killed their kind, Alina, when their packs have threatened our animals in the heart of winter, if that threat is real, or when their older and weaker kind have turned into man-eaters."

Alina looked at Ilyan in surprise, but she accepted this grave truth.

"Yet if we have to do such a thing, it is never with gladness," added Ilyan warmly, sensing the young woman's concern. "And then we raise torches and sing our own lament. Sing the song of the Helgra. Your mother would sing it to you as a little girl."

Ovidu looked up, and his eyes, heavy with wine, were glittering like dewy petals. He rose to his feet beside Catalin and swayed a little, but there was a huge smile on his face.

"The Song!" he cried drunkenly. "Let one amongst us sing the Song of the Helgra once again. To remind us all of the days when poets and bards lit our lives with hope and love and courage."

Ovidu raised his hands to a youth who had been serving them, a tall, beautiful boy with flowing black hair. He stepped forwards, and Ovidu rapped his fist on the table to silence the gathering.

Then, before Alina, Catalin, and the assembled Helgra, the youth
began to sing.

> Out of time, the Helgra come, loving spear,
>> admiring drum,
>
> Knowing, from the depths of night, how the heart
>> must praise the fight.
>
> Life's a journey filled with pain, teaching loss
>> in snow and rain,
>
> Death is sure the mortal's way, change a law of
>> night and day,
>
> Yet the heart must never die, raise your voice and
>> break the sky.
>
> Like the wolf on mountain clear, howl it out
>> through bitter tear,
>
> Everything that lives and dies, longs to find
>> the real prize,
>
> Longs to know what made this place, longs to
>> touch a gentler face,
>
> Fears its nature in the dark, loves the song of
>> rising lark,
>
> Turns to darkness in its pain, shames to feel
>> the sun again,
>
> Knows the finest place of all, proud in sunlight,
>> standing tall.
>
> Search the mountains and the sea, for the truest
>> way to be,

Honour all that marvellous horde, even as you raise
        your sword,

Men and women, know your worth, lest you fail
        the striving earth,

Then in union bring again, bursting joy from
        falling rain.

Free your children with your song, teach with
        love the right from wrong,

Teach them what the poets know, that in loving all
        things grow,

But that human hearts can make chains that
        every thing would break,

Feel as well, in brook and stream, how the earth
        itself can dream,

And that power that passes through, greater
        than the works we do,

Let it hold you safe and strong, like a hand with
        tender bond,

Breathe a breath so deep and calm, that no thing
        may do you harm,

Lest the harm that's done to you, comes like sorrow
        in the dew,

Or a canker in the earth, robs this lovely life
        of worth,

Sing this song from heaven sent, thank the world as
        you lament.

The boy stopped his haunting melody, half spoken and half hummed in the glowing tapers, and the two young storytellers watched the shadows flicker across those upturned Helgra faces, changing their aspects from things in part a little demonic, to faces at once tender and utterly beautiful. Alina WovenWord felt the tears come to her hazel eyes, as she heard that song that now she remembered as the lullaby of her dreams, and smiled softly at Catalin. She felt as if she had a family at last.

Yet there was another feeling there too. The feeling that she had been here before. Not in the Helgra village, for that she had, but eating at this table. It was the vision she had seen of herself in the forge. The future. But if it was, then the terrible prison awaited her, too.

All the while Fell sat alone outside, under the wooden awning that was the Helgra meeting place when the summer suns shone down, and none dared approach the black wolf, except the girls who were sent to serve him. Nervously they would totter forwards, with arms outstretched, place their platters of meat before the wolf, and run away. Fell delighted in giving short growls, or suddenly flashing his piercing eyes to frighten them a little, for he sensed that he was in no danger from these Helgra.

Never before or since has a wolf had a meal like that, and for a time Fell was not sad he had stayed, although he felt a dreadful guilt about Huttser. Fell lay there though, like some ancient king served by humans, as if the wolf had lain down with the lamb, and sniffed at the platters, suddenly snapping at a whole chicken, or taking a juicy haunch of boar down his hungry throat. He ate at his ease, cleaning his muzzle with his long, pink tongue at his leisure, until his belly was so full and fat that Fell thought he might burst open, while a million stars looked down, and sparkled at the incomprehensible miracle of being.

One of the Helgra had left him a bowl of ale too, as the song resounded in the hall, and the wolf lapped at it, tasting the pleasant bitterness of hops and feeling the strange effect it had on his thoughts. So strange that he got up suddenly and wobbled a little, then started to spin around, snapping at something in front of him that kept eluding his jaws. Like a young cub again, the drunken wolf was chasing his own tail.

Fell lay down again, a little shamefacedly and, closing his eyes, began to listen to Alina's thoughts in the hall beyond. The thoughts of the heir of Castelu, and a Helgra woman.

"Well, my child," Alina heard the kindly old elder whisper inside. "Tell me what you intend to do now."

Alina shook her head. "I must leave for the palace," she said, "although I would stay here awhile. I'd hoped that some Helgra could show me the way."

Catalin looked up from his food and was nodding.

"Show you the way we can indeed," said Ilyan, though with little enthusiasm. "But then what? If Lord Vladeran knows of your approach, he'll try to kill you again."

Alina nodded.

"If you seek revenge, child, and your rightful place," said the elder softly, "know too that Vladeran has long surrounded himself with a band of trained killers. The inner corps of his

Shield Guard are hand-picked and chosen to strike without mercy."

"A single arrow can pass twenty men easily enough," said Catalin suddenly.

"True, my boy," whispered the blind old man with a laugh, looking into the distance, as if trying to read the future, "but what matters is that which comes after the arrow has done its work."

"And I'd not let you do it for me," said Alina, looking at Catalin. "I'll confront Vladeran and fight him myself perhaps. Confront my mother too. Though whether it's revenge I seek, or simply to understand, I don't yet know."

"You fight Vladeran?" said the old man with a chuckle. "You may have a wolf at your back, Alina WolfPaw, and a sword too, but you're still just a girl."

Alina rose suddenly, and the noisy room fell silent.

"You think my sex weak, perhaps?" said Alina proudly. "And it's true I've not the strength of a man. But a Helgra woman has a heart as true as any man, and a skill just as fine."

Alina grasped the wolf handle of her sword. She drew it cleanly and, with a sweeping glide, brought it down towards the table and a boar's head that lay on a crowded platter, with an apple in its mouth. The stroke was perfectly measured, for it split the boar's head in two, leaving the apple pinned on the very tip. Alina Sculcuvant smiled, and turning gracefully, she offered the apple to Ovidu.

"That bounty should be a thousand gold pieces," he cried,

taking the thing with a smile. "Thank you, gentle Eve. That was well done."

"Well enough to tempt the Helgra to fight?" said Catalin suddenly, almost without thinking. He looked around the gathering, then stood up boldly. The young man felt nervous in front of them all, but he kept his chin raised.

"Fight?" whispered Ovidu.

"Fight against the tyrant who oppresses you, Ovidu. Fight too for the heir of Castelu and a Helgra woman."

Catalin was looking at Alina, and her heart stirred with his brave words, but there was fear in her too. Not only for herself, but because of what Catalin's father had told her of real fighting and of war. Alina wondered suddenly if her nature was weak.

"With what, lad?" snorted Ovidu. "You saw my men, armed with nothing but staff and hoe. Our best fighters were killed long ago, and our youth know nothing of the sword."

"Alina could teach them," said Catalin warmly. "Teach them all my father taught her. And this time I'll learn too."

Some of the women around the table were nodding admiringly, and the men's eyes were filled with questions.

"Well," whispered Ilyan, "they say that wisdom is a woman, and loves a warrior."

"Hush, Catalin," said Alina, sheathing her sword again. "I'd not ask others to fight my battles for me, and your father said war is a terrible thing."

"That may be, Alina, but it's the Helgra's battle too, from that mark on your arm, and what we hear of Lord Vladeran's rule. From what we've seen here too. You have wood from the forests to cut a thousand arrows," added Catalin, turning back to Ovidu. "And so learn their strength and power and speed."

He clasped the bow that leaned against his seat, and pulled an arrow from the quiver hanging there, strung it in front of the assembled throng, and sent an arrow singing down the very centre of the room, burying itself deeply in the wooden door beyond. There was an approving murmur about the great room, and Alina felt a deep pride in her belly for handsome Catalin, and thought how much he reminded her suddenly of his father, Lescu.

Not so pleased was the figure who had just slipped in through the door, and who had almost been grazed by the arrow. It was Cascu, Ovidu's younger brother, and now some of the Helgra were laughing at him. Cascu smiled coldly and, reaching up a hand, tugged the arrow from the wood angrily as he looked at his father and his elder brother, seated by these strangers at the head of his table.

"Bravo, lad," said Ovidu, next to Catalin, "but Helgra strength is born of the sword not the bow, and our swords Lord Vladeran took from us long ago. Our smiths too he butchered, boy, or took to work in his palace, and rot in his dungeons."

Catalin looked back at Ovidu with a sudden grin.

"Then you've two teachers," cried the young storyteller, "for my father was a great smith who taught me skills I'd willingly pass on. You've metal from the wheels of your carts. You can move on foot instead, like the wild wolf."

Ovidu's eyes were sparkling.

"But it would be a bitter thing to attack Vladeran's palace," he said. "He has so many at his command, not to mention that river to guard him."

"And the King?" said Catalin.

"You say that parchment was lost, Alina," answered Ovidu, "and even if we could get to the King, I doubt he'd think this anything more than some wild fairy tale, let alone spare a single man from his wars."

They had all fallen mournfully silent, and Catalin stared cheerlessly into his wine.

"Besides," muttered Ovidu, a little shamefully, "these fine lords, Vladeran and Tepesh, even Stefan, they stick together, do they not? Perhaps not even the King has quite the taste for justice I've heard he does."

"Then we must fight alone," said Catalin softly, raising his head again, his blue green eyes locked unwaveringly on Ovidu's. "My father always said that bold thoughts are stronger than a mighty army."

Ovidu seemed at a loss for words, but he looked at Alina, the true heir of Castelu, an heir with Helgra blood, and Catalin the archer, and slammed his fist on the table, with a belly laugh that seemed to shake the whole room.

"By Fenris," he cried, "I talk like a Sikla. It does my heart good to see a boy speak this bravely, and I'll argue no longer. It shall be so. Once more the Helgra shall forge weapons."

Ovidu's voice was swelling with courage, and it rang out around the Helgra hall.

"Once more we shall raise our heads high, for is it not better to live standing tall, than to die on your knees?"

Ovidu was gazing challengingly about the room, and many of the Helgra had begun to nod enthusiastically, although Ilyan's youngest son, Cascu, was not amongst them. Ovidu suddenly stood up.

"And the Helgra have other weapons too."

He strode over to the wall and plucked something from a shelf. When Alina and Catalin saw what he was holding in his two powerful hands, they shivered. It was a single antler tusk, from a large red deer. It look liked a curling branch, but not with fat twigs coming from it, but ten hard points, like daggers.

Ovidu swung the antler left and right, and both saw immediately how dangerous it could be in Helgra hands, but Alina suddenly thought of her dreams. She was no changeling perhaps, but she remembered how she had dreamt of these antlers, and suddenly Alina felt as if she were deep inside some goblin stronghold.

"We'll send the Helgra out to the forest, to collect fallen antlers and sharpen their points," cried Ovidu. "Only the Helgra know the skill of it."

Some around the table had jumped up too.

"And we'll light the forges, and go out amongst the mountain villages, calling out the Helgra to do battle and end this suffering forever," said Ovidu. "Then send messengers to the King while we train. There shall be justice again in our lands. "

The gathering suddenly rose, and one after the other began to take up the call, a chant that roused Fell from his drunken slumbers that had begun beyond, and made him whine in the night.

"Alina!" they chanted, as Alina thought that it was good indeed to have a pack, but worried too at the thought of war and the knowledge that Fell would not be at their side at all. "Alina WolfPaw!"

Fell and Alina stood together in the shattering morning, on the edge of the Helgra village. A new hope was in the air, and brilliant shards of sunlight had armed the heavens with spears of pure gold.

"I hate to leave you, Alina," came Fell's growling mind.

The chorus that had woken the Helgra that morning was still on the air—not birdsong, but the sound of hammering metal. Five days after the feast they had already lit the fires in the forges, and Catalin was hard at work. But Fell's yellow gold eyes were full of worry. He had delayed too long.

"You've friends now, Alina. A pack indeed."

"Yes, dear Fell. I'm part Helgra. I hardly believe the story of it. Yet I have no friends like you."

Fell gave a soft, contented growl. "You've a great destiny, I think. But I must find my father, Alina. Maybe I'll return to you. Who knows? Maybe I can still find the Guardian."

"Worry for yourself now, Fell, and for those you love."

The wolf raised his tail. "Love" had been such an unfamiliar word to the Kerl, but he knew suddenly he loved the girl, and it hurt him to leave her again, perhaps forever this time.

"A legend told us once that a courage is needed, Alina. A courage as deep as despair."

"Despair?" said Alina fearfully, worried about what she had

brought to her own people. Alina had never meant to bring sadness to anyone, and Lescu had taught her that war meant sadness and death.

"Yes, Alina, and I know what it means now, I think. I thought once that it meant that life itself is despair, and so we must make the darkness our ally."

Alina frowned.

"But it doesn't at all. It means that real courage is not to give up hope, even in the most terrible darkness, and to carry on. That if courage and love are as deep as despair, deeper, then light may come again."

"I pray it, Fell. For all of us."

"Pray?" muttered the wolf's troubled mind, thinking suddenly of Ottol and his talk of the Great One, and of his fruitless search for the Guardian too. "I'm a Varg, Alina, and so should pray to Tor and Fenris. Yet you're a human and pray to your own gods. They cannot both be real, Alina Sculcuvant. Perhaps none of these stories are. As I think now the Guardian is nothing but a myth."

Alina's mind was silent, but her heart was beating faster.

"Unless they're just names and human words, and it's the very thought of things greater than ourselves that really matters, wherever they come from," thought the black wolf, with a hopeful, defiant growl. "That by reaching out with those thoughts, we somehow reach into something far deeper than even words, and so touch something beyond what we think we know. So I shall reach out to what is beautiful."

"Yes, dear friend," said the storyteller. "But go now and find your father. Hurry."

Fell was seized with worry for Huttser, and he was suddenly running, out beyond the village towards the mountains, as Alina of Castelu turned back with a heavy heart towards her Helgra own, and the fight ahead. As she went, she did not notice the cowled Helgra mounting his horse hurriedly, and turning its head towards Lord Vladeran and his palace, beyond the Stone Den on the mountain.

EIGHTEEN

ELU

Another beading red droplet, like a holly berry broken from its leaf, plashed into the font, and Lord Vladeran's voice came cold and fearful, as he held out his hand again and clutched at the air.

"Morgra. They've escaped me again, damn you, and now this boy aids her too. A blacksmith's son."

The she-wolf's scarred features appeared once more in the water, lit by shadows thrown by the seemingly holy candlelight.

"And Fell," thought Vladeran, "we did not turn him."

"Turn him?" Morgra's ears came forwards in the water, and those wolf eyes glittered. "His nature dwells in darkness, human. Many times he's wanted to turn on the girl. Only some pact has held him back, but the Sight has shown him her death also. He needs only accept his destiny. He should have done so long ago."

Vladeran's eyes darkened. He wondered now about his own destiny. Twice the girl and the wolf had slipped his clutches, and the fear of it had made him set twenty Shield Guard about him permanently. But Vladeran had other worries too.

Although he had suppressed his enemies in his own lands, and the Helgra were crushed and broken, his armies had suffered great losses against the Turks already, while his own serfs and subjects, stretched to breaking by the taxes of food and provisions raised for the wars, and by the loss of their loved ones in Vladeran's battles, were breathing discontent. Vladeran's rule had become more and more ruthless, and now his dungeons were full.

"The Gift," said his mind, "they say it brings the power of prophecy."

Morgra seemed to be remembering, and her ear twitched.

"In the Red Meadow, although we lie suspended between your world and the final journey," came her thoughts, beginning to whisper like the wind in Fell's cave, "the Sight brings ways to touch the living world, indeed, through dream and prophecy, if nothing more. Just as the fortune-tellers once did in the land beyond the forests. There are indeed ways to see into the pattern of things, even from here."

"Tell me then, wolf. See for me now."

Vladeran was thinking hungrily of one of the sacred Oaths of the Order of the Griffin, the pursuit of knowledge.

"Of what would you know, human?"

"Of the future, and the girl. Redheaded Alina. Above all, of my own destiny. Is she really a danger to me?"

The scarred she-wolf nodded and closed her eyes in the water.

"Let me see into your future then, human. By Wolfbane, the Evil One, and by the great Varg god Fenris. By all the powers of the Sight."

Morgra suddenly opened her muzzle and gave a howl so strange and dark that Vladeran stepped back in fear, and the hunting dog in his hall whined bitterly. The cry rose, a cry that had once been one of summoning from the world of the living, and suddenly vanished into silence.

Morgra was silent for a long while, and Lord Vladeran thought that the spectre might fade once more, but at last her thoughts began to murmur, and her head to sway from side to side, as if she were seeing things before her dead eyes.

"I see the child, human. The changeling girl. WovenWord. SkeinTale. So important. I see a father, and a lifelong friend. I see your death."

Vladeran grasped the sides of the font and glared at the she-wolf. "My death?"

The wolf's eyes opened again, and the silence seemed to echo about the little chapel.

"Tell me," cried Vladeran. "What did you see of my death?"

"SkeinTale's no danger to you, human. For though her fate is bound into the very fabric of being, and Larka sent her spirit from even beyond the Red Meadow to tell Fell of it, you can only be killed if her father is in sight of these very halls."

Vladeran felt a great power swelling in his chest, as though he had just donned a breastplate of impenetrable armour. Alina's father, Lord Dragomir, Vladeran's best friend and his wife's first husband, had died on the battlefield before Vladeran's own eyes. When his troops had ridden down to collect his broken body, his soldiers had seen all their dead humped into pits, flaming like torches in the deathly air.

"You're certain of this, wolf?"

"Oh, yes, human. As certain as I am that only a love like Larka's could have reached her brother from where she is now, and talked to him as she did. That charm surrounds you."

Vladeran smiled, and suddenly it seemed as if he did not need the Inner Shield Guard to protect him at all. Did not need anyone.

"The girl was always a thorn in my side," he said, "but she's hunted everywhere and unjustly accused, too. I have set a bounty on her. It's as it should be."

Something came into Morgra's eyes, a dark memory. Had Morgra herself not once been unjustly accused? It had been the accusation that she herself, set apart by the strange powers of the Sight, had been a cub killer (when what Morgra had been trying to do was protect the infant) that had truly driven her into the shadows.

"Yet how can we guide Fell back towards his destiny," asked Vladeran, "and be certain that he will fulfil his nature, and kill the girl?"

"Pain," answered Morgra's bitter mind, "for Fell now faces a pain he has never known before. His father is dying. I see the shadow of these things from the Red Meadow."

"And then?"

"Then I shall touch him when he is most vulnerable, for it is only when we're really in pain that our strength, our courage, and our faith are truly tested. If we give up hope then and question all we believe, then we may truly be welcomed into the shadows, and taste the dark joy of the Sight. Fell has tasted it once, and he shall do so again. I shall help him."

Yet Morgra knew something she did not say, a terrible secret that none on earth knew, and which would surely drive Fell towards the dark forever.

Vladeran nodded gravely. "I will trust you then, Morgra. For I sense your nature, she-wolf."

Morgra's eyes glittered at this talk of her nature, but Vladeran heard a sound from the chamber beyond. A boy's voice.

"Father. Are you here, Father?"

He plunged his fist into the water, as if breaking glass in a mirror, and Morgra was gone. He turned and, sweeping through the tapestry once more, stepped back into the main hall. The fire was no longer lit, and great beams of heavy sunlight slanted through the windows, making the whole place glow and shine, glittering especially on Elu's golden head. His son was sitting in the great carved chair—a throne if Vladeran had been a king— and swinging his legs happily.

"You *are* here," said Elu, with a cheeky grin. "Mother said to find you."

Vladeran stopped and looked strangely at his own son.

"Elu. You look fine sitting there. Like the Lord of Castelu already."

The child beamed and Vladeran walked closer, with something almost jealous in his eyes.

"Where's your mother, Elu?" he asked softly.

The boy seemed distracted.

"Oh, she's at tapestry, and it's so boring. She sang to me though. A pretty enough song."

"I like to hear your mother's song, Elu. What did she sing?"

"It was a Helgra song. You love Mother, don't you, Father?"

Vladeran felt something tighten and catch in his throat, and again he was surprised by how direct children can be.

"Yes, Elu. Very much."

"Mother says you'll always protect us. That you always have done."

Vladeran leaned forwards, scooped his son up in his powerful arms, swung him round, and, sitting down himself in the chair, perched him on the arm of the chair next to him.

"You're a good boy, Elu," he whispered. "And so I do, but we must teach you to protect yourself too, mustn't we? One day you'll wield a sword."

"Oh, when, Father?"

"Soon, boy. But first comes the dagger."

Vladeran slipped his hand to his side and pulled the dagger from his belt, then brought it up beside his son's face. Elu's eyes sparkled. Vladeran turned the dagger slightly in his hand, thinking suddenly of his son on the throne and almost of how easy it would be to make the move, and pass it across the boy's throat.

He pushed the horrible thought aside, and flipped the dagger in his grasp, then offered it to his son.

"Oh, thank you," said Elu happily. "It's very fine. You love me too, don't you, Father?"

Vladeran felt something stir in his gut. He had long taught himself to disregard his own feelings, in the search for his own mastery.

"Yes, Elu, of course."

Elu smiled and leaned against Vladeran's shoulder with a happy sigh.

With that there was a great knocking, and the huge doors to the chamber swung open. Six soldiers entered, all in armour and none less than six foot tall. They wore leather breast shields and visors, and each bore an insignia like Vladeran's own.

Yet now the cross that had symbolised the Order of the Griffin was painted as black as night, and those yellow gold wings at each tip had turned red. The Inner Shield Guard marched towards Vladeran, flanking a man in a cloak and hood, whose clothes were spattered with mud after a hard and urgent ride.

"Go play now, boy," whispered Vladeran. "And tell your mother I'll come to her soon. I have high matters to attend."

"Yes, Father," said the child, jumping up.

The boy stopped for a moment to survey the soldiers admiringly, and then ran through their ranks from the great chamber. The Shield Guard all saluted their master, one to the right thumping his bare fist on his insignia, but it was the cloaked figure who stepped forwards and pulled down his hood.

"Well?"

"Alina and Catalin," whispered the spy, in a thin, nasal voice, made dry and weary by his long ride. "The storytellers are with my people now."

Vladeran stood up, with flashing, angry eyes.

"Alina with the Helgra, Cascu?" he hissed in amazement.

Ovidu's brother nodded.

"My brother and father welcome them. They know who she is. She is with her own again."

"Her own? What are you talking about?"

Cascu smiled thinly.

"She is marked, is she not?"

Lord Vladeran seemed confused.

"She had a mark, yes. What of it, man?"

"The opening eagle is the mark of a Helgra woman. The same mark the Lady Romana bears."

Vladeran's eyes were suddenly touched with doubt. Romana had never told him what the mark really signified.

"And could you not dispatch them easily, Cascu?" he whispered. "Kill them both."

"They're protected now, day and night. No weapons are allowed in their presence."

"Protected by those weaklings? A pack of cowards and foolish old men."

Cascu lifted his head slightly, and something like anger flickered in his face.

"Not all of us are old men," he said softly, with some pride left in his voice, "even if our best are already dead. My father and my brother have sworn to help them."

Vladeran smiled.

"With what? I've taken your weapons, poisoned your rivers, killed your smiths, broken your power. Forever."

Cascu's eyes narrowed, almost with a challenge.

"The boy teaches them the arts of the smith once more, and

now tales of a Helgra girl and a black wolf raise our kind to revolt throughout the Helgra lands. My people arm themselves again, Vladeran, encouraged by the appearance of a wolf who serves a human."

Vladeran stepped forwards furiously.

"This wolf," he hissed, "this cursed black wolf. Then can you not kill Fell, Cascu?"

"It's gone from their fold, my lord, into the mountains on its own once more. It goes to its dying father. But news of it stirs my people."

Vladeran's eyes glittered. Then Morgra's words had been true. He could surely trust the she-wolf and her prophecy.

"But the Helgra's pride begins to flow again," said Cascu. "It swells like a river, fed with snowmelt. The villages are rising, and they'll march soon towards the palace. They raise banners that carry the mark of a Helgra woman, in the cause of the heir to these lands."

Lord Vladeran's eyes blazed, but as he stood there he suddenly started to laugh.

"Do you hear that, Landu?" he cried, turning to the man who had saluted with his fist. "Do you hear that, my loyal Shield Guard? Fools come to test us in our own halls, but you shall protect me, shan't you?"

"In blood we serve," cried the Shield Guard as one, stamping their right feet.

"The oath," hissed Vladeran. "Repeat the oath of the New Order of the Castelu now."

"The conquest of the earth," Landu snapped back, standing even straighter, "the pursuit of war, and the glory of treading down the weak."

The soldiers were looking straight ahead as he repeated the five inverted principles that now bound them together, but there was something strange and caught in Landu's look as he finished the oaths. "The mastery of the feminine and the search for power, my lord."

Vladeran smiled approvingly.

"Exactly, Landu. And my soldiers too shall swat our enemies like flies. A girl and a boy lead an army, even a Helgra girl? Mere children. It's a silly dream."

But a new fear grabbed at Lord Vladeran.

"News of Alina, Landu, and this Helgra rising. It reaches the palace already?"

Landu shook his head.

"Not yet, my lord. It's spoken of in the countryside now, like a dark fable, but here there are only distant rumours, dismissed as mere fancy. As stories."

"Very well," said Vladeran. "You may leave."

Landu nodded and led his men from the room, and Vladeran did not notice the tapestry over the secret stairs stir.

"So, Cascu," said Vladeran, when they were gone, "your reward."

He strode over to a chest and, opening it, drew out a heavy bag of gold. Much heavier than the one Catalin had carried.

"I must use your services more often," he said coldly, throwing it to the Helgra traitor, "if you're so willing to betray your own people. Your own family." Vladeran was looking at Cascu with amusement.

"My people are superstitious fools," said Cascu with a scornful snort, as he caught the gold and weighed it in his hands, "with no learning and even less thought. They believe in fables and dreams, and the blind wonderings of . . . of a man who was strong once, but who has grown weak and old."

"It's strange that you talk so coldly of superstition, Cascu," whispered Vladeran, "when it was you that taught me the Helgra art of mixing blood with water to summon visions of the wolf. Taught me the words. When I sought out the truth of what had happened to Elu."

"Taught you?" said Cascu, raising an eyebrow. "I told you something of the silly stories I'd been told as a little boy, my lord, nothing more."

Vladeran smiled knowingly. He was holding his scarred hand in its glove. It now had many cuts across the palm.

"You don't believe in the power?"

"Of course not, my lord. Too long my people have sweated in superstition and ignorance, and I will trust to the reality of power and of gold," answered Cascu, wondering why Vladeran was looking at him so strangely, "and take my rightful place in the world."

"There's plenty more gold where that came from, Cascu," said Vladeran.

The Helgra stepped forwards.

"You're not frightened then, my lord?"

Vladeran looked back at him.

"Come with me," he said suddenly, striding over to the corner of the room. He led Cascu to a window, and they looked out onto a field beside the palace that ran far along the edge of a great river, which protected it from the plain beyond. There Cascu saw hundreds and hundreds of heavily armoured soldiers with bright new weapons. Vladeran's army was in training.

"I raised them to fight the Turk," whispered Vladeran with satisfaction, "but now they shall crush the Helgra. But come, we were speaking of gold."

"It's not even gold that I truly seek, my lord."

"No? Then tell me. Perhaps, if it's in my means—"

"I seek my rightful place, my lord, as Helgra elder. No more."

Vladeran turned and smiled.

"Ah yes, and it shall be so. A younger brother shall step up indeed."

Vladeran was thinking that after he had finished with them, there would be no Helgra left alive for Cascu to command at all, and the first death would be this Helgra woman.

"But first I would prove my strength and loyalty to you," said Cascu. "In your palace, my lord, as captain of the Shield Guard. I know the place lies open."

Vladeran looked at him doubtfully, thinking of Vlascan's death.

"You would take the oaths of the New Order, Helgra?"

"I would."

"The place is open indeed, with Vlascan gone, though Landu has his eyes on it, and he is loyal and strong."

Vladeran paused, weighing the benefits and possibilities in his clever mind.

"Very well then. But you must earn this honour, first."

"Earn it? Have I not already—"

"My soldiers shall prepare to meet these rebels, Cascu, and my spies ride out again, but you alone are Helgra, and so may walk freely amongst them still. Go back to them now and get to her, Cascu, somehow."

"They allow no weapon in her presence, as I said. All are searched. For many come to marvel at the storytellers. They think it is magic."

"Then use your mind, damn it. I want to know all they do."

Vladeran was thinking not of Alina suddenly, but of the wolf.

"Then I shall kill her, my lord?" said Cascu.

"No." Vladeran hesitated. "Now the Helgra rise, I've a better plan. Bring her to me somehow, Cascu, and in their eagerness to free her the Helgra shall walk straight into my trap. If you do so, you'll have your heart's desire."

Cascu paused and then he nodded.

"And Cascu. Any that speak of it must die. It must not be rumoured abroad that Alina Sculcuvant has returned from the dead, to seek vengeance."

• • •

"They have returned?" asked the man with the kingly bearing, in that throne room far away. The man who, like the mythical Guardian, kept his identity a secret. The leader of the Order of the Griffin. The armoured knight he had addressed before was in front of him again in the great hall.

"Yes, but found nothing."

The man bowed his head in the chair.

"But you believe the little girl's story?"

"Yes."

There was silence.

"What will you do?" asked the knight respectfully.

"Do what I should have done long ago. Set out."

"Don't blame yourself. The wound was very deep, even when you came."

The leader of the Order felt a wound now, but in his heart.

"Yes. And I've worked hard and long to sit where I do. Yet what use is my power if . . ."

He paused and shook his head bitterly.

"Justice means nothing in the land beyond the forest," he whispered, "and men set their eyes only on gold and war, thinking them an end in themselves."

"Lord Vladeran," said the knight, and his master grasped the arm of his throne. "He grows worse by the day. Vladeran breaks all our laws now. He's as bad as Draculea. And both are of the Order. Or were."

The man in the throne looked up, and his eyes glittered angrily.

"Since King Sigismund's death our Order has fallen into neglect," he said sadly. "Men, with their dreams and madness and fear, turn it to things dark and occult, as they always do when they feel powerless themselves. They think of the Griffin as a beast, and do not know what an ancient symbol it is. A symbol of sleeping power, that always guarded the lands beyond the forest."

"Still, I ask. What will you do?"

It sounded like a rebuke, and there was guilt in his master's eyes.

"For too long the Griffin has been eating its own tail," he answered.

"You shall summon the Order then? With so much fighting it will take time indeed for them to gather."

"Yes, but the Griffin's claws have wings," came the voice from the throne. "Summon them indeed. Send out secret word. The Griffin must awake."

PART THREE

THE PRESENT

NINETEEN

THE SALMON

As Fell ran, the humans and Alina WovenWord seemed to recede in his mind, and the wolf's thoughts turned more and more to Huttser. Would he be in time to reach his father and speak with him, before he went to the Red Meadow?

Fell thought of Morgra as he wondered, and it suddenly made him glad to have left his friend, for he knew that while he was away from Alina, at least she would be safe from his anger, and the vision the Sight had shown him.

He had seen her death at his teeth, and Fell wished to protect her, to protect nature too perhaps, although what that really meant he could not fathom. But he feared that every moment he was with her he was a danger to her.

Yet Fell felt the pain of separation from Alina like an ache in his mind. For it was as if it was only with her that Fell's mind opened to the full powers of the Sight. *Why?* he asked himself. Because the storyteller, because all humans, were further along in their journey than most of the uncomprehending Lera? At Alina's side Fell felt connected to something even deeper than the wild instincts of the wolf; he felt connected to the whole world.

He climbed into the mountains and plunged down into deep

wooded valleys. He was alone again, but he did not feel so alone now, for at least Fell had a purpose. He knew the valley his brother Kar and the Vengerid had spoken of, and it was not too far, though there was no time to delay.

Day and night he ran, using the eyes of the wolf to see in the dark, as Catalin worked in the forge, and Alina began to train the Helgra at balance and swordplay, and they wandered the hills collecting their antlers and listening to Catalin's and Alina's stories. At last the wolf reached the Great Waterfall. It fell in a mighty cataract, nearly a hundred feet down the side of the mountain, and it sang in Fell's ears like a glorious cry. He felt the air on his fur like a great wind, and saw sunlight broken into a seemingly endless ribbon of colour around the cataract's churning waters.

The rich, green mouth of the valley, where he knew his parents were, lay beyond the falls and the river, and Fell felt nervous at the thought of seeing them again. But on he hurried along the river, which now began to fall in dangerous rapids down the slopes. Fell already knew a place to cross lower down, where seven great boulders made a kind of bridge through the water, and soon he had sprung onto the first, as fearfully as ever, now he was so close to water again.

At his side was a smaller waterfall, or at least a drop of some twenty feet, where the river banked steeply, creating a kind of curtain of fast-flowing water, and as Fell sprang onto the second boulder, he froze. Two faces had appeared in the river, fine young Alpha wolves. Their muzzles were strong and proud, and Fell recognised them immediately. It was Huttser and Palla. The Sight was showing him the past. They seemed to look back imploringly at him, but suddenly the image of a huge wolf was behind them, with a great streak of silver down his back, and he was snarling angrily. It was Jalgan. Fell felt a jolt of fear, but something silver flashed in the side of his vision, and the images disappeared. With a great splash the shape came again, bursting out of the river, flying straight towards that curtain of water.

It was a huge salmon, and for a moment it seemed held suspended there, as its quivering body fought to carry it upwards against the current. But the salmon could not make it over the top of the falls, and at last it was swept back down into the water below.

Fell had crossed to the third boulder when the fish jumped again and this time it fought even harder, dancing there for even longer. As Fell watched it, he thought he saw a dark recess in the rocks behind the water, but the salmon's efforts to climb the river were in vain and it fell back again. Fell was in the very middle of the boulder bridge, when the salmon tried a third time, and something vaguely irritating in its fruitless battle made him swing his head and growl angrily at it.

"What are you doing, foolish fish?" he snarled.

To Fell's amazement the salmon answered him, and its voice seemed to come not from the salmon alone, but from the whole river, echoing around the wolf like the Great Waterfall upstream.

"Doing, wolf? I'm going home."

"Home?"

"Home to the river that made me, home to the waters that gave

me," sang the struggling salmon. *"Never be free, turn from the Sea. Fighting to sporn, dead by the morn."*

"But why do you fight so hard, fish?" growled the wolf.

"Because I must," sang the salmon, *"because I can. It's the pattern of all I am. But if you could only help me, I would tell you the secret of the whole world."*

The salmon fell backwards again with an even bigger splash, and Fell stared deep into the waters, suddenly aching to know. There was no possible way that a wolf could help a salmon, and no madder idea either, yet Fell wanted to help it indeed, and as he looked on wonderingly, he saw his own young features peering back at him.

With a splash the salmon came again, bursting out of the water with its splendid body.

"Tell me the secret, O Great Salmon, I beg of you," cried the wolf, "even if I may not aid you."

"And because you treat me with such respect I shall," answered the leaping salmon. *"The secret is that nothing knows, the secret is that all life flows, the secret is that thoughts and hearts are different beings, split apart."*

The whole river seemed to be singing now around the wolf's quivering ears.

"And though we change in skin and bone, each being has its truth alone, while dreams and wondering take you far, accept yourself in what you are, there comes the time when close to home, your self must please itself alone, then sing beneath the lovely sky, the earth asks simply that you try."

The salmon fell back again, exhausted by its fight and its strange song, and a groan seemed to come up from the water.

"But for me it's over, wolf," cried the river bitterly. "I cannot make it. I'm too tired."

The voice seemed to be sinking deeper and deeper, and Fell sensed that the poor salmon was floating downwards into the murky, silent depths, and suddenly he gave a great growl.

"No, salmon," he snarled furiously, "don't give up yet. Try. One more time."

"I cannot. My heart is too tired. I've seen the great world. I've swum through its mysteries. I've known its wondrous beauty, and its terrible ugliness. I've lost my own to predator and to hook."

At this Fell growled at it angrily and it spoke again.

"You've been with man, have you not, wolf?" asked the salmon.

"Yes, fish."

"Man, who thinks his mind knows everything. But what does man know of the great blue whale, moaning in the belly of the sea, or the flaring squid that show their anger and fear in their red skins, yet turn blue when you stroke them gently with your tail? Man cares only for himself, in his fear and hate."

The voice was fading, and Fell suddenly felt guilty at having protected Alina.

"Fight, by Fenris," he growled. "Fight."

"No more fight, wolf, not even by the great fish god Carpan. Too much fighting. I go to the greatest sea."

"But what you are," cried Fell, hardly knowing where the

thoughts were coming from, "all you know and all you've seen will be lost. Unless you continue now. Unless you pass that on to the future."

"The future?" came the voice sadly, and it sounded closer to Fell. "And do we really pass anything on to the future, except mirrors of ourselves? What if the future is as painful as the past?"

"That we can never know," answered the wolf angrily. "That's for the future. But what we can know is the importance of what we owe to the present. Here and now, and nowhere else. For nothing else exists, except in our minds. What we owe to ourselves, and to those we're bound to. And we can at least hope to make a better future, for everything. You sang the song. Told me the secret. So do it now. Try."

There was silence, except for the churning waters, and in his mind's eye Fell saw the once graceful salmon falling in the depths, turning on its side and sinking to the muddy river bottom. Its shining scales failing, its skin beginning to break apart like broken leaves, and the tiny creatures of the waters starting to take it for their own struggle. Fell's great black tail came down sadly. *Death,* whispered his darkening thoughts. *There is nothing but death.*

Suddenly the surface of the water erupted and Fell's heart soared, as the salmon came bursting from the river for the final time. It's jump was much higher this time, and it almost cleared the rapid. But still it hovered on the very edge, as if on a precipice, as if on the precipice of being that Larka herself had faced on a bridge up at Harja, when she had jumped to safety and, for a moment, she might have fallen or might have made it.

In that moment it had been as if the very thoughts of those that watched her, that followed her story, could have affected the outcome. As if that is always true, of everything that lives. That everything that exists, exists within its element, and so we all both influence and reflect one another all the time. The great interconnectedness of things.

Fell gave a great growl.

"Yes," he cried, "yes."

The very energy of Fell's cry, the will to help the thing, seemed to give the salmon that last bit of strength, as though the unseen movement of the atoms in the air and water had made the difference, and it cleared the lip of the falls and was gone. Moving like a current itself, back to where its parents, themselves made and driven by their own mysterious, searching natures, had spawned it. Many had fallen in that race. Many would fall again. But this creature, touched by Fell's strange journey, would continue for long enough to remake just a tiny part of the extraordinary, beautiful world.

Fell himself was already on the far side of the bank, racing towards the valley where his father might have reached the end of his own journey. As he went, he looked up and saw a huge group of starlings, which had been migrating from the Great Delta that formed a part of these strange lands to the south, and he stopped to watch them.

Evening was coming now, and as the lovely skies blushed purple, he saw the myriad birds darting and diving through the air, moving not as one, but like a great shoal of fish, a turning mass of black. Left and right the flock turned in the air, and up and down, swirling and winding and spiralling, like the currents of the river where Fell had seen the salmon, and it suddenly seemed to Fell the most beautiful sight he had ever seen.

Was it because, unlike the Kerl, these winged creatures were moving together, he wondered, as though some mind were directing them? And how did that great cloud of birds, each one a separate individual, form such a perfect organism? It seemed so purposeful, yet so instinctive, so beautiful and free. But had not each one somehow given up their wills to the whole?

Fell had will, and had learnt so much during his lone travelling. Yet all this knowledge, all this experience hurt him too. In that moment Fell wanted to be a part of that flock, to move unconsciously through that wondrous element, like the rivers that race to the seas, and the great waves that crash against the shores of the world.

Fell almost thought he heard a voice on the air, and suddenly he knew another great secret. Perhaps it was the Sight, or perhaps it was all he had seen and done. The secret was that Fell knew more than these birds and saw further, precisely because he had pulled away from the rhythms of nature and from the cycles that the world itself was caught up in.

Fell thought of man and of woman, and of their great journey through the world. So often with their wooden dens, and their weapons and their tools, they did all they could to separate themselves from nature. With their strange words too. Man sought to become more and more individual, and his very purpose, his mind's purpose, seemed to be to manipulate the world about him, to name it and conjure it with his language and dominate it. And so he did, and so he learnt more and became more.

But in the end, thought Fell sadly, was that knowledge and that way of seeing any more useful to man? Did it make him any happier, especially if he threatened to destroy all, as the Lera had seen in the vision? Like the Lera, man faced the same struggle as all living organisms, and in the end he too had to face his own death.

Dawn was breaking, grey and heavy, as Fell crested the rise of a hill and came down into the first valley beyond the Great Waterfall. It was edged by tall trees on every side, and the sward of green was thick with the summer. Fell saw Kar first, sitting with two large male wolves in the sunshine and telling them a story, searching through its words as he spoke, to find its meaning and its purpose. Fell padded up behind them and heard a little of the strange tale.

"And it was long ago," Kar was saying, "when Tor and Fenris themselves still walked the world and a beautiful Drappa, with a tail like white clouds and eyes of green gold, lived in a wondrous valley, where the birds sang all day long and no harm ever came to trouble the Varg or the Lera. So gentle and kind was this Drappa that even the butterflies loved her. But a creature lived in a cave on the mountain, and this beast was so angry and lonely that all kept away from him, for they feared him and said that Barl had cast a spell on him. So ferocious and ugly was he that he might have had human shape. Indeed, when he looked in the rivers and streams, he saw there such a terrible reflection that he appeared to be a monster, and thought that none could love him."

Kar paused, for he was trying to remember a story told to him when he had only been a cub himself.

"Then one sun the monster stole the beautiful, gentle Drappa away and kept her in his cave. The lovely she-wolf was so appalled with the Varg's human appearance that she hated him, while the monster would go down into the fields and terrify all the Lera, to keep them away from his prize. He brought the Drappa food and soft branches to sleep on though, and was so tender and caring around her that she could not believe his human shape was real. She realised that this form was not his at all, but the shadow of a spell, and that he was only angry because he was frightened and in pain. Then suddenly the Drappa knew that she loved him, and Barl's spell was lifted and there stood the most wonderful grey Dragga."

"It's a good old story, brother."

"Fell!" cried Kar, seeing the black wolf. "Palla said you'd come."

Kar sprang up and padded towards him, wagging his tail.

"Huttser?" whispered Fell. "Has . . . ?"

"He lives, Fell," answered Kar, swinging his head down the valley, "and Jalgan has not come. Down there, Fell, in a cave by the creek. Palla tends to him. There's time."

Fell relaxed a little. The two other males, as big as Fell, but without his form, moulded by experience and effort, were staring at him suspiciously.

"Come. Don't you recognise your elder brother Fell?" said Kar. "Greet him, Khaz. Give him our blessings, Skop. He's welcome beyond these boundaries, with a blessing or not."

Khaz and Skop, thought Fell with amazement, remembering the tiny little cubs that he had seen all those years ago. How they had grown and changed—from those little moving bundles of fur—as all things change. How fine they looked now, these males of five years old.

Khaz and Skop had paused, completely unable to speak, and Fell realised that their noses were cocked towards him warily, their senses hard at work, questioning him with their dimmer understandings.

"It's the scent of man," said Fell calmly.

"Then it's true," cried Skop, looking at his elder brother rather aggressively, "all they say of you."

"That you're a living legend, he means, brother," said Khaz more softly, and he wagged his tail too. Fell smiled at the wondering wolves.

"A legend?" he answered, with a chuckling growl. "Oh, I hardly think so, Khaz. And the thing about legends, Skop, is that they come to be so much more than the truth, don't they? Because we all need legends, for good and bad, just as we all need to believe . . . in something."

Skop's eyes flickered.

"But you have the Sight, brother?"

"Oh, yes, Skop. Do you think I'd be fooling with humans if I didn't?"

"And you'll use it, won't you, to challenge Jalgan yourself, then fight off the Vengerid if they come?" said Khaz suddenly, wagging his tail eagerly. "Father can't face this challenge now."

"Hush, now, Khaz," growled Kar, looking at him reproachfully. "Your elder brother's tired and he wants to see . . ."

Fell had already turned his head. Three she-wolves were racing towards them across the valley. Fell's heart quickened strangely as he recognised Tarlar, but it was the wolf at Tarlar's side that had caught his interest now.

She was very beautiful, the same age as Skop and Khaz, and her eyes flashed brilliantly. The third wolf was also a fine Varg, but not as fast as the other two. The first two wolves approached. Tarlar was as keen to greet Fell as he was her, but it was some delicacy in her that made her hang back awhile, and let her companion speak first.

"We were hunting, brother, when we saw you from across the hill," said the beautiful she-wolf boldly. "Mother knows of it already. We ran to tell her."

"Larka?" whispered Fell, feeling very strange to speak the name she had been given after his first sister, but looking her up and down proudly. At five she was almost as large as his Larka had been, but her coat was just a normal, healthy grey instead of white.

"It's good to see you again," he whispered.

"Again?" said Larka cheerfully. "Well, I don't remember you at all, I'm afraid, brother, although I knew it was you from the colour of your coat. But I've heard so much about you, and we make up stories too, don't we, Kipcha? About *you*."

The third she-wolf had come alongside too, wagging her bushy tail.

"Yes, we do," said Kipcha, "many, many stories."

"All bad?" asked Fell a little sadly.

"Of course not, Fell," answered Larka warmly. "We often make you the hero."

"Not always, though," added Kipcha, not looking the slightest bit embarrassed. "I mean, heroes can be so dull, can't they?"

Kipcha was looking openly at her elder brother, and Fell's eyes smiled.

"Yes, I suppose they can."

"And heroes and legends are not quite real, are they?" said Larka. "Not real flesh and blood like us."

"But you need them of course," said Kipcha, "for sometimes when we think of Jalgan we need someone really savage and brave in our thoughts to fight him," she added, looking suddenly fierce. "We know what stories are for."

"Oh, you do?" said Fell, feeling surprised at the wisdom of the young, but oddly reassured.

"Your stories get so dark though, sisters," said Khaz suddenly, shaking his head disapprovingly.

"Perhaps because the times seem to be so dark again, Khaz," said Larka sharply, "and shouldn't we tell the truth?"

"When times are dark, we should tell more cheerful stories," said Khaz.

"Perhaps we should." Larka turned to Fell and added warmly, "But you're very welcome here, brother."

"I am, am I?" Fell growled, with a smile. "You give me Larka's Blessing, do you?"

"Don't tease me, brother," said Larka, "We all agreed not to use that term here. Not often anyway. I'm Larka now, am I not, and not some fable. And we're a real family. As difficult as those can be."

Larka dropped her eyes.

"I'm not saying that she . . . that our sister was just a fable," she went on. "We're so proud of what she did. What you all did for us. But . . ."

"But?" whispered Fell.

"But when parents tell stories what should they say to their children? Do you think they should fill them with a courage they can't live up to, or an idealism about the world that might simply break their hearts in the end? Shouldn't they just tell them the truth, that they should try to love each other and be happy?"

"Yes," whispered Fell. "Perhaps they should."

"Besides, it was in the past, and I'll live my life as I see fit."

Fell looked at Larka in admiration, so confident and wise was she. He realised that what he had reached for by the river was true, and that was what really mattered. What was here and now.

"Good for you," he said warmly.

"Besides, to give Larka's Blessing makes Mother so sad. All she thinks of now is the past."

Fell raised his head, and his ears came forwards. His mother, Palla, was there now with his father, Huttser. Somewhere nearby.

"It's time," he said, looking nervously at Kar.

"Come then, Fell, I'll show the way."

They all ran together, the seven of them, like a bonded wolf pack, with Fell and Kar leading the group. Tarlar made sure

376

that the other wolves hung back, as they mounted a slope and rose up through the trees towards a low cave, beside a mountain stream. Fell stopped as soon as they reached the edge of the trees for there, in front of the cave mouth, was an old grey she-wolf, lying on her paws and lapping weakly at the stream.

"Go on, Fell," whispered Kar kindly, "we'll all talk together later."

Fell nodded, and as he padded forwards, Kar and the others turned away.

"Mother," Fell wanted to say as he stopped in front of the stream, but something suddenly choked in his voice. He just stood there trembling. The old she-wolf had caught a scent though, and looked up. Or might have looked, if Fell hadn't seen that Palla's old eyes were watery and filmy with cataracts. She wasn't blind, but her sight was so dim that although she knew immediately by its shape that a wolf was standing before her, she couldn't make out its features.

If his mother's eyes shocked Fell, almost more shocking was that Palla looked so old. In his memories and dreams he had always seen Palla as she had been when he left the pack. Tired and hurt by Larka's death, and all that had happened perhaps, but still a relatively young wolf. But now the hair around her beautiful muzzle was almost entirely white and she looked so thin and weak. She was older than any she-wolf to live in the lands beyond the forest—thirteen long, adventurous years. Fell suddenly realised how the world always changes around us, often before we even know it.

"Kar, is that you, Kar?"

"No, Mother, it's me."

Palla had risen and she was suddenly shaking.

"Fell?" she whispered. "Can it really be you, my Fell? They said you had come."

"Yes, Mother, it's Fell."

Fell wanted to run towards her, but something still held him back. A delicacy.

"Oh, Fell, it's so good to hear your voice again, and yes, though my eyes are weak, to see you once more."

Palla's eyes were straining, but she could see now that it was true. Suddenly Fell leapt forwards through the water and he was in front of her, taking in her scent, changed with age, and touching her dry nose with his.

"Dear Fell," she whispered, "you fill my old heart with joy. I thought I might go to Tor and Fenris without ever setting eyes on you again. Or hearing your song once more. That song that you sang to us from the mountain when you went, five long years ago. It so hurt my heart to hear it. It was so pained and full of longing."

"Oh, Mother."

"But I've never blamed you for going away, Fell. Not once. I knew you had your own path, and your own questions."

"And you had the new cubs too," whispered Fell.

"Ah yes. The joy of my heart. They're all strong and healthy. Though I worry for Khaz, sometimes. He's so thoughtful and, well, gentle."

"Every pack has its Sikla," whispered Fell, "if we should call them that."

"He's the brightest of all of us, and the kindest," said Palla proudly. "He just doesn't like fighting very much. But my darling Fell, tell me how you are."

"I'm well, Mother. I've been on a strange journey."

"Yes. As have we all. Life is a strange place indeed, isn't it? Whether we're touched by the Sight or not. So full of wonder and mystery, of beauty, yet so full of struggle and sorrow too. Of cruelty. Nature's cruelty."

Palla shook her head.

"Or is it cruel? I thought it bitterly cruel when my eyes began to go. Stealing away visions of so much colour from me. And yet they've lasted me more years than most wolves. I looked around me as the darkness crowded in, and realised that everything that is suffers in the same way. Not because anything makes it suffer, although that happens too, but because we all bloom and then fade. We're not Varg, Fell, not wolves at all. We're plants and trees, leaves and flowers. Like them, we all have our seasons."

"Yes, Mother."

"We bloom and then we fade," sighed the old she-wolf. "And I've bloomed indeed. But now my mind turns backwards more and more to the past. It fills me with sadness, for I wish it had not been so dark sometimes. Dear Larka. I think of her often."

"And I."

"But she comes to me in dreams."

Fell looked up and thought of that voice on the wind.

"Or I think they're dreams. And she's always smiling. That makes me feel much better, and gives me a courage too. Beyond even despair."

Fell's heart ached.

"Yet as I look back, and remember it all, I still wonder whether it all had any meaning, Fell. Or whether it's all simply as it is. Have you found a meaning to it?"

Fell cocked his head, but he could not answer, although he thought of Ottol and the salmon.

"And I wonder more and more too if there is anything up there." Palla had raised her old eyes to the heavens. "If the wolf gods Tor and Fenris are there at all. Or only lovely stories."

Not always so lovely, thought Fell, and he was going to speak, but suddenly there was a low growl from inside the cave.

"Palla. Where are you, Drappa?"

"Huttser," whispered Fell.

"He's bad today," said Palla sadly. "The wound is deep. He did not sleep all night. I must go to—"

"No, Mother. Let me."

"But Fell. I haven't told him yet of your return. He's too proud to ever have called on your help."

"Then I will tell him myself."

Fell padded forwards apprehensively, and as he did so the sun emerged from behind a cloud and illuminated the stone recess. He could already see his father, lying at the back of the cave. Huttser looked much stronger than Palla, in form at least. Although now fourteen, he was nearly the Dragga that Fell had always known, although his deeply greying head was slumped on his paws. Fell's feelings were suddenly confused, for he remembered a day long ago when his father, so strong and powerful, had grabbed him by the scruff of his neck and made him fearful and angry and resentful.

"Palla. Hurry up, will you?"

"It's me, Father."

Old Huttser had raised his head and was looking at his son in astonishment, for his eyes and ears were almost as strong as ever.

"Am I dreaming? It can't be."

Huttser was trying to get up, but he was too weak for the effort. Fell could see now the livid wound across his flank that was caked with blood, and Huttser slumped again.

"It *is* you, Fell. You're well, I see. I always knew that you were strong like your father."

"Yes, Father."

"Stronger than me now. Those damned Vengerid and that cur Jalgan, challenging all the Varg to fight him. His curs wouldn't have done this if they hadn't crept up on us. I may be old—sometimes I wonder at it—but there's fight in me yet. I've challenged him."

"There was always fight in you," whispered Fell, even a little reproachfully. "You are the Dragga, Father."

"Yes, quite right. And so I must fight, and lead, and protect you all. Hunt when the game is slow, scavenge when it's fast, mark the boundaries, keep out intruders, raise spirits, tell stories. Look out for the little ones, for dear, clever Larka and brave little Fell. And that new cub, Kar. He's not mine, but he's all right. Palla wants to help him very much, but you know what Drappas are like."

Fell could see that Huttser's thoughts were rambling, locked in the past, and that his father was in great pain. He was pierced by a pang of love for the old Dragga.

"We must be careful, you know. There's so much that faces a wolf pack in the wild. And all these silly rumours and legends, about a stolen human and that snake Morgra, and the stupid Sight."

Huttser was looking straight at Fell, but he wasn't talking to him at all, but to one of the Betas in his pack, long ago. Fell wondered suddenly if that isn't all we really are, our thoughts and dreams and memories. If it was so, then hadn't we a duty to make our memories the best they could be?

"Father, it's me. Fell. Your son."

"Do you think I've lost my wits?" growled Huttser angrily, breaking from his trance. "Of course it's you, Fell. And a long time it's been too. The years seem strangely out of shape."

Huttser growled again.

"But you're here now, that's what counts, and there's work to be done. This damned Jalgan has to be beaten. He wants that Drappa Tarlar, and I must say if I were a younger wolf I . . . Don't tell your mother I said it. But these Vengerid respect nothing at all. I must patrol again."

Fell was glad to see his father suddenly restored, and yet he was bitterly sad too that Huttser did not realise the nature of his own injury. It was fatal.

"And I'm glad to see how strong you've grown," growled Huttser. "I always knew you had my strength in you."

Fell felt very strange as he said it. He wanted to say, *"No, Father, I am not you."*

"Yes, Father," he said.

"It does my heart good to see you, Fell. Because you must help us."

Fell stepped forwards.

"Not *must*, Father," he found himself saying suddenly.

Huttser growled.

"Then why on earth are you here, damn it?"

Fell's voice choked. He did not say, "I am *here* to say good-bye."

"I mean that I'll help you if I choose to help you," he answered steadily. "Of my own free will."

Huttser growled again.

"Oh, don't talk rubbish. You'll do as you're told. You're of the pack, are you not, and I'm your father."

Fell was furious with his father in that moment for talking to him as if he were still a little cub, but because of something else too. Huttser had often talked to him of duty and of responsibility, so dutiful was he to his own family and his pack. But why do adults, why do parents not realise that children desperately wish to do things not so much out of duty, but out of love? And you can't force anything to love anything else against its nature. Not with talk of family or pack, not with talk of greater borders, or the truths or lies of Tor and Fenris.

Fell felt a deep pang in him now as he looked at Huttser, for he knew that all his life his father had lived with words like "must" on his tongue, when he, like everything else, craved love too. Well, Fell had come, not out of duty, but out of love.

"I'll help you, Father."

"Of course you will. Well done, Fell. And we must plan. You and I together. Father and son. It'll be a bitter fight, and if I fail the challenge, the Vengerid will try for Tarlar. But your claws are sharp and teeth strong."

"And I've another weapon," whispered Fell. "The Sight."

Huttser's eyes clouded and he growled uncomfortably. Fell remembered how, for so long, such a practical and rational wolf as Huttser had dismissed any talk of the Sight. How he had argued with Palla, and forbidden any mention of it, until the truths of their journey had forced it on them all.

Huttser had already closed his eyes, and laid down his old head again, and Fell turned sadly back towards the cave mouth, but as the sun shone on his muzzle he heard Huttser behind him.

"Fell. It is good to see you again."

"Thank you, Father. It's good to see you too."

Palla stood staring at her son as he emerged again into the day, and her failing eyes were full of pain and worry.

"I don't know what I will do when he's gone," she whispered.

"Hush, Mother."

"I love him so, Fell. Oh, he can be foolish and unreasonable at times. Angry and irritable, now more so than ever. But he's always been strong and true. But perhaps I must bear it. They say the Drappa often outlives the Dragga."

Palla shook her old head.

"For all your bold talk of fighting and strength and courage, it's we females that must birth the cubs in the den, and suckle them at our bellies. Must hunt and scavenge too, and direct the pack when it goes astray. So nature makes us strong. Stronger even than Draggas."

"I'm sorry, Mother. So sorry."

There was nothing else to say.

"When he goes, I don't think I want to be in the world anymore," said Palla, more in weariness than sorrow.

"Hush, Mother."

"It's true. Why should I? What is there for me? You are fine. The cubs are fully grown now and will be fine too, and it is high time they found their own packs. I think I would walk with your father through the Red Meadow, towards the Wolf Trail."

"Mother, please don't say it."

"Fell," whispered Palla suddenly, "I know the Sight has brought you much trouble, but Larka said that it has a power to heal."

Fell's eyes flickered. "So it's said. I think it has kept me young."

"Try to use it then, Fell, to help your father."

Fell felt strangely at a loss. He did not know how to use the Sight to heal.

"Yes."

Even with her dim eyesight Palla could see that something was wrong.

"What is it, Fell?"

"Mother," growled Fell sadly, "I've had dark dreams. More than dreams. Visions."

"Like the terrible vision we all saw on the mountain?"

"Something even worse. I've been travelling with a human. A girl."

Palla looked shocked, but she nodded as wisely as she could.

"And though I care for her, the Sight shows me the future. That I'll kill her. But there's something else, Mother. In these visions a wolf speaks to me. A she-wolf."

Palla's ears had come forwards suspiciously and Fell hesitated.

"Morgra," he said.

"Morgra!"

Palla was shaking furiously at the mention of her half sister, and the old Drappa had begun to growl. The lips on her muzzle were curling up, and Fell suddenly remembered her in her prime, that night of a terrible thunderstorm, when she had threatened to kill Morgra if she did not leave her cubs alone.

"Morgra alive? How can this be? We saw her death."

"Not alive, Mother," said Fell. "Calm yourself. But her spirit seems to live on. She calls to me with the Sight."

"Seems to live on?"

"She talks from the Red Meadow, through a human connected to this girl that I've journeyed with. And the boy child we returned to the village."

"She's evil, Fell. Beware her. Will this legend never be finished?"

"I fight with her," said Fell. "But evil? Yes, she's evil. And yet, the injustice that was done to her, when she was unjustly accused."

Palla had dropped her misty eyes now.

"I know it," she whispered. "And injustice spreads injustice. I often wonder if Huttser and I had taken her into the pack that day, would any of it have happened? Would Larka still be alive? And as for the Red Meadow, they say it's a preparation for what lies beyond. That Varg may linger there, if they are somehow bound to this world, by anger or pain or love."

"Or hate," growled Fell sadly.

HUTTSER AND PALLA

F or many suns Fell hunted for Huttser, and in the cave his father ate fresh red meat. The others gathered round Palla, waiting, and there was a strange expectation in the air as the days passed. Fell sat with Huttser as he fed, and as he watched the tired old Dragga try his weakened teeth on the flesh, Fell closed his eyes and tried to use the Sight to help him.

Fell sensed or hoped that the connection was doing his father some good, moving energy about his body, yet he felt something else even more powerfully as they lay there. That his father Huttser was dying.

He could sense that the spirit inside Huttser was growing very weak. Not just the wound, but nature itself was at work now, and Huttser was very old. The oldest Dragga in the lands beyond the forest. All things die, Fell realised, so perhaps the Sight could only aid living things to use their own strength, and if that natural strength itself was failing, perhaps not even the Sight could intervene.

But as two moons passed there was no sign of the Vengerid, and Huttser talked once more of Jalgan's challenge, of the younger wolves and of defending the pack. He talked like a true Dragga again and refused to accept what was happening to him.

"Father," whispered Fell one day. "Do you . . . do you believe that anything lies beyond the Red Meadow?"

"I don't know why you're talking like a foolish cub," said Huttser angrily. "The Vengerid threaten us and, when I'm better, we shall fight them side by side."

His son could see that Huttser didn't want to face the question, and Huttser suddenly gave a furious whimper from a bolt of pain from the infection that had gripped his side.

"Damn it."

Fell winced.

"I believe there must be something beyond, Father," Fell said softly, as Huttser settled again, although he thought of his failure to find the Guardian, and now he was lying. "I mean, if the Sight gives me the power it does, everything is stranger than we think."

As Fell said it, and almost felt it true, he could not say what it was he really believed in, even if he desperately wanted to give his father some consolation.

"Wolves like your father and I go straight to the Wolf Trail," said a soft voice suddenly, "to run forever with Tor and Fenris."

Fell swung his head and there was his mother, standing in the cave mouth.

"And they climb the skies and join those little lights in the heavens. It's nothing to fear."

Palla's very words had calmed Huttser's body, and made him relax again, and Fell was suddenly angry with himself. For all his searching and journeying, for all his struggles with the Sight, he had not had the wisdom, or the belief and certainty, to say such a thing to his father, when it was most needed. Fell was desperately glad that his mother had though.

Fell turned sadly and padded outside. He lay down by the stream in the moonlight and watched the waters gurgling and churning over the stones. As he looked, he calmed himself a little, and he thought that if he hadn't been so frightened of it, he would have always liked to live near the sound of water.

Fell shook his head. He no longer believed the Guardian existed, and it made the heavy weight of responsibility worse. He suddenly felt angry with life for throwing so many difficulties in his way, yet he was glad too that he was here at all. Glad of the responsibility.

"He's sleeping now," said a voice softly, behind him. "But he's bad today."

Palla lay down beside her son. He thought again how very old his mother looked.

"I'll sleep too. I'm so very tired, Fell."

Palla's beautiful old head was already on her front paws and her eyes were closed.

"Wake me, my dear, if he stirs, or needs anything. For I've always been at his side. Watch him for me."

"Yes, Mother. But can I get anything for you?"

Palla was already fast asleep. Fell lifted himself on his paws and looked down at her. She was breathing so faintly that Fell could hardly see her body stir, as though the spirit in her had become but a dream, or a memory itself, tying her but faintly to her own body.

"Rest, Mother," said Fell gently, "I'm here now."

Fell padded up the slope and laid his great black body down in the cave mouth, between his mother and father.

He slept fitfully that night, and it was in the early time, towards morning, after the fifth of human hours, that Fell suddenly flashed into consciousness. He got up immediately, and the wolf knew something was wrong.

Fell sprang into the cave and saw that Huttser had almost rolled onto his back. His body looked so feeble and old now, fully his fourteen years, that it was as if some force was sucking the life from him. Huttser was muttering to himself, as his tongue lolled from his mouth.

"Home. Take me home. I should be—"

"What is it, Father?" whispered Fell.

"I'm dying, Fell."

Fell knew it was not the time to lie, even to be kind.

"Yes, Father."

"Your mother, look after your—"

"You don't need to worry. Palla will be cared for."

"We've walked so long together, your mother and I. Hunted in the forests and mountains. Drank from the wild, fresh streams. Fought and laughed and cried. She's my blood mate. My . . ."

"Oh, Father."

"Meaningless," muttered the old wolf sadly. "It's all meaningless, isn't it? All our rages. All our battles and storms. For what? So we may become carrion, and feed the tiniest of beings. A bitter thing. And . . . And . . ."

"What is it?"

Fell's muzzle was straining forwards, and Huttser's voice was so faint that he could hardly hear him. He thought though that Huttser suddenly whispered, "I'm frightened, Fell."

Then Huttser's body flexed and the wolf was reaching out with his paw. It touched Fell's own, and Fell felt a new, unexpected force in Huttser, a renewed vigour, as if will itself was making him hold onto the world.

"Have I been all right, Fell? Have I done well in the world?"

"Yes, of course, Father."

"Your mother and I, did we argue too much?"

"Life can be a fight, Father. Draggas and Drappas argue. It is nature's way. Perhaps."

"And I'm a fighter."

Alina's word came into his mind at that moment—*a warrior*. He nodded.

"I am the Dragga," growled Huttser faintly.

"Yes, Father."

"Open, Fell." Huttser's body was struggling with pain on the earth floor. "Open like a flower."

They were the strangest words that Fell had ever heard, in that sad place by the stream, but Huttser's body was suddenly feeble again and broken. Fell bowed his head. He hated to see his father like this, with all his heart.

"Leave me, Fell. Go away."

"What do you mean, Father?" said Fell desperately.

"Leave."

Fell backed away. He suddenly thought of Palla, or any she-wolf, and how when they birthed in the den they always wanted to be alone. Was death like that too? Like the very beginning of life. Something you always had to do alone? As though it is life itself, and the living, that bind us to the world.

Fell stood there, his head bowed, for what seemed like an age, and when he looked up again he knew that Huttser was gone. His body had stopped moving altogether. Fell heard the fluttering of birds outside, and in the cave was nothing but emptiness.

He didn't know what he felt in that moment, for within himself he was partly glad that the horrible struggle was over. He had known it was coming, and known it had to be, that not even the Sight could do anything about it. Yet he could not comprehend it either.

As Fell looked at that body, once so alive and full of vigour, a wolf that had walked with him all his life, even as a Kerl, he felt as if something in the world had split apart. Light was coming outside, morning, but although the sky was blue and there was a brightness in the air, Fell felt a strange, slow darkness about him.

What is death really? he wondered. How can such a powerful, vivid, living being, and one that had marked Fell's whole life, just disappear? Just stop and go away. It was a question that only those near to death really understand. It seemed impossible.

Fell felt a deep sorrow inside himself then, and something else too. Guilt. With all his powers, with all the force of the Sight, Fell had not been able to heal Huttser. When his father had snapped at him too, he had almost wished him gone, and as he thought it, Fell suddenly had the most terrible feeling that he himself had killed his own father. Surely he could have done more. Surely he could have made it easier. *Am I wicked?* thought Fell. *Am I really wicked?*

Then came another feeling, like a lonely hunter: a resentment that Huttser had said nothing to Fell to wish his own son well, for the future. For we all have to face death, thought Fell angrily in that moment, because nothing can conquer that. Fell had needed something desperately from his father that had not been given, a blessing for his own hard journey and for his uncertain future.

As Fell stood in the cave the strangest feeling of all was that Huttser had not gone at all. Not that he was still in the cave, he wasn't, that place had an empty air, yet Huttser was still there, as real as ever, and where he was was in Fell's own mind.

Then the memories began to come, in such extraordinary detail that it was as if Fell were living these things again. Memories of his father when Fell was a cub, memories of hunting together, memories of being scolded, and of feeling safe at Huttser's side, memories of arguments and bitter quarrels and longed-for reconciliations. The past.

Fell padded over to Huttser's body, and as Huttser lay there, an unmoving carcass, he seemed stronger than he had seemed in the anguished throws of death. His muzzle was calm, his body no longer contorted with pain. It was as if that strength he had had in life had suddenly been given back to him. Huttser was restored. A warrior once more.

Fell turned from his father and padded slowly from the cave to wake Palla. He felt dizzy and sick, and although birds were singing and the sun was starting to shine brightly, it felt like a grey, gloomy day.

"Wake up, Mother. It's finished."

Fell was surprised that Palla didn't spring up with the news and rush to Huttser's side.

"Mother, this is important."

Fell's eyes opened in bewilderment. He could see now that Palla's body was as still and lifeless as Huttser's. The breath had only just left her tired form. Palla was dead too. Her heart had given out.

"Oh, Mother."

Fell felt like a tiny little cub, abandoned and alone.

"No, Palla. Not you as well."

"Fell," called a voice.

Kar was coming up the slope with the others, and they could see instantly that something was wrong. They rushed forwards.

"Is it Huttser, Fell?" said Kar.

Fell swung his head and his eyes flickered as he saw Tarlar and his younger brothers and sisters looking fearfully back at him.

"They've both gone."

The younger wolves stared at Palla, and all their tails came down in disbelief. Khaz whined, and Kipcha gave a low growl.

"I should have been here," she said bitterly.

"I must see Father," whispered Larka, looking towards the cave.

Fell knew that all of them, suddenly faced with this news,

were looking for him to say something bold and stirring, but Fell had nothing to say. He wanted to be alone. These were his family, yes, and yet he hardly knew them. Not even dear Kar.

"I'm so sorry, Fell," said Tarlar's soft, kindly voice. "May I do something for you?"

She alone did not seem overcome with the news.

"No, Tarlar. I . . . I must walk now. And think."

Fell sprang away. The black wolf ran like something hunted, sucking at the air, his mind feeling as if it were entering a dark dream. He wanted to be away again, away from everything.

For hours Fell ran, and the sun, burning with its unfeeling fire, millions of miles away in the heavens, began to sink in the skies, or rather the great, mysterious earth turned in space like a water droplet, and light began to dim and fade over the lands beyond the forest.

Fell was hardly aware of the ravishing landscape all around him, bursting with life and vigour. As he ran he thought of everything that had happened in his life. Of Huttser and Palla. Of Larka and Kar. Of the dark adventure that had marked his existence. But it was not as if he were seeing these things unfolding naturally before his eyes. Instead it was as if everything had been slowed down, as the action of cold works to slow water into ice.

Fell's powerful mind had fully entered the past, and now it was as if it were sucking him backwards, drawing him back in time itself, although Fell knew that none of these things he was seeing could he really touch or affect. Although he ran fast, his mind was inching along, like one stumbling through mud, or creeping through a freezing fog, so slowly that it was as if time itself might stop.

Huttser and Palla's powerful, vivid lives had simply come to a stop. Fell felt shadows flutter around him, like huge black birds, and it was as though the outside world, the grass and the rocks, the fields and mountains and the great, living trees, appeared through a dim, intangible film. There was a sickness in the wolf's stomach, as though he were turning inside himself and could no longer breathe.

Fell came to a small lake, and forgetful now of his own greatest fear, death by water, he stopped and stared into its reflecting mirror. He blinked as he did so. For the first time in his life he could hardly recognise himself at all. Or hardly cared. As Fell looked, he felt as if he were not looking at himself, but plunging through the water, back into his own thoughts, and into the past. Always the past. There was no longer any defineable barrier between himself and the world. Between the past and the present, and between his bleak, slow thoughts and reality.

Fell was lost in time and in space, and in that moment he felt as if he were going mad. A sparrow fluttered by, and Fell felt it move by him like a ghost. "Bird," he wanted to say. "Don't come near me now, bird, for I am not of life. My father, bird, and my mother, they're dead and gone. Forever. Will you howl with me?"

Because all living things fear death, because all of them fight with everything they are in order to avoid it, the sparrow sensed it immediately and its course through the air swerved far away from the strange lone wolf by the lake.

"That's right, bird," thought Fell bitterly. "Avoid me like a sickness. Like an evil."

Fell felt bitterness at life then and something deeper—fear. Why did death engender fear? Because death meant change, a change greater than we have ever known, and because death was indeed a mirror that made us see ourselves as never before. A mirror that we should cover, as people in olden days covered mirrors when someone died, for fear of an evil. For with all our care and pain for those who had gone, it was ourselves too we felt the agony for. Perhaps ourselves above all.

Fell wanted to shrug off these thoughts and feelings, but the wolf could no more do so than he could use the powers of the Sight to bring his mother and father back to life again. He suddenly thought of the story of Sita, and how she had been sent down by Tor and Fenris to suffer for the Varg. Of how she had been laughed at and reviled and killed, but had risen again after three suns. Because of the love of Tor and Fenris. Because there is no death.

Yet now the wolf knew the truth of it, as only those who experience life may really know. *So the story is a lie, as the Guardian is a lie,* thought Fell, *as there is no real magic in the world. We do die, as Huttser and Palla have just died.* Somehow that was stranger to Fell, or bleaker, than even Larka's death. Larka had struggled and fought with dark forces and the wicked actions of the Varg, and it had caused her end. But Huttser and Palla had gone for no reason except that life must end.

Try as he might to think clearly, or shrug away the darkness, Fell could not. For something was happening to him that, although he had no name for it, was as real as rock or branch or stone, and as inevitable as sadness is to joy. As much as Fell wanted it to stop, to think it all away, it was in his mind and his breath and his very veins. In his body too. The wolf was grieving.

Night had come as Fell found a clearing on the edge of the valley and lay down to rest his exhausted being. He felt sleep approach him like a welcome friend, and the terrible struggle of his mind began to ease, but as Fell lay there, once more his body started to twitch, and there was a face before his eyes. His aunt.

"Morgra."

"Yes, Fell, I'm with you. I've always been with you."

"What do you want, Morgra?" growled the angry wolf.

"To give you solace, for I know they've gone. My sister and her Dragga."

"Yes, Morgra. Are they with you now in the Red Meadow?"

"I sense they're here," answered Fell's aunt, "in this place of dream and memory, before the final journey. But the number of Varg here are legion and it is to the living that I speak now."

"Speak of what?"

"Of death and loss. Of pain and anguish. Of meaninglessness."

"Leave me, Morgra. I'm so tired."

"Then why resist me, my friend? I helped you once. Let me help you again, and stand at your side and howl with you into the shadows."

Fell's weary, sorrowful thoughts could hardly resist the terrible she-wolf, and he was glad to have someone, anyone, there with him. Not to be alone.

"I used the Summoning Howl once, Fell," said Morgra. "The cry that sounds like no other, to bring the spectres from the Red Meadow to fight at the Balkar's side. As your sister Larka used it to journey herself to the meadow and speak with the dead, or the memories of the dead." Fell remembered it well. "I can teach you, Fell DarkThroat, to make a fresh kill and use it to talk to your parents. Teach you to call into the night. You are with me. Your nature has always been with me."

"But the Pathways were closed," whispered Fell. "The Pathways of the Dead."

"Then open them again. Now Larka has truly gone beyond, even her power fades. Perhaps you could do it, Fell."

"No, Morgra . . ."

"Let the pain and the sorrow, the fury, cry through your strong, black voice. You may summon us now."

"For what, Morgra?"

"Anything you wish. We shall be your servants amongst the living. To save the changeling girl."

"To save her? The Helgra fight at her side."

"No, SlackNews, she is taken."

Fell's face twitched violently in his dream.

"Taken?"

"Yes, Vladeran's spy drugged her and took her to the palace. Each day Vladeran thinks of slitting her pretty throat. It's only his fear of the army that he thinks to draw into his trap with the girl that makes him hesitate. While the Helgra, those miserable wolf lovers, lock their eyes on the palace. They've moved closer. You could go to her, and take the spectres to her aid."

Fell stirred at the very thought.

"A powerful black wolf leading an army of the dead through the lands beyond the forest. Think of the fear and terror it would spread amongst the humans again. Think of the legend you'll really become, my dear. For her, Fell. To save the girl. To save nature itself."

Fell's heart was beating furiously, and yet as he looked back at Morgra, talking of saving Alina, tempting him with the idea, the black wolf knew that her eyes were saying something else entirely.

Morgra's dark, subtle mind was at play, and she knew that if Fell went to Alina's aid, then he would be near her again, and so closer perhaps to fulfilling the vision that had foretold Alina's death at his own jaws. Morgra knew that Fell's dual nature, his desire to protect the girl and to fulfil his own animal instincts, would go to war indeed, and draw him nearer to the darkness again. Morgra sensed Fell reading her thoughts and she growled.

"And why not, Fell? Why do you fight your own destiny? Huttser and Palla are dead, as all things die. Don't be a slave any longer."

Fell was growling in his dream, or his vision, but his growls were as low and black as his injured thoughts. Why not be free at last? Perhaps these Vengerid were right, and the only way to conquer suffering was to make other things suffer. Too long had Fell wrestled guiltily, and now he wanted to live.

"I feel your pain, my dear," said Morgra. "Don't deny it. Use it and feed on it. Still you try to hope, but hope is for fools and liars. Give in. Taste the dark joy once more."

"No, Morgra, no."

"Yes, Fell. You're close to me again. How I've missed you."

Fell had begun to growl, and Morgra's thoughts could feel how strongly the black wolf was fighting her.

"You hate me still, Fell?"

"I must not hate. Larka showed us that hate makes us weak. And Alina too."

Again the mention of Larka seemed to work like a talisman and push back Morgra in the dream, but she fought it hard, and then she was with Fell again.

"Foolish Fell. Hate makes us strong. Hate made me strong enough to linger still in the Red Meadow, and continue the battle your sister thought she had won. A battle with nature itself, that I shall truly win if the girl dies. Hate then, Fell. Hate me. Hate life. Hate man."

"No."

"Then I'll make you," growled Morgra. "If you will not go to save this girl you say you love, for the sake of love, then go for hate. Go to take revenge."

"Revenge?"

"On the human that holds her. On Lord Vladeran."

"Lord Vladeran? I would protect Alina indeed, but why should I hate Lord Vladeran?"

"I'll show you why," whispered Morgra. "I'll show you the secret."

Suddenly Morgra, or the memory of Morgra in the Red Meadow, used the powers of the Sight to do something so terrible that the Lera in the land beyond the forests themselves might have turned once more from their busy, struggling lives, as they had once on the mountaintop, and fix their eyes in horror.

"Look, Fell, and see."

Morgra's muzzle began to fade, and there was the human Fell had seen before, through whose mouth she had first spoken to him. Lord Vladeran was craning over the font in the palace again, looking down with his dark, empty eyes, and it was as if Fell himself were peering back at him out of the water.

"See, Fell," whispered Morgra. "See what the human wears about him."

Fell looked and saw the great collar of fur that rose around Vladeran's neck.

"You know what it is, don't you, Fell? His cloak?"

"Wolf," whispered Fell's darkening mind.

"Yes," hissed Morgra.

"What of it. The Helgra elder wears the wolf too, to honour us."

"Not just any wolf, Fell. Look at the old, grey colouring. The marks that I bore long ago."

"You?" said Fell's wondering mind.

"Yes, Fell. His hunting dogs found my body torn and broken, when he had ridden far to talk with their King. Even before he knew of the history of the Sight."

"And I should hate him for this?"

For a moment Morgra looked almost hurt.

"Not for this, but it takes more than one old wolf to make such a cloak, and two of us died that day."

Even as she said it, Lord Vladeran seemed to hear a noise from the palace behind him and as he turned, Fell's throat choked and his mind span. The cloak, Lord Vladeran's cloak, the collar was formed of Morgra's fur and the front and sides too, but the back of the cloak, stitched to Morgra with threads of leather, was a pure, snowy white.

"Larka," whispered Fell, seeing that two forepaws hung there as well.

"Yes, Fell," said Morgra triumphantly. "It's Larka. Your sister."

"Larka. Dear Larka."

Fell's mind was resisting his aunt still, and although the sight of Larka's pelt on Vladeran's back had filled him with sorrow, he shook off the feeling.

"It doesn't matter, Morgra. It's only a pelt. Once the spirit is gone, the body is nothing. Perhaps it brought some warmth."

Fell suddenly felt more at peace about his parents lying there at the cave.

"Not only a pelt," hissed Morgra. "Her body lay broken there too, next to mine, but when the humans rode by, Larka was not quite dead. It was Lord Vladeran who, thinking himself powerful and strong, took his dagger and slit her throat. The human killed Larka. Then they set to work skinning us, and so we're united, as I said we always were, even in death. Pelts to adorn this human Dragga, and warm him in his cruelty."

Fell was shaking furiously, but the revulsion of it was pushing his mind back towards consciousness and pushing Morgra away. Vladeran and his sister's pelt had vanished now, and Morgra was staring at Fell again, but her face was fading too.

"Think what it would be to revenge yourself on Vladeran's throat," whispered Morgra temptingly, "to revenge yourself for dear Larka's death. For everything that's happened. Go to them, Fell. Punish these filthy humans, at last."

"Yes."

"I'll come to you, again, Fell. Soon," said Morgra. "You're with me now. You've always been with me."

Twenty-one

THE STONE MOUTH

Morgra was gone and Fell sank deeper and deeper into sleep, feeling more than ever that his true power lay in darkness. He knew that images of his journey were with him, and of everything that had ever happened to him. There was Ottol and the salmon and the squirrels, and they all seemed to be talking at once. But suddenly someone else was there too.

"Help me, dear Fell."

"Human?"

Alina stood before him, holding out her hands pleadingly.

"I'm in danger, Fell. I'm in a dark place. A prison. I saw it before. Can you not help me?"

Fell wanted to push the dream off, like the sorrowful thoughts of Huttser and Palla, but he couldn't. Then Fell realised something startling. That voice was not in a dream at all. It was deep in his inner mind. Alina was using the Sight, even at this distance.

"Alina?"

"Yes, Fell. I know you can hear me, my friend. You're far away now, but my need is great."

"You wish me to come to aid you?"

"Oh, Fell, I think it's too late. Catalin and the Helgra are walking into a trap, beyond the gorge near the palace. Vladeran's spies have found out all their plans, and his soldiers lie in wait to ambush them. But you could warn them."

"How, Alina? I may not talk to the young Dragga's mind."

"I don't know, Fell, and I hate to ask it of you. You've done so much already. But if you care for me . . ."

Alina's voice was fading, and Fell heard the scraping of metal, and suddenly his eyes were open. The sun was shining brilliantly, and above a buzzard and its mate rode the heating air. The black wolf rose slowly on his paws and stood there, wondering. Alina was in need and that Dragga, Catalin, too. The humans were calling to him.

Yet why should he answer? He was a wolf, a Varg, not a man to wear wolf skins on his back, and if the fate of all nature was somehow in danger, it was a dim and distant thing to Fell now. He had found no Guardian, because no Guardian existed. He wished suddenly that the Sight would leave him forever, and that he could curl up and listen to the stories in a den, with Huttser and Palla.

The sorrow came like a wave, moved by a ghostly wind, and swamped his thoughts again. It was still true. They were still gone.

For an age Fell seemed to stand there, choked and motionless, seized once more by the past. He did not even see Tarlar, until she was almost at his side, and when she spoke urgently, for a time her voice sounded as if it were speaking to him from some distant country, like a hollow echo that had no pull.

"Thank Fenris, I've found you, Fell."

Tarlar could see the state that Fell was in, and her heart ached

407

for the black wolf, for she too had grieved bitterly at her brother Kenkur's death.

"I wish I'd been with you last night, Fell," she whispered. "I see it hurts you still, and know that it will for a long while. But, dear Fell, now we must look to the living."

"The living?"

"Your pack is in danger. Skop spotted them after dawn, coming down the ravine towards the valley. There must be thirty or forty Vengerid. And that scum Jalgan is at their head. He has come for the challenge."

Fell heard her words, dull and hollow, echoing as if from a well, and he felt nothing.

"Are you listening to me, Fell?"

The wolf did not answer.

"What's wrong with you?" growled Tarlar suddenly. "They're gone and it hurts, as life often hurts, but that doesn't mean we should give up. They were old, very old, and it was their time. It was natural. But others matter now. Think of what Huttser would have done."

Fell growled slightly.

"Wake up, Fell. Now's not the time for grief. Your pack is in terrible danger. What of your duty to your family?"

"My duty?" growled Fell. "And what if my father had been Wolfbane, the Evil One? Would I then have a duty, just because it's my family?"

"But your pack?"

"My pack?" said Fell softly, thinking of Palla lying there motionless by the stream, and Larka's pelt hanging on Lord Vladeran's back. "My pack is gone, Tarlar. Long gone. My mother and father, and dear Larka. All our friends from long ago. If I've any path now, it's not here, but with the humans. I'm closer to their minds than to the Varg's. But even they . . ."

"But your brother and your sisters all need you, Fell. Now. Need you more than ever. You must come."

"Don't order me," growled Fell, though dully and without passion. "I left the pack long ago, Tarlar. I'm not here."

"You're thinking of the past, and you mustn't," whispered Tarlar. "Larka is wise, and she often says that above all, cubs try to solve what seems wrong between their parents. They mustn't do it. For their own sakes."

Fell said nothing.

"Are you a coward, damn you? Are you frightened of the Vengerid?"

"I'm frightened of nothing anymore," answered Fell simply, "except lies. For they're the real killers. And any pack, any true wolf, must learn to fight for itself. For that's the law of life. There's no sorrow in it, and no pity. It's just the way it is."

"Stop it. Please, stop it. Come with me and fight at my side, or lead us away to safety. Don't give up now. We'll grieve together, you and I, for Huttser and for Palla. And then, Fell," whispered Tarlar, "we'll grieve for each other too, and our own mysterious lives. You'll grieve for me, and I for you."

Fell looked up at the beautiful brave she-wolf and his heart stirred. For a moment his eyes cleared a little and he saw Tarlar as she truly was, not just another struggling, frightened soul asking for help, but a passionate, beautiful living creature doing the best she could, as most things do the best they can, perhaps all things when they understand themselves. But the heaviness came again, and his eyes misted over.

"Grief?" he whispered bitterly. "I've been grieving all my life."

"Then stop it," snapped Tarlar furiously, "end your grieving now. Come and fight."

"No, Tarlar. I can't. I won't."

Tarlar knew that he was beyond her persuasion, and besides, there was no time.

"Very well then, Sikla," she snarled. "I'll go to their aid alone, and show you how a wolf should live."

Tarlar turned scornfully, and with her great bushy tail raised in the air, she began to run down the slopes of the valley, towards the pack that had taken her in. She had the wind at her back and Tarlar was quick to reach the stream, and the cave where Kar was beginning to address the others nervously.

Palla was still lying there on the ground, and around her Larka and Kipcha had scraped away the grass and the earth, to make sure that ants and beetles and grubs could not reach her body.

"Tarlar," called Kar as he saw her, "is he coming?"

"No, Kar," answered Tarlar guiltily, then seeing the look of shock on the others' faces, she added, "I think he's in too much pain."

"Too much fear, don't you mean?" growled Skop.

"Hush, Skop," said Kar. "You know nothing of what your elder brother has seen or suffered in his life. It's not for you to judge him."

"I know what I see now," said Skop angrily, "and judge too. I know he cares for humans more than us, and he's my brother no longer."

"Whatever Fell is," said Tarlar bitterly, "you must lead the pack, Kar."

Kar looked bewildered and surprised, but the aging grey wolf nodded. He stood there thinking for a while, and shaking too with the responsibility of it all.

"Very well then," said Kar at last, "I'm decided. If Fell had been with us, I would have said we stand and fight. For although they're many, the Sight's a powerful weapon and this is good ground, that we all know well. But now we must mix valour with wisdom, and turn to our other path, flight. So the pack flees. As fast as our legs can carry us."

"Flees where?" said Khaz nervously. "Skop said he saw Vengerid scouts all over the valley."

Kar's deep eyes flickered, for he was no more used to fighting or leading than the others.

"Then we'll use the cover of the lower tree line to head west, moving in single file and making as little noise as possible. We'll have to cross open ground to the south, but it should be night by then and the darkness will shield us."

"Wolves can see in the dark," whispered Kipcha nervously, "especially the Vengerid."

"The darkness will help us, Kipcha," said Kar as boldly as he could, "then we make for the Great Waterfall. The river will mask our tracks and scent, and after that is open country and escape."

The others seemed reassured a little by Kar's pretended certainty, and they stood there nodding.

"We go then, now," said Kar urgently, suddenly looking like a Dragga himself and beginning to pad down the slope. "The pack is on the move once more."

As the others followed, Kar noticed that Larka was missing and he swung his head. She was still standing by her mother's body.

"We can't just leave them like this, Kar."

"We must, Larka. If Jalgan catches us here, we would join them quickly enough. And Hutts . . . your father and mother, that's the last thing they would have wanted."

"But shouldn't we do something?" implored Larka, scratching at the ground with her right paw. "Bury them in the earth, or something. To protect them."

"Oh, Larka," said Kar warmly, "they're not there. Their spirit has gone somewhere else. You need protect them no more, for although it seems horrible in your thoughts, they can feel nothing now. No pain at all. We'll leave them together then, with honour, for the birds and the living Lera. So that everything may continue."

These wise words seemed to reassure Larka, but she suddenly lifted her throat to cry a howl of mourning.

"No, Larka," said Kar urgently. "The Vengerid will hear you."

Larka stopped her voice, and with a sad, last look at her mother, Palla, and the cave where Huttser lay, she sprang forwards. The pack was on the move, and fleeing for its life. They went in single file, as Kar had suggested, with Kar leading and Tarlar behind him. Skop came next, then Kipcha, while Larka and Khaz took up the rear.

It was a desperate sight, for all around them through the trees the Vengerid were approaching fast, springing silently through the undergrowth like trained killers. No more powerful wolves had the land beyond the forest ever seen, for Jalgan only accepted the strongest into their ranks, and because there were both Dragga and Drappa amongst them, and they lived such free, wild, and healthy lives, they were even more vigorous than even Morgra's Balkar had been.

Only a short while after Kar's decision to flee, Jalgan himself was standing above Palla's body by the stream, surrounded by his Vengerid. Jalgan opened his huge jaws and yawned, running his tongue along the jagged line of his teeth, as he looked down at Palla's body.

"And her mate," he growled. "Where's her mate? The meddling old fool who challenged me."

"Dead too, Jalgan," said a voice up the hill by the cave.

Jalgan sprang upwards angrily and pushed past the speaker, as he cowered in submission in the cave mouth. As soon as Jalgan saw Huttser lying there too, he gave a furious snarl.

"By Fenris," he cried. "Am I too late, after all? So you flee me, Huttser, into the shadows. You could not face the challenge."

Huttser's body just lay there, and Jalgan growled again.

"You were lucky when you fought my scouts, Sikla," he hissed. "But I would have taken you easily enough. Jalgan never misses his kill."

THE PRESENT

Jalgan padded forwards and placed his front left paw on Huttser's dead muzzle and pressed it scornfully into the earth.

"It would have been no great victory though. For you were old and the old must make way for the young. It's no matter, for I killed you anyway with that wound my Vengerid made, did I not? That'll teach you to oppose me, and steal Tarlar away."

As Jalgan thought of the beautiful she-wolf, he swung his head back to the sunlight and a look of greedy longing came into his eyes. Tarlar. Soon she would be his once more. Jalgan had not finished with Huttser and Palla though, and he turned back to the dead wolf.

"What shall we do with the likes of you though, Huttser, my friend? How shall the Vengerid really take its revenge?"

There was a growl from the cave mouth and another wolf was standing there.

"Jalgan."

"Silence," snarled Jalgan angrily. "Don't interrupt my thoughts. Would you rob me of the sweet fruits of victory?"

It was Jalgan's bitter mind that helped Kar and the others in that moment, for the wolf that had just appeared had picked up Tarlar's scent below the stream and had come to tell his leader of it. If they had followed the pack then, they would have caught them before nightfall and killed them easily. So Jalgan's hate, and his desire to humiliate even the dead Huttser, came to their aid.

"I'll ponder it," said Jalgan, lying down beside Huttser. "Think and savour."

The scout knew that he should tell his leader, but he was frightened to interrupt him too. A long while Jalgan lay there in the shadows, playing with the possibilities in his mind, and when he at last rose, what he said shocked even the watching Vengerid.

"Very well. Now you shall learn how the Vengerid treat scum like you. You'll be dragged from the cave, Huttser FailedPaw, and placed next to your dear, dead mate. Then, one by one, my Vengerid shall mark every inch of this valley, rock and branch and stone, to tell every living Lera that this place is ours, forever."

The other wolves' ears began to tremble.

"And then we'll mark you and Palla too, and laugh as we do it, before our muzzles and our jaws tear and rip your cowardly bodies into little pieces. We'll find the lowest and meanest holes and crevices, and place the parts of you there in the darkness, in shame at your dishonour."

The two wolves in the cave mouth were shaking, but Jalgan suddenly swung round.

"You," he growled, "order it done. And drag this . . . this thing out into the open."

The two Vengerid leapt forwards and bit at Huttser's legs, hauling the dead weight of him out into the open next to Palla.

"Good," said Jalgan, as they stood over the bodies outside. "Now summon the others to do this thing. But send some scouts to find Tarlar and the others too, or to try and pick up their damned scents. I want them to watch."

"But, Jalgan, I tried to tell you," said the scout. "We picked up their scent before. It was Tarlar."

Jalgan's eyes were suddenly burning furiously.

The Present

"And they're fleeing towards the Great Waterfall, Jalgan."

"Fleeing? Why didn't you tell me, idiot? You'll pay for it. But later. As Huttser and Palla must wait until later. Come. We go in pursuit, and now."

Jalgan howled, and the Vengerid sprung forwards after the little family.

Fell was wandering, alone, still in that dark, gloomy cloud. He was glad to be on his own, and although Tarlar had warned him that the Vengerid were close, he little cared. Fell had given up on everything now, and he had no wish to help anyone anymore. He had tried to help Alina. He had tried to help everyone. But his journey had led him nowhere except towards death.

Suddenly a jackrabbit shot across Fell's path, and almost out of reflex, the wolf turned to follow it. His pace rose steadily, as he jumped rocks and boulders and skirted sudden trees, feeling a little better with the effort and the chase.

The Sight and its visions did not come this time to impede the wolf's instincts in the wild, and the rabbit was locked in his sight, running desperately towards the edge of the valley and a sheer cliff, where Fell could see no chance of escape, as he felt his stomach begin to churn. The wolf pounced, and his paws were about to close, when the rabbit suddenly vanished under him.

Fell rolled with a whine, and thought for a moment it was some kind of magic, until he spied the hole that the rabbit had found to flee down. He had picked himself up, panting and disappointed, when he heard a voice all about him.

"Run, wolf!" it cried, seeming to shake the very mountain. "Run for your life."

Fell swung round with a furious snarl, but he could see no Lera around him at all. Instead he heard the voice again, like a low echo or the roar of the sea.

"Fear!" boomed the voice, shaking the very earth. "It's a good thing to see it in others, no? But not to feel it yourself."

Fell was shaking with terror.

"Who are you?" he growled. "Where?"

He swung left and right, but still saw no one at all.

"And who are *you*, Fell ShadowPaw?" came the booming answer. "For did not the ancient humans, who came to this land long ago and worshiped the wild she-wolf who suckled them at her belly, have oracles that told them this above all—*Know thyself.*"

An oracle? Fell was staring at the mountain suddenly, and he gasped as he realised just where the echoing voice was coming from. It had been hidden in the shadow of the cliff before, but the movement of the sun had just revealed it—there, in the side of the mountain, was a high cave, like a giant mouth. Fell's eyes opened in astonishment. A giant stone mouth was talking to him.

"And do you know yourself yet, Fell of the Sight?" the mountain seemed to ask, as Fell thought he saw a shadow move inside the cave. The wolf was shaking furiously, as he listened to that echoing bellow, like a god speaking from the Underworld. What had Ottol said? *A Guardian that spoke with a mouth of stone.* It was true.

"Are you the Guardian then?" Fell whispered in a petrified voice, lowering his tail. "You do really exist?"

"That I am, wolf," came the voice from the belly of the cave. "Of course I exist."

Fell dropped his muzzle and sniffed the air.

"The Sight," said Fell nervously. "You know of the Sight?"

"Yes, Fell," said the cave, "and we've been watching you."

"We, Stone Mouth?" growled the wolf.

"All the Lera watch you now, perhaps all the world, Fell LegendPaw, you and these humans. The winter robin tells me of it, and the great herons. The leaping trout carry it in the colour of their scales, and the wood lice in their trails through the forest."

Fell blinked in amazement at the cave.

"The very ants trace it, as they build their archways in tiny, secret places, and the slithering snake wraps it deep in her belly, like the hardening eggshell she prepares to birth her young. All nature watches you, Fell of the Lands Beyond the Forest," boomed the Guardian, "as the animals watched Larka when the vision came at Harja, and all nature listens too, wondering what you are, and what you shall do. What future you shall choose to make, as you struggle with the paradox of life, for their survival may depend on it."

For some reason a single word sang in Fell's mind then, and the word was "choose."

"So what is it you want here, wolf?" asked the cave.

Fell blinked. He hadn't come here on purpose at all.

"I . . . I don't know. What are you? Are you a Lera?"

The ground seemed to shake under Fell's paws, with the answer.

418

"That you shall never know," bellowed the Guardian. "For some things can never be known, and the Guardian's form is a secret. Though I shall tell you my name, if you wish it. For my name itself is the greatest secret of the Sight."

"Yes," answered Fell. "Your name."

"My name . . . is . . . ," the cave's voice seemed to rise to a gigantic boom and a wind to stir the grass, "PANTHEOS."

Fell shuddered, but he fancied now he could smell a musky, feral scent on the breeze, like a lynx or a Borar, a bear.

"Now leave this place, wolf," said Pantheos, "before I teach you the true meaning of fear."

"Leave?" growled Fell helplessly, feeling himself in a dream. "But I've been hunting for you, Pantheos, for so long."

"Many hunt me. What would you know then, wolf? Why do you search?"

"What is happening amongst the Lera?"

"Happening? The Sight is filling the world, of course."

"Filling the world?" said Fell in awe.

"Yes, wolf. Larka began it," cried the cave. "So can you end it, Fell? End it well."

"But how? Why?"

"Larka showed all the Lera the Great Secret that man too is an animal," cried the cave. "But does man know it himself yet, and will he ever accept it? For so often he thinks himself God's chosen. And when he does, will he love us animals any the more because of it, or will he simply hate himself all the more, and so destroy all around him?"

"You said *us* animals. Then you *are* a Lera," growled Fell doubtingly, stepping angrily towards the cave and remembering Ottol's strange words of tricksters in the land beyond the font. "Just an animal, like me. Are you trying to trick me?"

There was suddenly a terrible roar, like a giant Borar's, from inside the stone mouth, and Fell froze and his tail crept between his back legs.

"Fool!" cried Pantheos. "Why do you always need to know, like those restless, searching humans? Can't you just accept, wolf? Do you not know yet, Fell DoubtHeart, that the very power of myth is that it is myth. Why do you think the ancient Roman oracles always spoke in riddles? Trust that power. It comes from deep inside, and it has purpose."

"Purpose?"

"Like thought itself perhaps, or words. Where do they come from, and why do the humans' stories so often echo each other?" asked the echoing cave.

Fell shook his head, feeling himself in a story again, and wondering why.

"Perhaps because they carry inside them the secret journey that all things make," said Pantheos. "For does not everything feel itself to be somehow inside a story, like an unconscious being struggling towards thought? Struggling to see what it really is? As man evolves, does he not wake to that, as a child wakes from a story into adulthood?"

"Yes, Pantheos," whispered Fell, understanding but dimly.

"In the caves of their own growing minds, Fell, the humans

make gods and they make demons too, but tell me, Fell BlackCoat, which would you be? Would you bring light or darkness to the world?"

Fell thought of Alina and their journey together, and he felt a pang for her.

"Light," he whispered.

"Then know, wolf, that the Sight now moves through nature like a great mind, joining together to try to show man the mirror of himself. Perhaps the Lera shall unite to do it at last, or perhaps it is your lonely path. A path that will free you at last, wolf."

Fell shivered again and wondered if he would ever be free.

"But the Lera unite for another purpose. All nature unites to protect this child."

Fell's tail quivered, and his eyes opened wide. It was the most extraordinary thing he had ever heard, but he felt a strange jealousy too, having protected Alina himself for so long.

"Will you not help her too?" asked the cave.

"But why, Pantheos?" growled Fell. "Why is the girl so important? Tell me at last."

"Think of her mark. A Helgra woman. It is a steppe eagle, like the great Helper Skart. The first power, to look through the eyes of birds, began with the ancient steppe eagles."

Fell nodded slowly.

"With the Helgra's faith and love of nature, the Sight has passed to man, or rather woman."

Fell growled again.

"Alina Sculcuvant is the first. But not the last. For all she learns now in her journey shall be passed to her heirs, if she lives. And not just her heirs, but those of another great storyteller."

"Catalin!" said Fell in amazement.

"Yes. It is their distant children who will one day play a role in protecting all the world."

"All the world?"

"Yes, Fell. For one sun when you are gone, wolf, when they are gone too, when I am gone myself perhaps, there will come a time when man will threaten everything there is. Even the very forests that breathe the clean air of the world. Not because of a wickedness or evil, but simply because he will know a success greater than all the Lera, because of the cleverness of his mind and hands."

The black wolf nodded gravely and shivered.

"A time when that success will threaten the very elements themselves," said Pantheos. "But these heirs of Sculcuvant will help teach man balance once more, and will turn his greatest and most dangerous arts, the arts of scientia, that will themselves have been a cause of the growing disaster, to the very cause of nature itself. For it is there, in the power of scientia, along with the self-awareness that each human must learn, that man's true salvation will lie. And the earth's."

The wolf's yellow gold eyes flickered. He knew these things were beyond him.

"But there will also be a sun when scientia will threaten to rob man of spirit and hope and love," said Patheos. "For he must overthrow his gods to come to his full power, but in doing so may forget the wonder and mystery of it all. So these heirs of Sculcuvant will remind man that although his fables and beliefs, his religions and all the conflicts they will cause, are a terrible danger in the world, the world is also a miracle beyond even man's understanding. Teach man that he must cleave again to the spirit and the power of wonder. Like you, he must be reborn."

"But, Guardian," Fell whispered, thinking suddenly of his vision of Alina's death, "Pantheos, if man is so dangerous, why do we not rise up against him?"

"You think man cruel, wolf?" said the Guardian softly. "You think man terrible?"

"I . . ."

"You have seen the ravening wolf, Fell. And if you had swum in the seas, you might have seen a pack of Marjan— orcas, man calls them—moving in packs too, to hunt a great grey whale mother and her calf," said Pantheos. "Seen how they batter and strike her mighty sides, turning the sea blood red, and how she will never leave her child, but swivel her giant body and balance her own baby on her belly, to raise it safely out of the waters. Nature can be terribly cruel, Fell, and terribly brave. Is man any worse than that?"

"Yes," growled Fell, "for animals do not know what they do, but man has knowledge of his cruelty. So why do you not lead us now, Guardian, and send out Draggas to defeat them?"

"Draggas?" cried Patheos. "Have you walked alone so long, wolf, because you think the force of the wild Dragga the greatest there is? As the Balkar once did?"

Fell remembered his thoughts before he had met Ottol, but he was remembering too what Palla had said of the strength of the she-wolf.

"I . . ."

"Wake up, fool," cried the Guardian, and Fell felt as if his muzzle had been struck. "Do you not yet know that two forces live in nature, wolf, the Dragga and the Drappa, the masculine and the feminine? What is one without the other, for how else would the world exist? But each one contains elements of the other too. So use your power, but when others are too strong, be soft; when softness loses vigour, be strong."

Fell blinked and growled.

"But be wary too, Fell. For those humans whose language still echoes in the lands beyond the forest, and who built Harja, taught this above all—health to mind, health to body. Balance."

Fell thought of his vision after Morgra had visited him again, and his tail dropped.

"But something else is happening too," whispered Pantheos.

"Something else?"

"To you, Fell. Can't you feel it? Inside you, as it lies inside all the Lera. *Know thyself, wolf.*"

The cave seemed to shake, and the moving sunlight covered its face again.

"Now be gone from here," bellowed the Guardian.

Fell was trembling furiously, and in the shadows surrounding him, in front of that terrifying, hidden voice, he felt as if he were inside the birthing den again.

"Please. There's so much I need to ask you, Pantheos. So much I need to know."

"And my answers would be riddles," said Pantheos, "not to deceive, but to show you your reflection alone. For I do not lead, I teach. And you do not seek riddles, Fell ClearEye, you seek answers. Yet a riddle I shall give you, wolf. To end this the clawed Putnar must fly, and a wolf be reborn in the water and sprout two heads."

Fell shivered. They had been Skart's parting words too.

"But ask yourself this. Can you trust and believe? Can you face life's challenge? Now be gone."

Fell turned and slunk away and began to run. He wondered if he could trust or believe. And all around him, in the grass and the trees, in the clouds and the very sky, the terrified wolf felt the lingering presence of the fearful Guardian, Pantheos.

"I'm so tired," growled Kipcha loudly as they fled through the darkness. "I've got to rest."

"You can't, Kipcha, not now," said Larka, at her side. "There'll be plenty of time to rest, when we're beyond the waterfall and safe."

"If we ever get beyond it," whispered Kipcha desperately. "I wish Fell was with us."

Up ahead Khaz had just stopped, and the wolves' ears came up. Somewhere a lonely owl hooted from its solitary bower. They had come to the end of the forest, but they sensed it was already near dawn, and ahead of them stretched clear, open ground, all the way to the neck of the valley and the falls.

"From here on we'll be in the most danger," whispered Kar gravely, turning to the others. "You're all with me though?"

"Yes, Kar," said the other voices, almost as one.

"Then run, wolves, run like the wind."

They sprang forwards, the six of them, feeling as if the loss of the forest had stripped them of all safety, a feeling that grew worse and worse as they went, for light was coming fast now, and dawn breaking all around the terrified pack. Tarlar ran the fastest, but she kept turning too and circling, to give encouragement to the others, especially to Khaz, whose spirits seemed most overawed in the flight.

"Come on, Khaz, don't give up."

"I'm trying, Tarlar, honestly. Perhaps I'm a Sikla after all."

"And what if you are? You're part of a pack too, and we'll never leave you behind."

Light had broken fully over the fleeing wolves and the clouds in the skies were a deep and tender mauve, as they heard a sound that thrilled through them like hope. It was the sound of crashing water. The great falls were beyond, and the river. Kar didn't slacken his pace for an instant, as he showed the others how to spring from rock to rock, in the very same place where Fell had listened to the salmon.

As they passed that smaller curtain of water in the rapids and the threat of the Vengerid receded behind them, they felt as if they were passing out of a horrible nightmare, into another world entirely, and part of the magic of that feeling was the very sound of rushing water and the massive, thundering falls upstream.

They all made it safely across, although Khaz almost slipped on the rocks as they went. Kar had a desperately proud look as they reached the bank and he swung round to the others.

"We made it," he cried delightedly.

Kar saw the expression on Tarlar's face though. She was looking behind him and her beautiful eyes were filled with horror. Kar swung round again, and from the right and the left, beyond a range of scrub trees, he saw them coming on—the Vengerid. They had not tracked Kar and his pack through the forest at all, but had raced straight for the falls and lain in wait on the other side of the river.

"Quickly," cried Kar, "back across the water."

As they looked back though, they saw that more Vengerid had come up behind them, waiting on the far bank too, growling and snarling. The little pack swung left and right, forming a circle instinctively, their tails raised, and beginning to growl and, in Khaz's case, to whine a little.

There were more than forty Vengerid, males and females, far larger and more powerful than the six of them. Then, from the right, padding forwards slowly, as one who knows that his victory is already assured, came Jalgan.

"So, my love," cried the great, grey-streaked Dragga, staring coldly at Tarlar. "You thought you could escape me by masking your scent with the river?"

"What do you want with us?" answered Tarlar.

"You know what I want, Tarlar."

Kar dipped his head slightly, preparing to attack, but Tarlar whispered to him immediately. "No, Kar, don't. It's me he wants."

427

"But, Tarlar, we must fight."

"Against so many, Kar? It's hopeless. Not even Fell could help us in this."

"That coward," said Skop furiously behind her.

"I *will* fight, Tarlar," growled Kar, surprising himself yet again, "and die with some honour, at least. I've lived long enough."

But Tarlar had stepped forwards and her tail lowered.

"No, Tarlar, don't," growled Larka behind her.

"It's me you want, Jalgan," she said, "and if you let my friends go, I'll come with you willingly and run at your side as your Drappa."

Jalgan had cocked his head, as though he were interested in the bargain, but the wolf began to laugh. It chilled the little pack to their bones.

"The others shall die this very day, Tarlar my dear, by the Great Waterfall," he said, "as all things meet their rightful end, in time. For they're not worthy to be Vengerid, and so not worthy to live free and wild in the lands beyond the forest."

"Then I'll never run at your side," growled Tarlar.

"They will all die, Tarlar, nothing can change that now," Jalgan went on, yawning slightly. "But what can change is the manner of their deaths."

Khaz looked up fearfully.

"Come with me and it'll be a quick kill for each, nothing more than a torn throat and a sudden end."

Behind Tarlar, her friends were all shaking furiously.

"Resist, Tarlar, and never in the history of the Varg shall such suffering be seen. It'll last for suns on end, and by the time their

428

finish nears, each of your shivering pack shall be begging for death."

Jalgan's voice seemed to sing like the waterfall, and Tarlar stood there in horror at the terrible bargain. Not even she had thought that Jalgan could be so terrible.

"No, Jalgan, please."

"Yes, my dear. For know who and what I am, as your dear brother, Kenkur, learnt to his cost."

Tarlar was trembling furiously, but she began to walk forwards, as if in a trance. She had seen wild nature for herself and learnt how hard and ruthless it can really be. Suddenly Skop leapt in front of her, thinking to kill Jalgan himself to protect her.

The Vengerid around Jalgan were too quick for the brave wolf, and two of them sprang from the group. There was a flash of teeth and twisting fur and Skop was on his back with a yelp, the huge wolves pressing down on him and snarling and snapping at his muzzle. Kar sprang to his aid, but two more wolves came from the right and knocked Kar over too.

There they froze, with Kar and Skop pinned to the ground by four snarling Vengerid. Tarlar stood near them and Kipcha and Larka behind her. Khaz stood behind them, utterly incapable of action, and a voice was echoing in his mind: *Am I just a coward, nothing but a coward?*

"Please, Jalgan," cried Tarlar, "don't harm them."

"They show some spirit, at least," said Jalgan, "but you know the bargain, Tarlar. So choose."

"I can't consent to their deaths, Jalgan," she said desperately,

"Kill me, if it's blood you need and the bloodlust is on you. Kill me."

"You, my love?" said Jalgan softly, "I'll never kill you. I'll protect you always, like a true Dragga should. Now make up your mind. Say yes, and I'll give the word and, with just a strong snap of sharp teeth, it's over for these two. Then the others. Painlessly. It's easy. And of course, your word is good enough."

Tarlar's body seemed to slump, but she could see no alternative. If she resisted Jalgan now, then her dearest friends would be made to suffer terribly, and she would have to go with Jalgan and the Vengerid anyway. But if she said yes, then it would be over in a flash, and at least poor Tarlar would have a lifetime to take a terrible revenge on Jalgan. She would become Vengerid indeed.

"Very well then, Jalgan, I accept your filthy bargain."

Jalgan's cruel eyes flashed triumphantly and his tail rose even more.

"Do it then," he ordered. "Kill them swiftly, and let it be finished with. I'm bored of this place."

The Vengerid's powerful jaws opened above Kar and Skop, their hungry eyes aiming for their throats. A Vengerid muzzle flashed towards Fell's adopted brother and there was a terrible squeal of pain, and then another.

But not from Kar or Skop or the others, but from the Vengerid. The two wolves that had been primed for Kar and Skop's throats had suddenly rolled on their sides and were squirming in agony.

"What's this?" cried Jalgan. "Are you weaklings? Kill them."

The other two still held Skop and Kar and their mouths opened in turn. But then it was as if a great wind had suddenly struck them both, they were hurled into the air and went rolling onto their backs, growling and whimpering. The watching Vengerid were as appalled as they were amazed, and some began to whimper and drop their tails.

"Are we haunted?" cried Jalgan furiously, swinging his head left and right, but seeing no opponent at all. "Are there demons here?" Then a voice seemed to answer him, as if in his own mind, but from the river too.

"Demons, indeed, cur. And those who live by demons, Jalgan, must die by demons."

"Where are you?" cried Jalgan nervously. "This cannot be."

He turned to where that voice seemed to be coming from, from the drop in the falls itself. "Are you a god?" Jalgan shuddered. "Are you Fenris himself?"

"I'm Fell," cried a real voice now, from out of the water. "So behold and be afraid."

Fell's great black shape came moving out of the river itself, leaping through the curtain of water, behind which he had seen and heard everything that had just happened, in the cave scoured out of the stone by time and the river. The Vengerid saw him like a vision of rebirth, and it doubled and trebled their fear. Fell leapt onto the great rock and sprang onto the bank, shaking out his beautiful black pelt in a stream of flickering droplets.

"You!" growled Jalgan.

The Vengerid backed away behind their leader, as the black wolf came growling angrily through his brothers and sisters and stood proudly at Tarlar's side. Jalgan alone held his ground, and Fell's tail rose as he looked at the great grey wolf.

"Take him," cried the Vengerid leader, as bravely as he could.

A few of the wolves moved forwards, but they suddenly stopped, for Fell's mind and the powers of the Sight were moving amongst them again. Their eyes were filled with fear and doubt, and several of them dropped down on their forepaws and began to whimper bitterly. One though, on the bank behind them, was out of Fell's sight line and too far away to be touched. In several leaps he was springing out across the river, followed by many others.

"Fell," cried Khaz suddenly. "Behind you, Fell."

The black wolf swung his head, and the closest Vengerid suddenly spun on one of the rocks and was cast with a howl into the churning waters. The others stopped immediately, muttering furiously, and crept back onto the far bank, terrified by Fell and the strange powers of the Sight.

"So," growled Jalgan, "it's true what I've heard of you, Fell BlackWolf. And you're strong indeed, as I saw that day. Strong enough to join the Vengerid, perhaps."

Fell's eyes were locked on Jalgan's.

"Never, cur. I'm no Marjan. "

"Why not, wolf? Do you fear the truth of nature? Perhaps though, after all my years of wandering and searching, at last I've found a worthy opponent to face my challenge. Worthier than that foolish Sikla, Huttser."

Fell snarled.

"And I've looked into your mind, Jalgan," he said dangerously, "and seen there what you plan to do to my father and mother. In hate and dishonour."

Something like real fear crept into Jalgan's brutal face.

"Huttser and Palla were your . . . ?"

"Yes, Jalgan. They were my parents. And now you would try and kill my brothers and sisters too. So I'll kill you instead, Jalgan, and show you the meaning of pain."

Even Jalgan was shaking badly, but his blood was up too.

"Bravely spoken, Fell," he whispered, "for one who would use the forces of darkness to fight, and not nature. For one who's not a true wolf at all."

Fell felt the insult deeply and snarled again.

"For one who has not the courage to fight with honour," Jalgan went on, feeling his own courage returning, "like a Dragga and a true wolf, but one who uses tricks and lies instead."

"I've the courage to fight you like a wolf," growled Fell, "and to kill you too."

Jalgan smiled.

"Without the Sight, Fell? You'll face the challenge without the Sight?"

Fell hesitated only momentarily.

"Yes, Jalgan, without the Sight. But now I'll make a bargain with you. If I do this thing and kill you, then the Vengerid leave this place, never to return."

Jalgan did not hesitate, for he was larger than Fell and much more powerful. He thought it an easy pact, and one he would never have to fulfil.

"Hear that, Vengerid," he growled to his comrades. "It shall be so. And none shall intervene. Jalgan has spoken."

"But, Fell," whispered Tarlar at his side, "use your powers. Then we'll all fight together."

"No, Tarlar," answered Fell sadly, thinking of Pantheos's words—*Know thyself*, "I've given my word and I would be a wolf again."

"But, Fell, dear Fell, he's larger than you and—"

Jalgan heard the tenderness with which Tarlar addressed Fell, and it hurt his angry heart.

"Fight me, dog," he snarled furiously, "and die like the Sikla you are."

Jalgan and Fell sprang at each other, as the Vengerid and the little pack looked on. The two great wolves clashed in midair. For a moment they seemed suspended there, and then they both spun round, snapping and snarling in the grass, a flailing mass of muzzles and jaws and teeth, their prone claws searching for each other's body. Two giant males at war.

The snarls were terrible, and in any normal fight one Varg would have retreated into submission immediately, for nature's first art is to warn off the danger of battle, but this was a fight to the death. First Fell was knocked backwards and Jalgan nearly caught him in his throat, but Fell rolled away and, leaping up again, he sprung forwards and knocked Jalgan back in turn. But his bite missed too, and the wolves both sprang to their feet and faced off again. On and on it went, their terrible duel, but as the sun began to dip, once again Jalgan saw an opening, and lashing out with his right paw, he caught Fell in the side and raked his claws viciously right down the black wolf's body.

"No, brother," gasped Larka helplessly.

Fell yelped, and now his great black shape was spattered with blood. His own paw caught Jalgan in the muzzle and opened that brutal face, but as they fought on, it was Jalgan's size and strength that began to tell in his favour. Both wolves grew tired, and slowed too, but Fell's wound was far worse, and his strength was being sapped faster.

Jalgan could see it, and knew that it was only a matter of time. The ranks of the terrible Vengerid had begun to growl approvingly. Then, as they sprang apart, Jalgan turned to see that Fell had faltered. His right paw had buckled under him in exhaustion and he had nearly fallen over.

"No, Fell!" gasped Tarlar bitterly. For she knew now that she loved the wolf.

With his last ounce of strength, Jalgan leapt through the air in triumph at the failing wolf, and it was as if his mind could already see the vulnerable opening at the back of Fell's neck that would end the business forever. As if Jalgan had the Sight himself to see it with.

Fell had made an oath to Jalgan, and he did not use the powers of the Sight, but at the moment before the leap, Jalgan's angry thoughts flashed through Fell's mind and he knew what was happening. He had no time to spring away, but suddenly it was as if Pantheos was whispering to him again—*when others are strong, be soft*—and instead, just as Jalgan reached him, Fell let his front paws buckle beneath him and he rolled, turning his head and closing his teeth around Jalgan's forepaw.

The bite made Jalgan's legs buckle in turn, and he was tumbling on the ground with a snarl. Fell was almost too tired to move, but move he had to, and one thing above all drove him on. It wasn't hate, it was anger at Jalgan's cruelty, anger at what he had wanted to do to his parents' bodies, but something else too—Ottol's words, although they had changed slightly: *Strike upwards, Fell, if you strike at the Wolf Trail.* What did that mean? That it was easy to show natural strength against that which was weaker, but not so easy to strike at what was more powerful. The words and Fell's anger rose inside him like pure energy and hurled him up through the air.

Fell landed on Jalgan's back, and opening his jaws as if to howl to the heavens, he brought them down and snapped them shut around that line of fur at the top of Jalgan's neck. There was a terrible squeal of pain and then silence. Jalgan went limp in the grass. Fell had broken his neck.

Fell lay on top of the Vengerid leader, panting desperately and dripping with blood, and the Vengerid pack looked on in amazement. Some of them wanted to act, others to howl. But they were pack wolves, trained to obey by the most powerful of Draggas, and now all they knew was the last order of their leader. One by one the Vengerid began to turn away, and then, as the shadows came in, they were gone.

For a while the little pack just stood there, in amazement at all that had happened and how the complex fortunes of life could change so quickly. But change they had, from utter despair to elation and joy. Suddenly they were all around him.

"Oh, Fell," cried Skop, "I thought you a coward, brother, but I was wrong. Will you forgive me?"

"It was a brave fight, Fell," said Kar, in admiration, tinged with only a little jealousy. "I'll remember it forever, brother."

"Fell," growled Tarlar, "you're hurt."

"Yes, Tarlar," said Fell, raising his head and stepping wearily off Jalgan's body, "but it will heal."

"And then you'll lead our new pack, and we'll all be happy again," said Larka warmly.

"Oh, yes," cried Kipcha delightedly.

The others were nodding, and wagging their tails at their elder brother, the true Dragga amongst them, but the black wolf swung round to face them.

"No," he growled, though not angrily, "and now I must be gone. There's little time, I think. I may be too late already."

"Gone?" said Kipcha in astonishment. "Gone where?"

"The human," answered Fell, thinking of Alina and of Larka's pelt as well. "She needs my help too. They both do."

"But I thought you'd left them," said Khaz.

"And that you want to be a wolf again, Fell," agreed Tarlar.

"Yes, Tarlar. But we're linked, she and I, and first I must face my destiny. For I have taken the challenge, as Father would have done, life's challenge. It is for all of us that I go now. For nature itself."

Fell realised that he was still sopping wet, not with blood but water, and as he heard the falls thundering beyond and spoke of destiny, he gasped. Pantheos's words came back to him again and with them thoughts of what had just happened. He had come once again from a river, just as Skart and the Stone Mouth had foretold. He felt as if he had been reborn.

With that, and to the total bewilderment of the little pack, Fell the lone black wolf turned and went leaping away. Leaping into darkness once more, and back towards the humans.

TWENTY-TWO
NOISES

Don't fear, Alina. Don't give up hope.
All nature unites to help and guard you now."

The voice seemed to be in Alina's mind, but she couldn't tell if it was Fell or the wind outside her prison.

"Fell, are you there, dear Fell? I can't reach you anymore."

Alina Sculcuvant opened her eyes and stared into the shadows. She heard the wail of the wind, and the distant moans about her too. The young woman knew that the wolf could not hear her searching mind anymore, and she was suddenly thinking of another presence, Catalin.

Yet thoughts of the wolf returned. Once before, on her bed of straw and stone, Alina had managed to reach out across the distances and touch Fell. She was sure that at least the wolf had understood that she had been kidnapped by Cascu, to be chained in this prison in Vladeran's palace. The prison she had seen with the Sight.

Understood too that her father's old friend knew all their plans and was laying a terrible trap for Catalin and her people. Alina had not wanted to trouble the black wolf, on his journey to see his dying father, and had felt the dreadful pain in Fell as they had first spoken, but it was the only thing she could think of to do to fight Lord Vladeran.

He had visited Alina only once in that terrible place, just after the traitor Cascu had left her there to rot. That great bolted wooden door had swung open on its hinges, and a man, six foot two and wearing a wolf cloak of grey and pure white, with a strange red cross on his chest, had strode into the prison, surrounded by his Shield Guard.

Alina had not remembered her father's friend at all, but Vladeran had recognised Alina Sculcuvant immediately.

"Yes," he'd grunted, smilingly. "It's the changeling, all right. She looks even more like her father now than she did then."

Then he had taunted her by whispering with Cascu in the corner, of their plans for the Helgra. "There's only one way for so many Helgra to approach the palace. They'll be like a wolf, seized in metal teeth that they'll never escape. And all because of her."

Alina had listened in horror, before Vladeran had turned towards the door again, but he had said something else, almost as an afterthought. Her father's best friend had swung around angrily and, looking Alina WovenWord in the eye, he'd hissed. "And don't think I fear you, child, because you've returned and walk with the wolf. I fear nothing, don't you see? For *she* has told me that I'm safe. Forever. That's my destiny now."

The prison door had slammed, to the sound of laughter and stamping boots, and Alina had been left alone again, wondering why he had said it, and who he could mean by "she," wondering if he could have meant her own mother, Romana. For it was the truth of Romana she now feared above all.

Since then days and nights had passed in a terrible dream, with hardly any differentiation between light and dark. There was only one meagre little window in her prison cell, looking out onto a gloomy cloister far below, and the nights were as black as pitch, filled with the wails and moans of the souls who suffered in Vladeran's dungeons.

Alina felt she would have been better off back in Malduk and Ranna's barn, so hungry was she, forced to exist off little tin plates of food that were pushed through a slit in the bottom of the door every two or three days, along with a beaker of rank water, or a bowl of thin, grimy porridge and a crust of weevil-covered bread. But Alina knew instinctively that if she didn't eat she would surely die, and so, holding her nose and taking sips of water, she forced the evil-tasting fare on herself. Now the young woman even looked forwards to the sound of that flap opening, not only because it meant food and so survival, but because it was the one thing that broke the dreadful monotony of her days. That was almost the worst of it, the ghastly boredom of that place, along with the terrible noises.

Noises. The days and nights were filled with noises. Her nose and mouth had long closed themselves to the foul odours that circulated in that place of horror, but her ears had become more sensitive to all around her: the sound of the door flap and of metal scraping on stone, and the jangling of a prison warder's keys, or the heavy tread of his boots. The sudden scuttling of a mouse, or a rat, in the shadows. Human sounds came too. Muffled conversations in the tiny passageways beyond, or the occasional burst of cruel laughter in the dark. And those cries, those terrible, imprisoned cries.

Lescu's training had come to Alina's aid, for although the girl no longer had her sword, which Cascu had taken from her when he had drugged her and the men who guarded her in the Helgra village, she still had Lescu's words about calming the mind and directing her thoughts. It eased her fear a little, and helped her concentrate on all that was happening around her too.

As she waited and listened, Alina WovenWord noticed that her hearing, in comparison, seemed to have doubled in strength. It was as if senses are not things at all, or absolute facts, but parts of us that can grow or diminish in strength. As if the very fact of using them is the key to what we are, or might be, and that there is an art to their use too—the arts of seeing, and the art of taste and smell and touch. The arts of hearing also. Listen, Alina WovenWord, listen.

As Alina lay there and listened, she seemed to be able to send out her hearing in different and precise directions, and it allowed her to build up a picture of what was directly outside. It was not without danger though, this journey of her senses, for a noise might suddenly come as she turned a corner in her listening mind, a scream or a wail or a blow, and Alina would recoil immediately and then she was back in her lonely cell again. The young woman realised there was another sense involved in all this too, that also seemed to be growing stronger, the sense to imagine things. Perhaps the most powerful sense of all.

Or was it a sense? For Alina realised that it was only experience that allowed her to recognise certain noises, like dripping water or the turning of keys. She had heard them before, and so she knew what they were, like recognising words that give meaning to things.

What would it be like to hear these things though and not know what they were, or to not have the human words to describe them, and thus picture them in her mind?

Then Alina wondered about the black wolf, with his snarls and growls and howls, and what Fell heard in the night with his ears. The other Lera too, all of them in the wild. Was thought itself only possible with language, and if it was, where did that come from? Fell had a kind of language, because of the strange powers of the Sight, yet those creatures that did not, whose minds and words had not given them a map of the world, and of reality, what did they hear in the shadows of their lives? Only the ghosts of longing, struggling towards consciousness? It gave Alina a pain to think of it. How could it all be? It seemed quite miraculous.

Yet was that other sense, that sixth sense, to imagine, really just an act of recognition, or something far deeper and more powerful? And where did it come from too? Just as Alina had always had the sensation that she could know things before they happened, and had seen the Helgra halls and this place in her vision, so too she felt that she knew things about this palace that no physical sensation was really telling her.

She knew, for instance, or sensed, that there were many floors below her. She sensed that the cells around her were crowded almost to bursting, although that may have been from the number of cries she heard in the night. She sensed that there was a great body of water nearby too. A river.

But what use was it all? If the Sight was a power, then it was nothing like the goblin powers she had imagined when she thought herself a changeling. It was a power that gave her little command of the real world, and one that had brought her to this horrible place. There was no magic in the world, the young woman told herself bitterly in her prison, and no gods either.

Alina had one other sense, though, that kept nagging at her, like a worried friend, tugging at her sleeve. She sensed that her mother Romana was somewhere nearby. She knew it of course, or knew at least that she must be if she was in Lord Vladeran's palace. But it was more than that. It was a feeling deep inside her, as though she could feel her mother and her half brother too. As though they were all connected. Were people really all connected? The thought would wake her sometimes in the night.

Alina got up now and stretched herself with a yawn. The thinning darkness heralded a new day, and pulling her chain to its full length, Alina walked over to that small patch of window and peered out miserably through the metal bars. Bars that only humans make.

Again a warning voice came to Alina, one that she had first heard at the table of the Helgra—*Lord Vladeran, he loves your mother dearly.* What if Romana loved him too, and had colluded in his plans and betrayed the Helgra? Perhaps she had known that Alina was in this cell all along, perhaps it was she who had ordered her kidnap and murder seven years before. Alina would not believe it. She could not. It was not the mother of her earliest dreams.

A noise sent her lunging back to her bed of straw—the bolts being drawn back on the cell door. It swung open with a horrible creaking, but rather than the guard, Alina was amazed at what walked into that prison cell.

It was a dog, large and thin, but it was old too and its eyesight was not good. It growled with distaste at the rank smells that assaulted its nostrils and began to sniff the ground as it dropped its head.

"Out of the way, damn you, Vlag," came Vladeran's voice, as he gave the animal a kick and entered the cell too. The dog slunk to the side of the cell. Vladeran wheeled round and looked down hatefully at the young woman, but there was something else in his veiled eyes too, Alina was sure of it—fear. Could he really be frightened of her?

"So, child," he hissed, "you're awake?"

"I'm no child," said Alina angrily, straightening herself and glaring back at him.

"No, perhaps you're not," whispered Vladeran, with something close to admiration, "and even this place has not entirely sapped you of your damned spirit, I see. A spirit that so nagged at me when you were a little girl. You're quite a survivor, Alina Sculcuvant."

Alina felt the stirrings of memory, the memories of feelings for her father's best friend. She hadn't hated him then.

"And I'd show you my true spirit," she hissed, "if my hand were free and I had my sword."

"Such a fine sword," said Vladeran with a smile, "fine enough for the head of my Shield Guard, Cascu, to want it for himself. He tells me that you can use it too, like a magic wand, to bewitch the Helgra. Or should I say your people, Alina WolfPaw?"

Vladeran flexed his right hand painfully.

"And are not such things man's true power? Not magic and the lies of a feeble storyteller, but swords and tools and weapons. Look at you now, with your cropped hair and your boy's jerkin. Isn't a girl ashamed to walk so unnaturally through the land?"

"Unnaturally?" said Alina proudly. "Is it not you that is unnatural, friend of my father?"

Vladeran's eyes narrowed.

"You who talks to the shadows," said Alina scornfully. "You whose duty should have been to protect me, but who instead tried to kill me, and stole my mother's love. I know now that though they tell us how dangerous the world is, a greater danger always lurks closer to home."

Vladeran's eyes flamed.

"And your father's dead, changeling. Which is the only reason I haven't slit your pretty throat, WolfPaw," he whispered dangerously. "Do you know why, storyteller?"

Alina looked up. She had wondered it in her prison. Seven years ago he'd tried to do away with her, but for some reason had stayed his hand, and instead had her stolen away beyond the borders of Castelu, risking her survival.

"It's true that if my plans misfire with the Helgra I might use a Helgra woman as a bargaining counter," said Vladeran. "But now they are coming towards my trap. The real reason is that I myself once stood on a battlefield soaked with blood, and saw a brave man fall from his charging horse. Saw your father, Dragomir, get up once more, only to have his heart pierced by a Turkic spear. It's full of chance, the battlefield. Like life."

Alina didn't understand what Vladeran was saying.

"Why does this keep me alive, murderer?"

"Because it proves you are no threat to me. I can only be killed if your father is in sight of this palace. It has been prophesied."

Alina looked at the man in amazement.

"And that, my dear, brave Alina, is impossible."

Vladeran smiled coldly again.

"Real life is hard, no? Harder than children know. But you had one thing almost right, calling me a murderer, though you still live," he said. "It's too strong a word perhaps, but that day there was a reason you father fell from his horse, after his saddle slipped from its back, as the girth broke. For a sharp knife in a stable at dawn may do much to loosen the cords that bind us all, and so change many fortunes."

"No," gasped Alina.

It was as if her eyes were misting over and the bloodlust had come on the young woman. She saw herself turned into Fell, leaping across the cell and burying sharp claws in his throat. She wanted to hurl herself at this man and tear at him, and as Vladeran looked at her, he suddenly stepped back.

Vladeran shook his head, telling himself what he thought he had just seen must have been a trick of the light, and instead Alina wrapped the chain that held her angrily around her fists. A voice came to her too, out of the past: *Beware of hate, Alina.*

"You want vengeance, don't you?" said Vladeran, with a laugh. "After such a long, brave struggle. For that's the true law of life. Hate and revenge and need conquer everything in the end."

"And it is the law that should take you," said Alina coldly, thinking of Lescu's words about justice, "the law of King Stefan that should condemn your dark heart."

"Law?" Vladeran spat the word contemptuously. "I'm the law in Castelu, changeling. Men make their rules and their laws, when really they're just words that cover up the true laws of nature and survival. The laws of gold and struggle and of victory. The laws of life."

Alina could hardly argue with Vladeran. So much she had seen of the real world had taught that it was a cruel and ruthless place, stripped of magic. But her heart beat against it.

"I pity you."

"I don't need your pity, changeling," said Vladeran. "You're barely more than a child, so what can you know of ambition and true feelings? Such feelings, and such ideas too. Why should King Stefan rule this land, and why should I not sit on his throne? There's no birthright, fool, least of all for a woman. There is only what you can take and pay for later."

Alina glared back at the man.

"And your beautiful mother, Romana," he said softly, "how I loved that creature and longed for her, how I do still. A feeling so deep and powerful it's like breathing itself. As deep as the hatred I felt for you when my son was taken by wolves."

Alina shivered.

"Until you're gripped by that, what can you know of real life, child? It forced me to do what I did, while every day I have to carry the burden of power and responsibility," said Vladeran angrily, rubbing his scarred hand through his glove again, as though trying to rub the marks away.

Although Vladeran had said that he did not need Alina's pity, it seemed to her that in some way he was pleading with her, almost begging her to understand him.

"What do ordinary people know of true hunger and of true glory, Alina? What do they know of destiny? And what of the sorrow that comes like a thief, and of the cold facts that I must admit only to myself in the darkness?"

Vladeran's clouded eyes had grown dull. The light had gone out of them completely, as he struggled with the paradox of being.

"How sometimes I force myself down on my knees, like a king forcing a serf to bow before him, and lift my head to pray that God and the heavens may understand what I am, and what I had to do."

Alina blinked and her face set hard.

"But though I pray to God and all his silent, judging saints, my words hang dully on my lips and I feel nothing," said Vladeran. "Because though I've touched strange visions, I don't believe that there is anything up there at all. Not even Morgra has shown me anything beyond the Red Meadow."

Morgra, thought Alina, *he speaks with Fell's aunt. It must be she who prophesied with the Sight. As the Sight had prophesied this terrible place. It is true then. Vladeran is invulnerable.*

"So when I pray, I mouth the rite but my thoughts turn only to the shadows and to the future. To what we all must lose in the end, but also to what we may enjoy before we lose it—power."

Alina was trembling, and as she heard his confession, she thought that, although it was she who was lying here in the straw, chained to the dripping prison walls, it was really he who was in a prison, far deeper and more terrible than anything human hands could build. As she listened, she remembered Lescu's words again, *And remember, Alina, it is what we do ourselves in life that harms us.*

"No, Vladeran," she whispered sadly. "You want me to understand, but you had a choice, as we all have. "

Vladeran's face, racked with the passion that had overcome him, suddenly grew calm.

"Do we?" he said coldly. "Does my dog have a choice when he sees the squirrel flash from the undergrowth, and his belly and his soul tell him he must hunt?"

"We're not animals," said Alina, and she had a strange feeling that she was somehow betraying Fell. "We're much more than that anyway. We have a higher mind."

Vladeran stared hard into her clear, hazel eyes and her beautiful face.

"That's exactly what we are," he said. "But you speak of animals, Helgra woman. Very well then, storyteller. There's another reason you're still alive. I want to know, girl, about the wolf. Mastery of the creatures has obsessed me since Elu was taken. Tell me what it's like to walk the world with a wild beast at your side. To know its very thoughts and to command it."

Alina's eyes flickered protectively. How could this man ever understand her feelings for the wolf? To have Vladeran even talk of him felt like a desecration. Fell was wild, yes, and free, but he was far more than a beast. Yet what was Fell?

Though they talked with the Sight, his mind was like a foreign country, where she did not really travel. Where she did not even want to travel. As for commanding Fell, Alina did not command the black wolf at all. Vladeran could never understand that because of his obsession with power and control. That Fell had chosen freely to walk at Alina Sculcuvant's side, to protect her, and that was why she felt so safe in his presence. That was why she loved him.

Vladeran put his hand in his pocket and he pulled out a little brass key, like the key Mia had once used to open a chest.

"Tell me, storyteller, and I'll unlock your hands," he said. "It's not freedom, but at least you'll be more comfortable. Don't think to ask your guards either, for this is the only one."

Alina stared back at him, but said nothing of Fell.

"Very, well, changeling," growled Vladeran. "Though I could torture it out of you. If you will not speak of such things, answer this at least: Where does the power really come from to talk with the wolf? The Sight."

Alina wanted to say one thing alone, "sensitivity," but instead she lifted her chin defiantly.

"Why do *you* want to know, Vladeran?"

Vladeran's eyes flickered.

"My oath," he whispered, "one of the oaths of the Order of the Griffin. The pursuit of knowledge. And, as I say, they took my child!"

Alina paused. She was so tired.

"I don't know," she answered with a sigh. "It was just there.

Perhaps it's something to do with Elu and our Helgra blood, and what happened. Perhaps it is just as it is. Why do you ask me these things?"

Vladeran grasped the key angrily in his fist.

"This gift you have, that's a true power, and if I could have it too, then I would seek out many things, and could control all men. See into their minds. Then perhaps I could really look beyond too, and really believe. Prove that no one should be frightened of what comes after."

Vladeran dropped his eyes, and suddenly felt that he had admitted too much of his own fear in front of the girl. His dog turned his head and began to growl and Vladeran looked up again.

"You accuse me, storyteller," he whispered bitterly. "But what about you? Because of you and your fairy tales and lies, there is war within Castelu itself. Because of you real men will die tomorrow, and fire will light the land. How many are you willing to have die for you, Alina WolfPaw?"

Alina shivered. Perhaps Vladeran was right. Perhaps she should never have thought of wielding a sword. Perhaps she should never have gone amongst the Helgra at all. Was it all her fault?

The door opened again and one of the Shield Guard stepped inside.

"What is it?" hissed Vladeran.

"My lord, the Helgra have crossed the mountains and approach the passes to the palace. There are many."

Vladeran's eyes sparkled and Alina sat bolt upright.

"And the trap is laid?"

"A thousand trenches wait sewn with wooden stakes to impale them. Barrels of pitch are ready to be lit, and hurled on catapults into their midst. While like the pits your troops are hiding in wait in the forests to fall on their retreat and push them back into the jaws of death. The trap is ready to be sprung at your command. They shall not escape."

Alina's eyes were full of tears and horror, and Vladeran smiled.

"Good. And I have summoned other help too," he said. "Now go."

"Yes, my lord."

Alina's heart sank utterly. She had tried to reach Fell once more, but in vain. Catalin and her people were walking straight into a trap. For all her courage and skill, for all her training and the supposed wisdom it had brought, Alina was chained up in a miserable cell, and no more help to them than a useless prayer. It was hopeless.

Vladeran was deep in thought, still plotting and planning in his quick brain, but he suddenly turned to his hound.

"Come, Vlag," he whispered. "I'm sick of the stench of this place, and we shall feed you. Together we'll listen to the news of the Helgra's destruction from a safe vantage point. The hunt begins, and it will be finished by the morning."

The dog whimpered and lifted its tail hopefully, but Vladeran did not look at Vlag with kindness. He wanted a wolf at his side now.

"And you," said Vladeran, turning again to Alina, "I leave you to the shadows. If the trap fails, we still have your blood to force the Helgra to our will. If it succeeds, as it shall, then you'll swiftly meet a fate you were always destined for. For to me, child, you're already dead. You always have been."

The young woman looked back coldly at the man, and her courage rallied.

"Is that your final blessing?" she whispered scornfully. "Friend of my father, protector of our family. You are true to your nature at least."

Vladeran's eyes flashed. "Blessing? You're a believer, then, storyteller? Well, if it's a blessing you want, then the priest shall visit you, but only to bless you at the moment of your execution."

Alina WovenWord shivered as the door slammed and she sank her head sadly.

Catalin raised his blue green eyes as he stood next to Ovidu in the night, on a thin mountain ledge, above a high chasm that made his head spin. The mighty sweep of the twinkling stars above formed a glistening canopy to what lay below them now, beyond the narrow gorge.

In the distance was a palace, buckled in shadow, and in front of it snaked a great churning river. It flowed down out of the giant mountains, driven by the forces of nature, and the palace was set beyond it, at its widest part. The river was strong and looked difficult to cross, spanned only by a thin wooden bridge.

Before that was a rough plain, divided by a defensive ditch, that would leave them dangerously exposed when they crossed it in the morning light. Catalin suddenly thought of Baba Yaga and the brave Vasilissa, who dared to enter her gate of bones, and it gave him courage. Many times as the Helgra had marched towards the palace, Catalin in turn had sat by their fires and given them spirit by weaving brave stories.

"The night deepens, Catalin," whispered Ovidu at his side, smiling at the nervous young man. "We should rest now, boy. We must be up before the dawn."

Catalin's hand came down to the bow slung over his shoulder, and as he thought of Alina Sculcuvant, he realised that he loved the young woman.

"I wish we could fly to her now," he whispered, "like birds."

"Wishes can make fools of us, Catalin," said the Helgra softly, fingering the sword at his side, but clutching tighter the sharp antler he held in his left hand. "We're only human, boy. And we've the gorge to navigate first, and then the plain. A hard battle faces us, lad, and I'm sorry to take one so young to face it."

"You'll be at my side," said Catalin simply, though he thought of his father.

"Yes, young man. Watching your back, as you face the future with your arrows."

Ovidu swung his head.

"Unlike my dear little brother Cascu," he whispered, "I fear his disappearance, fear some dark fortune."

"But the Helgra are ready, Ovidu?"

"Many have come," answered Ovidu proudly. "Though more would have, I think, if Alina WolfPaw led us."

Catalin looked down from the ledge to the Helgra campfires, twinkling in the darkness far below them. He had never been to war and had no idea what was to come, except that his father had told him what a terrible thing it was.

"I hope we've not led you into a trap, Ovidu," he said guiltily.

"You've led us to nothing but the recognition of what we are. And your courage has taught us to forge our strength again. For a Helgra woman. And a young man I'd honour as Helgra too, storyteller."

Catalin smiled gratefully, but he suddenly wished he were back home with Lescu and Alina.

"I wish the black wolf were with us at least," he said.

"That would be a fine sight indeed," agreed Ovidu. "Yet the men carry him in their hearts, as they do the girl. The Helgra shall never forget them."

Catalin heard a noise in the night, and it seemed to him that the mountains around were suddenly alive with noises, like a strange whispering, as though the very undergrowth were speaking.

"Are you frightened, Ovidu?" he asked.

"Yes, my boy. And only a fool wouldn't be. Yet proud too. Come, let us return."

The two swung round, and almost instinctively they started to run, jumping and swerving down the track towards the campfires below. They were on foot, as they had been since the army had set out from the Stone Den. The Helgra, carrying their homemade weapons and antlers, had moved fast, like mountain warriors, but Catalin feared they had delayed too long.

The Helgra camps seemed to grow in the night like red flowers as they came down the mountain, revealing an army of nearly a thousand men, but as Ovidu and Catalin neared the foothills of the gorge, they saw a Helgra scout running towards them. He saluted Ovidu and stopped, gasping for breath.

"There's news, Ovidu. The messengers have returned from King Stefan."

"But not with welcome tidings, from the looks of it?"

"No, Ovidu," whispered the scout, bowing his head bitterly. "Stefan Cel Mare has fought a great battle against the Turk and many have died. It was a victory, yet he laughed at our story. He called it a foolish dream."

"And no doubt builds one of his sainted churches to mark his glorious success," whispered Ovidu bitterly, "while real lives are still in the balance in his own lands. I wish this were a dream. I wish the battles of men could be solved in their heads."

He turned to Catalin.

"And now we're alone, lad."

Catalin felt the hand of fear all about them.

"King Stefan promises a court of enquiry," said the scout, trying to lift the mood, "but it will not come for months."

"By which time we'll all be dead," said Ovidu, "or the good Lord Vladeran."

Even as he spoke it and they stood there, unaware that they were about to walk into a terrible trap, they heard a sound in the twinkling darkness that stirred the Helgra by their war fires, and made Catalin the storyteller wish bitterly that Fell had never left them. It was the howl of a wild wolf.

Twenty-three
BLESSINGS

T he storyteller stood in the bright
sunlight in the neck of the gorge, and around him the
Helgra carried their swords and antlers, ready for the fight. Their
hearts were heavy, for their spies had told them of the strength of
Vladeran's army, and of course the girl they had set out to fight for
was in his clutches, but the pale dawn had brought new courage
and the way ahead looked clear.

Yet the Helgra did not know what terrible secrets were hidden in
wait for them beyond the narrow gorge. The ground ahead strewn
with Vladeran's pits, and his soldiers waiting hungrily in the forests
that edged the valley. If the Helgra moved ahead, they would be
caught like flies in a trap.

"Well, storyteller?" said Ovidu, smiling at Catalin. "Shall I give
the order to advance?"

The young man looked surprised that the Helgra should ask
him, but he nodded, and Ovidu raised his arm.

"Alina!" cried the fighters as they began to move off. "Alina
WolfPaw!"

Suddenly, from the side of the mountain, a shape came streaking
towards them. Fell's black coat was drenched in sweat, from so many
nights without sleep as he had rushed to their aid, and Catalin saw

a livid scar on his right side as the wolf reached them. Fell could not speak to the human, but the wolf stood there with raised tail, growling furiously at Catalin, as if he wished to bar their way. Fell had scouted the forest the night before and seen Vladeran's soldiers in the trees, and he knew their traps only too well. Alina's warning had been real.

"Fell," whispered Catalin in amazement. "You've come. But what is wrong?"

Lifting his paw and clawing softly at his leg, Fell whined in frustration, as he tried to reach Catalin with his mind and warn him of the terrible danger they were in. Catalin knelt down, and placing a hand on the wolf's head, calmed his panting snarls, but the wolf kept swinging his head towards the neck of the gorge and growling again.

"There's something out there," said Ovidu suddenly, stepping forwards. "The wolf senses it."

"Yes," whispered Catalin. "You think it's a trap?"

"I don't know, Catalin, but we must take counsel."

The wolf calmed a little as he saw the Helgra leaders gathering together now and whispering amongst themselves, looking back at him and the pass. There was argument amongst them, for Ovidu was only first amongst equals with these men and many thought a direct attack the best, but the wolf's sudden appearance and his demeanour had alerted them all. Catalin had his hand on Fell's head still, as the council broke up and Ovidu strode towards him.

"We're agreed," he said. "We'll split our forces and go around. Something's wrong here."

THE PRESENT

Fell was filled with pride as he took the lead at Catalin and Ovidu's side, out along the mountain path that skirted the neck of the gorge, and he sensed that his presence had renewed the Helgra's courage. But the black wolf's heart was heavy. From the forest, he had seen far more than those soldiers and those traps. He had seen Vladeran's palace and that great river that protected it, and if he had to cross it to reach Alina, he would have to face his old fear, death by water. The wolf had seen the size of the human army too, and he was only a lone wolf once more.

Yet far more than this clouded his heart and mind. Morgra had come to him once more in the night, tempting him to use the Summoning Howl. Like a blue spectre, she had stood before him in his dreams, promising that she would see him again, urging him to seek revenge. But worse, she had laughed at his talk of a Guardian and told him that tricksters were spreading lies eveywhere. Fell had thrown her off once more, but his heart was filled with his old terror for his aunt and her power.

It was a power that seemed so much stronger than his own now. What could a lone wolf do in a human battle? Nothing at all. Pantheos had spoken of a great mind, moving through nature, of the animals turning to help Alina Sculcuvant, help for their very survival. Yet as Fell had neared the armies, he had noticed that the land about them was strangely devoid of animals, who seemed to have run away in fear, just as they feared the wolf. Was Morgra right?

It was a foolish dream, Fell told himself. Somehow he was being tricked. The Lera would never come to their aid. Fell was now convinced that this Guardian had been nothing more than a Borar. Perhaps the bear had believed his own words. Even Skart's words, so many of which had come true, seemed absurd to the wolf. A human male had spoken through a wolf, and Fell had touched the elements and risen from a river again, but it was the last words of that riddle that had put a final doubt in Fell's mind. A clawed Putnar open its wings? Or a wolf sprout two heads? It was utterly impossible. It was all a stupid story.

As they ran, Fell tried to tell himself to believe and trust, as Pantheos had urged him, but he doubted even Pantheos now, as he doubted so many of the stories that mingled with the real, hard life of the wolf, only to sow confusion. Fell thought, with a certainty he had never known, that he was running to his own death, and the death of these humans about him too. Yet the wolf would face what was to come, not to fulfil a destiny and save nature itself, but for Alina Sculcuvant alone.

"Fell. It is you, Fell. You're near now, I can feel it. I knew you wouldn't abandon us. You must save the Helgra from the trap. Must save my people. I wish I'd never brought them to this."

In Alina's vivid dream she felt hope swelling in her heart. She could hear the panting wolf nearby, and felt her feet touching the fresh, clean grass, running free through the forest.

But the images changed and she saw a terrible vision of men and banners tumbling into open wolf pits, their bodies pierced by sharpened sticks, like a thousand ghostly vampires with stakes plunged into their hearts. Alina groaned, as she had in a barn long ago with her dreams of goblins and fairies. Her journey had taught her that there was no magic in the real world, and it was she that had brought her people to despair and destruction.

"*No!*" she screamed.

"Alina."

"Yes, Fell. It's me. I'm here. Where are you, Fell? I can't see you anymore."

"Alina, wake up."

Fell's words had been nothing but a dream, and the whispering that was telling her gently to wake wasn't Fell at all, but a human voice in her prison cell. Alina WovenWord opened her eyes and stirred in the straw. A tall figure in a grey hooded cloak—a monk—stood before her. She felt the sudden rush of terror. The priest. Her final blessing had come at last, and so had Alina's execution.

"Get up, child. Hurry now."

"You've come for me then, Father?" she whispered sadly. "The Helgra are vanquished so quickly? Is Catalin dead?"

"Has it been so very long, Alina of Castelu? Don't you recognise my voice?"

The monk had raised his hands to his cowl to uncloak his face, and Alina's heart clenched. Before her was that face of her dreams and that tumbling, curling black hair—her mother, Romana.

Then Alina saw the dagger she was clutching in her hand.

"So it is you who has come to kill me, Mother," she hissed bitterly, "because you really love my half brother. And want him to rule in Castelu."

Romana looked down at the dagger. "Kill you, Alina?" she whispered. "Never. This is for him. For Vladeran."

Doubt filled Alina's hazel eyes.

"Then you . . ."

"Knew nothing, I swear it. Until I overheard Vladeran talking in the great chamber."

Alina's eyes flickered. She so wanted to believe. "Oh, Mother," she said.

The beautiful woman held back, as if still uncertain, then suddenly she was kneeling before her daughter, holding Alina's face in her trembling hands and dropping the dagger.

"Yes, I'm your mother, Alina. If one so foolish and wicked as I deserves such a name. Can you ever forgive me?"

"Forgive you?"

"I treated you so coldy, Alina, after I lost your father. You so much remind me of him, and I turned my love towards the baby. I was angry too when the wolves took Elu. It blinded me to my true feelings, and made me believe Vladeran's filthy lies."

Romana reached out and clasped her daughter's hands. Tears were streaming down their cheeks, and she pulled the girl towards her and began to kiss her face desperately, between her anguished sobs.

"Forgive me, Alina. Please."

Romana pulled back again and looked deep into her daughter's hazel eyes, with the strange fleck of green.

"If I'd ever known, my child, ever suspected for a single moment, I wouldn't have rested until I found you, I swear it. But I thought you were dead. Taken and murdered by Turks, like your father, Dragomir."

"Then you know everything now?"

"I knew nothing until I overheard Vladeran talking of a young woman in the great chamber and a wolf and our people," answered Romana's shaking voice, between her bitter tears. "Since then I've hardly been able to sleep or rest, worrying for you and them. I knew as soon as the Shield Guard came they were trying to keep all knowledge of you from me, but that you must be near."

Romana was looking about in disgust and anger.

"I felt it though, Alina, sensed that you were close, but I hardly dared believe the magic."

The young woman could hardly believe that her own mother was suddenly here, holding her hands so lovingly.

"Dearest Alina, let me look at you and see you with restored eyes. For years I've been blind, daughter."

Alina almost blushed as her mother lifted her chin with her hand and looked at her. She rubbed away some of the dirt on her face and touched the fringe of her short, boyish red hair.

"What have they done to you, my darling?"

"It's all right, Mother. I came disguised as a man, for I had man's work to do. And I can fight like them too, as a Helgra woman."

Romana's tearful eyes glinted proudly.

"And more, from what I hear of you, Alina," she whispered wonderingly. "They speak of a black wolf and a power. It's like the ancient myths."

"It is the Sight," said Alina, wondering where Fell was now and thinking with sudden worry of Catalin and the Helgra. "It's all so strange, Mother, as though I've been living through a dark dream. There's a bond between us, and somehow we're linked."

"As the house of Castelu seems always to have been linked to the fortunes of the wolf," said Romana, nodding. "As your brother Elu was taken by wolves that night, but then restored to us, just as mysteriously. I blamed you then, my child, for Elu's disappearance and almost wanted you banished. It closed my heart to the truth too. Forgive me, I beg of you."

"And I shouldn't have left him alone," said Alina, "though I was very young. It's all right now, Mother."

"Yes, Alina," said Romana more cheerfully. "If only your father could see you now, if only he hadn't died . . ."

"Been murdered you mean."

Romana's hands closed around Alina's wrists.

"What are you saying?"

"The day Father fell from his horse on the battlefield and was cut down," said Alina angrily, "his saddle had been tampered with."

Romana pulled back in horror, as if she feared to hear what she already knew in her own secret heart.

"By his best friend?" she whispered coldly. "By my husband, Vladeran?"

"Yes."

Again scalding tears were falling from Romana's eyes.

"Can you ever forgive me? You must forgive me."

Alina's kind heart suddenly melted.

"Hush, Mother. There's nothing to forgive now."

"I would have acted if I'd known anything, I swear it, but I had turned in on myself, when I should have been looking outwards to my people. I didn't know that Vladeran had been persecuting the Helgra. I should have known, I should. But after Elu came back I wanted nothing more to do with wolves."

"Mother," said Alina urgently, struggling to get up, "our people, and my friend Catalin, are in terrible danger, and I brought it on them. They come to save me, but Vladeran has set a trap for them. We must do something before it's too late."

Before her mind's eye, Alina could see the Helgra tipping towards those ghastly pits fanning the gorge. Catalin too. She had to stop it.

"Peace, Alina," said Romana softly, raising the young woman to her feet. "Somehow they learnt of this trap and broke ranks, circling the main body of our army, and avoiding the pass towards the palace. They are on the plain before these gates and they try to cross the ditch."

Alina's heart leapt. Had Fell somehow managed to reach Catalin and the Helgra and warn them after all? Had she summoned him with the Sight? As she stood there, she began to hear faint sound from the corridor outside. Not the wails and moans of prisoners, but distant cries and shouts beyond. The blaring of horns and the clash of metal on metal.

"There's hard fighting," said her mother, "and all will be swept up in it. We must hurry."

A man moved out of the shadow of the prison door. It was a Shield Guard.

466

"It's all right, Alina," said Romana, looking sternly at him. "Landu has remembered his true loyalties at last. It's how I discovered you were here."

"And you're right, my lady, we must hurry," said Landu gravely, and guiltily too. "Elu waits in your chamber. There are fresh horses saddled and ready in the courtyard nearby. We must get you all away behind the Helgra lines, or even better, and far safer, to the armies of King Stefan."

"King Stefan?" whispered Alina hopefully.

"He's far, but if we can get to him, perhaps we can persuade him to send help."

To help the Helgra, wondered Alina, or to aid his own overlord in surpassing his rebellious subjects? Besides, from the sounds outside, if the King was far it was too late for any help. Alina's heart was thundering.

"But my manacles," she said. "Vladeran has the only key."

Landu stepped fully into the prison. He was carrying her own wolf-topped sword and Alina stood away from the wall and pulled the chain taught, as he raised the beautiful thing and struck. Alina was free. She rose, rubbing her wrists, and Landu took the sword by the blade and, turning it, offered her the hilt. She clasped the thing again and felt a sudden flood of strength, as she balanced its trusty weight.

"Now we flee this place," said Landu.

"No," answered Alina, feeling herself restored again. "I must go to their aid and fight. We've a pact."

"It's too dangerous," said Landu. "And it will be of more

help to the Helgra if we can reach Stefan and tell him the truth of this."

Alina could see the sense of flight, although she desperately wanted to be at Catalin's side, and secretly determined to join him as soon as she got her mother and half brother away in safety. But Romana had stepped forwards too, snatching up the dagger again in her elegant hand.

"The way to the courtyard will lead us past the steps to the arras and Vladeran's chamber, will it not, Landu?" she said.

"It will, my lady."

"Then I've killing to do myself," hissed Romana. "For, daughter, are we not both women who run with the wolves?"

"No, Lady Romana," insisted Landu. "If you get close and strike, the Shield Guard will strike you down in turn. Leave justice to the King, Romana. And to heaven."

The thought of her mother being struck down, so soon after Alina had found her again, made the young woman terrified.

"Landu's right, Mother. Besides, you can't strike Vladeran down. Some oracle speaks to him of the things that will be, and he may only be slain when . . . when my father is in sight of his own palace."

"But Dragomir is . . ."

"Yes. So let us leave Vladeran to the shadows."

Alina's strange words had amazed both her mother and Landu, and Romana lowered the dagger fearfully in front of the storyteller. Romana was not a fighter, and although she hated Vladeran with all her heart now, these words of witchcraft made her wish to be away in the open, free air and the warming sunlight.

"Come," said Landu, pulling at Romana's arm. "Hurry."

They stepped out into the corridor and began to run, and as they passed the cells Alina began to see how many people Vladeran had locked in his prisons. Yet the moans were stilled now, as the prisoners heard the dim sounds of battle beyond, and wondered how the fight of great ones would affect their own bitter destinies.

They came out into an open courtyard and suddenly Landu raised his sword. Five Shield Guard soldiers had seen them and drawn theirs instantly. It was Alina WovenWord who stepped fowards, pushing her mother aside, and she began to move as if in a dream, the warrior smith's sword cutting and slicing through the air, turning and jabbing, unafraid. In her mind the warrior storyteller remembered Vladeran's accusation that it had all been her fault, but she threw it off. Landu fought at her side, and at last the soldiers stood no more. They all lay dead.

Romana was amazed at her daughter, but it was Landu who was staring at her in disbelief. At Alina's eyes. As she had fought they had flashed with yellow gold, and Alina Sculcuvant suddenly had the eyes of a wolf. They cleared again as the three of them stood there, but with that a note came to them on the air. A piercing animal cry.

"Morgra. Why did you not show me this?"

Lord Vladeran's bloody hands clutched the sides of the stony font again, as he too heard the cry outside the palace. He glared down at the she-wolf in the water, with fury and hate, and the scarred creature glared back coldly.

"The Helgra are on the plain, Morgra. And Fell is with them. Why did you not warn me, damn you?"

"Warn you?" came Morgra's scornful thoughts. "Did I say that I may foretell everything, human? And does a human need to know every step of the way, before he can show true courage and continue? I once thought your kind the greatest of Lera, but now . . ."

"But it was you that convinced me in all this. You that reassured me."

"Was it indeed? Is that why you wear me on your back, like my dear niece, Larka?"

Vladeran fingered the fur on his wolf coat, made from two dead Varg.

"You said we would turn the black wolf, yet even now that beast leads the Helgra against me. If they cross the river, the palace may be lost."

"There's plenty of time yet, human," whispered Morgra's shadowy mind, "for how can an army cross that water, even if they breach the ditch? I've spoken to Fell and even now the bloodlust grips him, as he kills and maims. It shall not fade before he comes within the presence of the girl."

"What are you saying?"

"When his teeth are at Alina's throat, he'll truly be ours. It was not I who saw Fell kill her, it was Fell himself who saw it with the Sight, and the Sight does not lie. As it did not lie when I looked into the shadows and prophesied your future."

"And so saw that I'm invulnerable," whispered Vladeran's calming mind, "unless a dead man walks the palace."

Vladeran seemed to swell in stature again, and he lifted himself to his full height.

"Word has come with my spies from King Stefan too, Morgra. He'll not come to help these Helgra scum. Nothing comes to aid them now."

Vladeran smiled as he thought of the King and of his cousin Draculea too.

"So I'll fear nothing and no one. And when Fell comes, I shall command him myself, and he shall lick the Helgra's blood from my hand."

Vladeran suddenly looked magnificent, yet something veiled came into Morgra's watching eyes. Vladeran was too lost in a dream to see.

"Command him and lead the wolf, still dripping with the bloodlust, to that little cell where the young woman lies, to fulfil his true destiny and make him what must be."

"The girl is not there," said Morgra's thoughts. "Even now I see her hurrying through your prisons with her mother."

"Her mother," gasped Vladeran in horror. "Romana knows?"

"She knows everything. As we all know in the end."

"Where are they going? Tell me, quickly."

"They go to fetch the boy and take horse and flee."

"To take my son!"

"Yes. Aided by one of your blessed Shield Guard, Landu. Perhaps you should not have promoted Cascu in his stead."

"Damn you," cried Vladeran, breaking away from the font, as Morgra's image faded in the water. "Damn you all to hell."

Vladeran turned and tore aside the tapestry, bringing it crashing to the floor to reveal the little chapel, and strode back into the great chamber, where thirty soldiers were waiting.

"Guards. Rouse yourselves. Cascu."

Cascu and the Shield Guard were already roused, for they could hear the sounds of battle beyond all too clearly, and their hands had been poised on their weapons as their master prayed. They were sworn on their lives to protect Lord Vladeran whatever came, and their courage was far from wavering yet. Cascu thought Vladeran's eyes looked so dark and sunken though, as if he had not slept in a month, and he saw the snarling fury on his lips.

"Hurry to Romana's chamber," cried Vladeran. "They're trying to flee. Stop them and bring them here. Bring me my son. My heir."

Ten of the Shield Guard saluted and went rushing from the hall, as Vladeran sat down wearily in his great chair. He cast a look to the tapestry where once Romana had appeared, then sunk his head on his fist and for a while seemed lost in thought.

"Lord Vladeran," whispered Cascu, fearful of disturbing him. "Should we not go forth to fight my people?"

Vladeran looked up coldly at the Helgra spy but was silent.

"Or flee?" said Cascu.

Vladeran's eyes were suddenly filled with pride and defiance, and he got up.

"I'll never flee, Cascu. I'll not lose this battle either."

"But how can you be so sure, my lord?"

"I've sent for aid. Even now riders come to help us. My cousin Tepesh. But I know I cannot be harmed, and as for the battle, if my soldiers or Draculea's fail, then the wolf is the key."

"The wolf, my lord?"

"To control Fell, Cascu, is to win the field whatever happens," hissed Vladeran. "For if we do that, we'll control your people too. When they see him meekly at my side, they shall worship me, even as their swords and bows glance off the impenetrable shield of my own destiny. Is the wolf not really why they march?"

"But how can you control it?"

"The Helgra woman, of course," hissed Vladeran. "Alina SkeinTale."

Alina was following Landu and her mother through the grimy passages still, and as they went they heard that sound more clearly now, and it stopped her in her tracks. It was definitely an animal cry. The high, angry note that carried both courage and power in it. The howl of the wild wolf.

"Fell," cried Alina, as her heart soared. "Fell is really here."

As Alina Woven Word said it, the black wolf stood on a mound of raised earth before Vladeran's fearful palace and the great river that protected it, spanned by the single wooden bridge. He looked magnificent. His tail was raised like the Helgra banners about him, carrying that open-winged eagle, and his cry rumbled from his belly and rose through his rippling throat, out of a black muzzle red with blood. The bloodlust was on the wolf.

Catalin stood to his right on the mound above the wide ditch, and although the storyteller was terrified, the young man's bow arm was working at speed, threading arrows and sending them deftly towards the enemy soldiers lined in front of them. Fell kept swinging his head towards the young man protectively. If any of Pantheos's words had been true, then Catalin was as important as Alina now, for it was their children's children who would one day come to help them all.

The young storyteller had never seen anything as terrible as this battle, and his heart was heavy as he looked about the field at the dead, but he kept his courage, and thought of Alina alone. At times as he fought he was gripped by such terrible emotions that it was as if he hardly recognised himself, as if he had somehow been transformed into a wild animal, and it was only the image of Alina's beautiful face that made him feel human again.

Ovidu was on the wolf's left side, raising an antler also red with blood, and turning to call to the Helgra warriors flooding into the breach behind them. How proud that Helgra man looked as he went to battle again at the side of the wolf. Ovidu knew, as he called the charge again, how important Fell's presence was to the Helgra attack. These Magyar-Dacian tribesmen carried the wolf's call in their dreams and legends, and it was as if their ancient songs and stories were coming true. Many dogs had played a part in past struggles, trained to march ahead in packs to frighten their foe, but never a wild wolf. And never a wolf like Fell.

Which was why what happened next threatened to destroy their morale once more, and turn the wavering tide of the battle against them entirely, even as they swung with their swords and antlers.

In Fell's desire to press forwards and find Alina, the wolf overreached himself. Until now they had pressed ahead together, in good order, fighting in hand-to-hand combat, with the weapons that Catalin had helped them forge again in the Helgra village and the antlers they had collected in the bracken. But two dozen Shield Guard soldiers had come on horseback over the long wooden bridge that crossed the widest part of the river.

They charged left and right, and some of the Helgra wavered on the mound, while more of Vladeran's foot soldiers charged towards the centre of the fight. Fell saw them coming and leapt towards them, with fury in his belly. He thought of himself sailing over that ice chasm. The wolf leapt too far though, for his powerful spring allowed him to cross the wide ditch below the mound they were on, and cut him off completely from the Helgra behind. Ovidu, knowing Fell's importance to his warriors, had ordered that his soldiers guard his flanks with their swords and bows and antlers, but now the wolf was alone and undefended.

"No, Fell," cried Catalin desperately, even though he knew that the wolf could not understand him. "Come back."

The storyteller strung another arrow and sent it scything towards a soldier who had leapt from the side to strike at Fell. It ended the threat, and the man dropped dead, but it was too dangerous for the Helgra to flood into the ditch and lose the advantage of height, while the black wolf was completely surrounded.

Fell swung in a half circle, snapping and snarling furiously, baring his teeth and his anger. The soldiers had seen the wolf from a distance, and now his proximity kept Vladeran's men at bay. But as they began to realise that Fell was a real animal, and not some demon of the night, as they saw from the scar on his side that he could certainly be injured and killed, the soldiers' own courage was returned. This was nothing but a wild dog.

A single soldier came running towards Fell, more dangerous to him than any of the others. It was an archer who was already stringing his bow to shoot. Catalin saw him and the terrible danger to Fell, but he realised that he had just fired his last arrow, and did not have time to retrieve any others.

"Ovidu," cried the storyteller desperately, lowering his empty bow. "We must help Fell somehow."

"The ditch," shouted Ovidu. "We have to get over the ditch."

They could both see that it was useless. The deep ditch itself was already piling with dead Helgra, and thus difficult to cross, and the gulf was too far anyway. In a moment Fell too would lie dead, and with him all hope might well break amongst the ranks.

The archer lifted and drew back the bow string, and in the sight of that metal arrow tip, Fell saw death pass into his own soul. But suddenly a grey shape came flying across that ditch of death. It landed next to Fell and then sprung again, reaching the archer before he released his arrow, and knocking him to the ground. Wolf teeth struck at him as the advancing soldiers shrunk back in terror, and now before Vladeran's men was not one but two wild wolves. A black and a grey.

"Tarlar," cried Fell in astonishment, sending not words but furious snarls to the ears of the defending soldiers, as the she-wolf lifted her muzzle and turned to him proudly. "You're here too, Tarlar?"

In another bound the she-wolf was at Fell's side.

"You think I'd leave you to fight alone, Fell," she growled angrily, "after what I said that day, and what you did for the pack? When the survival of nature itself depends on us? I've been following you, dear Fell, though it was hard to keep pace with a Dragga such as you, and in the end I had to track your scent. But I'm here now."

Hope swelled in Fell's pounding heart. And something else too. Belief.

"But you should not, Tarlar. This is a destiny the Sight has forced on me, in my long, lone journeying. But not you, dear Tarlar."

"Fell," whispered Tarlar softly, "can't you see it now? You're no longer alone."

Something strange rose in Fell's belly, as if a kindly hand had stroked the black wolf, and his words felt choked and his heart about to break.

"The humans may kill us yet, Tarlar."

"And all things must face that end," said Tarlar boldly. "So let us unite our destinies, come what may. But not with the madness of the Vengerid, with purpose and meaning."

The wolves both turned, the Dragga and the Drappa, and began to growl and snarl at the soldiers. In that moment the Helgra, who had seen Tarlar's strange appearance, sent up a great shout. Like the salmon breaking from the manacles of the lower river towards the future, they rushed the ditch and began to push back Vladeran's soldiers. They inched on towards the palace and the bridge across the furious river.

Yet the battle was not to be won so easily, if won at all. At that moment another wave of Vladeran's men came riding across the bridge, hundreds of them, and to a man they bore those black crosses on their armour.

They were the most hardened of Vladeran's feared Shield Guard, and little impressed with the presence of two wild wolves, as they fanned out across the plain. Although the Helgra protected Fell and Tarlar's flanks, these fresh troops quickly engaged the surrounding attackers, who began to waver again. There were just too many Shield Guard soldiers and the Helgra were hopelessly outnumbered. They were losing the fight.

"It's no good, Tarlar," cried Fell bitterly. "We're lost. This has all been a story. A bad dream."

Tarlar whimpered, but suddenly a sound came to the air that froze Fell and Tarlar in their paw marks and made their tails rise and their ears twitch.

"What's that?" whispered Tarlar, although she knew already.

It was a wolf howl. Yet not one but ten, twenty, forty voices, crying and howling through the air. From the surrounding mountains they came, those calling wolf throats, howling from the echoing hills.

The attacking Shield Guard paused fearfully, and Fell and Tarlar looked up and were quite astonished to see, there in the distance, forty wolves on the mountain. They did not move forwards, or join the attack; they were not there because of some strange enchantment. They were there, howling and calling, with one purpose alone. The Vengerid had come to salute Fell.

And there were five other wolves there too, set slightly apart from the rest. Kar and Larka, Kipcha and Skop and Khaz. The Helgra heard the wolves and rallied, while the Shield Guard wavered again, truly fearful now, and their frightened horses began to buck and whinny in terror.

But still their discipline held, and it would have vanquished the day if it hadn't been for another extraordinary sound, a rushing, like a great wind, or a wave breaking on a shore. Fell thought he was in the river again and behind the waterfall, except all around him the moving cloud was so black it blocked out the sun.

"What's happening?" growled Tarlar fearfully, feeling a presence about her as ominous as Pantheos had been to Fell. Shapes were moving all about them, swirling and eddying around the Shield Guard's starting horses, and suddenly Fell realised what it was.

"Starlings," he cried.

The giant wave of starlings turned and swirled and broke around the humans and wolves, and Fell almost expected the salmon to come leaping amongst them too. But as they watched, Fell realised that within that great organism, individual birds were breaking away and rushing at the visors of the Shield Guard. And as those wings fluttered, Fell seemed to hear a voice whispering around them, but as loud as the voice of the Guardian: *Ask this then, wolf, if you seek the wonder and magic of the world,* it seemed to say. *Ask only what consciousness is. Consciousness, that does not live in man alone.* Fell shuddered and remembered Pantheos's words of a Great Secret carried on the air. Skart had prophesied it too.

"But how?" cried Tarlar. "It's impossible."

"The Sight," answered Fell. "The Sight is filling the world, like a great mind. The Lera have come to show man what he is, and to help the girl and boy. The Helpers are here."

"And to help you too," growled Tarlar.

It was indeed as if all nature had risen up, and suddenly the Shield Guard broke completely. The way to the bridge was open. Yet even as the wolves led the Helgra through, their hearts sank. They saw that long ropes had been strung from supports of the thin bridge, back across the churning river to Vladeran's palace, and soldiers on the far bank were pulling now. Suddenly there was a thundering crash, as the attackers reached the shore. That long, thin bridge, the only way across, collapsed on itself and crashed into the swirling waters.

Fell thought of Alina and the ice bridge, and felt his heart go with it. The river was so wide, and its waters looked so angry and deep, that the wolves and the Helgra had little chance of crossing it safely. Their swords and antlers would only weigh them down, while if they made it at all they would be easy prey for the Shield Guard.

Fell began to growl helplessly, hearing a voice in his mind, too, *Fear it, wolf, fear death by water,* but even as the wolves and the humans stood there, defeated again in their attack, the most extraordinary thing happened in that extraordinary fight.

Ovidu pointed at the river in disbelief. Through its swirling current, shapes were moving rapidly upstream. The Helgra thought it witchcraft, as the logs made for the shore, as if guided by an unseen hand. Some of the logs had come moving rapidly up the river, while parts of the bridge itself now turned towards the shore and the Helgra. Fell's tail rose, as a wide, flat part of the bridge reached the shore where he and Tarlar stood, and he padded forwards onto the little platform.

"Come, Tarlar," he said softly.

The she-wolf was growling in terror behind him, her tail between her legs.

"But Fell. It's witchcraft. And death by water."

"You've nothing to fear now," growled Fell. "You're with me, Tarlar."

Tarlar padded onto the platform nervously, and immediately the wolves found themselves turning in the water and moving across the river. The wolves had given the lead and now, everywhere,

Helgra were springing forwards onto those little boats to cross the river too.

"I don't know what power you have, Fell SpellWeaver," whispered Tarlar, "but I think it a good thing."

"Power?" said the wolf, gazing into the waters and suddenly believing with all his heart. "Only the power that is all around us, Tarlar, always."

Fell had already guessed what was driving those strange boats on, and suddenly two familiar little heads popped up from the river.

"It *is* you, Ottol," cried the black wolf, with pleasure, "and your mate."

"And zo it is," answered the beaver, squirting water from his mouth, "and many others, Fell. Beaver and otter too. It is a strange zing, no? It's as if vee couldn't resist, and zumthing was zummoning us. As if you were speaking to all of us."

Yes, thought Fell, thinking of what Pantheos had said and that great mind, moving through nature.

"But one came to us too. A bear."

Fell blinked in surprise. A bear? Then perhaps Pantheos was just a Lera . . .

"So you left your kits to help us, Ottol?" he growled.

"Only for avile, voolf. Vile you help zees humans. You've found your vay I zee."

"That we will know soon," answered the wolf gravely, "but hurry, Ottol, hurry."

• • •

In the palace the song of the wolf, multiplied fiftyfold by the Vengerid and Fell's family, was lost again, but Alina WovenWord was standing now, beside her mother, in a chamber far from that prison, looking at the face of a boy. Her own little half brother.

"Come, Elu," said Romana softly, beside them, "do you recognise your elder sister?"

"But you're dead," said Elu nervously, looking up at the strange changeling storyteller. Alina looked at him just as warily. But he was just a little boy, she told herself.

"No, Elu, not dead," she whispered, taking his hand and smiling with eyes filled with tears, as she remembered the baby in the cot. "But I've been away a long time. I've been in a different country, far away. A strange country."

"Was it a nice place?" asked Elu cheerfully.

Alina thought back to that shepherd's hovel and dear Mia, but to Malduk and Ranna too.

"No, Elu," she answered sadly, "it wasn't a nice place at all. Although I had friends there too."

"And are you our friend?"

Alina remembered the love she had felt for the little baby of her dreams.

"Oh, yes, Elu. I'm your sister and I love you dearly. I always have. I won't let any of this touch you anymore."

"I like your sword," said Elu. "Will you show me how to use it?"

"Yes, I will, but first we must all go on a journey. Mother, you, and I."

"Is Father coming with us?"

"No, Elu."

"You're funny. Why do you look like a boy?"

Alina laughed and ruffled the boy's blond hair.

"Perhaps I'll tell you one day," she answered. "Tell you of changelings and goblins and Baba Yaga. But do you trust me now?"

The boy thought for awhile, and at last he gave a firm nod.

"Good." Alina smiled. "Now we'd better hurry."

As Alina said it though, they heard raised voices outside and Landu hardly had time to draw his sword before the Shield Guard burst into the chamber. Landu did not expect them to have foreknowledge of all that was happening, or to be moving with such intent, so he hardly had time to defend himself as the lead guard's sword knocked him aside and plunged into his gut. His startled eyes went blank and lost their light entirely.

Elu cried out and ran to his mother, grasping her middle, as Alina's sword came singing from its sheath and again her eyes flashed with wolf gold. Alina struck, cutting the attacker's forearm, but it was too late for Landu. He sank to his knees and crashed to the floor.

"My lady . . . forgive . . ."

Alina turned, sinking her weight through her body, all her training returning to her. The storyteller was poised and her mind was crystal clear, ready to fight again, but the Shield Guard were many and she hesitated.

"If you resist us, you both die, woman," said the soldier who had struck, coldly. "You and your mother."

"Lord Vladeran would not allow it," cried Romana furiously.

"Vladeran has ordered it, woman," hissed the soldier scornfully. "And has summoned you to the great chamber. He wants his son."

Alina WovenWord paused. A pain had come, but not from the soldier's words. It was that ache in her head, and Alina pretended to be listening to the soldier as she heard the voice in her mind.

"I'm close, Alina. We're crossing the river and some of the Helgra are already on your side, and entering his stone den."

"Fell?"

Alina's heart was racing.

"There's fire and blood about us and has been much death. Sometimes I cannot hold my own savagery. The bloodlust is on me. On us all. Are you safe, human?"

"Not yet, dear Fell. And you and Catalin?"

"We've all survived. The boy is strong, and the Helgra leader too. I'm proud of them both and myself, for Catalin is important to this destiny too, Alina. And the Lera have come to help us too. To help you."

Alina felt amazement in her heart and hope too, even now.

"Be careful, Fell. Vladeran has summoned others to his aid."

"Where are you, human cub?"

"I don't know, Fell, but they take us to Vladeran's great chamber."

"Then I shall come."

"How, Fell? I do not know how to guide you in this place."

"I'm a wolf, remember, with senses more powerful than yours, and I have your scent."

THE PRESENT

The link snapped and slowly Alina lowered her sword arm.

Romana and her children were hurried through the palace by the Shield Guard, and Elu was terrified, for there was the sound of fighting everywhere now. The Helgra had begun to breach the palace. Flames licked at the rich tapestries in the chambers below and bodies lay in the passageways, while several times the Shield Guard had to strike out to defend themselves, but of Catalin and Ovidu and Fell, Alina saw nothing.

As they burst back into the chamber, Vladeran sprang from his throne and the doors were slammed behind them. His eyes blazed with hate and jealousy, as he saw that little family together, the two women and the boy, and he strode forwards and caught Romana by her cloak. With a growl he threw his wife to the ground near the throne. Elu went running after her and tried to help her up, as Romana slid on the hard marble.

"Mother."

"My boy," whispered Romana bitterly.

"So you know everything, Romana," said Vladeran, glaring down at them both, "and there's no reason to dissemble anymore, is there, my love? And you would have stolen my son."

"He's my son too!" screamed Romana.

Vladeran turned and looked at Alina, held there by the Shield Guard.

"I should not have dissembled then, Romana, should I? I should have killed the lying little whelp myself, in the palace, all those years ago when she failed to protect my child. Then this never would have been."

"As you murdered Dragomir, Vladeran?" wept Romana bitterly. "As you've murdered my heart. Assassin."

Madness came into Vladeran's eyes as he saw his beautiful wife sobbing on the floor, madness and utter despair.

"No, Romana. You can love me again. All this has been for you, don't you see? I love you, the only creature I've ever loved, and all shall soon be well, I swear it."

Vladeran knew it was foolish, and suddenly he reached out and grabbed Alina SkeinTale's arm, pulling her furiously across the room towards them. He thrust the storyteller backwards into the throne, near her mother and his son.

"Sit there, my fine Lady of Castelu," he said mockingly, "for that's what you seek, is it not, against all the Salic laws? Against nature itself."

"You're mad," whispered Alina.

"That may be," snarled Vladeran, suddenly pulling the dagger from his belt and jumping behind the throne, "but here you shall be sitting when *he* comes."

"Fell's here already," spat Alina, "somewhere close, and my wolf shall tear out your throat."

Vladeran put his dagger to Alina's own throat.

"Shall he?" He smiled, pushing his brutal face into hers. "I hear them outside now. I have always known he was coming, all my life."

"Shall we bar the doors, my lord?" asked Cascu fearfully, as the sounds of fighting rose even louder. Vladeran stood at his full height, but still he held the dagger against Alina WovenWord.

"On the contrary, Cascu, throw the doors open and welcome the wolf into my fold."

"But, my lord. The Helgra."

"Do it, fool, do it now."

Cascu bowed, and fearing more and more the approach of his people and his brother Ovidu, he waved his hand and four Shield Guard soldiers pulled open the doors again. Seven bodies lay in the passage beyond, and flames were flickering against the palace walls, the shadows of candles and tapers that had been overturned by the desperate fighting in the corridor, though the Helgra who had killed these men had passed on. The corridor was empty.

The captives and their captors stood there in Vladeran's great chamber, hearing the shouts and cries from beyond, wondering what would appear in that doorway, and waiting for Fell to find Alina WovenWord's scent amongst the complex, confusing web of smells that filled his nostrils in the palace. Smells of earth and stone and human blood. Waiting for him to catch it like an echo and let it draw him along an Ariadne's thread of sensation, up a stairway, round a corner, down a long, body-strewn corridor. It seemed like an age, but at last they heard it. A wild growling beyond.

TWENTY-FIVE
MORGRA

Alina started as she saw Fell's silhouette magnified against the wall in the candlelight, and even more so when that head suddenly seemed to sprout two muzzles, like some mighty dog guarding the gates of hell. Just as Pantheos and Skart had foretold. A wolf had sprouted two heads.

Cascu and the Shield Guard soldier looked at each other in horror, but they held their ground. And there they suddenly stood in the doorway, not one but two full-grown wolves. The black and a grey. The male and the female. Tarlar and Fell came side by side, and it seemed as if there was blood and fire reflecting in their glittering yellow gold eyes. Even Alina was amazed as she saw them together.

"Fell, dear Fell."

Fell stopped and gave a low growl, as his eyes took in the armed humans around the chamber. Alina felt almost jealous of this she-wolf that walked at his side. As the Shield Guard all stepped back, Elu buried his head in his mother's breast and started to cry.

"Alina," came Fell's angry thoughts, "I can hardly see you, Alina. Their damned blood clouds my vision, while the bloodlust has me."

"But you've come, Fell."

"And if I move, human, he'll strike with his dagger."

"Yes, Fell. He's full of tricks and traps. Beware his men too."

Fell's head swung around the room, and in an instant, as if he were sensing it, he had taken in the precise number of the Shield Guard watching him. Their position in the room. Their distance from him and Tarlar.

"I have them in my eye, Alina, and they'll pay bitterly if they strike."

"You're talking to it, aren't you?" whispered Vladeran, glaring at Fell and pressing the knife even tighter to Alina's throat. "Tell it to speak to me, girl. The real wolf."

Alina simply smiled. "Even if you had the gift, Fell would never speak to one such as you," she answered coldly. "He may see your thoughts if he chooses, but he will not speak to you. Any of you."

Vladeran pressed the knife tighter and Fell snarled.

"Remarkable," growled Vladeran, "it's as if he acts beyond the instincts of a mere animal, and understands everything we say. Then speak to him for me, girl, and tell him that I offer him a bargain."

"What bargain?"

"You're a part of this bargain too, storyteller. For if the wild wolf walks to me now and stands at my side, in return I swear by the halls of Castelu that you'll live, and the wolf shall be honoured here, as the Helgra have always honoured his kind. The forests where he hunts shall be made sacred, and the land itself that is his home shall have my protection."

Fell was growling again, for he had looked into Vladeran's mind and seen the pact and what it meant. Fell was looking at Alina's half brother too, huddled there with his human mother, next to the great chair. The very human whom Fell had once called Bran, the infant Larka herself had protected in the snows, and whom Fell had carried on his back to the village below the castle. The child he had made a pact with too, and a promise to remind him of the wildness and beauty of the world, in exchange for his protection of the Lera.

Fell remembered a vision he'd had of the boy, standing tall, with two dogs at his side, ready to protect the animals. But he felt guilty, for wolves had brought a great darkness to this little human family.

"No, Alina," growled Fell furiously, glancing back at Vladeran, "you may not trust this Dragga scum."

"I know it, Fell, and I would rather have a curse on my head than his protection."

"So, Alina," said Vladeran, "will you not order these beasts?"

"I've told you before, they're not mine to order."

"Very well then," cried Vladeran, "in my kennels my whips bend the dogs to my will, and wolves shall learn too what it is to be tame. Now!"

Vladeran had been waiting for the best moment for the trap he had laid when he had sent his men to fetch Romana, and at his cry four concealed Shield Guard soldiers came running from their hiding place behind the arras, in that recess at the top of the secret passageway. They ran straight at Fell and Tarlar, carrying a net in their arms, which they cast towards the animals, and before the wolves could react, they found themselves struggling in strange bonds made of coarse black rope.

Fell snarled furiously, and Tarlar flailed out with her right paw, but found it sliding through one of the holes in the net and entangling her even more. The net closed around the wolves, as if they were giant, furry fish, pinning their paws under them and wrapping them in a tight bundle, their snouts poking uselessly through a grilling of black cords.

"What's happening to us?" growled Tarlar.

"Don't struggle," whispered Fell, as the soldiers tugged at the ends of the net. "It'll only make it worse. I know of human traps."

Vladeran was smiling contentedly.

"So I have you all," he said delightedly, "as I knew I would in the end. You cannot deny true destiny."

"Your orders, my lord?" said Cascu.

Vladeran swung his head.

"First slay that beast at the black wolf's side."

Fell growled, for again he had read Vladeran's thoughts.

"Stop him, Alina."

"No," Alina started, "I'll do what you ask. I'll persuade Fell to take your pact."

"Even if I thought you weren't lying," said Vladeran, "what use is the other wolf to me? We're animals, and animals we kill."

Vladeran pushed Alina back and, walking around the throne, gave Cascu the dagger.

"Hold the storyteller," he ordered. "Kill her if she moves a muscle."

Vladeran turned and walked forwards, his wolf cloak sweeping across the marble floor. He circled the struggling wolves in their net, and as he did so his back came into Fell's vision and the wolf whimpered as he saw his sister's pelt. Fell hated this human. In that moment he hated all humans. All but Alina. Vladeran was triumphant, feeling invincible indeed with the spell that surrounded him.

"Let our soldiers spread the word," he cried. "Tell the Helgra, under a white flag of truce, that we have the black wolf and if they do not throw down their weapons, Alina Sculcuvant shall die instantly, and salt be sowed over her bones."

The Shield Guard ran from the chamber, as Vladeran began to laugh.

"So then," he cried, "let us wait and see what comes."

Alina was looking helplessly at her friend.

"Oh, Fell," whispered her mind bitterly. "Have I really brought you to this?"

"Don't blame yourself, Alina. A destiny marks us all, no matter how we try to struggle against it, and I'm glad I came. Although I'm sad the she-wolf is here with me."

"Dear Fell."

"If I could just get loose for a moment, I'd rush him now," growled the wolf. "The human who holds you is not so ruthless as Vladeran. I see it in his thoughts. I think he would not kill you as easily as your father's friend."

Vladeran turned and gave Fell a brutal kick through the net, knocking the wind from the wolf and sending up an angry yelp. Fell was struggling to breathe, and as he lay there he suddenly noticed Vladeran's old hunting dog, watching from his place near the throne. Fell gave a low, angry growl.

"Help us, dog. Help those of your kind."

The dog lifted his head wearily and blinked across the chamber floor.

"Help you?" he growled sombrely. "There's no help for it, wolf, even if you were of my kind. I've learnt to accept their power, and to take their meat in return, with the warmth of their red flowers. Besides, there was a time when I myself hunted the wild wolf."

"But now you're nothing but a tame cur," growled Fell angrily.

"Tame I may be," said the dog, with a sigh, "but life tames us all in the end, wolf. Don't fight against it, and it'll be easier for you. It's those that fight hardest for freedom who are never free."

Fell turned away his muzzle in disgust, and suddenly there were more running footsteps. Some of the Shield Guard had returned.

"My lord," cried the first, "your cousin's men have come. Draculea's soldiers. The battle's turning, and many of the Helgra are handing over their weapons."

Alina was at her wits' end now.

"Fell, can't you do anything?"

"I can't control human wills, Alina, even their weakest."

Suddenly a thought flashed into Fell's struggling brain though. A thought that Morgra herself had placed there. Not man, but Lera.

"Yes," cried his mind, remembering what Morgra had suggested. "Yes."

"Fell, what are you doing?"

"There are other armies, Alina. I have seen them before. It'll be dangerous, Alina, for I fear the shadows. I fear they will take me again."

Tarlar was amazed, for beside her Fell's black body had suddenly gone limp. His eyes were closed, and as he lay there a sound came from his throat that terrified all in that great chamber. It came low, and then rose like a ghastly demon, taking to the air, a howl like no other. Only Vladeran suspected what it was, for he had heard something like it before, and it made him tremble. Fell was trying to call the dead from the Red Meadow to come to his aid, just as Morgra had once done. The Summoning Howl.

"No," said Vladeran, rounding on the wolf. "Stop his throat."

The guards were not looking at Fell, or listening to their leader at all. They were staring at the font in that little chapel in utter horror. There, in the shadows, a ghastly silver shape was appearing. Romana slunk back even more, hugging Elu to her, and Alina felt a cold wash of fear through her whole body. She sat back in that chair, and suddenly, as if she were fainting from fear, the storyteller's head went back and just for a moment her eyes became wolf eyes again, before they closed.

Fell blinked and opened his own eyes again, for his call had suddenly ceased, but there, in the arch of the chapel, in front of the font, stood a spectral she-wolf.

"Morgra," he whispered in terror.

The scarred, silver spectre was growling, as Morgra blinked and looked about her, like a sleeper waking from a ghastly dream. Even Tarlar whimpered at Fell's side, as Morgra's angry growls rose, and then her voice came echoing through that hall, as the she-wolf spoke, growls mixed with human words that all assembled understood.

"So then, Fell. You use the Summoning Howl, after all, to restore the dead."

The soldiers and the Helgra and Vladeran understood Morgra, not because a wolf had suddenly been given the power to speak in a human tongue, but because those strange words did not come from Morgra's muzzle at all. They came from the throne and Alina WovenWord's mouth, and Cascu stepped away in horror.

The young woman's eyes had opened again, yellow gold, though they seemed asleep, and her body had gone rigid, as Morgra spoke through Alina's mind, and on the young woman's lips. A wolf was talking through a human Drappa, as Skart had prophesied.

"But the howl is not strong in you, is it, Fell?" Morgra whispered.

Fell flinched and growled back at them both.

"For the others will not come, Fell, I promise you that," said Morgra through Alina's voice. The spectre of the old she-wolf padded slowly from the recess towards the girl and stood beside her.

"No army of ghosts to help you and the Helgra now. But I came. You brought me forth again. Then I was keen to come, and smell blood once more, and taste it too."

Lord Vladeran was even more transfixed than the rest of the assembled humans.

"Morgra," he said wonderingly, not knowing whether to look at the storyteller or the she-wolf. "This grows better and better. If

Fell will not serve me, we'll work together then. My power united, not with a mortal wolf, but with a wolf of shadows and darkness, howling the howls of love and hate."

Vladeran smiled as he stared back at the spectral she-wolf, and Cascu looked at him in awe, not only because of the ghastly apparition, but because Cascu knew that it was he himself, in his doubt, who had given Lord Vladeran these dark Helgra arts. He knew too that the power was real and that he had betrayed more than his father and brother and his own people. But the presence of the spectral wolf kept all away from Alina Sculcuvant.

"Together we'll rule in the land beyond the forests, Morgra," said Vladeran. "Rule the Helgra, my cousin Draculea, and King Stefan himself. You'll show me more and more of the shadows, Morgra, and together we'll conquer death itself."

"Silence, fool."

Alina had swung her head to Vladeran and cried out, and Morgra's spectre was growling beside her, her lips curled into a snarl as she swung her muzzle towards Vladeran, who took a step backwards from them both.

"Silence? But, Morgra . . ."

"Did I not say silence, human, and now I command it."

Vladeran was peering straight into Morgra's eyes, and his hand came down to his dagger.

"Command a human? You dare, animal?"

"Yes, Dragga, I dare. And more than dare. For you think you're invulnerable and that you've won, but even now knights ride towards the palace. Even now the turning Helgra see their banners, and their thundering approach from the mountains, and charge once more. Even now Draculea's men turn away and fear turns to hope again. As it always will."

A look of doubt came into Vladeran's eyes, but outside he fancied he heard the distant blaring of trumpets and a great shout.

"King Stefan's men?" he hissed.

"Not the King, human fool. Knights to whom you swore sacred oaths, long ago, to protect the world."

Vladeran touched that red cross on his chest.

"The Order of the Griffin?" he gasped in terror.

"Yes, Vladeran. And their veiled leader knows you have broken the sacred oaths to which you bound yourself. The oaths to which he is Guardian."

"It does not matter," said a trembling Vladeran, "for you told me that I could not be killed unless Dragomir is in sight of the palace, and I saw my friend die myself. Unless you lied."

Morgra's eyes twinkled as viciously as Malduk's or Ranna's had.

"I did not lie, Vladeran, unlike your own eyes. For you saw Dragomir fall to the Turk, but you did not see his body, on the point of death, recovered by them too and taken to be healed, even as others were burnt."

"Healed?" said Vladeran.

On the floor near the throne, Romana had looked up. Dragomir alive? Her own daughter was telling them this thing. It was impossible.

"There, with the arts of Eastern healers, they gradually restored him, and there, after years in captivity, he was ransomed to the

Griffin Order, only to rise himself amongst their ranks and finally to become their leader."

"No," cried Vladeran. "Dragomir leads the secret Order?"

"Yes," snarled Alina, "for I do not lie."

Through Alina's mind, and Morgra's snarls, Fell could understand the spectre entirely, and he wondered why she was bringing the human this strange news, if she had served him all along. But hope had once more swelled inside him, for the dead were restored indeed, and, if he had known it, the Griffin, a clawed Putnar, had opened its wings again.

Vladeran's body seemed to slump. All his belief in himself, in his own invincibility, seemed to vanish in that instant, like Baba Yaga's broken spell, and now it was as if the slightest touch could shatter him into pieces.

"But why, Morgra? Why didn't you warn me?" he whispered bitterly. "Why have you tricked me?"

Fell was suddenly growling from the net.

"Tell him, Morgra. I do not understand this either."

"Oh, Fell," cried Morgra through Alina's mouth, and the young woman turned her wolf eyes towards Fell. "Don't you see it yet? I've come to help you. To help nature itself."

"Help me?"

"Even now you do not believe me, dear Fell, as I knew you would never believe me, when I spoke to you from the Red Meadow. For once we see another being as one thing, too often we see them as that forever."

Fell growled again.

"At first I thought to help Vladeran, it's true, and I looked into the future for him and saw a part of the truth about his destiny and the girl's. But as I watched you, I began to remember the life of the Varg, and I longed for forgiveness, and for my sojourn in that terrible meadow to end forever."

Fell's golden eyes were flickering doubtfully.

"I longed for the hate that has kept me a prisoner for so long to cease and release me. For hate imprisons us, Fell, and what I did in life, tried to do, made a terrible purgatory for me, that bound me in confusion tighter than your ropes." Morgra's silver spectre looked almost beautiful now. "I once sought to rule the Lera, rule through man, to take revenge for the injustice that was done to me all those years ago. But I knew too that I hated the human who summoned me, and knew it more than ever when he spoke of the injustice that has been done to this girl. For now I know that the only answer to injustice is this. It is justice."

"But what you told me of my own nature," growled Fell, "of nature itself. And what I saw myself of Alina's death."

"I'm sorry, Fell. It was a dangerous path that I walked, but I had to maintain my mask of hate. Firstly because I knew that you would not believe my intentions, unless you saw them with your own eyes. Secondly because I had to hide these things deep within my own mind, almost from myself, so that Vladeran would not suspect me for a moment. Like some secret jewel hidden at the bottom of the sea."

Vladeran was glaring at Alina WovenWord and the spectral

she-wolf, and he could not believe that he had met a mind even more labyrinthine than his own.

"But, Morgra," growled Fell, "the pain and darkness when my parents went. What you tempted me with?"

"I had to be sure too that you would come, Fell, and be here now to complete your destiny. For when this is over, you must know that we are not meant to be with these creatures, Fell. That we must be ourselves alone."

"And Alina's death?" said the black wolf.

"Remember, Fell, that although the Sight can show the truth of the future, like stories it can lie too, or rather destinies can change. As the vision of man's destruction of the wild turned from cold to heat, but also to a wondrous garden. Our destinies are our own, Fell, if we have the courage to take control of them."

Morgra's voice had become softer, calmer, as if she were making a confession and it gave her release.

"And the Sight lied to me, Fell, when it told me all is shadows, and that the answer to injustice is hate, when it's really love. Not a guilty, caught, and needing love, like a child trapped by too much talk of duty, but real love and real strength. Because in all my own searching, I know now what the true meaning and purpose of life is. It is to be happy. To feel joy. That is why evil will always conquer itself in time."

"Oh, Morgra. You did suffer injustice. They thought you a cub killer, when you were simply trying to save it. And like me, the Sight set you apart."

Morgra lifted her tail hopefully.

"There isn't long now, Fell, and soon I'll vanish like a dream," she whispered through Alina, and even now she seemed to grow translucent at the young storyteller's side, as Alina's eyes flashed hazel again. "For your call was not strong, and you are for this world, not the next. But, Fell, can you ever forgive me? For them. For your pack. For dear Larka."

Fell raised his head in the strangling net. An extraordinary strength had suddenly entered the black wolf, and he remembered what Tarlar had said of the need for all things to ask forgiveness.

"I laid a trap to make amends, dear Fell, but not a trap for you, for this human Dragga, one whose kind have hunted us forever with their minds and their spears. I ask your blessing. Fell's blessing."

Morgra's pleading spectre was fading, vanishing, dissolving into thin air. Vladeran stood there in confusion, paralysed by doubt, quite unable to act, and Fell suddenly felt a fury inside him, as he swung his head to the hunting dog once more.

"Help me, damn you," he snarled, "or I'll use the Sight to force you."

Fell knew it was not so, for the Summoning Howl had exhausted him entirely, and near him he sensed Vladeran move. Just his dagger hand at first. Only one thought was in Vladeran's vicious mind, and Fell saw its terrible simplicity immediately. To kill the young woman who had brought Morgra's message. Who had brought his ruin.

"Force Vlag?" said the dog scornfully, across the chamber floor.

Fell's ears cocked forwards immediately. Still Vladeran hesitated, held back by that spectre that seemed to be protecting Alina.

"Vlag?" Fell whispered in astonishment, pierced by a sudden memory. "Is that your name?"

"It is, wolf. What of it?"

"But it was you, Vlag. Long ago, when I hid with my mother, Palla, and my little sister Larka in an abandoned badger's set by the river. It was you that hunted us, Vlag, when a fox came by and you missed the scent."

Vlag's old eyes were peering hard at the wolf, as his master, Vladeran, began to walk slowly towards Alina WovenWord, forcing himself forwards in his hate.

"Remember, Vlag, you must remember. It was when the human child was stolen and the humans were hunting wolves. They wanted revenge."

"Yes," muttered Vlag, "I remember it now. And I said if they wanted revenge then we should give it to them."

"But you said something else too, Vlag. You said you wished the humans would let you hunt what you wanted. Always chasing after wolves."

"I did?"

"Yes, Vlag. Remember your nature and the wonder of the world, and what it is to be wild and free. To hunt what you want, not what they order you to."

Vlag stood up suddenly, but Vladeran was nearly on Alina and Morgra had almost vanished.

"I . . . I . . ."

"Do it, I beg you, Vlag. The soldier. I must get out of this net."

For a moment the old hunting dog, roused into life by the

power of memory, hesitated, and then, as if he were gasping for air and youth, he sprang forwards and bit the nearest guard hard in his calf. With a scream the man leapt back, releasing an edge of the net, just enough for Fell to push himself through the opening. The amazed men were frozen into fear, and Fell leapt straight over Romana and Elu at Lord Vladeran, just as he reached Alina WovenWord.

The storyteller saw again through her startled hazel eyes, and Morgra's shimmering spectre vanished, as Vladeran's dagger hand rose to strike Alina down. But Fell's great paws struck his back and knocked him to the floor. Tarlar was wrestling herself free from the net too, and she sprung out and held the guard back with her teeth, as Vladeran rolled and looked up at Fell in horror.

Fell felt Alina's mind in his, questioning and doubting, even now wanting to show kindness and humanity, in the gentleness of her nature, even now caught by the duality that follows all human animals, but Fell pushed it away.

"No, storyteller," came his liberated thoughts, "the bloodlust is on me and this thing took and wore my sister Larka's coat. Slit her throat and skinned her. Let wild nature do this thing then, Alina WovenWord, let it bring justice, and you shall be guiltless of more blood."

Fell bit, deep and hard, severing Lord Vladeran's windpipe, and in a gush of red the life expired from the shaking body of the man who had killed his sister Larka. It was over. Some of the Shield Guard drew their weapons, but Cascu raised his hand.

"Hold," the Helgra cried. "It's enough. It's all enough. There has been enough darkness and bloodshed here, and now the reason for the evil is dead. We are men, not beasts."

The Shield Guard were held, partly by their leader, partly by Tarlar's snarls, and partly by the hopeful thought that this Helgra might protect them from the fighting beyond. The black wolf growled in satisfaction at his work, and then Fell padded softly towards his friend on the throne.

"You're safe now, changeling, but I must ask your forgiveness, for taking one of your kind."

For a moment Alina stared at the wolf, for though she had been locked in the vision, she had understood all Morgra's words and knew now that her father was alive and here in the palace, as the sounds of battle continued round them, and she knew that still she would have to fight. Then, with a cry, she hurled herself to her knees.

"Oh, Fell, dear Fell," she cried, and as the tears streamed from the young woman's lovely hazel eyes, Alina WovenWord threw her arms around him and hugged that great black wolf.

TWENTY-SIX
FELL'S FAREWELL

The terrible battle was done. Now a tall, visored soldier stood calmly on his palace walls, and as he looked at Romana and Alina and little Elu, his eyes glittered through the slots in his face armour.

On his chest, like the knights around him, patrolling the battlements, or wandering amongst the fallen on the plain below, he bore that symbol of the red cross, with its tongues of yellow flame, like wings, and, since he led that Order, the curled griffin beneath.

Alina thought of Baba Yaga's riders as the man lifted his gauntleted hand and pulled the visor from his head. The women's hearts trembled as they saw that fine, sad face, and that red hair, drenched in sweat. The face of Alina's dreams. Romana could not believe its reality, but her dead husband stood before her, and Alina's father too.

"Dragomir," whispered Romana fearfully. "Can this really be, husband?"

Around the mysterious leader of the Order of the Griffin, his warriors watched silently, as did Catalin, standing in the background with his bow. It had not been their charge alone that had won the fight for the Helgra, and Alina had raced to Catalin and Ovidu's aid, with the wolves guarding their backs. But it had turned the tide again, and driven back Draculea's men, as that swathe of secret riders had thundered across the plain into battle. Their banners had streamed in the wind like mighty sails, like Guardians, marked with the image of the sleeping griffin.

"I would hardly believe a tenth of it myself," said Dragomir softly, "if I were not standing here now, Romana. Can you forgive me, wife, for taking so long to return?"

Alina remembered that voice immediately, so deep and full of feeling, like a river mumuring amongst stones. "It is not I that has anything to forgive, husband. It's you," said Romana.

Dragomir looked down. On a wooden pallet, beneath a bloodied cloak of wolf fur, lay the dead friend of his youth, Vladeran. Although now it was just a body, and that terrible spirit had departed. Little Elu was looking at him too. He was bewildered and horrified, but he had seen his father's darkness and cruelty to his mother.

"I was sick to the point of death, Romana, when the Turks took me amongst them," said Dragomir guiltily, as he clutched his painful left arm and wondered what had done that to Vladeran's throat. "When they ransomed me, I rose to lead our Order, but so far off in the lands of Hungary, I did not know how my best friend plotted, and then I heard of your marriage and the birth of a son. Then my own daughter's death. It nearly killed me a second time."

Romana's eyes flickered guiltily and Alina's heart ached.

"For a long time I did not know what to do, until recently, when I learnt how Vladeran had desecrated the oaths of our kind and then that my darling Alina was alive. I had to be sure when I came that I could defeat him, and save you all. But we are here now at last. The Order. To make accounting."

"Oh, Dragomir," whispered Romana.

Dragomir looked at Vladeran's son and smiled at the little boy. He felt nothing but compassion for the child.

Alina took Elu's hand. Her own red hair was almost as wet as her father's, and she looked tired from the fight they had taken up after Vladeran's death, but her sword was sheathed again on the storyteller's back.

Alina remembered that face and her changeling dreams, remembered how this man had stood aloof, yet how safe he had made her feel too. How much she loved him. Romana stepped forwards suddenly to hold her husband. Then the two adults turned and put out their hands towards the children, Romana to her son, and Dragomir to his daughter.

Elu ran to his mother.

"Will you not embrace me, daughter?" said Lord Dragomir softly, as the young woman stood there still, her beautiful eyes glittering with tears. "You've much to forgive, I think, my child. I thought you were dead, until the Order managed to follow your tale, Alina, if only in part. One was especially helpful to us. The girl Mia."

"Mia," whispered Alina in astonishment, remembering how she had seen her in the forge, though with hardly as great a wonder as she now looked on her own father.

"The Order of the Griffin found the little girl in the snows, Alina, fleeing with that old woman Ranna."

Alina shivered.

"The shepherd's wife was on the point of death, but Mia had tended to her faithfully at her end. She told your story and of the parchment. She was desperate to speak of your innocence."

Alina smiled and shook her head, her heart filled with gratitude to the little girl for all she'd done.

"Mia asked me to give you this," said Dragomir, reaching into his jerkin and holding out a small carving, part ram, part wolf. "Until you meet again."

"Where is she, Father?" asked Alina, stepping closer and taking the thing with a smile, but feeling the word "Father" so strange to say.

"Safe in the halls of the Order, Alina. She lords it about the place like a little queen. Oh, Alina, I'm sorry I was not there to protect you. So sorry. Must we not protect children with all we are? And so the future."

"Yes, Father," said the young woman, "but we must help them grow too. And it was not your fault."

Dragomir dropped his eyes. There were still tears in Alina's, but she held them back. Instead she put the carving safely in her jerkin and walked forwards slowly. She took her mother and father gently by the hand, no longer a changeling at all. A real girl with a real family.

"Perhaps we must all protect one another," said the storyteller softly. "And listen carefully."

Then the family were holding one another once more. Romana and Dragomir, and Alina—restored—and little Elu with them too.

509

"Perhaps we'll all find peace now," said Romana, as they drifted apart, "when the strong hand of justice moves to contain the savage hearts of men."

"Peace?" said Dragomir, looking sadly at that terrible battlefield. "Is there ever peace in the world, Romana? The King has his troubles, and even now the Order of the Griffin must ride out. There is other accounting to be done."

"Who?" asked Alina.

"Tepesh," answered Dragomir. "Draculea. Vladeran and he both touched the left-hand path."

"You must ride soon, husband?" asked Romana.

"We may stay awhile. And then set out," answered Dragomir, "But when it is done, I will step down as leader of the Order. For there has been too much secrecy here. Too much darkness in these lands."

"I'm glad of it, husband," said Romana tenderly.

Dragomir looked around at the Helgra below, still wandering across the battlefield, tending to their wounded.

"But you must tell me more of this, daughter," he said. "And of the strange rumours that envelop these halls."

"Rumours, Father?"

"Of a boy who walked the mountains with a wild black wolf. Not even the Order of the Griffin has heard of such a thing before. I little believe most of the tales, for I've seen real children suckled in the wild, Alina, and know how hard it goes with them. How their minds are hurt by it, so that it seems they can never be human again. For people need each other to grow."

Perhaps that's the truth of it, thought Alina, *if there were no such thing as the Sight.* She thought of Fell, waiting out of sight nearby.

"It's like the stories you used to make up as a little girl, Alina," said Dragomir, with a sudden laugh, his heart filled with joy and peace he had not known in years. "Do you remember, child? You loved reading so much, and were a marvel at it, but at inventing even more. You hated it when the priests tried to tell you what the truth is, and instead kept trying to teach us all about the world with your tales." Dragomir laughed again. "All the palace called you a liar, but I knew it as a healthy thing. All those animals and those imaginary friends. Those stories of how you could tell the future, and how one day you would protect the whole world from harm. But your favourite was about how a fine noblewoman went once amongst the people in disguise."

Dragomir smiled and shook his head, but Alina WovenWord said nothing. She was thinking of that house in Baba Yaga's valley and wondering.

"Perhaps I should have spent more time with you," Dragomir whispered, "but there are many things I would have done differently. Will do differently, if you'll let me."

Alina nodded.

"Yes, husband," said Romana keenly, "how terribly we argued too, before you went to fight the Turk. And when you went, Dragomir," she added, turning regretfully to Alina, "I became so terribly . . ."

"Hush, Mother," said Alina. "Peace."

"But this morning, when we mopped up the rest of this traitor's men," whispered Dragomir still, "I almost thought I saw them amongst the men. Two wild wolves."

Alina smiled. Fell and Tarlar had hidden themselves in the battle, watching Alina and Catalin as they fought, and protecting their backs, while in the fray all had been confusion. As it always was in the ghastliness of war.

"They must have been drawn down by the smell of death, husband," said Alina's mother softly, and Dragomir looked hard at her, but at last he smiled too.

"If you say it, wife. The Helgra have had reason enough to throw off my friend's cruelty, yet they too revere the wild, and the wolf."

"They do, husband."

Dragomir could see that Alina and Romana would say no more though. They were protecting the real wolves from the fears and stories of men.

"But now the Helgra shall be safe in their villages again, beyond tyranny," said Dragomir, "and all of us may honour the five once more."

"The five, Dragomir?" said Romana.

"The five oaths that bind our Order. That once bound my 'friend' Vladeran, until his jealousy and hatred made him betray them and us. The pursuit of knowledge," said Dragomir, lifting his strong head and looking at that scorched ground and the weary Helgra. "The support of the downtrodden, and the upholding of peace. Peace, and the protection of the earth. And one last."

Dragomir's eyes were glistening as he looked out across the lands beyond the forest, and he seemed lost in thought.

"What is it, Father?" said Alina. "What are you thinking?"

"It's so strange, daughter. As I was healing amongst the Turks, tended to by Muselmen physicians, surrounded by the voices of their mystic Sufi poets, I had a kind of dream. More than a dream. A vision. It was of the whole world and all the animals in it. Not just the animals, but the trees and plants and flowers, and it told me that man, for all that religion teaches him, is an animal. The Order of the Griffin teaches it too."

"Yes," said Alina, thinking of that shape clambering down from the trees.

"But of all the animals, man holds the fate of the world in his hands. And woman too, Alina. To know such a thing might drive mankind to terrible ends," said Dragomir, "or might teach humility and care. For there is such power in nature. Power to heal us all. Is it not as beautiful as all the works of man? Perhaps we must simply choose where the knowledge takes us."

"Yes, Father, we must."

"So although I shall be your father once more, the Order shall continue, for generation on generation if I can help it, into the distant future," said Dragomir, looking proudly at his daughter, and that sword at her back, "and perhaps one day women shall join it too. Warriors. Who knows, Alina, perhaps one day your heirs shall come to lead it."

Alina's eyes shone and she sensed Catalin nearby. Dragomir raised his hand and took his wife's in his again, but he was looking suddenly towards his daughter, and he shook his head wonderingly.

"But of all the five oaths perhaps the greatest is the last, child."

"The last, Father?"

"The defence of the feminine, Alina WovenWord. Come, Romana, let's go into the palace and talk of this. There's much to tell, I think."

Romana held her son's hand firmly, and Alina walked over to Catalin, who was gazing back towards the passes and the mountains he had come from, and the two young people heard a note rise around them that made their hearts stir. Human voices were suddenly all around them, exhausted from the fight and mourning their own, singing to the young storytellers, Catalin Fierar and Alina WolfPaw. It was the song of the Helgra.

In that moment Alina Sculcuvant knew that of all life's great journeys, perhaps the greatest was to come home, and to know the place for the first time.

"It was a brave fight," whispered Catalin.

"But a painful one," said Alina softly, "and I'm tired of swords for now, and of bows too, Catalin," she added with a gentle smile, squeezing Catalin's arm. "I'd learn what Father spoke of. The upholding of peace. And I will let my hair grow. For why should a woman not head the Order, and sooner than Father said?"

Catalin looked back at those brilliant hazel eyes, with that speck of green, and his heart beat faster. He no longer resented this fine, high lady, this heir to Castelu. He had never seen anyone so beautiful in his life. Suddenly Catalin grasped Alina to him and kissed her, holding her beating heart to his own.

Then the storytellers parted and stood staring into each other's eyes. As they saw each other then it was as if nothing of that strange story had happened, and none of it mattered.

"So the wolf is gone, Alina?" whispered Catalin.

"Fell," cried Alina suddenly. "Will you wait here for me, Catalin? There's something I must do."

Alina ran down the steps to the battlements and out across the plain. Darkness was coming now, and as she hurried towards the trees on this side of the river, her heart was thundering. She knew that what Morgra had said of man and wolf was true, that they were not meant to be together. Alina WovenWord had her world and Fell had his. They were set apart, but perhaps they could learn to honour each other.

"Fell? Are you there, Fell?" she cried as she reached the trees. No sounds came back, except the chattering of birds and the shadows put a fear in Alina's mind that perhaps Fell had gone already. It couldn't be.

Then she saw the wolf, standing quietly by an oak tree, waiting.

"Oh, Fell, dear Fell. I was worried I'd be too late."

Fell growled, but Alina felt the ache in her mind, though faintly now, like a memory of childhood.

"I could not leave, human, without saying farewell."

"You have to go?"

The wolf whimpered slightly.

"Yes, Alina. I have my own. I . . ."

As Alina knelt down, she heard Fell's thoughts turning to growls, and she felt a violent tugging at her heart. It felt as if it were breaking.

Alina lifted her hand and touched the wolf's muzzle softly, then she stroked his dear head. The tears were streaming down her face.

"Thank you, Fell. For everything you've done. For bringing me home."

Fell's great yellow gold eyes blinked slowly, and he raised his black paw and placed it gently in Alina's hand. She grasped it.

"Everything we have done together, friend."

Alina was filled with sorrow, yet she knew that her friend had to be wild and free, and bravely she tried to hold back her tears and be strong for him. Fell whimpered again, and licked one of the tears from Alina's cheek. Then again she threw her arms about the wolf's neck and hugged him, before she pushed him away for a final time.

"Go, Fell. Quickly. I cannot bear this pain. I will remember you always."

Alina stood, and Fell growled one more time, before he turned to the shadows and was gone. There were still tears in Alina's hazel eyes as she mounted the palace steps again, and now great flickering tapers had been lit, which reminded the young woman of the halls of the Helgra. Catalin was still standing there, waiting for her.

"Oh, Catalin," said Alina desperately. "He's gone."

The young storyteller stepped forwards and took her tenderly in his arms and held her again.

"Come, you two," said a voice suddenly.

They turned to see Romana walking towards them once more. "Mother?"

"There's much to be done, Alina, and undone too. First we shall feast, and give thanks for our blessings. You must tell us some of your stories, while this handsome young man shall sit by me, Alina," said Romana, "if you, and your father, will allow it."

Alina almost blushed as her mother took Catalin by the arm.

"And you, Ovidu," said Romana, as she saw the Helgra leader mounting the steps to the battlements too, leading a proud old man, with tears in his blind eyes, by the arm. "You'll sit by me as well, with your father, Ilyan. For I would talk of my people and hear our songs again."

Ovidu smiled, but there was a great sadness in his eyes. He was thinking of his brother.

"If we have the heart to sing, my lady."

"Cascu's own actions have punished him," said Romana softly, understanding the look, "but the Helgra must decide his fate."

There was laughter in the party as they began to walk towards Dragomir through those burning tapers, but suddenly Alina turned and looked back. It was no sound that had made her turn. No howl. It was the sense of it.

There, high on the hill above the palace walls in the moonlight, where the Vengerid had saluted him, was a single black shape. Fell stood all alone and Alina shivered. As she gazed at her wild friend, he dipped his muzzle.

"Good-bye, Fell," she whispered, as the others' laughter rose around her. "You shall walk with me, always. If not in fact now, then in thought at least. No, in memory, and in stories."

There were tears in Alina's eyes again as the storyteller turned, but turn she did, for she heard the irresistible pull of human voices, and high up there on the mountainside, another shape stepped up next to Fell in the darkness.

"Come," said Tarlar softly. "It's time."

"Time?" said Fell almost sadly. "Time to let thoughts of these humans go?"

"Why not, Fell? Time to remember our own world, for the humans are dark indeed. More even than for each other, they seem to have a fondness for demons."

"The only demons are in their own minds, Tarlar," growled Fell. "And such strange minds they have."

"What do you mean?"

"It's as if they have the power to make things that are impossible come true. Yet perhaps, because of their minds, they are not impossible at all. Would not that vision seem impossible if the Lera hadn't seen it with their own eyes?"

Fell seemed lost in thought.

"But I've seen evil amongst them, Fell."

"Evil? Yes, there is evil, very great evil, but it is not outside them like some sickness, Tarlar, or a winged grasht, it's inside them. Or the potential for it. Perhaps only if they recognise that will they be free. Perhaps too, if they recognise that they've a right to some of their darkness and anger and pain. If they know and love their own clever natures. And now the animals have shown them too."

"Are you all right, Fell?"

The black wolf was lifting his gaze then to the heavens and the stars that were beginning to glitter wonderfully above them. The Wolf Trail.

"I had a dream, last night," he answered, gazing up longingly, "in the thin, formless hours of the morning after the battle."

"A dream, Fell?"

"I saw you, Tarlar, standing on a hill, calling to me. But somehow I was afraid. Then as I began to walk towards you, there were spectres all about me from the Red Meadow, and as I went they began to talk to me."

"Talk to you?"

"With sadness, Tarlar, and longing and accusation. It was like the Gauntlet that my parents spoke of once, when they were with the rebel wolves. I was in a Gauntlet of voices, and all of them were trying to hold me back, because of their own fear and pain and confusion."

Tarlar lifted her paw and touched him on the flank.

"But I remembered those old words about a courage as deep as despair, and then I heard another voice. 'No, Fell,' it cried passionately. 'Go to her. Live and be free.' At that voice I began to run, as fast as a river, and it grew stronger, like a wind I heard in a cave. 'Yes, Fell. Life is wonderful, so revel in its beauty. Be all you can be, and let go of the past. It is nothing but shadows.'

"And then I had broken out beyond that terrible Gauntlet of doubting and self-doubt, and I no longer felt sad or guilty, and as I swung my head, I saw her standing there again, shining like moonlight, my sister Larka, watching me kindly. She said one thing to me then. 'It's a lovely place' was all that Larka whispered."

"Perhaps she's been watching over you all along," said Tarlar.

Fell thought of the voice that had begun it all and Larka's great face in the ice cliff and he wondered.

"Even if Tor and Fenris are nothing but stories, or fables for cubs, perhaps she has," he said. "Because she's been there, if only in my memories. And I knew then too that even though my father had not the words, he did say good-bye, and give me a blessing when he died. Because if he was only working it out within himself, it does not mean it was not directed towards me too. 'Open,' he said, 'open like a flower.'"

Tarlar nodded.

"And then I had another dream," said Fell, "of Huttser and Palla together. They were young again and smiling at me from the highest mountaintop. It was night, but the air was filled with a shining glow from the stars, that seemed to reach down from the heavens and glitter like dewdrops in the grass around them. Their tails were raised and suddenly they began to run, and the carpet of the stars lifted them up and carried them heavenwards, racing up the skies, up there towards the Wolf Trail."

"How wonderful, Fell," whispered Tarlar gravely, looking up.

"Yes. I knew they were going to Tor and Fenris. Just as I know now that the world is made up of far more than what we call real. Perhaps that reality is only what we see, Tarlar, but the true reality is what lies beyond us, and our struggling, clouded understandings, which seem to change all the time."

Tarlar nodded.

"And suddenly another shape was running at their side, young and innocent and free, but not with the innocence of childhood, with the innocence of knowledge and self-knowledge, and of joy. Running beside her dear sister, Palla. Running happily, her ears raised above her head. It was Morgra."

The wolves were looking up at the Wolf Trail together, and suddenly, just as it had been with Catalin and Alina, it was as if nothing of the terrible history of the Sight had happened at all, and the world was as young and happy and fresh as ever.

"Death," whispered Tarlar, "you do not fear it, Fell? By water, or any other way?"

"What is there to fear?" answered the black wolf. "If it is an end, then so be it. For there is no pain in that, except the pain left to the living. I once thought, and felt with the Sight, that I could see the pain of the whole world, and it grew and grew like a sea. But though all feel pain, it does not join together like individual droplets in a pool. A million deaths is really only one death. And if death is not an end, then what more wonderful journey, if we do not fear it? We must have courage to face the truth, and the future."

"Come, Fell," said Tarlar, "we'll run happy and free through the world, together, until we too must walk the Wolf Trail in our turn. For that is as it must be."

"Wait, Tarlar, there's something I must do first."

"Do?"

Fell had stepped away again and raised his muzzle.

"I must howl, Tarlar. For I must ask their forgiveness too. Only they can let me go, I think."

Fell's sleek black muzzle lifted and his cry rose in the air. *Aaooow.* It sang in the night, weaving a mysterious wildness over the gathering revellers below, as if casting a wild spell to protect them from any harm. But Fell was not talking to them alone.

"For you," cried the black wolf's howl. "For all who are lost, or alone, or frightened in the world. For we are all lost, and all frightened. For any in pain too, or in sorrow, and for any who can no longer tell the light from the darkness, the sadness from the joy. I must leave you now, for I've found my way, for a time at least, and I wish you well."

The howl went on in the night, like a wonderful song, yet both more and less than a song, and as it did so it seemed to the black wolf as if the world was changing. As if the things he saw about him, the trees and the forest and the palace, he no longer had words for at all, and so he no longer knew what they were.

"But I let you know that I too have seen what you have seen, and felt what you have felt," cried Fell. "I have suffered as you have suffered. For all things walk the same way. But now, for the last time, I, Fell of the Mountaintops, give you my blessing. So listen well, for love's greatest art is to listen."

Fell's mind was already losing the memories of the journey he had made with Alina Sculcuvant and the humans, and as it did so the smells on the wind became stronger, the ground firmer beneath his paws, the mystery of the wild, of life itself, deeper and deeper. Then a distant voice was whispering to the wolf, yet not a voice at all, a boom from the mouth of a cave: *A path that will free you at last,* it said.

The beautiful song ceased and Fell turned back to Tarlar.

"Come then," cried the black wolf, although his words had become nothing but powerful wild growls.

Then the two of them were running, side by side, their brilliant yellow gold eyes flashing like stars, searching through the darkness, as the Dragga and the beautiful Drappa vanished down the chasms of the welcoming night.

ABOUT THE AUTHOR

David Clement-Davies is the author of such highly regarded novels as *The Sight*, *The Telling Pool*, and *Fire Bringer*, which *Booklist* called "a masterpiece of animal fantasy" in a starred review and which Richard Adams, author of *Watership Down*, hailed as "one of the best anthropomorphic fantasies known to me." His books have been named *Booklist* Books of the Year and Book Sense 76 selections. David is also a travel writer, and his wide-ranging journeys are often inspiration for his vividly set stories. He is a graduate of the University of Edinburgh, where he studied English literature and history, and lives in London.

This book was art directed by
Chad W. Beckerman. The text is set in
12-point Adobe Garamond, a typeface
that is based on those created in the
sixteenth century by Claude Garamond.
Garamond modeled his typefaces on
those created by Venetian printers at the
end of the fifteenth century. The modern
version used in this book was designed by
Robert Slimbach, who studied Garamond's
historic typefaces at the Plantin-Moretus
Museum in Antwerp, Belgium. The display
type is Lafayette.